Sam

Tha

joy!

KAT xx

# STRINGS

KAT GREEN

ISBN: - 10: 1500345288
ISBN-13: 978-1500345280

# DEDICATION

This book is dedicated to my Mum, who I miss every day. It seems like yesterday you had to leave us, but you showed true strength during your last days, and I'm proud to have known you. You raised me, and shaped me into who I am today, and I hope you are proud and you are forever in my heart.

# CONTENTS

# ACKNOWLEDGMENTS

Firstly, thank you for purchasing my novel. I hope you enjoy reading it as much as I enjoyed writing it. There are some very special people I would like to thank, without their help and support, it might never have happened. My husband Jon, for his support, and for his advice and input. I had to realise this was a project that needed time and patience. I don't like waiting or having control taken away. As usual he was completely right. Thank you for making my dream come true and for being my best friend. My small team who helped during the first stages, and gave me feedback, or a kick up the ass, when I began to doubt myself. Anouska, Claire, Tracy and Linda, you have no idea how much you helped. Liz, who had the job of editing my draft, which was a job and a half, it was my first attempt and we all have to start somewhere. My family and friends who supported me throughout this process, and didn't let me give up. There are too many names, but you know who you are. I love you all. My son Leo, for being my reason to breath, giving me the strength to be all I can be.

This book started another passion of mine. Music, finding new bands to rave about, blog about and help, if I can. Some have helped me through this process, their music has inspired me and lifted me when I most needed it. So, White Clouds and Gunfire, Sabella, Phoenix Calling and The Castellars, Thank you for making music that not only inspired but kept me going. I wish you all the best on your journey, and I will see you at a gig soon

An eagle will mate for life,
only seeking out a new one if theirs were to die.

# Hospital (1)

October 13TH 2014

'Are you sure I can't get you anything?' Liz, the nurse, asked. She looked sympathetically at Melissa as she fluffed up the pillows.

Melissa shook her head and leaned back. 'No thank you. The only thing I want, you can't give me.'

Liz sighed and took her hand. 'It's a terrible business. You poor girl. But I'm sure things will work out.' The nurse was in her late thirties and had been taking care of Melissa for the past twenty-four hours, quickly becoming very fond of her. There was a buzz around the hospital due to the presence of the new patient but Liz refused to become a gossip. This girl had been through enough and she wouldn't add to it. She was amazed to discover how different a person could be to what the media would have you believe they were like. Melissa Webb was one of the sweetest girls Liz had ever had the pleasure of caring for, and she knew she would not believe another word printed about her. Liz prayed that things would work out. 'The police will be here soon to take your statement,' she said as she released Melissa's hand and gently placed it back on the bed.

Melissa nodded, but didn't make eye contact. Instead, she continued to stare at the leather cuff in her hand, knowing that if she looked Liz in the eye, she would lose control, and she didn't want to cry in front of a stranger, regardless of how nice she seemed to be. There was only one person who could make her feel better. His comforting arms were all she wanted and needed, but she knew he wasn't coming. He wouldn't be here to dry her tears if she cried. He always did those caring and loving things for her, and nobody else made her feel safe like he did.

'Press the button if you need me, and I'll be straight in,' Liz said as she left the room.

Finally alone, Melissa turned over, buried her head in her pillow and sobbed. The pain was so intense it felt as though her heart was being ripped out of her chest. She was still trying to piece it all together; how her life had turned from a dream to a nightmare so quickly and dramatically, and what she would do if he didn't come home. She ached for him. Melissa knew the world would be talking and the rumours spreading, but she didn't care, not today. They could gossip and speculate all they wanted, but as far as she was concerned, the world had ended and she wanted to die. She cried for what seemed like hours and didn't hear her mum come into the room until she turned her over and embraced her.

'Come on, sweetheart, let it out. You're safe now.' She rocked her daughter like a small child while trying to hold back her own tears. Although her daughter was twenty years old, she was still her baby. Jean Webb was a small woman with golden blonde hair that sat just above her shoulders. Her pale blue eyes were welling up as she kissed the top of her daughter's head. She pulled Melissa's hair back into a loose ponytail, to see her beautiful face better. Melissa had the same colour hair as her mother but it was much longer. You could tell they were mother and daughter, or at least you could usually, but maybe not today. The dressing on Melissa's face hid the true extent of the injury caused to her left cheek. Jean knew her daughter was heartbroken and recovering from a trauma, but she also knew that it was important for her to talk while everything was fresh in her mind.

'Talk to me, please. You should have come to us when this all began,' she said softly.

Melissa cried into her mum's shoulder. 'I know, I was so stupid ... this is all my fault. He should have just walked past me after that gig and kept on walking. I should never have got involved. I should have stayed out of his life!'

She wasn't thinking straight and Jean told her not to be so silly. This was clearly not her fault, none of it. He had a choice, and he chose to spend his life with her. They simply fell in love, and there was no way they could have known how their lives would change as a result. They definitely shouldn't apologise for it. He was a star with a talent that most people could only wish for. He deserved his status, and Melissa had every right to walk proudly by his side. He had said to Jean once that she was his angel. She had saved him and changed his life. They weren't perfect - they had been through bad times and sometimes argued just like any other couple. But if you believed the gossip, they were at each other's throats twenty-four seven, which was so far from the truth it was ridiculous.

'This shouldn't be happening. You don't deserve it, and *he* doesn't deserve it,' Jean said, the thought of what had happened making her angry.

Melissa asked what was being said about them, but Jean told her not to worry about that. 'I assume they're saying it's my fault - it always is.' She was used to taking the blame when it came to Luke. She wasn't good enough in some people's eyes, and it irritated her intensely, but there was nothing she could do about it. People on the outside didn't know them – they didn't know anything. The people close to him all agreed she was perfect for him, and vice versa. Luke would listen to her, and she could calm him when no one else could.

'Babe, they're idiots. Don't waste time worrying, it's bullshit,' her mum said.

Melissa looked up at her and smiled. Jean didn't usually swear but she was mimicking Luke in an attempt to make Melissa feel better. 'Thanks Mum' she replied.

She felt as though they were never going to let her recover in private – the vultures were already circling, and picking for information as to what had happened. Jean had dodged two of them as she'd come into the hospital and that wasn't even the beginning. There would be more – lots more. She wanted to scream at them to leave her daughter alone, but what would be the point? She was an intelligent woman and she knew that the lifestyle Melissa and Luke had chosen came at a price. But surely there had to be a limit? Apparently, her broken and terrified daughter was even more exciting to them than she was before. It was just another scoop for them to sell their trash, she thought. They didn't care that two families and their friends were going through a terrible time, which would only get worse if he didn't return. Millions of fans around the world waited to discover the fate of their idol. But to Melissa he was her boyfriend, her soul mate, her world.

Melissa finally cried herself to sleep, and Jean stared out of the window, watching the rain. She listened to the tapping sound of the drops against the glass, and found it soothing. The room was as private as they could make it, with only a select few medical staff allowed in – not because she was a diva, but for her own safety. Jean heard the door open and turned to greet her husband, who had brought coffee and food. They knew they would be staying put for quite some time.

'How's my baby girl doing?' he asked as he passed a skinny latte to his wife. As he did so, he saw the fear in her eyes.

Jean shook her head, and stared down at her sleeping daughter. 'Not good. Look what that lunatic has done to her! How could we let this happen? How could one person do all this?' Jean cried. She didn't want to wake Melissa, but she was so angry and upset that the emotions flooded out. She felt that she had let her daughter down.

Mick put his coffee down and hugged his wife. 'We didn't know this would happen, nobody did. We had no idea there was a problem. You mustn't blame yourself. We're here now and we'll make sure she is fine,' he assured her.

'Everything was going so well after—'

Mick interrupted her. 'Shhh. That's over with and they got through it, so they can get through this too.' But while it was his duty to be strong and reassure his wife, privately even he wasn't completely convinced this time.

'They can't get through this if he isn't here! How will she cope, Mick? He's the love of her life! This isn't a break up. I wish it was. At least there'd be hope, and an explanation,' she said.

Mick kissed his wife's forehead. 'They will find him. Someone like Luke can't just vanish.'

'That's what worries me. No one's seen him for three days. Even the bloody paparazzi haven't seen him! This is bad, really bad....' She took a deep breath and they both sat down by their daughter's bed, silently sipping their coffee and watching her sleep, desperate for this to be over, but with no idea how that could happen.

The dressing on his daughter's face made Mick sad and angry. She was such a beautiful girl and she was his baby. Similar to Jean, the thought that he should have protected her was killing him. That's what a father is supposed to do after all, Mick thought. The doctors were worried that the cut on her face was deep enough to scar, and that thought made him feel sick. He needed to get out of the room for a cigarette, so he headed out through the maze of doors and corridors. He'd only had three puffs when he realised his mistake as the reporters and photographers swarmed towards him like locusts, some clicking away and competing to get the best angle, and others yelling questions at him and pointing microphones. The group of two had grown to at least twelve.

'Mr Webb ... how is Melissa?!' Click, click, click!

'Is Luke in there too?' Click, click, click!

'What happened?!' Click, click, click!

'Come on, give us something!'

Mick ignored them and decided he would finish his cigarette and not utter a word. He would give these bastards nothing – they'd write whatever they wanted anyway, so it made no difference. He recognised some of them, and in his mind had marked the cards of a few in the past. Every vile word they had written about his beautiful daughter was etched in his memory, and not a single one contained a grain of truth. They had branded her a cheat and a whore, a drug addict and a drunk. She was none of those things.

He threw the cigarette away and stomped back towards the hospital entrance. The vultures followed. He called them vultures because they circled and picked until there was nothing left. He promised himself that he wouldn't let them do it any more, not to his baby. He was just about to head inside when a group of girls caught his attention, congregated at the side of the main entrance. They seemed to be led by a girl of about eighteen, with long black hair with a blue streak on one side. Her hair was damp from the rain, and so were her clothes. Her mascara had started to run down one cheek. Or it could be from crying, Mick thought. This girl was definitely one of the Eaglets, avid female fans of the man who was missing, his daughter's boyfriend and one of the world's most famous musicians. The Eaglets would follow Luke and his band anywhere and everywhere. The girl's jumper was a souvenir from one of their recent tours. The front displayed their logo, four eagles in a diamond shape, one slightly bigger than the others. The eagle's eyes were savage and its beak wide open. The girl ran to Mick and grabbed his hand.

'Please, are they OK?' she asked, the desperation clear in her voice.

Mick pulled away from the girl politely. 'Sorry, I can't talk to you.'

Her eyes pulled at his heartstrings and he wished he could tell her that everything was fine – that Luke was fine and so was Melissa. But that would be a lie because they were not fine, far from it.

He was surrounded by the hoard of reporters again, and decided it was time to leave. He rushed back inside, feeling guilty as he heard the girl calling behind him.

'Please, I just want to know if Luke's OK. Please, please! I heard that he's dead! Please, Mr Webb, please!' the girl sobbed as the rain poured down on her, and her friends hugged each other as they feared for their idol.

*****

Melissa was awake when he returned to her room.

'Hi, baby, how are you doing?' he asked as he hugged her tightly.

She shook her head. 'I just feel numb.'

He stroked her cheek gently. 'I brought you the things you asked for. Don't worry about your flat, we'll make sure it's looked after.'

She worried about Luke's things as he did a lot of his creative work at home. When he wasn't away with the band, he stayed at home as much as possible. It was his choice, not Melissa's. 'Did you lock it? His guitars are in there,' Melissa asked.

'Yes, don't worry, my love. The keys are in the front pocket of your bag.' He pointed at the purple holdall on the chair in the corner.

'Thanks, Dad. Did you speak to Ray?'

'Ray's taking care of it. Stop worrying. Nobody will take anything from your home. They can't do that without your permission.'

'I don't want anyone touching his stuff, and I don't trust many people right now.' She knew it sounded as though she was being paranoid, but until Luke was found safe and well, she was on edge about everything. The police had already been to the flat to investigate and take fingerprints. The thought of strangers in their home bothered her, perhaps more than it should have. But it was their personal, private space, and it made her nervous, even though it wasn't particularly significant at a time like this.

'OK, but don't worry. They won't take anything, honey, I promise.'

Melissa smiled slightly as Liz returned to check her over. She liked Liz, who seemed to genuinely care for her well-being and nothing else.

'Melissa, darling, the police are here to take your statement. Are you ready?'

'Not really, but do I have a choice?' Melissa asked.

Liz shrugged. 'Probably best to get it over with sooner rather than later. Putting it off will only drag things out.

'You're right,' Melissa agreed, messing with her sheets to cover herself up properly. She started to look for a mirror to check her hair and make-up, something which had become an almost unconscious habit, but she stopped herself when she thought how pointless that would be while lying in a hospital bed. But it made her realise that life in the public eye had changed her, even though in every way that mattered she was still the same girl she had always been.

*****

Two men came into the room and stood at the side of the bed. One was around fifty, with grey hair and a matching grey suit that might have fitted him twenty years ago, but was now too small to accommodate his impressive beer belly. The other was younger, probably early thirties, with short brown hair. He was much more smartly dressed in a black suit and cufflinks. Beer Belly was clearly in charge.

'Miss Webb, I'm Detective Inspector Fox and this is my colleague, Detective Sergeant Noels from Thornvale CID. We are in charge of this investigation.'

'Hi,' was all Melissa could think of to say.

Mick stood up and shook hands, and offered them seats. 'You might need them. I believe this is a long story.'

They thanked him and sat down. Their training taught them to ensure that a witness felt at ease in an interview situation – it helped them to establish trust and obtain complete and honest responses to their questions. In an investigation like this the key witness was the most valuable source of information and must be handled extremely carefully. Melissa assured them she felt well enough to be interviewed, and so they began.

'Miss Webb, can you explain, in your own words, the events that led up to Mr Black's disappearance and your admission to hospital yesterday?' DI Fox asked.

'Luke. His name is Luke.'

DI Fox leaned forward in his chair. 'I'm sorry. I know this is difficult, and we'll try to make it as easy as we can for you. But you must understand that in order to find him, we need to know everything that you know. I understand that there have been some tough times between you since—'

Melissa cut him off before he could finish his sentence. 'Since what?' she snapped. 'Since they broke my heart for entertainment? Read the magazines. They seem to know all the gory details. Ask *them* what goes on in my life!' Tears streamed down her face. 'It was fucking *her*! All of it! Don't bring that up. I don't want to talk about it!' Melissa was yelling now, her fists clenched tightly. She was still hurt from their past problems; it still broke her heart to think about it, but she couldn't change it. DI Fox had touched a very raw nerve.

'Darling, calm down. They're just doing their job – don't upset yourself.' Jean was on the other side of the bed. She grabbed her daughter's hand, squeezing it tightly to emphasise what she was saying, then relaxed her grip when she felt the anger start to subside.

Melissa wiped her eyes. 'Sorry, I didn't mean to shout at you. It just wasn't a very nice part of our lives and I don't like talking about it. We are ... I mean we were ... great. We'd managed to move on from it. It's a pity the rest of the world won't let us forget.' She paused and took some deep breaths. 'Please find him.'

She had been winding the leather bracelet round her fingers and even that upset her more. He never took it off – it was a reminder to him of where they came from; those good old days, looking for their big break, before he became the star he was now. They were ordinary people who could walk down the street without being noticed. The bracelet may not have cost much – it had been just £15.00 – but that wasn't the point - it meant more to him than anything expensive they had now, because Melissa gave it to him.

She heard the door open and let out a cry as her best friend ran in, throwing her arms around her.

'Liss ... are you OK? Oh my God! What the hell happened? Have they found him?' Melissa hugged her back and the tears flowed again. 'Beth! I'm so glad you're here. It was *her*. She tried to kill me! She said ... she said ... I can't even repeat it!' Melissa sobbed again.

Beth's black curls rained down over her face, and her honey eyes were sad and angry. Her immediate instinct was the wellbeing of her best friend, and she held her tightly. She too felt full of guilt, thinking that if she hadn't left Melissa alone, none of this would have happened. But deep down she knew that nobody could have predicted what had happened. 'Twisted bitch! They'll find him, I know they will.'

Beth's boyfriend, Dale, hovered closely behind her, quietly greeting everyone in the room. His eyes looked tired and stressed and his long hair was tied back in its usual scruffy way.

Melissa broke from her best friend's hold and reached out to him. 'I'm so sorry. This is all my fault.'

Dale shook his head as he hugged her and kissed the top of her head. 'Don't be silly. None of this is your fault any more than it's Beth's.' He warmly held the fragile girl who had become like a sister to him.

DI Fox leaned forward and cleared his throat. In view of the exceptional circumstances, he had allowed the intrusion to take place, even though he was trying to conduct his interview. But he was conscious that it was a crucial interview in the most time-sensitive of investigations, and he had decided that enough was enough. 'Mr Baxter, I will need to ask you some questions as well. You've known Luke for ... how long?'

'Since we were ten. Ask me anything.'

'I will, thank you, after I've finished speaking to Miss Webb.'

Dale had grown up with Luke and they had spent most of their lives together. They were brothers in all but name, and he was the closest person to Luke after Melissa.
'Have you found Amber? She's a maniac and she needs to be stopped, you do understand that?' Dale felt uneasy that someone so clearly unstable was allowed to walk the streets freely in this day and age, especially after what had happened recently.

Fox knew it was essential to maintain his professionalism in such an emotionally charged situation. 'Please be assured that we're giving this investigation every available resource, Mr Baxter. But our first priority is to find Mr Black.'

Melissa shivered and Dale tightened his arms around her protectively. His thick jumper and his strong arms warmed her enough to stop her shaking. Dale was like a brother to her – there was nothing to be read into this long embrace except a friend taking care of a friend. He was one of the very few people in the world she trusted. The quizzical look on Fox's face showed what anyone else outside of their close-knit group would think, but she ignored it.

'Don't look at us like that! Luke is my best friend and I would never betray him. And anyway, my girlfriend is right there!' Dale was defensive. He was sick of the lies about Melissa. It was beyond ridiculous. On more than one occasion she had been accused of sleeping with the entire band. Yes, he thought she was attractive, but he didn't fancy her. He was in love and very happy with her best friend, who at that moment was pacing the room, looking ready to kill someone. Their glances met, and Dale gave her an 'Are you OK?' look.

'Yes, I'm fine', her expression silently replied.

'I wasn't looking at you like anything, Mr Baxter,' said Fox, although he knew he had been.

'Yes, you were!' Dale snapped.

'OK, I'm sorry, maybe it seemed that way, but I just noticed that you seem very close.'

Dale nodded, realising he had overreacted. 'We've all been through a lot together. Melissa is like a sister to me, that's all, and if this was the other way round and Beth was lying in this bed, Luke would be here doing exactly the same thing. We take care of each other, all of us – we're a family.'

Fox was still nodding and his younger colleague was scribbling everything down, quietly trying to look studious and professional and not the least bit excited at being involved at the centre of this hugely high-profile case. The rest of the world was on tenterhooks, wondering and speculating about what was happening in this room, and he was here, listening to it first-hand.

Melissa looked up at Dale like a frightened animal. 'She could come back to finish me off ... she hates me so much. I don't think she'll rest until I'm dead.' There was panic in her voice.

'No, she won't. But if she does she'll have to take me on first,' Dale said, and Jean, who had been silent for a while, patted her daughter's hand.

'Nobody will let her near you again, darling,' Jean assured her, although privately she was terrified that if they left her alone again, even for a minute, anything could happen.

'That twisted little freak of nature should be in a nut house! I'll take her down myself! Just give me two minutes with her, just two ...' Beth quietly raged as she paced round the room, flicking her curls as she did so. She was a tough girl, on the outside anyway. She definitely 'told it like it was' and made no apologies for it.

'What protection does she have?' Jean asked Fox.

'I've arranged for two officers to be outside her door at all times until we track Amber down. Now if you don't mind, I think we'd better return to your interview. Why don't you start from the beginning – when did you and Mr Black meet?'

It all seemed such a long time ago now to Melissa. But so much had happened in such a short space of time. It was like a bad dream and right now she wished she would wake up from it. She took a deep breath and began.

'I met him just over twelve months ago ...'

# Collide

*September 27th 2013*

'These guys are brilliant!' Beth had to shout over the music so Melissa could hear her.

Ruby's was packed. A local band was playing, and the place was jumping. The two girls were at the front, squeezed against the barrier at the edge of the stage. It wasn't a very big stage, and the venue had an intimate feel – they could reach out and touch the lead singer if they wanted to.

'Liss, stop drooling!' Beth laughed.

Melissa hadn't stopped staring at him since the gig started. 'I'm not!' she said defensively.

Beth flicked her hair. 'You totally were! Anyway have you seen *him* with the long hair? I like!' Long messy hair was Beth's thing.

'Now who's drooling? Anyway, will you shut up. I'm trying to listen,' Melissa said, her attention back on the band, or on him anyway. She blushed as he looked down and caught her eye. She could have sworn he smiled just slightly before turning away and looking at his bandmate. But she thought no more of it.

By the time the band had finished their set, the girls were definitely fans. They agreed that they couldn't quite place them into a particular genre. Beth thought they were alternative rock, but with a little something different, edgier perhaps. Some songs were much more aggressive and rocky than others, and some were softer with an acoustic touch. But all had more than a little attitude to them. The front man was an incredible guitarist, and they worked well together as a group. This band were clearly more than just a group of mates messing around – they were good. But it was definitely his voice that drew you in, commanding your attention. It was raspy but strong – even when the music was full-on, he sounded as though it was no effort at all. This band were unique, and the girls were hooked.

'That was epic!' Melissa gushed as they made their way to the bar. It was crowded after the show, and when they'd eventually got their drinks, they headed outside for a smoke. The smoking area was already busy but they found a space, lit their cigarettes and sipped their wine.

'Have you heard from him?' Beth asked.

Melissa had recently split with her boyfriend, Shaun, who she'd been with for eight months. He was a nice guy, but he was a bit boring and just didn't 'light her fire' as Beth put it. Melissa had been unhappy for a while but was afraid of hurting him because he hadn't done anything wrong. In fact he couldn't do enough for her. But the bottom line was that she didn't love him or want to be with him.

Beth had told her over and over, 'Just tell him. It'll hurt him no matter when or how you do it.' Beth didn't particularly like him, but she felt that Melissa had dragged it out longer than she should have, and it wasn't fair. He didn't excite her in or out of the bedroom, and that, ultimately, meant it couldn't last. But Melissa couldn't tell him that. She wasn't a heartless person, but she didn't want to be with someone who couldn't satisfy her. Her previous boyfriend, Leon, had satisfied her, but he was an arrogant jerk, who she discovered was also satisfying half of Portsmouth when he was supposed to be with her. She felt as though she couldn't win.

Beth was having no luck on the romantic front either. She'd been on a few dates recently, but none of them were right for her. They were either too clingy, came with baggage, or loved themselves way too much. She was supposed to be meeting one of them that night but had cancelled at the last minute. It hadn't gone down well. 'If it isn't working, it isn't working. He's not for me, so no point pretending otherwise,' she said before downing her drink and checking her phone.

Beth loved Twitter and would tweet everything. Melissa was more of a 'tweet when it really matters' kind of girl. They chatted about what to do for the rest of the weekend, and how good the band were, before moving on to the more pressing business of who was going to get through the scrum at the bar to buy the next round.

'They were really good – what were they called?' Melissa asked.

Beth shrugged, unable to remember.

*****

'We smashed it tonight!' Dale said, patting his best friend on the shoulder to congratulate him as they returned to the dingy backstage room which was their staging area for the evening. Another band were just leaving, ready to take to the stage.

The manager of the club came in to thank them for the show, and handed Luke their fee – the princely sum of two hundred pounds, which would pay for their drinks for the rest of the night. Luke high-fived Dale, his oldest friend and the band's rhythm guitarist, then placed his guitar on its stand. Toby, the band's drummer bounded in after them, shouting about drinking shots and getting wasted.

Everyone was in high spirits after one of their best gigs yet. But then Tom, the bass player, sighed as he noticed that the 'two shadows' were back. He looked at Luke, frustrated, but all Luke could do was return the look and shrug his shoulders. He glanced over at the two girls sitting in the corner, lying in wait for their prey. Luke wasn't happy that they were there either. They had seemed OK at first, and the band had initially been flattered by the attention. After all, these were their first 'fans' and as a new and aspiring band, fans were what they needed. Jenny wasn't that bad, although Luke had a feeling that she didn't want to be there any more than the band wanted them around. But she wasn't really the problem. Luke could feel the other girl's eyes on him. They were like lasers, and she was becoming more than a minor irritation.

'Amber, you're not welcome, go home,' Dale said pointedly, but Amber ignored him and continued to look at Luke, who was busy trying to pretend she wasn't there. She smiled and called him over. He didn't want anything to do with her but she continued to follow him around. Quite how they'd managed to get backstage he wasn't sure, but he knew that it was much easier for girls who could flirt with security and flash a bit of leg to get what they wanted. Luke wasn't a nasty person and didn't want to hurt her feelings, but he was beginning to lose patience.

'She's a bit weird if you ask me. How many times do you have to tell her to do one before she gets the message?' Tom whispered, as he opened two beers and passed one to Luke.

The band were growing increasingly tired of Amber, and if they were honest, her presence was becoming almost creepy. It was the way she watched Luke, as though she owned him and anyone who took his attention away from her was committing an offence. She was glaring at Tom now, and he was uncomfortably aware of it. He could feel her glare burning the back of his head like a laser. Luke continued trying to pretend she wasn't there, but it wasn't working very well. He resolved that he wasn't going to encourage her, and if she wanted to sit there and make herself look like an idiot, that was her choice. He definitely wasn't going to talk to her because that would be accepting her presence. It was becoming a very awkward situation, he thought, and one that needed to be dealt with sooner rather than later. He just wasn't sure how to go about it. Right now, he just wanted to get pissed.

Dale wanted to go for a cigarette and see if he could find the girl he'd spotted in the front row earlier. He thought she was hot, and Luke wasn't going to argue. It was a good excuse to get out of the room.

'Did you see her mate? Stunning!' Luke said and gave a wolf whistle. They all laughed and Luke admitted she'd almost put him off – she had the most amazing eyes.

'Wow, nothing ever puts you off!' Dale was shocked by this admission because his best friend was never distracted when they were playing. He got himself into "the zone" before they went on, and stayed there until they left the stage. Although they were an amateur band, his approach was extremely professional, and he set a perfect example for the rest of the band.

Dale declared that if they had almost distracted Luke from 'the zone', the girls had to be found because they must be special. Then, as though fate wanted to prove him right, they opened the stage door to go outside and almost collided with them.

'Sorry, excuse us,' Luke said as he jumped out of the way of the dark-haired girl. Beth also tried to step out of his way as the rest of his group walked past. She caught the eye of the long-haired guitarist and winked at him. Her heart fluttered a little as he smiled back. It was unusual because Beth didn't usually get flutters. She was quite hard to please, and she definitely knew what she wanted. Melissa side-stepped in the doorway, letting the band's singer past. He looked at her, catching her eye. He held the look a few seconds longer than was needed, and smiled warmly at her.

'Thanks,' he said, and walked on towards a group of people they knew.

Luke couldn't help but take one more quick glance back at the girl who had mesmerised him twice in one night. He decided there and then that she was going to be his before the night was over. He watched as a guy approached her and asked for a light for his cigarette in an attempt to start a conversation with her. The guy clearly had a lighter in his back pocket – Luke had watched him put it there as he walked over. Strangely, he felt uneasy about her talking to someone else. He knew it was a ridiculous feeling to have because he didn't even know the girl, but he knew that he wanted to change that. She is beautiful, he thought. The girl lit the guy's cigarette but showed no further interest. After the guy had returned to his friends and stared at her for a few minutes, he gave up and moved his attention to another target. Luke felt relieved.

'He is *so* checking you out!' Beth teased, once they were out of earshot.

Melissa knew that Beth was now on a matchmaking mission, and when she was set on something, it was a waste of time trying to talk her out of it. 'Beth, don't start with your cupid stuff, not tonight!' she moaned.

'Oh be quiet. Look, you get with him and I get with his mate. It's just meant to be! Look at him!' Beth wouldn't listen to reason now, her claws were out, ready for her prey, and Dale was that prey. Melissa laughed to herself, thinking, 'poor guy!', but she knew her friend wasn't a man-eater. Beth just didn't hang around waiting for things to happen. She decided what she wanted, and she went for it – that was just how she worked. Sometimes Melissa wished she could be a bit more like that. But at the same time it made her feel slightly uncomfortable when she was dragged along by Beth's unstoppable momentum.

'You know my motto, babe.' Beth flicked her cigarette away.

'Yes ... get on with it, you might be dead tomorrow.'

Beth grinned at her. She wouldn't be swayed. They heard loud shouts and shrieks from some of the band who had started play fighting, attracting quite an audience. It was the usual behaviour you expect when you put young men and beer together – 'peacocking' Beth called it. They knew people were watching as they tried to outdo each other and achieve top dog status. The good-natured brawl spilled into the crowd, knocking people over like dominoes. Suddenly, the girls were right next to Luke, who tried to move out of the way, but not quickly enough. He could see it coming, but the shove was much too hard and he lost his balance, falling into Melissa, the very girl he had decided he wanted to impress. She fell unceremoniously to the floor.

'Hey, watch it. You could have seriously hurt her! Idiots!' Beth yelled, holding her arms out over her friend and making sure she was OK. But secretly she was pleased. This was perfect.

'Shit. I'm so sorry!' Luke said as he looked down at her sprawled on the pavement. Beth tried to smother her laugh and Melissa shot her a deadly stare. This was *so* not funny.

'Are you OK?' Luke asked. He couldn't believe he had just done that, although it was a complete accident and he'd had no control over it, having been pushed by his friend.

Melissa tried to play it cool in front of him, but it wasn't easy whilst laying flat on the floor. He was gorgeous, in an 'ultimate rock band' kind of way. He had a cigarette in his mouth, and the smoke rose over his head as he looked down at her. Then he held out his hand to help her to her feet.

'I'm fine thanks. I don't think there are any broken bones.' She was, however, a little irritated that this had happened in front of so many people, many of whom were now falling about laughing. The rest of the band came over to apologise for pushing him and knocking her over.

'I spilt your drink as well. Would you like another?' He finished his cigarette and flicked it aside, feeling like a complete idiot. This was not a good way to introduce yourself to a girl.

'Yes, a bottle of champagne please.' Her expression was deadly serious. Beth sniggered behind her.

'Who do you think I am, Bono? How about another glass of wine instead?' he offered, smiling. He felt a bit better now, but he was still secretly seething at his idiotic friends.

'Fine, I suppose that will have to do,' she huffed, then shivered, realising how cold it was in the night air. She cursed herself for yet again not bringing a coat. The stage door was slightly open, and Melissa could see the band's equipment inside. She could also see that there were some chairs. Her feet were killing her and she wanted to sit down. 'Hey, it's freezing. Can we go inside to warm up?'

Luke could have sworn she fluttered her eyelashes, just for a second, and he thought she looked adorable. 'Sure, go on in. There isn't any wine but there are beers if you want one?'

'Beer's fine, thanks.' The girls followed the band through the stage door, down a dark corridor and into the backstage area, where they helped themselves to beers from a table. Luke turned to Dale, giving him an angry look because it had been Dale who had pushed him. His friend shrugged and pointed out that it had worked, so he should stop moaning.

'Mission accomplished!'

'You're still a dick,' Luke shot back, not at all amused. They left the two girls for a few minutes, promising to be back once they had said goodbye to some friends who were outside. There were several other people milling about in the room; a couple from another band and some staff from the venue.

Melissa sat on a tatty brown leather chair in the corner of the room. Next to it was a sleek, black electric guitar, resting on its stand. She noticed it was a Fender, which was a brand name she recognised, but that was the limit of her knowledge of guitars. It was beautiful, and she remembered seeing him play it earlier. She admired it, and almost reached out to touch it, but then had a vision of knocking it over and decided to keep her hands well away. It looked precious.

Bands were her thing. Real musicians. Boy bands made her cringe, big time. She loved to hear a group play live, preferably with songs they had written themselves. This was real talent, as far as she was concerned. The two girls had been to many gigs together, and loved watching both new and established bands. They'd been to a few festivals too. They both loved the same bands, and they lived for going to as many gigs as possible.  It was what their weekends were for, and what most of their money went on.

Beth perched on the arm of the chair, sipping her beer and smiling smugly. Phone in hand, she was tweeting as usual. 'That couldn't have worked any better! See, I know when to go for something. He definitely wants you!' she whispered to Melissa without taking her eyes off her phone. It buzzed and she read something which made her frown. She let out an irritated sigh and shook her head. Stu, the guy she had stood up, was asking when he could see her. What a cheek, she thought. 'Is he for real? He calls me a bitch and thinks I'll see him again.' She responded with a very short message, 'No, I'm too busy being a bitch right now. You blew it.' Then she blocked his number. That was how Beth did things – you very rarely got a second chance if you crossed her.

Beth then told Melissa once again that the guy she had just met definitely liked her, and that she should go for it. 'Anything has to be better than Shaun. Oh my god, Liss, how did you not die of boredom?' She leaned her head back, pretending to be asleep and snoring.

'You're so mean!'

'The guy likes staying at home at the weekend ... all the time!'

It was true. He was really quite shy and didn't like socialising much. It baffled her sometimes how they ended up together. Deep down Melissa felt sorry for him. But she didn't want to dwell on it, so moved the conversation on.

'You don't *know* that he likes me ... he invited me in for a drink, he didn't ask me to marry him!'

Beth shook her head in frustration at her friend. 'Open your eyes, babe, and go for it. What have you got to lose? Anyway, try to look interesting when they come back,' Beth ordered in her usual bossy way.

'I am interesting ... but maybe *I* don't like *him*.' Melissa leaned back in the chair, getting a little irritated with her friend. This was supposed to be a girls' night out, the rule being "no guys". She was fed up with men.

'Shut up, Liss, don't be an idiot. Of course you do ... and jeez, those guys are a brilliant band. Hot!!!' She whistled her approval. Deep down Melissa knew Beth was right.

They hadn't noticed the two girls at the other end of the room when they had first entered, until Beth realised that one of them was glaring in their direction. 'What's her problem?' she whispered. 'Are they the girlfriends?'

Melissa answered with a shrug, feeling slightly disappointed because despite what she had been saying to Beth, she really hoped he wasn't spoken for. But one of them was glaring at her as though she was about to charge over and punch her. Melissa had no idea why, so she tried to ignore the stare.

Luke jumped up the step at that moment and walked into the room. He glanced at the two mystery girls and his shoulders dropped a little. Melissa thought he sighed. If either of them were with him, he didn't seem pleased about it.

'You two still here?' he said in their direction, with more than a hint of irritation in his voice.

'Yes, waiting for you to buy us a drink,' one of them replied. But her expression changed and she looked ready to kill him as he turned, walked straight over to Melissa and Beth, and sat on the floor in front of them.

'Hi, I'm Luke.' He decided to start again and introduce himself properly. He apologised again for pushing Melissa over, an apology which she happily accepted. She then introduced herself and then Beth, but before they had a chance to say anything else, one of the other girls stood up and headed for them. Her brown hair was tied up in a ponytail and her 'little black dress' was way too little for her. It was impossible to walk gracefully in the black heels she was wearing, and she looked like she was walking on hot coals as she stumbled over. Her steely eyes glared down at Luke, and Melissa half expected lasers to shoot out from them.

'What do you want?'

'Are you going to ignore me all night?' she pouted.

'Looks like it. Amber, please give me a break.' Then he turned back to Melissa. The scowls went from Luke to Melissa and then back to Luke, and it seemed pretty clear that she must be his girlfriend. Melissa leaned forward, which with hindsight wasn't the best idea. 'I don't think your girlfriend's very happy with you. Perhaps we should go.'

Luke shook his head, saying that she definitely wasn't his girlfriend. 'She just won't take the hint,' he whispered. Meanwhile, the girl's friend now also glared in their direction.

'What?' Luke snapped at the second girl, who was sitting on a beanbag, still on the other side of the room. She jumped up and stormed over.

'You've said barely two words to her all night!' she said as the rest of the band piled into the room and began opening more beers. Melissa could see they were trying not to laugh at Luke's predicament, but clearly finding it all very amusing. She really didn't understand what was going on, but she had a feeling she was about to find out.

Luke didn't look up as he answered through gritted teeth, 'Jenny, I didn't ask her to come. Amber, you should go home.'

'Please,' she begged. 'Just give me five minutes alone to talk.'

He sighed before getting up and pulling her by the arm to a far corner of the room, where they had a hushed conversation. Melissa could only pick up snippets of what they were saying, but Amber was very animated, and she didn't look happy at whatever he was saying. Then she heard him say, 'You have to stop this. There is no us, and there never was. Why would you lie about me wanting to see you? I never said that.'

'Yes, you did!' she screamed, and grabbed his arm. 'Last night when I called you, I said I was coming tonight and you said you couldn't wait to see me!'

'Are you nuts? I didn't speak to you last night! I ignored your call, in fact I ignored all of them!'

The quiet discussion had now become a shouting match, and the whole room had stopped to watch and listen.

'I can't believe he's lying like this. He told me to come tonight!' she cried, prompting a roar of laughter from his friends and bandmates at the other end of the room.

'Shut up!' she yelled at them, but that just made them worse.

'Just leave him alone, Amber. It's gone on long enough,' Tom said. Tom was tall and skinny with black curly hair that was partially hidden under a grey beanie. Tufts of hair stuck out messily from underneath it. He wore red skinny jeans and a black T-shirt, and he looked to be the youngest of the group.

'Go to hell, Tom,' Amber fired back at him.

Tom made cuckoo signs behind her back, and the long-haired one had his hand over his heart mouthing silently, 'Oh, Luke, I love you, Luke!'

Melissa found it hard to keep a straight face – it was pretty obvious now that this was not Luke's girlfriend. He tried to move Amber from the room but all it did was anger her even more, and the argument spiralled.

Beth caught Melissa's attention, and leaned in to whisper, 'That girl is a nut job! Jeez, these guys have some mental groupies.'

Amber turned suddenly in their direction, kicked off her shoes and ran across the room. At first it seemed that Melissa was the target, so she jumped to her feet and Beth prepared to take a swing. But Amber's eyes weren't focused on either of them. She was aiming slightly to Melissa's left, towards the guitar on its stand. She could see what Amber was intending to do, and knowing how important a guitar is to its owner, she felt a strange sense of duty to protect it.

'Oh no you don't, lady!' Melissa shouted, but she was too slow.

'Liar! Nobody treats me like this!' Amber screamed, grabbing the guitar and holding it above her head. The stand toppled over and the colour drained from Luke's face. The other band members stopped laughing, shocked that the situation had suddenly become much more serious.

'Shit.' Melissa heard one say, but she wasn't sure who it was.

Luke took a step forward. 'Put it down now, you crazy bitch!'

Amber held it by the neck and prepared to swing it round towards the wall, which would smash it to pieces. It seemed to Melissa that this girl was actually mad enough to do it, so she grabbed the guitar as Amber swung it behind her, holding on for dear life. There was no way she was going to allow such a beautiful instrument (with such a beautiful owner) to be damaged. She could see the panic in Luke's face.

'Let go!' Amber screamed.

Luke stood with his hands over his eyes, helpless. 'I can't look. My baby!'

The two girls continued to wrestle with his most precious possession, neither giving in. Melissa released one hand, but still holding on to the neck she slapped Amber hard across the face. She did it instinctively, and it surprised them both. It caused the raging Amber to temporarily lose her grip, enabling Melissa to yank the precious guitar away from her.

'Seriously, chill out, love,' she said triumphantly, and a little smugly. But she then immediately began backing away from the girl who was practically hyperventilating in front of her.

'He told me to come tonight ... he said he wanted to see me,' she murmured. She looked around the room for support, but even her friend seemed shocked by her sudden, crazed outburst and gave her a pitying look.

'Come on, sweetie, let's go,' Jenny said to her gently before ushering her out of the room.

As they made their way out, Amber glared at Melissa, and the whole room saw it. She gave her a look of pure hatred, and it sent a chill down Melissa's spine. The girl was clearly obsessed with Luke. But they were not together, that much was clear.

Luke turned to Melissa once Amber had gone. She looked more than a little shaken up. 'Brilliant,' he thought to himself. 'First I knock her over, and then she's attacked by that nutter.' But she had selflessly stepped in to save his prized possession, and he had never been so grateful to anyone in his life. That guitar had taken over a year to save up for, and he'd dreamed of owning it for five years before that. If Amber had succeeded in smashing it, he wouldn't have been able to play until he had enough money to buy a new one, and that would have been a disaster.

'Thank you so much. I can't believe you did that. Are you OK?' Luke noticed that she was rubbing her hand, and there was a small cut on her palm caused by one of the strings.

She assured him it was nothing and smiled at him, looking rather dazed. 'I'll live.'

'Wow that was completely fucked up!' Dale said as he passed Luke a beer. Tom stared at the door Amber had just left through, looking disgusted. 'I need a smoke after that. You want to join us?' He asked Beth.

Beth was still bewildered by what had just happened but was very proud of Melissa. That had to win him over, she thought, and winked at her friend as she followed three of their new companions outside. The boys all agreed that Luke had shot himself in the foot with that one.

'Big mistake. Judging by how crazy she seems to be, he's gonna regret winding her up like that,' Toby sniggered. 'Wouldn't be surprised if he wakes up with a horse's head on his pillow!'

Melissa and Luke stood together awkwardly for a few seconds. Melissa was still holding his guitar by the neck, her hair hanging down to her waist rather messily after her scuffle. Her fringe was feathered and cut so it fell to the side but it was her deep blue eyes that drew you in. Her purple jeans hugged her figure tightly, showing off slender legs, and her tight black vest top displayed the message, 'Don't whistle, I'm not a dog' in gold letters across the front. She was a petite girl, and her black heels made her look much taller.

Luke thought she was stunning. She handed his guitar back, picked up her beer and took a sip. 'Thanks,' he said.

She shrugged. 'No worries, I couldn't let her damage this beauty.' He put it back on the stand after inspecting it, satisfied that there was no damage. 'How long have you been a band?' she asked. Melissa thought it must have been a while – they seemed too good to be newly formed, not that she knew anything about being in a band. But there was something about them, a chemistry and a presence which suggested they had been working together for some time.

'Just over two years, but I've known Dale since I was ten.' He flicked his hair out of his eye as he spoke.

'You're so good. Who writes your stuff? I noticed you didn't do any covers,' she asked and moved to sit sideways on the chair, hanging her legs over the arm.

'Thanks. The writing is *my* job.'

He talked at length about their music, explaining that it had been his ambition from a young age to play in a band. She listened intently, fascinated by his story and hearing the insights of someone in a real band who played in front of real paying audiences. He was clearly very passionate about his music, and was so animated as he spoke about it.

He told her how it was just himself and Dale at first, and later they'd seen Tom and Toby playing in another band. They had been impressed by them as individuals, but the band as a whole was not so great. Tom and Toby were good friends but they were on one side of a divide in the band. The other two members had been difficult to get on with, and neither Tom nor Toby felt they were going to be able to resolve things, so they decided to quit. It was perfect timing, because at that time, Luke and Dale were becoming serious about forming their own group. They got talking to Tom and Toby and they agreed to have a few practice sessions together. It was a great success and a lot of fun because they all got on like a house on fire. Everyone agreed they should play their own material rather than regurgitating the music of others, and so The Black Eagles were born.

Luke realised how comfortable he felt with this girl. He'd been talking to her for ages about things he would not usually tell someone he'd just met, but somehow this felt different. At the same time, he was very embarrassed by Amber's performance, and concerned that she was proving to be difficult to shake off. He had made a mistake, a drunken one, but a mistake nonetheless. Luckily for him, Melissa didn't seem to be put off. She carried on asking him questions about himself and the band, and he asked about her. They chatted while Beth interviewed the rest of the group, who she thought all seemed like genuine, fun guys. Tom was probably the most stand-offish but he was friendly enough. Toby was treating her as though he had known her for years - he seemed to just want a good time with no drama. Beth noticed how big he was, like a brick wall. He had no hair, although you couldn't really tell because the hood was up on his black sweater, which displayed the word 'Fucked' across the front in white letters.

'Is Amber his ex?' Beth asked Dale, who was standing beside her sipping a beer.

They all laughed, except Tom, who looked disgusted to hear the name again. 'That Bunny boiler needs to see a shrink,' he grumbled.

'No, she was just a one-off mistake. But now she's obsessed with him and won't take the hint.' Dale explained, shaking his head.

'Does he make mistakes like that often?' Beth asked. If he was a guy who slept around, then she didn't want Melissa anywhere near him. Beth hated people like that, and Melissa had already been through that kind of heartache with Leon, so she didn't want her hurt again.

'No, not at all. The episode with Amber was a few weeks ago and it was a wild night. Things happen sometimes, but not very often and never with a performance like that afterwards. He never promised the girl anything. It was she who said there were no strings attached.'

Beth always checked guys out first, to make sure they were suitable. Melissa was like a sister to her and she had always been there when Beth needed her, so she hated seeing her friend hurt and would do what she could to make sure it didn't happen. She felt a bit like her guardian angel, although she tried not to make it too obvious because she didn't want it to look like she was interfering.

'You're very protective of her.' Dale had noticed how she seemed to watch people around her friend – these girls were obviously very close. She was doing it now, continually glancing through the door at Melissa and Luke, who were staring intently at each other, deep in conversation.

'Yes, I am. Are you interested in her? You might want to get in line,' she said, feeling a little deflated by the thought that he might like

Melissa too.

'No.' He looked her in the eyes as he replied. 'It's just that you act like her bodyguard.'

Someone handed him a joint and he took a few puffs before passing it to Beth. She did the same and handed it back. She much preferred a cigarette to a joint. Too much weed made her sleepy and sometimes light headed, but a bit now and again didn't hurt. 'We've been friends since we were four years old. We met at nursery – I pulled her hair and she pushed me over, then we both laughed and played together for the rest of the day. We've been inseparable ever since.' Her black curls whipped around her face in the breeze. Dale wasn't interested in Melissa, he wanted this beautiful girl in front of him. The play fighting earlier had been planned, although they hadn't intended on it getting so out of hand. And so far it was working out just fine, Dale thought.

Dale noticed that Beth was much curvier than Melissa, and her black cords hugged her figure showing it off nicely. But mainly he liked her bossy, upfront, yet friendly, attitude. 'Melissa is not my type - I prefer midnight curls,' he said and winked. He then decided that having said that, he might as well just ask her before someone else beat him to it. 'Beth, would you—'

'Yes I would, that would be nice' Beth answered, like lightning.

'You don't know what I was going to say!' he laughed.

'Yes I do. You were going to ask me out,' she replied confidently, but secretly hoping she hadn't just made a complete fool of herself.

'You don't mess about, do you?'

'Nope. Life's too short,' she said, smiling sweetly at him.

He stood up straight and took another puff of the joint, feeling very pleased with himself. He liked this girl.

'It's a date then.'

Beth nodded. She had set her sights on him and had won him over in minutes, demonstrating once again that she always got what she wanted.

Tom and Toby were chatting to a few girls who seemed to be hanging on their every word, leaving Dale to it with Beth. There was a rule in the band that they never trod on each other's toes when it came to women. It was the age-old rule that you never mess with a mate's girl. Dale had laid claim to Beth, and Luke had done the same with Melissa. It didn't need spelling out to Tom and Toby that both girls were now out of bounds. In Melissa's case in particular, they both knew very well that they wouldn't have any chance even if they *were* to compete with Luke. Being the front man of the band had numerous advantages, and popularity with the ladies was definitely one of them.

*****

'Aren't you cold?' Melissa asked, pointing at Luke's bare chest. He was still shirtless from the gig –- he rarely wore a top when performing, claiming that he always got too hot, what with the lights and the energy of their show. Nothing to do with impressing girls though, definitely not.

Luke's hair was jet black, and although it was short he had one slightly longer piece of fringe which fell over his left eye, almost reaching his top lip. It was cut into a jagged shape, almost like lightning. Melissa wasn't sure if this was deliberate, but she noticed that he flicked it a lot, and part of her wondered why he chose to have it like that, if it got in the way so much. His eyes were sapphire blue and he had the most beautiful tattoos on the left side of his body. Covering his rib cage was a magnificent eagle, wings stretched back, and talons ready to strike at prey. The eyes and beak were savage and intense, and Melissa loved it.

Then she noticed his arms, which seemed to show fragmented parts of a picture. When she asked him about it, he simply smiled before bringing his arms together with his hands facing upwards. She could now see that on each arm was half of a picture, which was now complete. It was the same eagle, but the wings and talons were curled around a black guitar. It was much more vicious looking, but both tattoos were magnificent, and in a certain light Melissa thought she almost saw them move. She liked the way Luke dressed. At the moment, he was only wearing dark blue jeans with black and white Nike casual shoes but they suited him well. Over the back of the chair was his black hoody.

'They're awesome!' she said, giving her approval of the tattoos.

Luke told her they were something called "New Skool", a specific type of tattoo art. He laughed and said that Toby, the drummer, was like a human canvas, so if she was impressed by his, then she would love Toby's.

'It's freezing in here.'

Luke noticed her shiver and leaned over her to reach for his black hoody. His chest was inches from her face, and she had to resist the urge to do something inappropriate. He handed her the hoody and she wrapped it around her shoulders. She was disappointed when he put on a long-sleeved white T-shirt because she'd been enjoying the view of his toned body. He was the smallest of the band in stature, but seemed to be their biggest member in personality and charisma – he was unquestionably the leader. When he spoke, they listened.

He picked up a black classic guitar and placed it with the other one ready to pack away. She hadn't noticed it before, but this one was also his. He called it Chloe.

Luke was Melissa's idea of a perfect man, certainly on first impressions anyway. She already felt as though she could just sit with him all night and listen to him talk. His voice was soft and friendly, in contrast to the strong, masculine singing voice she had heard during the gig. He seemed to look deep into her eyes, and it made her heart pound because his diamond-shaped face and disarming gaze were like nothing she had encountered before.

She finished her beer, which gave her a reason to move away and regain some composure. She told herself to stop staring at him so much, although he didn't seem to mind, she thought. She returned quickly with fresh beers, anxious not to be away for longer than necessary, in case someone else moved in.

She decided she needed to know more about the scene that had unfolded earlier with the other girl. 'Your groupies are nuts by the way!' Although she wanted to know more, she thought that it was a bit too soon for personal questions, even though he did seem to have been talking very openly to her so far. Luke's smile immediately faded at her comment, but he had known it was coming at some point. He explained that Amber had been 'just a one-night stand' which he wished had never happened. But since that night she wouldn't leave him alone, despite his best efforts to let her down gently, and get the message across to her however he could.

He worried about how this would look to Melissa and he didn't want her to think he was a man who slept around, because he really wasn't like that. It was certainly true that he could be, if he wanted to – he wasn't short of offers. But he wasn't that sort of guy. Amber wasn't his type at all, and he'd regretted it ever since. Tonight more than ever. 'I know that wasn't the best way to make a first impression, so I wondered if you were free tomorrow so I can make it up to you?'

Melissa wrinkled her nose while she pretended to think about it and Luke held his breath, waiting for her answer. The first time you ask someone out is the moment you find out whether they have any genuine interest in you, and it made Luke nervous. He wasn't sure why, because he was usually pretty confident in these situations. But there was something about Melissa which made it different. He was desperate for her to say yes, and terrified of a rejection. Maybe it was something to do with him struggling to take his eyes off this girl he'd known for less than an hour, he thought. But at the moment all he could think about was kissing her.

'Maybe. I'll check my diary.'

'We're playing in Chichester tomorrow night, and it would be nice if you could make it. In case we need extra security!' He tried to make a joke of it.

'Do you need me to be your bodyguard?' she giggled.

'You're welcome to guard my body any time.' It was his turn to embarrass himself. You idiot, what a fucking corny line, he thought to himself.

They drank and danced the rest of the evening, and everyone seemed to get along really well. It had taken Beth one hour and twenty-three minutes to win Dale over, and he looked just as pleased with himself as she did as they snogged away. Her approach to life was not to hang around waiting for things, but just get on with it. Melissa felt that they were going a bit far. They really did need to get a room, she thought – they hadn't come up for air for ages. But she didn't mind her friend deserting her as her focus was on Luke.

She was making her way to the bar when a noticeboard caught her attention. It was full of flyers for various local and nationwide events, but one stood out. It was perfect! She pulled it from the wall, folded it up and shoved it in her bag, to deal with later. It needed thinking about first, as she didn't want it to seem like she was interfering. The band clearly meant so much to Luke. But she was sure it was a perfect opportunity for her new friends.

Everyone seemed to have formed friendships very quickly. Toby was hilarious and had the girls almost crying with laughter with his non-stop jokes and laddish antics. Despite his menacing appearance, he seemed like a lovely guy. Tom had warmed to them as the evening went on, and was laughing along with them, just as the others were. He'd chatted to Melissa, realising that maybe she wasn't a mental case. It was a great relief, in view of recent events. Dale was just a genuine, friendly type who seemed to really like Beth. Of course he was snared now, so he didn't really have a choice in the matter. But he certainly wasn't putting up much of a fight. He also seemed to have a calming influence on everyone, which she liked. Melissa was still trying to figure Luke out, but she was analysing him in much greater detail. Overall, they seemed like a typical group of lads, just wanting to have fun. She admitted to herself that they were a little wilder than she was used to, but it was all good-natured and she liked it.

'There you are. I'll get these,' Luke said, as he caught up with her. She tried to say no, but he wouldn't hear of it. She thanked him and gave him her order.

'You don't have to pay for my drinks all night. I feel guilty.' So far, he hadn't let her pay for anything. He brushed aside her protests. He was happy to pay, even though his fee for the night was already gone. He was enjoying the night and her company, so why not?

By choice, he had been single for six months, but now he was bored of being on his own. Although they'd only been in each other's company for a few hours, he was enjoying being with a girl again, and found it remarkably easy and comfortable to slip into that feeling with Melissa. It was as though he'd known her for months, rather than hours.

'Are you trying to get me drunk?' she joked.

Luke shook his head and laughed. If he was lucky enough to get close to her, he didn't want her to be drunk. She was the prettiest girl in the place, and he could see the attention she was getting from other men, and a few of the women too. He wasn't dropping the ball on this one. She was amazing, and what he liked most was that she didn't even seem to know it. He had known plenty of girls in his time who were drop-dead gorgeous and were all too aware of it, which often made them unpleasant people. It was a trait that Luke disliked intensely. Ironically, he was also oblivious to the attention he was getting. In the same way that men were watching Melissa, the women were watching him. After all, he was the lead singer of the band. They weren't famous, but that didn't matter in a small venue like this, filled with genuine music fans. They had a definite presence about them, and it felt as though they could be famous one day. Melissa hadn't missed the fact that there were eyes on him – she could see other girls lying in wait, hoping he would stop talking to her and present an opportunity to pounce. She laughed to herself. No way. He's mine.

'I have to go after this drink. I've got to work in the morning. Beth wants to stay out though, so will you make sure she gets home OK?' she asked.

Luke looked disappointed because he didn't want her to go. It seemed like only five minutes since he'd pushed her over. He looked at his watch and realised it had in fact been nearly four hours. He promised her that Beth would be fine, and they'd look after her. She knew Beth would be safe with these guys, but was aware that she wouldn't normally entrust her well-being to a group of men she'd only just met. But this was different somehow.

Luke tried to make her drink last a long time, playfully moving it away every time she tried to take a sip. He made her laugh, and kept reaching over and messing with her hair as she talked. They sat at a table and talked for what was supposed to be the last few minutes, while the others 'ripped up the dance floor' at Toby's insistence. Over an hour later, and not before making Dale swear over and over again that he'd make sure Beth got home safely, she said goodbye to her new friends and Luke walked her to her taxi. It was cold in the night air, and without thinking, and as if to prove how comfortable she felt with him, she linked arms with him and they cuddled up as they walked. He put his arm around her, tucking her under his jacket to keep her warm. She was so tiny, she could almost fit inside it with him. As they turned the corner, they saw her taxi waiting and Melissa suddenly felt irritated that she had to leave.

'I had a really good night. I'm sorry I have to go.' Luke seemed disappointed too. This was that moment when you don't know if you should get in the taxi and go home or kiss the person. Melissa wanted to kiss him, but what if she had totally misread his friendliness as just that?

'Did you check your diary?'

Melissa frowned as she pretended to think about it. 'Yeah, I think I'm free, and besides, you might need my protection.' Luke smiled, and pulled his phone from his pocket. They swapped numbers, then she turned to get into the taxi. At that moment he decided what he should do, and grabbed her hand, pulling her back towards him. They locked eyes and she willed him to kiss her. She'd been waiting all night for him to do it, but she wasn't as forward as Beth. As Luke bent his head slowly down, her heart beat faster and fluttered as she felt his lips on hers, locking her into a gentle, passionate kiss. He held her tightly around the waist, pressing their bodies together with one hand while his other hand cupped her cheek. He wanted to get in the taxi with her; all she had to do was ask him. But he was a gentleman, and he wouldn't get ahead of himself. This guy can kiss, she thought as she wrapped her arms around his neck and melted into him. She could taste the beer and whisky on his lips, and his stray bit of fringe tickled her cheek making her giggle. She backed away to move it but he held on to her, not wanting the moment to end.

'Please stay,' he almost begged.

Melissa wished she could, more than anything, but she had to go, and she promised that she would see him tomorrow.

Then he kissed her once more, before whispering in her ear, 'See you tomorrow, beautiful.'

She smiled all the way home.

*****

It was so tempting to stay out and not let the evening end, but she was already walking a thin line with her boss due to poor timekeeping recently, and if she was late again she knew she'd probably be in the job centre by Monday. She had no choice but to smile her way through a full working weekend in the busy café. It was hardly thrilling work and not really her calling in life, but it paid the bills.

She closed her eyes to avoid any conversation with the taxi driver, and twenty minutes later she was home and snuggled up in bed, still smiling from an incredible evening. A text arrived from Luke, checking she was home OK and thanking her for a lovely evening. She thought it was very sweet of him. She took a photo of herself all safe and warm, tucked up in bed, and sent it back to him. It wasn't rude in any way, but she did it just to tease him a bit. Luke cheekily suggested that if he could join her he'd be there in minutes, she just had to say the word. He made it sound like a joke, but they both knew that he meant it. The flirty conversation went on for a while and she started to think that he should have just come home with her. But she wasn't that type of girl. It was gone four by the time she fell asleep.

*****

'Bitch!' Amber hissed to herself, raging as she watched Melissa kiss him while the taxi waited. She couldn't believe that this girl had just walked into their lives and stolen him, without any shame or hesitation. And he had just let her do it. She promised herself that there was no way she was going to let this happen; Luke was hers, and she was going to make the Bitch regret messing with her man.

He was heading back inside the club when Amber grabbed his arm. 'Luke, please, I'm sorry about earlier. Can I talk to you?'

'No, Amber, I've told you to leave me alone and I meant it.' He yanked his arm from her grip. He'd never regretted anything as much as he regretted giving in to the crazy girl's advances, and he was really starting to lose his temper with her.

'I know I embarrassed you earlier and I'm sorry.' She pleaded with him, but he just shook his head and walked away, leaving her standing alone as he returned to his friends. He smiled as he walked through the crowd, Amber quickly forgotten as his kiss with Melissa still lingered on his lips.

Amber's rage bubbled inside and she felt a strange sensation coming over her, a feeling of disconnection from what was going on around her. She walked through the crowd of drunken teenagers and twenty-something's inside the club, and for a while just stood and watched him, her beautiful Luke. He was talking to his drummer who was laughing at something he had said, and patting him on the back. She heard him say her name and he smiled. She wanted to believe he'd said something nice about her, but deep down she knew it was the opposite. Amber scowled at Melissa's annoying friend who seemed to think she was centre of their attention now, clinging to Dale and laughing smugly as she passed Luke another whisky. Amber had seen enough, so she turned on her heels and headed home. She had to find a way to get rid of Melissa and her friend, whatever it took. She was not going to lose him to anyone. It wasn't his fault. It was his stupid friends, she thought. They didn't like her because she was closer to him than they were, so they were poisoning him against her.

# A great idea?

September 2013

'That's awesome!'

Toby was showing off his artwork. His entire back was one big piece of art, and Melissa was admiring the fallen angel which was arched over a girl who looked lost and scared. Her head was down, causing her long hair to flow over her face. It was a beautiful wave of hair and very skilfully drawn with an impressive level of detail. Her head was at a slight angle so that you could only see one eye. The wings were those of an eagle, and they arched over as if to shield the girl with their strength. It was breath taking and beautiful.

'It is pretty cool, isn't it?' Toby was very proud of it. It had taken weeks of planning and several long and painful visits to the tattoo parlour to create it, and he showed it off at every opportunity. Melissa noticed that the entire piece was painted in the most vibrant colours and there was a hint of black shading, like a shadow, around the angel. But one detail stood out – the girl's hair and eye had no colour at all. Melissa pointed it out, intrigued.

'They'll be coloured in when I find 'the one',' he said without a hint of jest. It was a small insight into the real character of Toby. Only a few people ever got to see this side of him. He was a lovable and caring giant, and behind the public façade, he took care of his own. He had a fun-loving and carefree attitude to life, but beneath that, he had an emotional side and he was looking for a special girl to settle down with. He would not normally have given this sort of honest answer to someone he barely knew, but Melissa's disarming personality had caused him to let his guard down. He didn't mind though - he liked her and felt as though her friendship with Luke and the band would not be a fleeting one.

They were all in good spirits, having played to a packed bar in

Chichester earlier in the evening. They seemed to have been well received by the crowd of mainly university students. They were again paid only a small fee for the gig, and it was already being handed back across the bar, where Tom and Toby were attempting to drink it dry. They'd hooked up with a small group of girls who were all giggling every time either of them cracked a joke, regardless of whether it was remotely funny or not.

Melissa thought again to herself that there was definitely something about this group of guys, and it wasn't put on or forced. They were just being themselves, and people liked them. The same was true when they were on stage. But unlike most men she'd known in the past, she felt as though she genuinely wanted to talk to them and listen to what they had to say. She smiled to herself, feeling very proud that they seemed to be her new friends. Beth and Dale were all over each other again, and might as well have just left to get a room, and Luke was having a heated discussion with someone he had met at the bar about guitarists, their opinions differing on who was better. Luke was clearly a Jimi Hendrix fan and the other guy favoured Van Halen. After a while Melissa got bored listening to the discussion going round in circles. She couldn't care less either way; they were both good, so why did it matter? She headed to the bar and found Toby lining up more shots. He passed her a Sambuca.

'Hey, get this down you!'

Melissa took it and knocked it back, immediately wondering whether it was wise. She'd struggled to get through work today, and had to go in again tomorrow. Luke found her at the bar when he too had finally got bored of what he'd eventually decided was 'the most fucking stupid argument ever'.

Melissa realised that she was now on her fourth large glass of wine, and the shot she'd just downed was not her first. She'd been attempting to keep up with Toby and had been carried along by his infectious enthusiasm. But it was clear that she was lagging badly behind, and so she decided it wasn't even worth trying. 'Have you finished talking about that Jimi Halen guy?' Melissa slurred her words as she threw her arms round his neck.

He laughed loudly. 'Yeah.'

She knew she must have said something wrong by the way he laughed. 'What's so funny?'

'Nothing, nothing at all,' he said and kissed her forehead. He didn't want to explain; it would just embarrass her.

'I need to go soon. Working at the weekend should be made illegal,' she complained.

'Really, you're leaving me again?' Luke made a sad face as he looked down at her. How could she abandon him two nights in a row? He was only joking but he was disappointed to be parted from her again. Melissa assured him that if she had a choice, she would stay. Luke had put a few drinks away himself, and felt confident to ask whether he could go home with her. Not yet, she told him. She never took a guy home until she knew him well enough to feel comfortable about it. That was her rule, and she never broke it, even though this time it was very hard to resist.

She was wearing a body-hugging short purple dress which showed off her perfect petite figure. Luke couldn't stop looking at her for the second night running, but he respected her for not jumping into bed with him, frustrating as it was. She'd almost put him off again while he was playing, and it was exciting but slightly unnerving for him. Nobody had affected him like this before. It was very different to the beginning of any other relationship he'd had.

Melissa gushed about how good the gig was, saying that seeing them for the second time was somehow better than the first. Probably because she knew some of the songs now. He just nodded and smiled, trying not to seem big-headed. But he liked hearing her say it; his last girlfriend never had anything positive to say. Then, as if to back her up, a group sitting at a table next to them got up and came over, saying they'd really enjoyed the gig and thought The Black Eagles had bags of potential. You should be selling CDs, they said. If they were, they would have sold six right there an then. That would have paid for another round of drinks for starters, Melissa joked. The idea of making an EP was something Luke was working on, but the problem was that you needed money up front to pay for a studio, production etc. With their current lifestyle, they woke up the morning after each gig night with nothing but a pocket full of change and a headache.

The good wishes were very welcome, and with her idea in mind, Melissa had been making mental notes all night about how the gig went down with the paying punters.

'See, I'm right ... you're amazing!'

He smiled broadly, and she could tell it had made his night.

Beth stumbled over, and threw her arms around their necks. 'Come and dance with me, lovers!' She didn't give Melissa a choice, grabbing her by the hand and dragging her to the front, where another band had taken the stage.

'Just one song. I have to work in the morning!' Melissa said.

'Work, shmirk!' Beth dismissed her weak protest, and carried on regardless.

Beth was happy, which was nice to see because she'd been a bit down recently. Dale was taking her mind off things and they were having fun, so maybe another hour wouldn't hurt, Melissa thought. The girls danced together, becoming the centre of attention as always. If there was one thing Melissa and Beth did well, it was take over a room. With Melissa in her little dress causing men to almost pass out, and Beth in an equally short yellow dress, also looking stunning, it wasn't a surprise when several chat-up lines came their way. They usually wore more comfortable outfits, but they were out to impress tonight. One very drunk man was quite insistent that Beth danced with him, and his friend was finding it difficult to understand the word 'no' from Melissa. Neither advance was welcome. Luke was outside with Tom, and missed the entire incident, but the two guys' faces were a picture when Toby and Dale appeared from nowhere and told them in no uncertain terms to back off. They practically wet themselves at the sight of Toby towering over them, and the girls found it hilarious. He was one of the nicest blokes you could ever meet, but with his bald head, ear piercings, and tattoos, he looked pretty formidable. He made Melissa look even tinier than she was, but he was very reassuring to have around.

'Thanks, Toby,' Melissa said, and gave him a friendly hug.

He smiled. 'No problem. They needed telling, couple of idiots. I don't like that sort of thing anyway, but even less so when it's my mate's girlfriend.' He was clearly very fired up, and had surprised himself by how quickly he'd become protective of these two girls. They had slotted into their group so quickly and effortlessly, and they were a lot of fun to have around. It didn't feel like an intrusion as far as Toby was concerned, as it could easily have done.

'Oh …' Melissa wasn't sure what to say. It had thrown her a little to be referred to as Luke's girlfriend.

'That's what you are, right?' he said, smirking a little because she was blushing.

'I-I don't know.' She didn't actually know where things with Luke were going; she hadn't really had a chance to think about it given that they had only met twenty-four hours earlier. It was true that the way they'd been getting on, it looked like it was going that way pretty quickly. If that's what people already thought, she certainly wasn't going to argue about it.

Toby laughed. 'He hasn't shut up about you all fucking day! Melissa this, Melissa that. Melissa is so great, blah blah blah!'

She went even redder. 'Shut up, you idiot!' She was embarrassed, but very pleased at the same time.

'It's true, I haven't heard him talk about a girl like that in the time I've known him.' he said, turning back to the bar to order more drinks. She smiled again.

Melissa turned down another drink, and decided to finally head home. Luke protested again, but she insisted that she had to go, and she'd already stayed out longer than she should have. The taxi driver wasn't impressed at having to wait an extra ten minutes while they kissed each other goodnight, but they didn't care.

'I'll speak to you tomorrow, if you can wait until then.' Melissa joked. Finally, released from Luke's hold, she got into the waiting taxi and apologised to the grumpy driver. It was after two o'clock and her groggy mind was turning to the prospect of dragging herself through another day at work. But after the fantastic evening she'd had, it was definitely a price worth paying.

*****

On Sunday night, once Melissa had finished her shift, she lay on the sofa at home with a bowl of strawberry ice cream – her hangover food of choice – and reflected on what had been an incredible and totally unexpected weekend's events. She was feeling the effects of having had a combined total of only eight hours' sleep in two nights, but she'd enjoyed every moment of their evenings out, and she wouldn't have changed a thing. Apart from having to work, maybe.

After a very long and at times funny phone conversation with Luke and his three mental bandmates, she was feeling much better. They were at Toby's, having some beers to round off the weekend, and congratulating themselves on two very successful gigs. Luke hated his day job too, but he confidently assured Melissa that one day, when they were selling out arenas on their world tour, she wouldn't have to work. It made her smile, especially when he referred to her as his girlfriend.

'If you want to be, that is?' he asked, realising that he'd better not sound like he was making assumptions.

'Of course I do. I don't go around saving guitars for just anyone, you know.'

After hanging up, Melissa looked at the piece of paper she'd picked up at Ruby's on Friday. The name 'Amplified' jumped off the page. It was a 'Battle of the Bands' competition to be held in Hyde Park, London, and she noticed that the closing time for entries was midnight that night. Only twenty bands would be chosen to compete, but she thought the Black Eagles would have a great chance, and she couldn't help feeling that it could be their big break. She debated the pros and cons in her mind for ages, thinking back to the audience reaction she'd seen. In the end, she decided that yes, they were definitely good enough, and they just needed a push in the right direction. Thinking that Luke wouldn't do it without some encouragement, she grabbed her laptop and fired it up. She looked at the application page and then nearly talked herself out of it before starting to fill it in. As well as the usual information, the organisers also wanted at least four minutes of footage from a gig, or even just a practice session. She'd got that much the previous night on her phone, so she uploaded it and watched it a couple of times, just to remind herself, and to make sure it did them justice. She tried to look at it from a neutral perspective, to make sure she wasn't just being biased (which was difficult), but she was convinced that they were too good to be playing to dingy bars forever – it just seemed like a waste of their talent. They needed to find their big break, and she felt excited that this could be it. She filled in the form, then hovered her finger over the 'submit' button, again agonising over the decision for what felt like hours. What if they thought it was a terrible idea and hated her for doing it behind their backs? But what about the possibilities if they were selected?

With five minutes to go until midnight, she knew she had to decide. Closing her eyes and taking a deep breath, she pressed 'submit'.

It was too late to change her mind now.

# Play for me

October 2013

'Please tell me that wasn't a joke,' Luke said in disbelief. He was expecting to be told that the phone call he had just taken was some sort of prank.

Melissa shook her head, smiling on the outside but terrified on the inside, unsure how he would react to her entering them in the competition without their knowledge. 'No, it really isn't a wind-up – as if I would do that!'

'I can't believe you did that for us!' Luke picked her up and kissed her.

They'd only been together for two weeks, but the feelings between them were growing stronger every day. They spent most evenings together, usually at Toby's, which was the venue for the band's practice sessions. His neighbours were used to hearing their music, but they tried to be considerate, keeping the noise levels reasonable and the times sociable.

Although he hadn't slept at his parents' place for days now, this was the first night Luke and Melissa had really spent the whole evening alone together. It was a rare night off from band activities, and they had decided to just relax together at Melissa's place.

The phone call inviting them to compete at Amplified had nearly ended badly. The man who had phoned Luke sounded a lot like Dale, and Luke had initially thought it was a wind-up. Luckily, Melissa was nearby and heard his confused response.

'Amplified? What the ... if this is you, Dale—'

Melissa had to intervene quickly, and pointed at herself whispering, 'It was me ... I did it – it's real!'

Luke quickly realised that she was being honest, and that the call was genuine. He accepted the offer politely, and sheepishly apologised for the initial misunderstanding. He looked a little dazed as he hung up, looking at her for an explanation of what had just happened.

'Wow, this is mad...' was the only response he could manage after Melissa explained everything and brought him up to date. He was still trying to comprehend what it meant for them – it was huge. But then it dawned on him that they had only two weeks to prepare, and he began to panic. Should he write some new material or stick with what they knew? He seemed to want Melissa's opinion, and it was a nice feeling for her.

'Luke, you'll be fantastic whatever you do, so just do what you feel is right. But if you ask me, you should stick with what you know and have practiced playing 100 times. There isn't time to write and rehearse anything new, and even if you did, would it be better than what you have now? I doubt it.' She did insist that whatever they did, they must include "Weekend High" because it was her favourite. Luke said she could have whatever she wanted.

'What made you enter us? You really think we can do it?' He couldn't get his head round the fact that she had done this for them. Deep down, he knew it was exactly the sort of thing he'd been wanting them to do for a while, but he just hadn't plucked up the courage to do it himself. It was a terrifying prospect, but at the same time very exciting.

'Of course you can do it! I entered you because you are an amazing band! You're much better than you give yourselves credit for.' He laughed and made a joke about himself. He didn't seem to realise how good they were, or he did a very good job of hiding it. Melissa suspected it was to protect himself from rejection or ridicule, and she knew that he wouldn't want to come across as arrogant.

She went on. 'I wouldn't have even considered it if I didn't think you were good enough. I can't explain it ... I just saw the flyer by chance and it was as though I was being told to do it, like destiny or something. I nearly did it the first night I met you but I waited until I'd seen you play again.' She told him how she nearly decided against it, and how she was undecided right up until the deadline. 'I know we barely knew each other back then, and I knew I was taking a big risk. I didn't even know if we'd be together—'

He cut her off by kissing her again. She didn't need to give any more explanation – he was delighted that she'd done it. 'Thank you. We'll make sure we do it justice, and make you proud of us.'

'Can I come with you?'

'You're definitely coming with us! That is not up for discussion. We need our girls with us, you know, for protection.' Her big blue eyes gazed into his, and her smile lit up her face. She admitted that she'd thought he wouldn't want her there, in case she was a distraction. He told her that was ridiculous.

Luke called the guys, and they rushed round to see them. They couldn't believe that they'd been asked to compete, and they were equally amazed that Melissa had made it happen for them. As an aspiring band, they'd had to struggle for every small break they'd got so far, and nobody had ever done something like this for them before.

'Melissa, you little beauty!' Toby ruffled her hair before giving her a huge hug and lifting her off her feet. Hair ruffling seemed to be his trademark way of saying 'Hi' to people, and she now always made sure she had a hair brush in her bag, to tidy herself up after Toby had arrived.

Melissa watched quietly as they stood in her kitchen, talking and laughing excitedly, and making plans for the big event. She felt a warm satisfaction that she'd made her friends so happy. Her gamble had certainly paid off. They were like children, boisterous and animated, debating which songs to use in their set and listing the things they'd need for the big road trip to London. The first thing on the agenda was a trip to 'Leo's Guitar Heaven' in Fratton. They needed to update some of their smaller bits of equipment, which they'd been putting off due to lack of money. But simply making do wasn't an option any more though, everything needed to be perfect.

Melissa noticed that Beth was standing behind Dale, quieter than usual and maybe looking a little annoyed. She was actually feeling left out – Melissa was the hero of the hour and Beth didn't like to be anything other than the centre of attention. To push Beth aside had never been Melissa's intention, but Beth needed to feel important – it was one of the scars left behind by her difficult childhood, a past she was still trying to heal from.

Dale looked up at her and took her hand. He knew her full story – she had trusted him so much that she had told him everything after just over a week together. It was a calculated risk in Beth's mind because he could have run a mile. But she had a feeling he wouldn't, and she felt that to be honest from the start was the right thing to do. She was right, because it had made them stronger. From Dale's point of view, he got to know the real Bethany Watkins that day, and he was pleased that she trusted him enough to confide in him. It also made him understand a lot more about the bond between the girls.

'Why didn't you tell me what you were up to?' Beth asked Melissa as they both moved to one side of the room. She'd been sulking, but trying not to show it. As well as feeling a bit left out, she was nervous that Dale would think she didn't care as much about him as Melissa did about Luke. She was completely in love with him, and she was just as proud of her man. If she was completely honest, she wished she'd thought of the idea rather than Melissa, or at least that it had been a joint venture between them.

'Sorry, babe – I just sort of did it and then forgot about it.' She felt a sudden pang of guilt and realised she needed to make her friend feel better. 'If it wasn't for you playing Cupid and making me talk to Luke, we wouldn't have met them, and none of this would have happened. So you played a part too, a much more important one than me in fact.' This went down well, and Beth's mini strop was averted. Looking back, it had probably been the boys' play fighting that had broken the ice that first night, but that didn't matter.

Dale looked over at Melissa, smiled and winked as if to say, 'Nicely done.'

'Liss, have you seen the date of the competition?' Beth suddenly started jumping excitedly on the spot. Her mood had clearly improved, and she felt part of things again.

Melissa grabbed the paper Beth was waving around and checked the date. In all the excitement she hadn't even thought about her birthday. 'Oh my god, I hadn't even noticed that!'

Luke looked up at her as he scribbled in the little notebook he always carried. He frowned and said he hoped that she didn't have other plans. He really wanted her to be there as their good luck charm.

'It's the weekend of my birthday, October 26th - it'll be a perfect way to celebrate!' The boys cheered at another reason to get, as Toby put it, 'absolutely fucking mullered!'

Luke realised that they'd never discussed birthdays, and it gave him another reason to panic. He was already planning to use every penny he had for Amplified, but he couldn't just ignore her birthday. After a bit of frantic brainstorming, one idea for a present came to mind. He thought it could work and wouldn't cost much, but he cursed himself because he wanted to be able to splash out and buy her a special present. He hated the fact that he couldn't spoil her as he wanted to. Then, to make him feel even more useless, she kneeled down next to him and whispered in his ear, 'I can help out with money if you want. I'll pay for our room in London and I know you need new guitar strings.'

She had a bit of money put away for a rainy day. She always saved a little each month – it was something she'd done since she got her first job. Her dad was a partner in an accountancy firm, and he had always taught her to be sensible with money. As a family they had always been comfortable financially, and as she grew up she looked back and was grateful for the security her parents had given her in her formative years. Her mum worked part time in a flower shop, not because the family needed the money, but because she enjoyed it and it was important to her to feel that she was making a contribution. She used her wages to buy little luxuries for the family, and she still helped Melissa out from time to time, even now that she was grown-up. She had paid for their tickets for the gig on the night they met the boys, as a treat, so Melissa gave her mum some of the credit for her having met Luke, as well as Beth.

Melissa had about a thousand pounds in a savings account, and it had taken about two years to save, but she decided she would use it for Luke if he needed it. He shook his head as he kissed her forehead, but she insisted that she wanted to help, so he reluctantly agreed, temporarily at least. 'I shouldn't be taking your money,' he whispered, feeling embarrassed. The others were chatting loudly in the living room, so their conversation couldn't be overheard.

'Why not? It's the twenty-first century – we're supposed to be equals, aren't we? I want to help, and I don't want you to be stressing about money on top of getting ready for the competition – you need to be fully prepared and focused. I know I don't really understand all the ins and outs of your equipment, but I know it doesn't come cheap if you want the best.'

Luke appreciated her generosity, but knew he would feel terrible if she had to dip into her savings to pay for their competition. 'I'll get what we can afford, if that means—'

Melissa held her finger to his lips to stop him. 'My Luke isn't stepping up in front of thousands of people using cheap equipment!' She tilted her head, smiling. 'I really want to help ... please.'

'You've saved for ages. You must want it for something.' He was feeling very uncomfortable with the whole thing, but he had to admit that it would really help them out.

'Nothing really. My dad always taught me to have something for a rainy day.' She sat on his knee, and wrapped her arms around him. 'Well, this is my rainy day,' she smiled before kissing him and suddenly wishing they were alone. But she knew there would be many beers and several hours before the others departed.

'What did I do to deserve you?' Luke said between kisses. 'Thank you.'

*****

After everyone had eventually left, Melissa and Luke sat together on the sofa. Luke was shaking his head after they'd had a full-on heart-to-heart. They'd been telling each other about their pasts. Melissa had told how Leon had broken her heart and humiliated her. She'd become a bit emotional after recounting how she'd walked in on him and some girl from work. They had been in her bed of all places! He could have at least done his cheating away from her home – that had really hurt her.

'The guy is a total idiot. Forget him,' Luke said, and wiped the lone tear that was running down her cheek. 'I promise I won't ever do that to you.'

'Please don't make promises if you can't keep them,' she said, feeling her guard going up a little.

'I always keep my promises.'

'Thank you for being patient,' she whispered, and he knew what she meant by that. Melissa had made him wait before taking that next step in their relationship. It made her feel a bit scared, because she feared that if she gave herself to him completely, it would all go wrong, just like all her past relationships.

'It really isn't a problem – we've got all the time in the world.' He meant it – he wouldn't rush her. But there had been times when they'd been very close, and he'd found it very hard to back away from her.

Melissa had fallen for Luke on that first night, from the moment he stepped onto the stage. Hearing his voice filter through the venue while he slammed on his guitar as he looked down at her, she remembered thinking that would be as close as she would get to him. She would just become a fan who would go to their gigs and dream about him. But now she was part of it all and regularly had to pinch herself to make sure it was really happening. She was with the guy everyone had wanted. He was now stroking her hair while he kissed her. Luke had surprised her with his patience and the way he treated her with respect – a rare quality in her experience.

'Luke,' she said, running her hand under his shirt as she pushed him down, knowing she was going to give in. She was falling in love with him and she couldn't stop herself – they had both waited long enough. 'I want you,' she breathed in his ear as she nuzzled at his neck.

Luke grabbed her and pulled her down, pressing their bodies together. 'Finally!' he thought. She was driving him to distraction, but he knew it was going to be worth the wait. The passion between them was raw and the feelings they both had for each other were new and intensely exciting.

'Don't break my heart,' he heard her whisper, making him stop for just a second to look her in the eye.

'I won't. Don't break mine,' he responded, making her smile as she pulled him back to her. She wanted his lips on hers again.

'You're so ... perfect,' he told her, feeling her soft pale skin under his fingertips. He had undressed her with some skill and was now taking in the view of her perfect body, something he had been imagining since they met. To him, there couldn't be anyone better – she was his perfect woman.

Melissa blushed as she admired him, now completely naked. The words caught in her throat because he took her breath away. His tattoos almost winked at her as he looked down, clearly liking what he saw. He was desperate for her, and she knew she was ready. Luke had never waited so long before, but he knew she would be worth the wait. Even her kisses made his heart race. When she touched him, a feeling like electricity flowed between them. It was something neither of them had ever felt before, and in this moment, nothing else mattered.

'You were *so* worth the wait,' he breathed into her ear as her nails dug into his back. She responded with the sweet sound of pleasure – the world outside could be ending and they wouldn't have noticed.

*****

The rain pounded against Amber's face as she stood in the garden, surrounded by darkness and hidden by bushes. She had been waiting for hours for him to leave. But he was still there, so she had to stay where she was. She couldn't let him see her – she couldn't risk it. Her face was twisted with rage under the hood of her jacket as she watched their bodies tangled together. She had been so smug when it had been her, and now it was agonisingly painful to watch someone else in her place. 'That should be me he's kissing.... me that he's making love to,' she thought. 'I'm the one he loves, and I'm the only one who really loves him.'

The curtains weren't fully closed, so she could see right into the living room. They were on the sofa together, both naked. 'She has no shame!' Amber thought. The slut didn't even shut her curtains, like some sort of shameful exhibitionist. She watched as Melissa ran her hand down his side, over his tattoo, kissing his chest as she did so. He kissed her with so much passion, she wanted to bang on the window and scream, but she knew she couldn't. She saw Melissa laugh at something he said, and pull him down closer to her, but it was his smile and the way he looked at her that hurt Amber most. Deep down she knew that he hadn't looked at *her* that way. Melissa was making him think he was falling in love with her, and Amber told herself that she was manipulating him, and she was taking him away from the one he was supposed to be with. They pawed at each other, their naked bodies completely entwined, oblivious to anything else. After a while, she decided that she couldn't watch this anymore, and she slipped away silently. Her rage was growing, and she vowed that she would win him back. And if she couldn't have him, then she would make sure that no one else could.

*****

'I sound shit,' Luke complained.

It was the night before Amplified, and the band were having one last practice session. They'd spent every day for the past two weeks getting themselves ready, poring over every detail of every song in their set, and a few they planned to keep in reserve, just in case. They always used Toby's place for their meetings, because his house had most space – the large back room was a perfect place to play and was permanently decked out with amplifiers, speakers and other assorted pieces of kit.

Luke was as usual much more stressed than the others, and Dale rolled his eyes at his best friend, who was always way too hard on himself. 'You sound like you always do, shit hot.' The other two agreed. It was nearly two in the morning and they'd been busy for several hours but were now running out of steam. They could tell that Luke was getting obsessive, and they all realised that they needed to nip it in the bud. He was their best asset, their front man, and the last thing the band needed was Luke suffering a crisis of confidence at the eleventh hour. This was going to be a long and important weekend for them, so making sure Luke was at the top of his game was the top priority.

'Am I being annoying?' he asked, already knowing the answer.

'Yes!' they chimed in unison, the frustration clear in their voices.

*****

Amplified was held over two days. On Saturday, all twenty bands would perform to a crowd of six thousand, and a panel of three judges would nominate five to go through to Sunday's final. The overall winner would be decided by the audience. Each person entering the venue was given a card at the turnstile which carried three voting credits. The cards could be swiped at voting screens around the venue, using contactless technology similar to credit cards. But votes weren't used to back the winner, they were given to the group you liked the least. This meant that less was more, in terms of votes, and the winning band was the one at the end of the competition with the least votes. The grand prize was £3,000 worth of studio time plus an assortment of new equipment worth £5,000, donated by the corporate sponsors. To bands trying to make their way in a tough and competitive business, usually on a shoestring budget, the prize would be a huge boost. But perhaps the most valuable reward would be the publicity and recognition the winner would receive. It was the chance of a big break that every aspiring band dreamed of. It was widely expected that the winning band at Amplified would be offered a record deal.

The event was sponsored and organised by Sky Storm Records, one of the UK's biggest labels. There was no promise of a contract for anyone, but according to Sky Storm, 'anything could happen'. This really meant that they would offer a contract to any band they felt was good enough. It was a very clever concept on the part of Sky Storm – effectively a public audition for a new act, which they could sell tickets for, and make money from. The winning act would already have been given a public seal of approval, so it was much less of a gamble than giving a contract to a band nobody had heard of.

The judges were big names in the music world, giving the competition credibility, but at the same time making it all the more nerve-racking for the participants. If the verdict from any of them was negative, you were in trouble because many of the crowd would vote according to their comments. The judges would also be writing reviews for the music press, and of course you wanted them to be singing your praises. The opposite could spell disaster.

Melissa had almost had a heart attack when they'd discussed it the previous day – she hadn't even thought about that side of it - the risk factor - and she desperately hoped it wouldn't go wrong for them. She was still acutely aware that their entry was her doing, and if it didn't go well, she worried that there could be serious implications for her relationship with Luke, as well as the band's prospects.

'That girl is driving me nuts!' Luke yelled at his phone. Amber was calling again for what felt like the hundredth time. He cut her off as usual, and reminded himself once again that he needed to change his number. He never answered her calls, and had no intention of doing so. He was starting to feel stalked. There had been a few times he thought he'd seen her, almost as though she was following him. But he wasn't sure if it was her, and nothing ever came of it so he shrugged it off. But he wished it would stop. 'I'm definitely changing my number if she doesn't give up soon. What can I do to get rid of her?'

There were several suggestions from the lads, none of which were legal or particularly helpful, but they were tempting all the same. He joked that with every nuisance call, he was getting closer to considering them.

After a final beer and some last minute arrangements, they called it a night. They'd initially agreed on getting a reasonably early night, to be ready for next day's adventure. But as usual, time ran away from them and it was the small hours before anyone got any rest. Most of them were out like a light, but Luke lay awake, running everything through his mind over and over again. He tried to create the perfect scenario of a flawless performance and a momentous victory, the idea being that if he could visualise it, there was more chance it might happen. He often did this before a gig, and it had served him pretty well in the past. Being the front man, he knew he would be the focal point of the crowd and the judges' attention tomorrow, and therefore he felt extra pressure. He couldn't stop his mind conjuring up thoughts of things going wrong, but he used that to identify potential pitfalls and make mental notes of problems to be avoided. He knew he was a perfectionist, and he didn't apologise for it. It annoyed the hell out of the rest of the guys at times, but they also knew that he was the most professional member of the band, and he was their leader. They wouldn't be the same band without his high standards and determination to be the best they could be. They always had fun, but only *after* giving a performance they were happy with, never before or during. He had a burning desire to succeed, and he was not going to let this chance pass them by.

His motivation was not borne out of greed – he wasn't interested in being filthy rich – comfortable and secure would be just fine. Nor was it a misguided sense that simply to be famous was the pinnacle of human endeavour, something he saw in a lot of wannabes these days. He wasn't the sort who would consider going on a TV 'freak show' or pulling a ridiculous publicity stunt just to get noticed. All he wanted was for their music to be appreciated by genuine music fans. For him, that was the only kind of success that mattered, and it would make all their hard work worthwhile. In Luke's opinion, to hear people say they liked the music he'd created was the best feeling in the world. It was all about the buzz of entertaining people, and making them smile. It made him smile too.

Melissa was also a big part of his plans. It surprised him when he thought about it, because with past girlfriends, his focus had never been diverted from his musical goals. More than once, this was the reason that his relationships ended. It wasn't selfishness on his part, or at least he didn't think it was. It was just that he'd never been with someone who he had pictured in his long-term plans. But she was in all of them now. He'd always found the thought of spending your life with one person a bit scary – never being close to another person or having that exciting feeling of a new relationship. But she'd changed all that. It may have been only a month, but he knew she was the one he wanted to be with. The fact that his friends seemed to like her too was a bonus; there had been one or two girls in the past who hadn't fitted in – usually too wrapped up in themselves to bother getting to know his mates. They were the people he spent most of his time with, and he was nothing without them – they were like family. Melissa had just slotted into the role of being his girlfriend so effortlessly, and vice versa. It just seemed natural. His plans for his future and the band's therefore naturally included her – it was as though she was their fifth member, even though she didn't sing or play an instrument. He trusted her and valued her opinion, so it meant a lot to him that she approved of what they did.

He was still awake, his thoughts flying around in his head. He decided that he needed to hear her voice, to settle him down and put that tiny bit of doubt out of his mind. So he dialled her number.

'Are you worrying?' She sounded sleepy when she answered.

'A little – everyone's asleep, but I can't shut off.'

'Can you get to me?'

'Of course, babe. I'll be there in half an hour.' He knew he should be sleeping, but there was only one place he wanted to be right now. He called a taxi, leaving a note for his sleeping bandmates to pick him up from her house in the morning. He just hoped they could be trusted to get up on time.

*****

'This van stinks!' Beth started complaining within minutes of finally getting on the road, an hour behind schedule. 'And seriously, what the hell is digging into my back?' She turned as best she could in the cramped space, revealing the edge of an amplifier as the culprit. It was wedged between two seats, along with a multitude of other pieces of kit which took pride of place, and forced the human passengers to squeeze into whatever gaps were left around them.

'I need a fag – I can smoke, right?' she asked, looking around the old and filthy Transit van. Toby was already lighting one, answering her question.

'Just don't flick ash over any of the gear!' Luke called from the front. After a game of Rock, Paper, Scissors, it had been decided that he would drive to London, the deal being that Toby would drive home. In reality, that depended on Toby being sober, and Luke suspected he might end up driving both ways.

'Yes sir!' Beth gave him a mock salute.

The journey was long and uncomfortable, but finally they arrived around lunch time and checked into their cheap and cheerful hotel near Brent Cross.

'It's not too bad, I guess,' Melissa said, slightly surprised. She had expected a complete dive judging by the cheap rates, but it was comfortable enough and seemed to be clean.

'Yeah, it'll do,' Luke agreed as he chucked their overnight bags in the corner before grabbing her round the waist and playfully throwing her onto the bed. She giggled naughtily, and it teased him but there was no time for any funny business because they had to get changed and leave for the venue straight away. They needed to get their equipment unloaded and ready before the event started. They didn't know how bad the traffic would be, where they were going to park, or how long it was going to take to get accredited and through security, so nobody wanted to leave it to chance.

'I believe you have to do your sound check?' she giggled. 'And I don't need sound checking, I'm always ready to play! But you'll have to wait till later ...' She enjoyed teasing him.

Luke knew she was right. But there was one thing he wanted to do before they joined the others. He was a bit embarrassed about not being able to get her much for her birthday, so he wanted her to have her present now. He hoped she would like it, even though it didn't cost much.

'I love it!' Melissa beamed as she held the small black box in her hand. Inside it, a silver heart-shaped locket with a pink rose on the front lay on a bed of velvet.

'Open the locket.'

Inside he had put a photo of them, taken at the gig in Chichester, the night after they met. Melissa remembered the moment – Tom had taken the photo on his phone shortly after the gig finished. It was simple, but it captured the moment perfectly. Luke was kissing her forehead, and she was smiling the beautiful, natural smile he loved so much. Receiving the locket produced one of those smiles.

'Happy birthday. I'm sorry it isn't much,' he said, still feeling embarrassed.

'Don't be silly – it's perfect! It's a lovely thought, and I'll treasure it. I don't need big, expensive presents. Being here with you is more than enough.' She turned and lifted her hair. 'I want to wear it today. Can you put it on for me?'

He took it from the box and placed it carefully around her neck. Then he fastened the clasp and kissed her. It completed her outfit perfectly.

'How do I look?' she asked, doing a little twirl for him. She definitely looked 'ready to rock' in purple denim shorts and white lace fitted top. She wore her hair down and her black Tom's shoes had come out for the weekend. Luke had raised an eyebrow when she'd pulled out some of her highest heels, and he reminded her that she'd be on her feet all day and night, so maybe something a bit more comfortable would be wise. She preferred the more natural look, so her make-up was subtle.

'You look beautiful, as always.' She barely had to try, he thought.

He was in his usual dark blue jeans and black hoody.

'Do I look fat?' she asked.

'Shut up and stop fishing for compliments!' he joked, but she pulled a sad face.

'Of course you don't!'

'That's the right answer.'

'I've something for you too, to bring you luck today.' She opened her travel bag and pulled out a small package.

'You didn't have to. It's your birthday, not mine!'

She waved his protest away; it was a big day for him, and she felt that it would be right to give him a gift too. It was a brown leather cuff which she'd seen in a music shop. She'd thought it would suit him and look good while he played. She placed it on his wrist carefully, winding the strap around several times so there were three layers, then fastened the small silver buckle at the side to secure it.

'It's great – thanks, babe,' he said gratefully as she wrapped her arms around his neck. Even though he tried to hide it, she could tell he was nervous.

'Play for me – don't worry about anyone else,' she whispered. The next few words came out of her mouth without her even thinking, 'I love you ...' She immediately realised that this was a big moment because they hadn't said it to each other before, even though everyone else could see they were head over heels in love. She held her breath, waiting for him to react, hoping he felt the same. It hadn't been planned, and she'd surprised herself as well as him, but desperately hoped she hadn't picked the wrong moment or said it too soon and scared him off.

'Glad to hear you say that, because I reckon I might love you a little bit too. Thank you so much for this weekend. You don't know how much it means to me.' He saw her frown, and knew why. Luke had always refused to say those three words unless he truly meant it, so he'd never said them to a girlfriend before. He realised what he'd blurted out was not exactly what she wanted to hear. Idiot! He cursed himself, knowing that he needed to do better. 'Liss, I love you too, of course I do.'

'Better,' she said, smiling fully now, and feeling very relieved. 'And I do know this means everything to you. It's who you are, and it is what you were born to do.' Luke's expression confirmed she'd got it right.

The door opened noisily, making them jump and abruptly ending their intimate moment. The others bounded in, almost falling over each other like excited puppies. They were all ready to go, apart from one thing.

Toby took a small bag from his inside pocket, and carefully poured four equal piles of fine white powder on the table. He used a credit card to turn the piles into lines. It was the band's tradition to give themselves a little something to fire them up before a gig. They weren't regular drug users, but they considered gigs to be 'special occasions', so as far as they were concerned it was OK every now and then. Toby handed Luke a rolled-up bank note.

'Let's get this show on the road, boys!' Luke shouted as he leaned down and snorted his line up his left nostril before gagging slightly as the cocaine hit the back of his throat. The note was passed on, and the others followed suit.

Toby laid out two more lines, and looked at the girls. He wasn't sure what their views on this sort of thing were, because it had never really been discussed before. He felt a little awkward because he didn't want to be seen to be leading them astray if it was not their thing. But on the other hand, it could appear rude to leave them out if they did want some.

Luke had picked up on this too. 'You don't have to – it's entirely up to you,' he assured them, not wanting them to feel pressured. They both nodded, and said it was fine. It wasn't a new experience for them. They had experimented in their time, but not for quite a while, usually preferring just to have a drink.

'Why not? It's a special occasion.' Beth shrugged. 'It can't hurt to have a bit, but not *that* much thanks!' She pointed at the Toby-sized lines on the table, which were more than generous, and he divided one in half for them to share. Deep down, Luke wasn't overly comfortable with it, but he couldn't be a hypocrite.

They left shortly after for the biggest weekend of their lives – so far.

*****

'They're giving it stacks – I love it!' Beth was enjoying the band currently on stage – a female rock band called Echo, who were half way through their performance.

'She's proper hot,' Tom observed, referring to the bass player and they agreed that the band reminded them of Paramore and the Yeah Yeah Yeahs.

The front girl gave off a sense of confidence and defiance, as though she didn't care whether people liked them or not; they were doing their thing regardless. In a strange way, it seemed to make the crowd like them more. She had her black hair pulled back in a short ponytail and her red and black dress hardly covered her butt. She'd kicked off her black canvas shoes during the first song, and was now jumping around barefoot, but still in control of her red guitar. They all laughed as she stuck her finger up at someone in the crowd who'd heckled them between tracks.

The bass player asked through her microphone, 'Do you have a small dick to go with your pea brain?' This was a great comeback, and the crowd roared. These girls had attitude.

‘Go on, girl, you tell that twat,’ Tom said under his breath. He was impressed; she looked and sounded like a badass.

The stockily built drummer played aggressively, and looked as fierce as her bandmates, if not more so.

‘They’re pretty good ... for a bunch of girls,’ Luke commented, earning him a punch on each arm from Melissa and Beth. He loved winding them up – it was too easy. ‘What?’ he cried, rubbing his left bicep. He’d forgotten how hard Beth could punch.

‘Women can play, you chauvinistic pig!’ Beth snapped. He put his arm around her shoulders and gave her a friendly hug.

‘I know. But you’re so easy to tease.’

‘Shut it, Black,’ Beth retorted jokingly. She couldn’t hide her smile – it was hard to stay mad with Luke for long.

They still couldn't quite believe they were here. The set-up was incredible. The competition was being held inside a huge marquee erected specially for the event, which was necessary because it was October and the weather was awful. It was dark inside the tent, and there were blue and red laser lights dotted around, providing the only illumination other than from the stage. It was packed to the rafters, and the sense of excitement had been growing all day.

Melissa was nervous now. Some of the acts were nothing to write home about, but some were really quite good, although a lot of it depended on taste, she thought. But what worried her most was the panel of judges. They’d been quite ruthless in their assessment of some of the performances. One band had been described as ‘disappointing’ and ‘boring’. The female singer had left the stage in tears, and the whole thing had been very difficult to watch. Melissa worried that they might react negatively to Luke and the boys, but she had to admit to herself that The Black Eagles were much better than the group who’d been slated by the judges. There were now five acts left, including The Black Eagles, and they were more nervous now than they’d ever been before a performance.

The first judge was Sonny Lee, a rock legend from a band called Jet-Lagged, who had their heyday back in the 1970s. Sonny was in his sixties now, and the years of drink and drugs were evident in his appearance and the way he spoke. He still tried to cling on to his youth by wearing black leather trousers, a tight top and a black bowler hat, but his long, grey hair and wrinkled skin gave his age away. He was still very passionate and excited about music, and had plenty of experience of the business, so he was well qualified to judge in this contest.

The second judge was Lou Miller, a music producer, who'd worked in the business for twenty years. She was in her late forties, but still looked thirty and was both beautiful and glamorous. Her blonde hair was pulled back into a bun, and her black suit hugged her body tightly revealing boobs that were definitely not natural. Lou had worked with some of the best in the business, and had not got to the top by being a pushover. She was hard to please.

The final member of the panel was Jay-Den Lake, the man representing Sky Storm Records. He was a significant figure in the music world, and he had discovered some of the biggest bands around. He was someone you wanted to know and impress, because his company was one of the UK's biggest labels. He was twenty-nine, about six feet tall, with tanned skin and blonde hair which stuck upwards in messy spikes. He was smartly turned out in a navy blue suit, portraying the image of a music industry big-hitter.

Lou Miller had been the one to make the female singer of the previous band cry. 'Darling, I might be good at what I do but I doubt even *I* could make you sound good. You don't even have the looks to help you out. If I were the rest of your band I'd be looking for a new singer.' She'd then waved her hand as if to dismiss them.

The boys were now in the backstage area, their turn imminent, with Lou Miller's harsh words ringing in their ears. They'd been whisked through security half an hour earlier and reunited with their equipment at the stage door. It was a very professional set-up, and they were well looked after, which helped put them at ease. But the underlying tension remained. All the PAs and roadies in the world couldn't help them when they stepped out on stage – they would be on their own.

*****

The distraught singer was still sobbing on her friend's shoulder nearby. She was a short, stocky girl with red spiky hair. The attitude she was clearly trying to convey in her performance had now disappeared, and Melissa felt very sorry for her. She wasn't that bad looking either. Lou Miller had been unduly harsh, she thought.

But now Melissa was thinking more about their turn, which was next. She felt sure they would do well and the crowd would like them, but she was not sure now about the judges. The poor girl and her band who'd been slated hadn't been *that* bad. The criticism was clearly designed for shock value, and to make the judges appear strongly opinionated. She could understand it from the competition's point of view; if the judges gave empty praise to all the acts, then what was the point of having so-called expert judges? Melissa didn't think it did much for the fairness of the competition though, because the crowd's vote would inevitably be swayed by what the judges said. It seemed to her that the organisers were effectively able to exert influence over the outcome. Nothing she could do about it though, so she tried not to let herself worry about it too much. And besides, since a serious mauling had just been handed out, maybe they would be due some praise.

'Are you OK? All ready?' Melissa asked, trying to sound calm and confident. There were only a few minutes left before they were on. She was terrified, but couldn't even imagine how the boys must be feeling. Luke looked as though he was thinking carefully about something, but then he nodded. 'I'm ready to go now – this standing around is doing my head in.' He wished they could have gone first – that way they'd have finished by now.

'Group hug!' Toby shouted, and they all gathered round him. The girls stood back but he waved them in too, reminding them that they were just as important and it was down to them they were in the competition. They all took that line now, to make sure Beth didn't feel left out.

'Good luck, everyone. Bring the goddamned house down!' Beth yelled as she jumped into the hug before grabbing Dale and kissing him.

Melissa joined in too. Before she left she leaned down and kissed the neck of Luke's guitar. 'Blow them away, baby!' she said gently before standing aside, leaving them ready to take to the stage.

Luke watched her and hoped he would do her proud. He was scared to death, but at the same time felt confident about what he needed to do. He knew that nerves were natural, and the key was to channel the nervous energy into the performance. He smiled and turned to follow his three best mates, who were waiting at the side of the stage.

The competition's host, a female TV presenter called Astler Brooks, whipped up the crowd and introduced them with a great fanfare. Luke closed his eyes, said a little prayer, then took a deep breath and stepped onto the stage. Dale patted his shoulder and nodded at him, meaning, 'We'll be great, let's do it.'

'Welcome our next act ... The Black Eagles!' Astler Brooks yelled into the microphone.

Beth and Melissa had found a perfect spot at the side of the stage, pressed up against some unsturdy looking barriers. They watched the boys make their entrance, and as expected Luke had lost his shirt.

Beth rolled her eyes. 'He's such a show off!'

'If you've got it, flaunt it!' Melissa threw back at her.

The boys took up their positions on the stage, standing silently, all looking at the floor.

'It's working,' Beth said. By doing nothing, they had instantly commanded the crowd's attention, intrigued at what was going to happen next. Lou Miller leaned forward to say something. But before she could utter a word, Luke whipped his head up and the band exploded into their first song, 'Games'. He couldn't have timed it better. The judges didn't seem to react until Luke began to sing. Jay-Den Lake instantly looked up from his notes, and smiled. He took his phone from his pocket and began to type something.

This was where they belonged, thought Melissa, on a real stage in front of a real crowd. They owned it.

The girls sang along, knowing every word and bursting with pride. The staging was spectacular, with laser lights and a huge screen behind them that came up with graphics that Tom had put together on his laptop and given to the stage crew. It felt like a real stadium gig – a million miles from the pubs they'd played in.

'Should we throw our pants on the stage?' Beth yelled.

Melissa smiled her wicked smile. 'I would, but I'm not wearing any!'

'Liss, you naughty girl!' Beth giggled.

'You did well putting them up for this! Look at them, they're tearing up that stage. Look at our boyfriends, woohoo!' She jumped up and down excitedly.

'Does that mean I'm forgiven for not telling you?' Melissa laughed.

Beth hugged her friend. 'There's nothing to forgive.' She pointed to the stage. 'You've just made their dreams come true!'

Melissa watched their boys living out their dream. Even if it was for one night only, it would be something they would never forget. Toby was jumping up and down on his stool with the beat, sweating profusely. She often wondered how he didn't make a mistake or even fall off the stool with such chaotic movements, but he never did – he was in complete control. Now they'd got into their stride and the crowd were reacting well, Tom was smiling – a rarity during a performance. Dale was standing next to his best friend while they sung the chorus together. As Dale stepped backwards Luke turned his head, spotted Melissa in the crowd, and winked at her. She blew him a kiss. His tattoo was more prominent under all the lights and he really did look like a natural rock star.

'Wow!' was all Melissa could say when they finished their second song.

The judges silenced the crowd who were going wild, cheering and chanting their name. Melissa and Beth linked arms, and after what seemed like a lifetime, Lou Miller rose from her seat and placed her hand on her hip. She turned her back on them and looked into the crowd for a few seconds, and then turned on her heels back to them. Finally, she smiled. 'That was one of the best performances of the day, well done' she said, and began clapping loudly.

'What's your name, young man?' Sonny Lee asked, pointing at Luke.

'Luke!' He was sweating and breathless, but buzzing with a feeling of adrenaline and euphoria he'd never come close to experiencing before.

'Luke, you have one hell of a voice, and your guitar skills are some of the best I've seen. Your performance was full of energy and enthusiasm, and you got the crowd on your side from the very beginning. You're one heck of a band and I'd say you have a very promising future. Who writes your material?' Sonny asked.

'I do,' Luke replied, and there was a cheer from the crowd who seemed to approve. So did Sonny Lee.

'That was excellent. You're a very talented young man,' was all Jay-Den Lake said. But that was high praise indeed, and all you needed from someone like him.

'I'm so proud of them!' Melissa sobbed joyfully as the emotions that had been building up all day seemed to spill out at once.

Beth nodded. She also had a tear in her eye –a significant display of emotion by her standards.

It had gone better than they could have hoped. The worst part was definitely over because they'd got through the performance with no mishaps, and they hadn't been booed off stage or slated by the judges. Quite the opposite in fact. Now all they had to do was wait to see if they'd made it through to Sunday's final. The vote was a few hours away, so there was an anxious wait ahead of them. But, Melissa thought, if Jay-Den Lake was impressed then *surely* they had to be through. She'd listened carefully to his comments about the other acts and was sure that none had been as positive as theirs. But she was trying not to get her hopes up too much or get carried away, so wouldn't allow herself to draw any conclusions from the reactions of the crowd or judges, even though it seemed to make sense to her.

*****

She walked behind them, through the crowd, her hood covering her face. Amber was so pleased that things had gone well for him – their performance was brilliant. But it was killing her that she couldn't celebrate with him, for now at least. They were laughing and talking to another band, and she could see that he had his arm around her waist. He had his shirt back on, which was a shame. Melissa looked smug as he kissed her neck, giggling as he whispered something in her ear. The whore. Amber forced herself to stay calm. She knew that if she went for her now, in front of all these witnesses, it would be over for her. She had to pick her moment carefully and find a time when she could deal with Little Miss Perfect properly. They were all to blame – his stupid moronic bandmates who would fuck anything that moved, and that other little whore who hung around like a bad smell. The two of them were nothing but shameless band sluts, who had probably been passed round the whole band anyway. Luke deserved better than a piece of trash like that. It wouldn't be long before he would see that ... she just had to be patient.

*****

'Good luck!' Luke shouted as they moved away from the band they'd been chatting to. Everyone they'd met so far had been very friendly and supportive – they all wanted the same thing, which was to succeed in the competition. But there was a sense of camaraderie rather than rivalry because they had so much in common; they all understood the life of an aspiring rock band. Perhaps when it came to the final there would be more tension in the air, but for now it was a very relaxed and friendly atmosphere.

As they headed to one of the many bars for drinks, a girl who looked about eighteen came bounding up to Dale.

'I think you guys are awesome!' The girl was practically drooling and Beth eyed her carefully. She was polite to her, but had her 'back off bitch' look on her face.

'Thanks,' he said, before the girl continued gushing about how fantastic she thought they were. Then she turned her attention to Luke, at which point she seemed to become suddenly mute. She just stared at him.

'Err...hi. Did you like our songs?' he asked, trying to start a casual conversation. He felt a bit uncomfortable – the staring was freaking him out. The girl just seemed to have lost the ability to speak.

'I-I-I love your voice. I, er, I think you're great ...' was all she managed to get out. She was shaking too.

'Are you OK?' Melissa asked, thinking there might be something wrong with her. The girl nodded, still staring at Luke. This wasn't a situation they'd ever had to deal with before, and none of them really knew what to say or do. The girl was dressed in black, with long black hair which had a blue streak down one side. She looked completely star-struck. The silence was finally broken as the girl gingerly asked Luke for his autograph. He obliged happily and quickly, and they were then able to continue to the bar.

'See, you have a fan already. I thought she was going to pass out!' Beth laughed.

If that reaction was anything to go by, Melissa thought, her faith in them would be vindicated and she would be proved right about getting through to the final.

The drinks flowed and the lads were getting quite rowdy. They were getting bored with waiting and were becoming impossible to control. A lot like little children, Melissa thought. They sang Happy Birthday for the fifth time to Melissa, this time getting others around the bar to join in.

'Come with me,' Luke said, pulling Melissa away from their group and through the crowd.

'Where are we going?' Several glasses of wine and a couple of tequila shots were now taking effect, along with the little something extra from the hotel room, so she was up for a little fun.

Luke led her out of the tent, and towards the stage gate. Eventually, after being stopped by a couple more people wanting to speak to Luke, they were back at the van. Luke opened the back doors and lifted her in.

'What are you doing?' she giggled.

'We've a little while to wait, so I've thought of a way to pass the time!' His naughty smile spread across his face as he laid an old fleece blanket down to cover the dirty van floor.

'What, in here? Are you mental?' she half-heartedly protested, but he was already kissing her neck and laying her down onto the blanket. She didn't argue as he quickly pulled off her top. She was becoming addicted to him, and right now she would do just about anything for him.

Likewise, Luke couldn't get enough of her – she drove him wild. It was a potent combination. 'You're a bad influence on me. I used to be a good girl!' she teased as she removed his shirt.

'You were never a good girl. You just hid it well!' He kissed her as the last bit of clothing was lost somewhere on the van floor.

*****

'Where the hell are those two?' Tom sounded irritated. All the bands had been called back on stage for the announcement of those through to the final, and they were nowhere to be found.

'Well, it's pretty obvious what they're up to ... and you say me and Dale are bad!' Beth laughed as she called Melissa, who again didn't answer. She left a message: 'Melissa Webb, put him down and get back here! He is needed, you know, here with his band. Get your knickers back on and hurry the hell up. Oh no, wait, you weren't wearing any to start with!'

Everyone looked at her, open-mouthed.

'You may think Melissa is a sweet and innocent choir girl, but believe me she has a wild streak. She just hides it well. She can be a badass chick, you know. Don't be fooled by the 'butter wouldn't melt' exterior.' She knew her best friend better than anyone, and she knew she wasn't quite as innocent as she liked people to think. They were definitely somewhere together, and they were not playing chess.

'Keep your hair on,' Melissa said, appearing at Beth's side, phone to her ear, looking pleased with herself and sounding slightly out of breath.

Luke had a very satisfied look on his face too. His friends mocked him and respected him at the same time. They headed to the stage to stand with the other bands, all looking nervous as they realised that the moment of truth was upon them.

'Slut!' Beth joked. Melissa wrapped her arms round her friend's neck and gave her a kiss, smiling and not feeling the slightest bit embarrassed that they had enjoyed themselves. She was definitely feeling a bit tipsy now.

'Eeeekkkkk, this is it!' Melissa squeaked, and gripped Beth tightly.

It was a nerve-racking moment for everyone, and Astler Brooks played on the tension, taking an age to reveal the name of each band. Melissa didn't pay much attention, although she did notice the name of the third band, Death Wishes. She had her eyes closed, praying to hear three specific words.

'The fourth band through to tomorrow's final is ... Echo!' There were cheers around the venue, and the female band hugged each other.

There was now only one space left, and sixteen bands still stood on the stage. The tension was unbearable – could they be out? It was starting to look like it.

From the side where they stood, Beth and Melissa could see Luke and the others on the stage. They patted each other on the back for reassurance as they waited for the final name to be revealed. The waiting was excruciating, and as usual with this sort of competition, Astler Brooks was drawing it out far longer than was needed, supposedly in the name of drama and entertainment.

'The last band into tomorrow's Grand Final is….' she then went silent for at least a minute - a minute of sheer torture for everyone - 'The Black Eagles!'

As they heard their name, the boys jumped all over the stage and each other, hugging each other like a football team who had just scored the winning goal. The crowd went wild too – it was the popular choice and they'd been left till last for that very reason.

'Woooohooooo, they did it! I knew they would … I just knew it! 'Melissa screamed, as she wiped away another tear.

Beth jumped all over her. 'They did it! Oh my god!' she yelled.

Melissa caught Luke's eyes and mouthed to him, 'I love you.'

He knew what she was saying, and responded by running over to her, grabbing her face and kissing her in front of six thousand people. 'I love you too,' he said before quickly returning to his band to celebrate with the crowd and be interviewed.

'Is he your boyfriend?' a girl next to Melissa asked.

Melissa nodded proudly. 'Yes, he is.'

'You lucky bitch!' the girl replied.

# Deep Breaths

October 2013

'You, my dear, are a legend,' Toby's thick speech was evidence of the number of beers he'd put away during the evening. Melissa had her arm draped around his huge shoulders, but it wasn't clear which of them was holding the other up. They were back at their hotel, celebrating in a big way, but it seemed like the sort of hotel where this sort of behaviour was common. It was nearly four in the morning and the night was finally winding down. They realised they should get a bit of sleep since tomorrow, or rather today, they had a very important job to do.

'I didn't do anything – you did all the hard work,' she slurred back, but Toby was shaking his head and waving his arms around.

'No way. No. Bollocks. That's bollocks. We wouldn't have even known about it without you. You're the man! Best day ever!'

He wasn't making a lot of sense now.

'I'm glad you enjoyed yourself. You were great out there, well done.'

Toby smiled. When he did, you could see the goodness in him. He wasn't bad looking either, Melissa thought, but not her type. If she had another friend looking for a good guy, she'd definitely recommend him. They'd had a good old fashioned drunken heart-to-heart tonight and they had definitely bonded.

*****

Dale and Tom were playing cards and Beth had been having a 'best friend talk' with Luke since they got back.

'Luke, I like you but I have to say this,' she said as she patted his shoulder. He was swaying on the chair and nodding at her, trying to look serious and as if he was concentrating. But he wasn't doing either very well. Neither was Beth for that matter.

'Say what?' He tried looking through one eye in order to focus on her better.

'If you ever hurt her,' she hiccupped, 'I will kick your ass. Seriously.' Her tone was firm, and it was clear she wasn't joking, even if it did sound a bit ridiculous. But he knew she was looking out for her mate, and he gave her a 'scout's honour' promise that he'd take good care of her. He worked hard not to snigger as she hiccupped again and nearly toppled off her chair.

'I mean it. OK? Alongside Dale, she's the most important person in my life and she always will be.'

'I know. You have my word, I will take care of her.' Luke hugged her as he whispered something in her ear. 'I know about your parents – I'm so sorry.'

She tightened her hold on him. They were clearly having a 'moment' and everyone else left them alone. 'Yeah, my family sucked, but what can you do?' There was sadness in her voice, but she had clearly decided not to dwell on the past. Luke liked her. She was good for Dale and despite her confident, sometimes brash exterior, she was a sweet girl when you got to know her. She came across as bossy, loud and confident, but deep down all she wanted was to be loved and to have good friends. Just the same as most people, thought Luke.

'Hey, you turned out just fine without them,' Luke reassured her.

'Liss and her family saved my life. Without them, god knows where I'd be now.' She gazed over at her best friend, smiling. Melissa was still deep in conversation with Toby. For no good reason, they were arguing about the very important art of making the perfect cup of tea. Melissa was horrified at Toby's insistence that you should always add the milk before the water. It was madness, she was telling him. She looked over, smiled back at Beth and winked at her.

Beth had been neglected badly as a child. Her dad, Jason, was a cruel, violent man, and her mum was too scared to stand up for herself, let alone Beth. He was pure evil and Beth referred to him as the monster in her closet. For her, the bogeyman was real.

Jason would beat her mum regularly. And as Beth got older, he turned on her too. She was six when he first took his anger out on her, just for spilling her juice on the floor.

Tragically, her mum had killed herself when Beth was ten. Her dad was jailed shortly afterwards, for GBH and armed robbery, and was given a ten-year sentence, meaning that Beth was alone. But it was definitely better for her than remaining with him as his sole punch bag.

'He was so cruel to her, and I didn't help her,' Beth had sobbed when she first told Dale about what she'd seen her mother go through. Of course, there was nothing she could have done about it, and she was just as much a victim as her mum, but it was natural for Beth to feel guilt. Her mum had put herself through hell trying to protect her. It hadn't always worked. Beth knew her mum loved her, and had ultimately given her life trying to keep her daughter safe. In hindsight, she should have walked away years earlier, but it is often easier said than done to escape from an abusive relationship. He'd had such a strong hold over her, psychologically as well as physically, that she couldn't think clearly or logically. She was too scared of him.

'You were just a kid – don't blame yourself,' Dale had told her as he held her sobbing in his arms, disgusted by the things he had heard. How could a parent do that to their own child? It made him realise that it was actually Beth who needed Melissa, despite how it looked from the outside. She utterly depended on her, and if anything ever happened to Melissa or their friendship, it would destroy her.

She missed her mum every day, and it never seemed to get any easier – not until she met Dale. He made her life brighter, making it easier for her to leave her troubled past where it belonged, behind her. The pain never went away, but it faded into the background when she was with him. In the past she had struggled to find anything to block out the memories and numb the pain, and she had gone off the rails more than once. But Melissa had always looked out for her and got her back on the straight and narrow. Nobody understood her like Melissa, who was like a twin sister to her, and whose parents had cared for her like their own. She'd lived with them for a while after her Mum died, until Social Services put her in the care of an aunt. Her aunt was OK but being her dad's sister it was difficult because she would make excuses for him, and Beth couldn't stomach that. There were no excuses for what he did, except he was a vile excuse for a human being. Beth had vowed that no matter what happened, she would never speak to or see him as long as she lived. She didn't care if he lived or died. Why did he deserve to live when her Mum had gone?

She had no real family left; her mum had lost contact with her relatives a long time ago because of him, so the only other person at her funeral was the aunt. She had decided then that if any of them ever did get in touch, she'd tell them where to stick it, and ask them where they were when she and her mum really needed them. Melissa's family had taken care of the funeral, allowed Beth to say goodbye and comforted her when she cried at night. They were her real family – they cared about her. And as soon as she was sixteen she got a job and a place of her own.

She still cried in her sleep sometimes, but it was Dale who was there for her now. He felt her heartache just as much and he hated her dad too. She'd told him how he locked her in the shed one night when she was nine, just for breaking a plate. He didn't let her out until dawn. She didn't make a sound all night because she was so scared of him. All she had were her blanket and teddy. And her mother did nothing. This was why Beth was the way she was – when she found something good, she held on to it for dear life and cherished it. Dale was one of those good things, and the band too, as a group of friends. She felt as though she belonged somewhere now, and that was why she was so protective of them. So she always tried to do what her mum hadn't been strong enough to do all those years ago, and look after those she loved.

'Luke' she slurred. 'I think I love your best friend,' before she unceremoniously slipped off the chair into a heap on the floor. This signalled that the night was over, and in truth it probably should have been over some time ago. Melissa was asleep on Toby's shoulder, and he in turn was snoring whilst leaning against the wall. Neither looked comfortable, but they didn't seem to care.

Dale picked Beth up, laughing at the state of her. 'Come on, babe,' he said as he cradled her.

'She's a good girl, she'll be fine.' Luke patted his friend on the arm. Dale nodded, smiling as he carried his semi-conscious girlfriend to bed.

Tom pulled Toby to his feet and with Luke's help, got him back to their room. Then Luke picked Melissa up and carefully placed her in their bed, tucking the cover around them both. He watched her for a while, noticing that she wrinkled her nose a lot in her sleep and occasionally muttered things he couldn't quite make out. She opened her eyes, just for a few seconds but she wasn't awake – her eyes seemed to look through him. She smiled and muttered something before closing them again.

'Happy birthday, my beautiful Liss,' he whispered, knowing one hundred per cent he was in love with her.

*****

'Please give a huge welcome to our final act of the night ... The Black Eagles!' the host yelled at the crowd, clapping as she walked off stage. The noise reverberating around the venue was deafening as they came on, giving them a huge lift. They were ready. They waved their thanks as they took up positions, and wasted no time as they launched into their first song, "Weekend High". It was fast and upbeat, a great number to open a set and get the crowd going. It was one of the girls' favourites and they all loved performing it. The crowd clapped, their hands above their heads as the boys gave it everything they had, moving around the stage, using every inch of it to make sure everyone got a good view and felt part of it. They fed off the energy of the crowd, and vice versa. There was no doubt they were producing yet another scintillating performance. Beth jumped up and down, screaming every word, while Melissa stood, leaning against the stage, grinning proudly from ear to ear. Luke turned and winked at her and she beamed back at him. Beth almost jumped on her friend's back with excitement.

'Come on, stop swooning and dance with me!' she demanded.

Melissa didn't argue. She turned and threw her arms in the air, singing at the top of her voice. Then she felt a tap on her shoulder, and turned round to see a guy in a black baseball cap and white shirt grinning at her. He had beer stains down one side and sweat running down his face and was breathless. Melissa had noticed him jumping around near them earlier.

'You know those guys?' he asked pointing to the stage.

'Yes,' Melissa replied.

'They're really good. How do you know them?'

'Luke's my boyfriend,' she said, again feeling full of pride. The lad raised his eyebrows and asked if Beth was also with one of the band. Melissa nodded.

'Cool,' he said, waving at Beth. 'So, I'm talking to the girls with the band?' He held out his beer to Melissa, but she declined. 'Shame, I was going to ask you out. I take it the answer's no?' He laughed, knowing perfectly well that she was with Luke because he and six thousand other people had witnessed their kiss.

'The answer is definitely no!'

'Aw well, you can't blame a guy for trying. You and your friend are the hottest girls in here.' He looked her up and down as he said this. She was wearing black denim hot pants, a white strapless top and her comfortable shoes again. Her hair was up in a ponytail, except for a few strands that she'd curled falling forward onto her shoulders. Beth was dolled up, in her tight red playsuit which left very little to the imagination. She'd kicked off her heels and was dancing barefoot.

Melissa thanked him politely for the compliment.

'I'll let you go back to your friend. It was nice to meet you. I hope they win.' He went back to his friends, excited that he'd spoken to the girl who was dating his new rock hero.

*****

'You did it again, Black Eagles, well done!' Sonny Lee had to shout to make himself heard above the cheers from the crowd, once the performance had finished. The judges were again impressed, and gave them positive, exciting feedback.

'You're gonna be big!'

'You're something new and exciting, just what music fans have been crying out for.'

'Fantastic, amazing, you have six thousand new fans right here!'

'Epic!'

Once the performance section of the show had been wrapped up by Astler Brooks, a recap was given on the big screens, and the crowd were given instructions on the voting process. Then they started heading towards the booths on the outskirts of the arena to cast their votes. The girls weren't allowed to vote, so they headed to the backstage area where they found the band talking to a member of the female band, Echo. The lead singer had her arm on Luke's shoulder and they were laughing about something. Melissa heard the end of their conversation as she approached.

'We should get together and play sometime,' she said, and Luke was nodding enthusiastically. Her black jeans were skin-tight, as was her deep red vest top. Melissa suddenly felt threatened – the girl was very pretty, and she was in a band. She could play the guitar as well as sing, and in that respect she was everything Melissa wasn't. She obviously shared Luke's love of music and performing. She walked over to her boyfriend, wrapping her arms around his waist and kissing him, to make a point. She threw a look at the girl, who took a step back, knowing exactly what this little performance was about.

'I take it this is your girlfriend?' She sounded amused, and Luke smiled smugly as he introduced her, knowing Melissa was more than a little jealous.

'I'm Cassie, nice to meet you.' She held out her hand.

'Hi,' Melissa said, then turned away.

Luke looked down at her and raised an eyebrow. She wasn't normally rude to anyone, so this was a little out of character.

'Liss?' he whispered.

'Darling, don't you worry. I'm not interested in your boyfriend, not in that way,' she said, laughing now. 'You're more my type ...' She winked, making her point as she looked her up and down. 'I like your shorts, they're nice and, err, tight.'

'Oh, thanks,' Melissa said, feeling like a complete idiot.

Beth couldn't suppress her laugh for long.

'I gotta go and find my girls anyway. See you later.' She was definitely laughing to herself as she walked away. Probably going to have a good joke with her band at my expense, thought Melissa.

'Oh god, tell me that didn't just happen,' she said, hiding her face against Luke's chest.

'You just got hit on by a chick, and you were totally ready to kick her ass. I like it!' Luke laughed, but Melissa didn't see the funny side. She just wanted to find a hole and crawl into it.

'You gave her your ultimate bitch stare. That was classic!' Beth cackled.

Melissa had been jealous just for a few seconds, but suddenly felt as though she'd probably come across as a crazy woman. 'Sorry if I embarrassed you, babe. Oh dear, I'll have to find her and apologise. I feel awful.'

'It's fine, I'm sure she'll get over it.' Luke was still trying not to laugh.

But Melissa decided she had to find her. Beth went with her and they searched the crowds for a while, but without luck. They were about to give up when Melissa spotted her sitting on the floor in the middle of a large group of people. They were talking and laughing very loudly. Melissa felt nervous – what if Cassie was annoyed? She wouldn't blame her if she was.

'Cassie?' she said as she approached.

'Hi.' Cassie smiled and stood up. She didn't seem annoyed in the slightest.

'I'm sorry I was such a bitch before. I don't normally behave like such a moron, honest.' She was still feeling about two inches tall.

'It's fine. How about we start again?' Cassie held her hand out, and they shook hands.

Melissa was relieved. Cassie seemed nice, and the awkward incident was forgotten. They chatted for a while, then Cassie introduced the rest of her band, who were Jo-Jo and Allie. Beth and Jo-Jo got on instantly, but Allie seemed more interested in arm wrestling a guy called

Aiden, a member of Death Wishes. Melissa noticed that he seemed to love himself way too much. He had that cocky look about him, a buzz cut like an extra from a war movie and a strut that gave off an aura of pure arrogance. Anyway, their music was just angry and hurt your ears, she thought, so there wasn't that much to be arrogant about. The judges' feedback to their performance hadn't been all that glowing.

'That guy is a complete tosser, and his band suck,' Cassie quietly said to Melissa. She giggled, glad that she wasn't the only one who thought so. Allie beat him no problem in the arm wrestling and Cassie yelled gleefully, 'Nice one, babe!'

Allie, Echo's drummer, was short and boyish looking. She had blue spiky hair and wasn't in the least bit girly. Although she looked like the stereotype of a butch lesbian, she was in fact straight. Cassie had explained that to Melissa before introducing them, because people always made assumptions about her, and it really pissed her off.

Aiden wasn't happy about being beaten by a girl, but taking her on again was not on his mind. He got up and made his way over to Melissa and Cassie, smiling smugly. Melissa was his target.

'Alright, darling?' he said, in an annoying, smarmy way. Melissa nodded and smiled politely, but didn't start a conversation. 'You're with those Eagle guys, aren't you?'

'Yeah,' she said, not wanting to be drawn into a conversation. She disliked him already.

'How about I show you what real music is? Come on, let's get a drink.' He was standing way too close for Melissa's liking, and her skin crawled as he looked her up and down.

'No thanks,' she said, and turned her attention back to Cassie to continue their conversation, and thinking that was the end of it. But suddenly he grabbed her chin, turning her face back to look at him.

'Ouch, get off me!' she cried, shrugging him off. But he did it again.

'Aiden, don't be a dick, leave her alone,' Cassie demanded. She had only known him a few hours, but he had already pissed her off with his behaviour. Aiden thought he was a star already. He thought his band were going to win and bragged about how they already had groupies. True, they did have a few girls who followed them around, but it was hardly rock star status, and Cassie couldn't give a tiny rat's ass – they all looked like fuckwits anyway.

Beth had appeared, ready to kick off in defence of her friend and the other four members of his band had also gathered round.

He kept hold of her face, his fingers digging into her. 'Think you're something special do you, blondie?' Melissa shook her head and pushed his hand away.

Beth yelled, 'Oi, douche bag, go play with the electrics, preferably with your tongue.'

He turned towards her, hissing, 'Who rattled your cage, you her bodyguard or something?'

'You rattled my fucking cage, and I'll kick your ass if you touch her again.' Beth was livid.

'Look, I said no to a drink. I didn't kill your cat so I don't understand your problem. Just leave me alone.' Melissa was getting angry.

'I don't like being told no,' he said.

Melissa raised her eyebrows – he really did love himself. 'And I don't like being spoken to by morons, let alone manhandled, so why don't you just fuck off!'

Cassie told him again to back off, but he wasn't listening. He seemed to be enjoying the attention. 'Your boy's band is shit. They'll never get anywhere,' he sneered.

'Fuck you!' Melissa snapped.

He laughed and grabbed her by the face again. 'That's what I'm asking for!' His band laughed with him, but they were the only ones who found him funny.

Melissa pushed his hand away again, disgusted at his behaviour. She'd rather kiss a poisonous snake than entertain that idea – he really was vile.

Aiden was about to say something else, but at that moment he was grabbed round the throat and lifted off his feet. Luke held him up against a pole in a choke hold. He'd just arrived and had heard the last little exchange. 'If you've got some kind of a fucking problem, I'm happy to discuss it.' Luke was seething, and the look on his face was almost murderous. The two most important things to him in the world were Melissa and his guitars, and you didn't mess with either. He turned to check Melissa was OK, and she nodded.

'I'm fine, just having a chat with her,' Aiden lamely replied, shocked to suddenly have gone from a position of strength (or rather bullying) to being half throttled. He clearly hadn't banked on Luke turning up and he'd been caught off guard. His band members were about to come to his defence, but so were Luke's. There was a stand-off with Luke and Aiden in the middle.

'Chill, man, I was just messing around.'

'It didn't look like messing around to me.' Luke kept hold of Aiden's throat. People had noticed there was something going on and gathered round. It was soon clear that Death Wishes were not as popular as they thought they were. Like a commentator, Cassie filled the spectators in on the situation, and they laughed when she repeated Aiden's suggestion that The Black Eagles were shit.

A shout from behind them summed it up, 'You got your wish on stage tonight – you died a death!' It got a good laugh, and then the chanting started.

'Black Eagles.'

'Black Eagles.'

'Black Eagles.'

'Echo.'

'Echo.'

'Luke, smash his face in!' someone shouted. 'That jerk needs to be taught a lesson!'

Melissa moved quickly, taking Luke's arm and gesturing for him to leave it. 'Let go. The asshole isn't worth it.'

It took several attempts to persuade him, but eventually he let go. 'Touch her again, and you'll be eating through a straw – you got that?' He slammed him against a pole as he let go.

Toby eyed each member of Death Wishes – they'd all noticed his size and wisely backed off. He knew he could take two of them on his own no problem, maybe three. They threw more cheap insults at each other, and one of them called Echo's bass player an ugly bitch. She hadn't said a word during the whole incident, and it was totally uncalled for.

Tom squared up to the culprit. 'I think you need to find a mirror, mate, or look up the meaning of ugly.' The guy wasn't prepared to follow up his insult, and Jo-Jo smiled at Tom and he winked as he turned back to look at her.

They'd started to break away, the situation seemingly calming down, when Aiden kicked it all off again, 'She's not all that fit anyway – I've seen better on the bottom of my shoe.'

Luke gave no warning as he flew at him, landing a crunching left hook on Aiden's right cheek sending him toppling to the floor. Luke jumped on him and they wrestled with each other until their friends pulled them apart and dragged them away from each other. Dale held Luke, but it took Toby and Tom to really drag him away. Melissa put herself between Luke and Aiden as they glared at each other. She moved closer to Luke, blocking his line of vision. 'Calm down,' she said, turning his face away from his target. 'Look at me, Luke, please stop,' she begged him. 'Please, don't get thrown out or arrested. Don't let him spoil this,' she pleaded with him, but he was still looking in Aiden's direction. Security had finally arrived, too late as usual, and he was being dragged away. 'Look at me ... deep breaths. I'm fine, and he isn't worth it.' She was relieved when he let out a sigh and seemed to calm, but he was still seething inside. She was right though, he wasn't worth risking this all for. He took a deep breath and counted to ten to calm himself as he checked her face. It had slight pink marks where Aiden's fingers had dug in and his blood boiled. Melissa assured him she was fine.

'My turn to be your bodyguard,' he said with a little laugh, despite his fury.

'Thanks ... but you need to go and stand on that stage with the others. Don't kick off, just ignore him. Please.'

*****

The five bands lined up ready for the results to be announced. Melissa worried about the trouble kicking off again, but luckily they all seemed to have brought their attention back to the competition, and stood at opposite ends of the stage, ignoring each other. She noticed that Aiden had a black eye forming, and he kept dabbing it with his sleeve. The Echo girls stood with the boys, and it seemed as though they were quickly becoming friends. Cassie was watching them both, seemingly trying to make sure that Luke didn't go for Aiden again. It was to protect Luke more than Aiden. Dale kept whispering in his ear, keeping him calm. His best friend knew how to handle him. Tom was ignoring all of it, instead checking out Jo-Jo, who was returning the glances. Allie was on Toby's back, giggling nervously.

Astler Brooks took to the stage to begin the announcement, and was greeted by a rapturous cheer from the crowd.

'OK, the votes have been counted ... [long pause] ... and the first band to be voted out, and clearly not the favourites today are ... [another long pause] ... Death Wishes!'

Luke threw his head back, laughing, as Death Wishes stomped off the stage, throwing profanities in every direction. It was like winning just seeing them voted out first. Astler Brooks took even longer to announce the names of the next two bands to be kicked out, Demon Boys and Rocking Dolls, leaving only Echo and The Black Eagles.

'Oh shit,' Beth said, because they were going up against their new friends. The remaining band members stepped forward, with one band standing on each side of Astler Brooks. They were all shocked to have got this far, but were bursting with nerves and excitement to be in the final two, and to have the chance of winning.

'Good luck,' Jo-Jo whispered to Tom, and he smiled back at her as she turned away. Her cherry brown hair hung around her shoulders, and she had the ultimate sexy rock chick look. Tom definitely liked her, but now was not the time to worry about that.

'I will now read out the winner of Amplified 2013.'

There was a roar from the crowd, then silence during the eternal wait for the name to be read out.

'The winners are ... Echo!!'

It took a few seconds for the name to register, because it wasn't the one they were expecting to hear. Echo jumped for joy, screaming and hugging each other, while the crowd cheered and chanted their name.

'Shit!' Beth and Melissa said together. Cassie threw her arms round Luke, who was congratulating them, and whispered something in his ear. Luke smiled. Tom hugged Jo-Jo, and Toby and Dale hugged everyone. Echo made a short, chaotic speech, managing to thank everyone who had voted for them, and played a victory set to mark the end of the event.

'Hey, no hard feelings, Black?' Cassie asked afterwards.

Luke shook his head. 'Of course not, well done.'

'Thanks. We gotta get going. I've to be back in Manchester tonight, but can we keep in touch? You guys are wicked.'

They all swapped numbers before saying their goodbyes and heading home.

*****

'Are you OK?' Melissa was worried that Luke was upset, but trying to hide it.

His smile told her the opposite. 'I'm absolutely fine, babe, honestly. I wanted to win and yes there is a part of me that's a little gutted. But we lost to a really good band, and we did way better than I ever thought we would.'

'Are you sure?'

Luke pointed out that six thousand people heard and liked their music, and a rock legend said they were 'awesome'. They had made some new friends, drunk way too much, won a fight and had sex in a van. 'And most importantly, we did our best and gave two really good performances. We definitely did ourselves justice. On the whole I would say it was one shit-hot weekend.' He put his arm around her, and she rested her head on his shoulder, happy that he was happy. She would need to sleep for a week to get over this weekend, but Luke was right, it had been well worth it.

'Thanks, Liss.'

'You're welcome,' she told him he could pay her back in kind – with designer shoes when he was playing to a sell-out crowd at Wembley.

Luke laughed, but thought briefly about not winning, and that maybe it wasn't their destiny to become global rock gods. 'It looks like it wasn't meant to be. But we gave it our best shot, so we can have no regrets.'

*****

Jay-Den Lake was on his way home from the competition. His driver was chatting away in his usual annoying way, but Jay-Den wasn't listening. He was still thinking about Amplified. He had been fully prepared for a complete waste of a weekend, but there were three bands that had caught his attention and one in particular. He was excited, and could see an opportunity for his label. He pulled his phone out, and called his boss. 'Russ, I'm coming to see you. You have to check these guys out.'

# Hospital (2)

October 2014

'Melissa needs a break. This is distressing her.' Jean was concerned that Melissa was in pain, and she could see in her eyes that talking about Luke was getting too much. She decided to ignore the fact that her daughter had just admitted to taking drugs. It wasn't really a secret, especially after one of Luke's episodes, but they were not addicts or anything like that. Lots of people experimented a bit when they were young and carefree, but they were good kids and Jean knew they wouldn't overstep the mark. Right now, there were more important things to worry about, like making sure she got better. And finding Luke.

Inspector Fox agreed that a break was for the best, and they would return in a few hours once Melissa had rested. He could clearly see she wasn't focusing now in the way he needed her to.

Jean went downstairs for food and coffee, because everyone needed refuelling after the session with the police. Melissa insisted she was fine, but she clearly wasn't. It had been days since she'd eaten a proper meal, and Liz went to get her something from the hospital kitchen. 'I can't do this, I can't. I just want him here.'

It broke Beth's heart to watch her friend look like she was slowly giving up. The fight seemed to be seeping out her, and it was painful to witness. Something needed to be done. Melissa had been through so much, even before all this, but she always bounced back, never letting the world bring her down. But how much can one young girl take before throwing her hands in the air and surrendering?

'Don't give up, not now. Don't let her win,' Beth said, trying to reignite her fire. Melissa needed to fight now more than she ever had – Luke needed her. And if Beth was honest she needed her too. Her family needed her, and so did Dale, Tom and Toby.

'She's already won,' Melissa sobbed, her hands covering her face. 'He won't want me now anyway,' it was her face that was worrying her –

she feared that he wouldn't want her if she was scarred. The combination of emotion, painkillers and tiredness were conjuring up some irrational thoughts, but that was understandable, Beth thought.

'Of course he will. He loves you,' Beth assured her, pulling her friend's hands away from her face so she could look her in the eyes before telling her yet again that it wouldn't change anything. Beth meant every word and had no doubt in her mind that Luke would stand by her; he would never leave her just because of a few scars. 'I promise you that won't happen.'

'Yeah, have a little more faith in him, Liss,' Dale said, looking a little frustrated. How much more proof did she need to believe he loved her? But then he realised that she wasn't really herself at the moment and it was natural to worry.

Melissa's head was scrambled and she couldn't think straight. Her whole body ached with pain from the bruises and her heart ached for Luke. She reached over to grab her phone from the bedside table and switched it on – it had been left charging at home since that horrible day. There were messages from friends and family wishing her well, and one from Toby that made her smile. It read, 'Chin up, baby girl, I'm here if you need someone's ass kicked! See you very soon, miss you xxx'

The messages were all so helpful, reassuring her that people cared, and were thinking of them both. Cassie and Jo-Jo, Tom and Megan all sent their love, and told her that they missed her. They were all hurting too, and she knew she had also to remember their pain, because they cared for Luke. Ray had left a message saying he was there if she needed anything. All she had to do was call, no matter what time.

Melissa stayed well away from the mad world of social networks – that was a shark pool she didn't need. She knew it would be going mental with gossip, and wouldn't make her feel any better, so best that she ignored it all.

Jean suggested she get some rest while she had some time. Melissa didn't even answer, but turned over, closed her eyes and let sleep take over her. She rested peacefully until Fox came back a few hours later, insisting that he needed to continue with the interview because it was crucial to their ongoing investigation. Time was running out. He asked if she felt well enough to continue.

'OK, I guess so.' She was still groggy as she sat up and took a cup of coffee from her mum.

# Pink Ribbons

November 2013

'Wow!' Luke was looking at their Facebook page. They'd set it up a long time ago, but hadn't bothered to keep it up to date. The girls had told them in no uncertain terms that it wasn't acceptable, and insisted on taking on the job of managing it. They'd worked hard to spread the word about the band, and had built up a significant online following. Beth had uploaded her pictures from Amplified, plus some from previous gigs. Twenty-four hours after the girls took charge, their ninety-seven members had jumped to three hundred, and a week later they were nearing two thousand. Their Twitter following was growing at an impressive rate too. Even their personal Twitter accounts were attracting plenty of interest.

Beth had been chatting all afternoon to people who wanted to know more about them. She was in her element, over the moon that she had what she considered an important role in the band now – she was their self-appointed publicist. There were so many YouTube videos from Amplified being uploaded, and the event's own footage was helping to spread the word about them. They laughed when they realised their most recent follower was Tess, the girl with the blue streak from Amplified. She was 'very enthusiastic', as Tom put it, but it was a nice feeling to know that people were interested in them and liked their music.

'This is great – you have actual fans!' Melissa was excited.

Luke was still serious about getting somewhere, and Amplified had given him a taste of the big time. Once he'd had a chance to reflect on the weekend, he'd realised that coming second was definitely not a failure, and it didn't mean their chances of making it were gone. Perhaps it had felt a bit like that at the time, but they'd been caught up in the competition and the 'win or bust' atmosphere whipped up by the organisers. But the number of online followers they now had was a good indication that they were starting to get somewhere. Besides, he couldn't keep working in that petrol station much longer.

It was Tuesday, and they were waiting for a pizza to arrive, having just finished a session at Toby's.

'What can I tweet? Give me something interesting,' Beth asked Melissa. It was getting addictive. Melissa shrugged and lit a cigarette.

'Oh *I* know, the group photo that guy took for us at Amplified.' Melissa found it on her phone, uploaded it to both sites and titled it, 'Us and the boys @ Amplified 2013'.

The picture was a typical group photo of a bunch of friends. Tom was on Toby's back, arms in the air, and Dale was hugging Beth, both laughing about something. Melissa was standing in front of Luke who had his arms round her waist. She had both arms up and around his neck. It looked like he was whispering something in her ear, and she was giggling. It was a lovely, natural picture, capturing their friendships perfectly. Melissa remembered exactly what he was saying – it was only ten minutes before their adventure in the back of the van, and she blushed a little at the memory.

'Love that photo. It's brilliant,' Beth said, smiling. It hadn't been more than a minute before people were commenting and 'liking' the photo on Facebook, and retweeting it.

'Boys, come here a minute. I want another photo for the page, of you four, in a behind the scenes setting.' Beth fluttered her lashes to make sure they did as she asked. They dutifully shuffled into line, next to their instruments. The picture was taken and quickly uploaded, and seconds later people were responding to it.

It was a strange feeling, having complete strangers so interested in what you were doing, but that was what they were trying to achieve to make the band successful, and was something they would have to get used to. Luke decided to post his own picture, and took a snap of Melissa, who was deep in conversation with Dale. He posted it, creating a buzz about how pretty the blonde was, and who was she?

'What the fuck is *she* doing here?' Melissa yelled as Amber, out of nowhere, casually walked through Toby's patio doors, and confidently made her way towards Luke.

'Hey, baby,' she purred, placing her hand on his chest. Luke immediately recoiled and swept her hand away. Her expression turned from a smile to a frown. She was wearing a tight pink dress, and her hair was a little windswept.

'What are you doing here?' Luke yelled.

'Is she mental?' Beth looked genuinely shocked, but ready to drag the girl out. Dale took her hand, and held her back.

'You didn't call like you promised. Last night was amazing,' Amber purred, looking up at Luke and leaving him open-mouthed in amazement.

'You have actually lost the plot,' Luke said, looking anxiously at Melissa, who was on her feet and obviously seething.

'What is she talking about?' A feeling of dread rose in Melissa's stomach as she checked his expression – she was encouraged that he seemed to be as confused as everyone else.

'I've no idea. Don't listen to her, Liss. You know she's nuts!'

'Amber, get out of my house. I mean it, leave now!' Toby intervened and attempted to take control of the situation, grabbing her by the arm and pushing her back out of the patio doors. But she yanked her arm from his grasp and turned to Melissa. Her grin was almost evil.

'Ask him where he was last night after band practice? He wasn't with you, was he?' She pointed at herself and mouthed the words, 'he was with me'.

It was Melissa's turn to see red. Toby sensed it, and picking Amber up he carried her outside, while she screamed at him to put her down.

Melissa thought back to last night. She'd tried calling him because he hadn't phoned her like he normally did when they weren't together. He hadn't picked up, which was also unusual (for her calls anyway), but despite this, deep down she knew Amber was lying. Of course she was. It was just a horrible feeling to think that someone wanted him so much that they were prepared to do this sort of thing, even though she was obviously unhinged.

Because she didn't actually know where he had been last night, the tiniest doubt remained, no matter how irrational it was. Luke needed to give her an explanation to put her mind at ease, and it needed to be a good one. Emotion had taken over, and she didn't exactly ask the question in a calm manner. The room emptied as she yelled at him to explain what the hell was going on. She was shaking with anger, although it was Amber she wanted to swing at, not Luke.

'I was at home, you know I was! I fell asleep, like I told you.' He reached out for her hand, but she yanked it back and turned away. She immediately felt bad because Amber was clearly lying. She was just so shocked by the very suggestion that Luke could have cheated on her, no matter how ludicrous it was.

Luke turned and followed the others out of the door, running after Amber who was now arguing with his friends in the street.

'Why?' he yelled, his eyes furious. Melissa followed closely behind him, and Dale pulled him back.

'Luke, calm down, mate. Don't let the nutter get to you.' But Luke wanted to have it out with her.

Amber carried on with her little show, claiming he was always calling her and turning up at her house, and how it was her he really wanted. They'd been sleeping together for weeks, apparently. Tom was laughing so hard he was almost crying, but she ignored him.

'You're lying. It's all bullshit and you know it!' Luke yelled at her, but she wasn't listening. He told her again that he didn't want her, and warned her to back off. Finally, he told her he never wanted to see her again. He couldn't be any clearer than that, he thought.

Amber looked like he had killed her puppy. 'Don't say that Luke, please. We're meant for each other.' Her demeanour and tone had gone from a confident swagger to looking decidedly desperate. This outright rejection was not what she had been expecting.

Luke turned, knowing that he now had to walk away, before he did something he would regret. Melissa took his hand. She'd had a few seconds to process the situation, enough to realise that there was no way he would have had anything to do with her.

'Leave us alone. You got it?' Melissa hissed at her.

Amber stood for a few seconds, her eyes locked on Melissa. The desperation had disappeared as quickly as it had taken over a few seconds before, and her claws were out again. Her body shook with rage as she glared at the object of her hatred. Without warning, she charged, grabbing Melissa's hair and dragging her to the floor.

'I hate you! I hate you!' Amber screamed as she pinned Melissa down. They struggled for a few seconds and Melissa cried out in pain as Amber slapped her hard across the face.

'Get off her,' she heard Luke shout as he grabbed Amber and dragged her off. Amber screamed and kicked out, yelling obscenities until he put her down. She turned and grabbed hold of him, tears pouring down her face.

'Please don't leave me,' she cried, her desperate side back again.

Luke peeled the pitiful girl off himself, and put her down. 'Don't you ever touch her again,' was all he calmly said, as he turned and led Melissa inside.

Left standing alone outside, Amber glared at the door as it closed behind them. Despite her skimpy dress, she didn't feel the cold in her emotional state. 'I will destroy you, Melissa Webb,' she whispered into the wind.

*****

'Luke, I want to go home please,' Melissa said quietly, once they were back inside. The evening was ruined anyway so he didn't argue with her. He couldn't tell if she was mad with him or just with the situation, but she almost threw his jumper at him and stormed to the car without saying goodbye to anyone.

'Are you mad with me?' he asked once they were in her car.

She shook her head and blasted her horn at a car that had pulled out in front of her, making her brake. 'Idiot!' she yelled, banging her hand back down on the steering wheel.

Luke put his hand on her leg, and she put hers on top of his. He pulled it to his mouth and kissed it. 'I'm sorry about Amber,' he said.

'It's fine. You had a one-night stand with a complete head case, and now she won't leave us alone. It's just brilliant,' she snapped. Luke dropped her hand. 'Sorry, that's not fair. She's just really pissed me off. And I'm scared of her. She really is nuts.' Melissa had noticed a darkness in Amber's eyes, and you could tell that she really did believe what she said.

'Don't be. She'll move on eventually,' he tried to reassure her, although he wasn't entirely convinced about that himself.

'What happened with her, really?' she asked him.

He let out a frustrated sigh. 'Not much. She was at a club we played at and we just got talking.' He explained that Amber didn't seem so intense back then; she was just normal and quite funny. It had been Amber who had said it was just a bit of fun, no strings attached. One-night stands weren't his thing, but she'd convinced him somehow that there was a first time for everything. They all headed back to Toby's place for a party, he drank way too much and before he knew it he was in bed with her – something he'd regretted ever since.

'Did you enjoy it?' Melissa knew it was a stupid thing to ask, and she didn't really want to know the answer. But it bothered her that he had slept with this girl.

'You really want me to answer that?' he asked, sounding a little annoyed. She shook her head and took a deep breath.

'Not really, sorry.'

Luke reached over and touched her cheek. 'You make me happier than any girl ever has. That's all you need to know. I just wish I'd met you sooner.'

Melissa reached out for his hand, feeling a bit guilty. He couldn't help it if the girl was insane.

'You can't change the past. Let's not waste any more of the evening on her. It's not that late and I've a bottle of wine at home with our name on it.' She was feeling much calmer now.

'Do you have any beers?'

She rolled her eyes, pretending to despair of him. Luke wouldn't drink anything other than beer, whisky or shots. 'Of course I have,' she said, still holding his hand.

'Good girl.'

*****

'Bitch!' she yelled as the tears streamed down her face. The room was dark apart from a light from a candle on the small table in the corner and she sat surrounded by pictures, hacking at one of them till the eyes were just dark voids.

'He would never have said that. This is her fault.' She punched the wall.

'I know that!' She screamed back at herself. The dress she'd been wearing was in pieces on the floor.

'The dress was a stupid idea.' She had torn it with her bare hands.

'You can't let her get away with it.' Amber looked behind her, and shook her head.

'Do you think I'm going to give up?' There was silence. 'Well I'm not. Be quiet anyway, I'm trying to think.' She scrabbled around in the photos that littered the floor, searching for a certain one.

'Ha, got it!' She clapped excitedly – it was a photo of her and Luke on the night they had spent together. She was sitting on his knee and they were both smiling at the camera. Luke had his hand on her knee. He was wearing black jeans and no top which seemed to be his trademark look. The band had just come off stage, and the picture was taken backstage. They looked good together, she thought.

She was so tired now– she hadn't slept in days – but the photo brought back happy memories and relaxed her a little. Hugging the photo, she lay down on the mattress and tried to get some sleep. But the voice just wouldn't stop talking to her. She buried her head in the pillow and screamed into it to drown it out. It was always so loud; there was nothing she could do to escape it.

'Stop talking. Please leave me alone. No, I don't want to do that!'

she begged. It was always so intense, and would only get louder if she tried to ignore it. She knew she had no choice but to do as she was told.

*****

The rain was so heavy that it woke Melissa and Luke up. It was as though stones were being thrown at the window. Melissa felt like someone was pounding her head with a hammer, from the inside. They'd had way too much to drink when they'd got back to hers, and now she was regretting it. She pushed Luke away as he started pawing her.

'Spoilsport,' he moaned as he gave up. She rested her head on his chest.

'I think I'm dying from wine poisoning, and it's your fault,' she complained.

Luke ran his hands through her hair, and mocked her for being a lightweight. He reminded her that she'd tried to play his acoustic guitar at two in the morning, and he'd thought it the cutest thing she'd ever done.

'I know I wasn't very good, but never mind.' He said he'd teach her if she wanted, but she shook her head. There was no way she could ever be as good as him, and besides, she wasn't cutting her nails for anything. Luke liked her nails – they were perfectly manicured, and intricately decorated. Their appearance was striking, and they definitely made an impression. In more ways than one, he thought, laughing to himself as he remembered the marks on his back. They'd earned him quite a bit of abuse from the rest of the band after they'd noticed them during a gig.

Melissa was still thinking about a song he had played for her last night, before her embarrassing attempt at playing the guitar. He'd played his acoustic version of 'Pink Ribbons', the first song he ever wrote. Luke wouldn't say who it was about, but just said it was a long time ago. She decided not to push him to answer but she had noticed how attached he was to his first guitar – he would just sit and play it for hours sometimes. There was a softer side to his talent, but he told her it wasn't what he wanted for the band. Melissa asked him why he named the guitar in the first place, and why he chose Chloe. There must a reason, and she wanted to know what it was.

'It's just something some people do, no big deal,' he said, shrugging. He didn't answer the Chloe question.

'Who is she?' she asked. Again he didn't reply, but he looked upset just at the thought of this girl. Whoever she was, she was clearly special to him.

'It doesn't matter.'

'Yes, it does matter. Tell me, babe, who is she?' He thought for a few seconds and his shoulders dropped. 'Don't worry. If it's an old girlfriend I won't be weird about it.'

Luke looked at her. There was hesitation, or maybe a look of loss in his eyes.

'Chloe was never given that chance. She wasn't a girlfriend, not like you think anyway.'

She took his hands and held them tightly. 'What happened?'

Luke explained that 'Pink Ribbons' was about Chloe. She was technically his first girlfriend, if you can call it that when you are six years old. He kissed her on the cheek every morning, and they held hands in the playground. But Chloe had died in a house fire on her seventh birthday.

'Oh, Luke, that's terrible. I'm so sorry.'

He looked so sad, it broke her heart. He was clearly still hurt by it, which was not surprising.

'It wasn't nice. Someone pushed fireworks through the letterbox one night, and there were some boxes by the door which caught fire. Her parents managed to get her out, but she'd inhaled too much smoke, and she didn't make it through the night. They never caught the culprit – some stupid kids messing around without thinking of the consequences. Anyway, it's called 'Pink Ribbons' because she always had pink ribbons in her hair.' The sorrow in his eyes showed that he still missed her, and had been greatly affected by the tragedy.

Melissa shed a tear for the girl she never knew. She'd obviously had a big impact on Luke's life, and her memory still did now. He had named his first guitar after her, and that alone meant she would always be in his heart.

Luke felt a sense of relief to have finally spoken about it after all these years, because he had never really done so before. He felt better just knowing that someone else understood how important the memories were to him. He had wanted to talk to Melissa about it before, but had never really been able to because he couldn't find the right words – he didn't know where to start. It wasn't the sort of thing you just brought up in conversation. But before her, he'd never been close enough to anyone to want to share it with them.

Luke told her how the funeral had been, and still was, one of the hardest days of his life. He had to say goodbye to his first best friend. It took him a long time to get over it. For the next two years, he spent a lot of time alone. He remembered thinking that there was no point in making friends because they might be taken away from him too. It was at that young age that Luke started to experiment with writing music. He would express the way he felt by turning his thoughts into words.

It was only after meeting Dale that Luke began to grow into the person Melissa knew. He would never admit that to Dale, and he made Melissa swear never to tell Dale that he'd said so. He told her how he had been kicking his football around in the driveway, on a Sunday afternoon. The sun was going down, and it dazzled him every time he turned towards it. He heard a shout after a misjudged kick, and then a crash. His football had hit another kid on the head as he rode past on his bike. He could remember it all as if it was yesterday.

'You complete moron,' the kid had shouted as he picked himself up. Dale didn't have his long hair back then, it was shorter but it was just as messy.

'Sorry, but you got in the way of my ball. I think you'll find that makes you the moron.'

After exchanging a few insults, they looked at each other and burst out laughing. They swapped names, and played football together until it was dark. Suddenly, Luke had a friend again. When he thought about it later, it made him realise how lonely he'd been. From then on, Dale would be at his house every day, football in hand, until they were teenagers and music took over their lives. Now, Luke couldn't even contemplate losing him. They were brothers in all but name, and although he would never say it, he loved him like a brother and the feeling was mutual. The funny thing was they went to the same school but had never really noticed each other before. Dale had always been the fun-loving guy who everyone liked. Luke would just flit between people, never choosing anyone as a good friend, until meeting Dale changed all that.

Melissa realised that talking about Chloe had saddened him, so she moved the conversation along. He didn't seem to want to talk any more about his lost friend, which was understandable, so she didn't push it and decided to lighten the mood and ask him about the band name instead.

'I love eagles, my surname is Black and it's my band, so it just kinda made sense,' was his fairly obvious reply. Luke had talked about his passion for eagles before, and he always liked watching documentaries about birds of prey. One of his dreams was to experience an eagle up close, to see one in the flesh, preferably in the wild. He and Melissa had agreed that they'd do it one day, when they were rich and famous. He often dreamed at night about being able to fly like an eagle, but he agreed that dream might be a bit more difficult to live out.

They had talked for most of the morning, lost in their conversation. Melissa admitted that she loved musicals, and *Annie* was her all-time favourite. She started singing 'Tomorrow' and before she knew it, Luke had grabbed Chloe and began playing it perfectly for her to sing along to.

'You're not a bad singer!' he said, with no hint of sarcasm, and she blushed.

'Thanks. I don't think I'll be selling out Wembley any time soon though!'

'I don't know. I think you could. And when you do, I'll be *your* groupie!' He felt better now – talking about Chloe had definitely lifted a weight from his shoulders. He had spoken to Dale about her in a drunken heart to heart moment a few years back, but it was one of those conversations that was forgotten by morning. And besides, it wasn't the same as talking to Melissa – women were more sensitive and understanding about things like that.

They were interrupted by Luke's phone, and he groaned as he picked it up and looked at the screen. He didn't recognise the number, so ignored it, but it went off again almost immediately.

'Just answer it and get rid of them.'

Luke picked up the call second time. As the conversation with the unidentified caller unfolded, Melissa watched his expression, which was initially confused but then changed to something she couldn't read. Then he said something which made Melissa sit bolt upright.

'No no, it's fine, of course we're interested, Mr Lake.' Melissa couldn't hear the other side of the conversation but there was only one person she knew with the surname Lake. Luke must be talking to Jay-Den Lake! Luke gestured to her to grab a pen so he could write down a number. Then he said, 'Megan. OK, sure. I'll do that straight away. Thanks so much for calling,' before hanging up and lying back down next to Melissa, looking like he'd just seen a ghost.

Jay-Den Lake had just asked them to make an appointment with his PA, Megan, to meet with him to discuss the possibility of the Eagles 'joining the Sky Storm family', as he put it.

Sky Storm wanted to give them a record deal.

'Oh ... my ... god! This is just epic!' Melissa couldn't believe it.

Luke frowned, hoping it wasn't a wind-up. He wouldn't believe it until he had proof. Ignoring the number he'd been given, he Googled Sky Storm's number, rang it and asked to speak to Megan May. The switchboard operator put him through, and he was greeted by a very polite girl who immediately put his mind at rest.

'Hello, Mr Black. Jay-Den said you might call. How are you today?' His heart raced and he tried to stay calm as he booked a meeting with Jay-Den Lake's PA.

'You're going to be signed! Shit!' Melissa screamed, jumping up and down excitedly.

'I've got to call the guys.' Luke grabbed his phone panicking. 'Dale ... fuck! Clear your diary for next Wednesday! Why? Because we've got a fucking record deal to sign, that's why!'

# I think you're mental!

December 2013

'I'm so sorry to bother you, but please can I have your autograph?' The girl standing nervously next to their table asked. It was the third time today they'd been stopped and asked to sign things or pose for pictures with a fan. This girl, just like the others, was shaking with nervous excitement. Luke signed the poster for her and Melissa took a photo of them both on the girl's phone. Her name was Anna, and they could tell they had just made her day. Melissa painted on her smile, but underneath she just wanted one day to have Luke all to herself. But that wasn't happening at the moment, and there was little chance of things changing anytime soon. Luke and the guys were heading to New York in a few days to promote their new record. So he'd taken her out in London for some shopping and dinner before he left.

They were sitting at a table at the back of the restaurant, attempting to keep a low profile. Luke's arm rested around her shoulder as they talked. 'That's the third time today – that one looked like she was going to faint.'

'Yeah well, I am pretty awesome – you are aware who you're dating, right? I'm a pretty big deal now!'

'Yeah, and you're so modest too!' Melissa mocked, and slapped him playfully on the arm. 'You do remember who made all this happen?' She raised her eyebrows at him smugly. She could feign arrogance just as well as he could.

He smiled and kissed her forehead. 'How could I ever forget? I suppose you're pretty awesome too.'

*****

The band had been busy for the past few weeks, ever since Sky Storm Records had signed them. Sky Storm were known in the business as a hard label to get noticed by, and Jay-Den Lake's approval was the icing on the cake. Melissa didn't fully understand all the details of how it worked, and although it was great to finally get some recognition and earn some money, she couldn't help feeling slightly disappointed by how little the band would actually receive from the music they sold. Twenty per cent of their record sales didn't really seem that much in the grand scheme of things, bearing in mind that the label would take the rest. Jay-Den had given them a long and complicated explanation of the expenses the label would pay on their behalf – production costs, marketing and promotion, staff, travel, accommodation, venue hire and ticketing to name just a few. But she still knew that the label would be taking a bigger profit than the band, and that didn't quite feel right to her. But it was a tough business and this was their first contract which represented their big break, so they weren't really in a position to call the shots or complain.

The label placed huge demands on the boys, and when they weren't doing promotional work Luke was expected to keep writing new material. There was some oversight from the Sky Storm people, who wanted to make sure their sound was consistent with the image being portrayed to the public. But on the whole he was given the freedom to write naturally. None of the band would have stood for excessive or overbearing influence over their music. From the start, Sky Storm had made it clear that because they were a 'real band', they would be allowed the freedom to stay true to their own style – provided it was of a high enough standard, and gave the public what they wanted. This was undoubtedly a commercial stance by Sky Storm, rather than being borne out of respect for them as artists, but the boys didn't care because it gave them what they wanted.

From a practical point of view, they found that doors opened for them wherever they went. In the past they'd had to pay for everything themselves, and find venues willing to let them play in return for a small fee and a guarantee of a decent bar takings. Sometimes they felt as though they ended up providing most of the bar's income themselves after the show. It wasn't easy to find places to play, when there were countless other aspiring bands competing for the same slots. They had often been disheartened when it felt like the doors were always closed. But now, everything had changed. Everything was organised by the label, who had the contacts, influence and financial might to book Wembley for them, if they wanted to. Maybe not just yet though.

Before Jay-Den had made his call, Melissa would watch Luke

phoning round, searching for somewhere to play. She felt his disappointment when he was told no, and although he would shrug it off as if it didn't matter, she could see in his eyes just how much it meant to him. She sometimes found it hard to accept like he did – some of them made no attempt to let them down gently or even be polite. She wanted to call them back and ask what their problem was. She could understand why so many bands never got beyond the garage practice sessions. There were only so many rejections most people could take, and you needed a special kind of determination and belief to keep going until you changed people's minds.

In stark contrast were the times when they did manage to get a gig. To have people paying to see them play, and reacting positively to their performance made it all worthwhile. For Melissa, seeing Luke beaming after a great gig was the best feeling in the world. She could only imagine how he felt – after all, it was his band, his performance, and they were his songs which he put his heart and soul into writing.

Their last gig before being signed nearly ended badly though. Their performance was flawless and as usual went down a storm with the crowd – so far so good. But afterwards, while they were at the bar, a guy talking loudly with his mates was making it very clear that while he was impressed by the playing skills of the band, the songwriter deserved a slap because he was shit. He obviously hadn't realised they were behind him, or maybe he didn't care due to his bad attitude and several beers. Either way they could hear every word, and even his mates looked embarrassed by his rant.

Melissa couldn't see Luke's face, but his body language told her he had heard it. She threw Dale a look which said, 'Watch him, I've got this covered'.

Beth saw the look too and cleared her throat, preparing for a showdown. She noticed that Toby was eyeing the guy, and gripping the neck of his beer bottle tightly in his hand. She nudged him to pass on the message. Nobody quite knew what was going to happen next, but everyone knew Melissa was going to do something. She casually ordered a pint of beer, took a few sips and edged a little closer to the guy, so she was touching his back. Then she turned, bumping into him and letting the pint glass fly out of her hand. She gave it a clever little flick as she let go, so that it somersaulted in the air and rained beer down on her target, soaking him from head to foot. At the same time, she pretended to stumble, lifting her heel and stamping it down on his right foot with considerable force. The guy screamed out in pain, falling backwards and taking two of his friends with him. They toppled into a table full of girls who were now covered in their drinks. It was a chaotic scene, and a row ensued between Gob Shite – as Melissa later called him – and a pack of angry, wine-soaked women.

Toby casually finished his beer and spun the bottle in his hand before launching it in Gob Shite's direction. It narrowly missed him, smashing at his feet. Toby agreed later that it was a stupid thing to do, and he was lucky he was such a bad shot.

'Fucking gobby little prick,' he boomed, towering over the heads of the shocked crowd. Before a full-scale riot kicked off, the doormen intervened and they decided it was time to leave, and fast. Luckily they managed a quick getaway as the van had been packed up ready to go before they hit the bar. Dale, much to his annoyance, was the designated driver. But rules were rules.

'You are one feisty little lady!' Luke said once they were on the road and clear of any trouble. He was secretly proud of her for defending his honour, stopping him from giving the guy a slap and producing a very clever assault disguised as an accident, all at the same time.

'Fucking idiot. So rude! Bet he's never written a song in his life.' Melissa still wasn't amused.

Luke played it cool, but she knew it must have hit a nerve. He hadn't given the guy any satisfaction by reacting to it, even if he had wanted to put his head through the nearest window.

They had then headed back to Melissa's to carry on with the party, feeling a little fortunate not to be in the cells for the night.

The clock showed just past six the next morning as Melissa stood in the centre of her small living room, surrounded by her friends, who were all snoring away and sprawled untidily where they'd collapsed. The surprising thing was that she was the last one standing, something that almost never happened.

For different reasons, she was completely in love with each one of them, mad as they were. She lifted Luke's head, which was hanging over the edge of the sofa, in what looked like the most uncomfortable position possible. She placed it on a cushion, hoping he wouldn't wake up with neck strain. He barely even noticed.

For some reason, she decided to go and check the van. The lock could be dodgy at times, and they had to be careful with it. It was lucky she thought of this, because yet again it had come loose, and one door had swung wide open in the wind, leaving all their equipment on show.

Luke's electric guitar had fallen over, and was hanging out of the door. Dale's Gibson Les Paul, which he called Ebony, was also leaning precariously, threatening to end up on the pavement. She picked up both carefully and tried to lock the van up securely, only after checking that nothing was missing. Strangely, she knew exactly what should be in the van, and she knew just how important every little piece of equipment was to them. The contents of this van might as well be the beating heart of the band. Then she spent several undignified minutes scrambling around under the van, retrieving Dale's spare picks which had also fallen out. She started to wish she hadn't bothered, now that her hangover was kicking in. She wanted to sleep, so she quickly finished up and went back inside, looking for a comfortable retreat. Before going in, she obsessively checked the lock to make sure it was now well and truly secure. She decided to take Luke's most precious possessions with her, because she couldn't get them to sit right in the van, and she felt uneasy about not having them in sight. If anything happened to them he would have a meltdown and they didn't have the money to replace them. If they'd been thinking straight when they got back, they would have taken it all in, but they were already half-cut. Apart from Dale that is, who'd been itching to get started.

'Fix that damned lock, Maxwell ...' she cursed as she went inside. It was Toby's van, but it had become the band's official tour bus. They called it Alf, because it was 'A Little Fucked' and it had its own song, which they sang for entertainment on long road trips to gigs.

Later that afternoon Melissa told her story to the others, and they all had a good laugh about it. Dale admitted that although he was grateful for her efforts, those picks were old and destined for the bin anyway.

'You are fucking kidding me? Dammit, I scraped my knee and nearly broke a nail!' she cursed him, and threw a pillow at him, knocking his afternoon 'wake up beer' all over him.

'Thanks, babe,' Luke whispered once she'd stopped attacking his best friend. Protecting his guitars – another telling sign that she was perfect for him, he thought.

*****

It was a very exciting time, and Luke had to pinch himself every day. Everything was top secret until the contracts were signed, but it was hard not to shout it from the rooftops. Melissa had never used her social networking sites as much as she had in the last few weeks, and as soon as she was allowed to, she told the world. She'd cried when he came home with a bottle of champagne in one hand, and a copy of the contract in the other.

'Sorry it's taken a while, but I got there in the end,' he said, referring to the conversation they'd had when they first met about hitting the big time. The studio time had been the most incredible experience; better than he had imagined. They were living the dream, and loving every second of it. They had shot a video in London for their first single, which was a surreal experience to say the least. They wanted an English feel to it, so they turned down the opportunity to fly to the States to make it. The theme was couples arguing because the song was about the mind games people can play when in a destructive relationship. It was gritty, but slick and stylish. The girl hired to play Luke's love interest was an Italian model, and Melissa had to take a deep breath when she first saw it. Some of the scenes were a bit intense – heated and explosive rows turned quickly into passionate 'making up', only to explode again. Each member of the band had an on-screen partner, with perfect model looks. Melissa had to remind herself that it was just acting, and Beth was in the same dilemma. But once they'd got over their initial urges to scratch the girls' eyes out, they agreed that they loved it.

Jay-Den worked very closely with them initially, providing them with the best studios and producers. He also had a say on which songs they would release, and in what order. But Luke was also very vocal on that subject. It had caused a stand-off at one point during the negotiation stages because Luke was very protective of his material and could be very stubborn if he didn't get his way. But Jay-Den and his colleagues were well used to dealing with artistic types and the situation was soon resolved amicably.

'I have a say too, Jay-Den. It's my work and I don't sit around writing for you to come along and tell me what is or isn't good enough. I know what's best for my band.' As always, the other three backed him up, although they didn't want to push Jay-Den too far, recognising that he was in total control over whether they hit the big time or not. Jay-Den agreed they could be involved and have their say, but ultimately if he really didn't think something would work, his word was final. They agreed that was fair enough and privately knew it was the best they could expect in the circumstances.

They'd been given an advance of £50,000 once they had signed the deal, but they knew they had to be sensible. Jay-Den had drummed that into them. It wasn't free money; it was more like a loan. They just had to hope that they made plenty of sales when the single and album were released. But the real key was making a success of the follow-up tour. Jay-Den had explained that these days the real money was in touring, because music sales were not what they used to be.

They'd spent the past few days appearing on as many UK TV shows as possible to promote the single. It was an exciting novelty at first, but the interviews became repetitive and annoying very quickly.

Today was their first day off in two weeks. Last night they'd been on *Breakout*, a music show for up and coming acts, along with their friends, Echo.

Echo's single 'Run and Hide' had already been released and was climbing the download charts steadily. Their album, *'Finally Found',* was also doing well. It had taken them nearly three years of hard work and plenty of rejections to get where they were now, a similar journey to the Eagles in many ways. They would be heading out on their first tour in a few weeks.

For the Eagles, the meetings had been endless recently. Being the songwriter, Luke would earn a greater share of the band's income from the pot of royalties, which wasn't a problem with the rest of the band. Melissa didn't understand a lot of it, but as Luke pointed out, she didn't really need to. She still couldn't help worrying that their cut was small in comparison to the amount Sky Storm would make.

'Babe, don't worry about it. That's just how it works. Besides, it costs a lot of money to put a single or album out and do all the promo stuff,' he tried to explain.

Melissa wrinkled her nose and frowned. 'I still think it sucks.' She wasn't sure he fully understood it either.

'Quit complaining. We've already got more money than we've ever dreamed about earning before!'

Melissa realised she shouldn't pick holes, but instead be grateful for what they now had. After all, she was now officially dating the front man of a band with a record deal – something Luke still hadn't got bored of reminding her about.

'Sorry – it is pretty cool.'

He kissed the top of her head. 'Thank you. I'm sorry you can't come with me, and don't worry about the press. I'll take care of you,' he promised.

*****

There had been so much speculation flying around about who Luke was dating, that Stan, the band's publicist, thought that Luke should be seen with Melissa more often. Just to calm the rumours a bit, for their own benefit. For a record company, whose usual attitude was 'there's no such thing as bad publicity', this was a turn-up for the books.

Luke didn't like all the media and gossip side of things. He didn't see why it mattered who he was dating, but apparently it was important to some people. 'Stan, I couldn't care less what people think,' he had said during one of their phone calls.

'You might not, but unfortunately, son, the public do. Your fans want to know, so you just have to play the game a bit. Unless you're happy with people thinking you're dating Cassie or Jessie J? That can be arranged.' That last name made him spit out his coffee. Stan could keep these stories going if it suited him, or he could make them disappear. It was his choice.

'What? I've never even met Jessie J.'

'Doesn't matter,' was Stan's predictable response. There were a million and one stories flying around about each member of the band, mostly groundless rumours started by bloggers or fans speculating on Twitter and Facebook. In the age of social networking, these sources routinely fed the media with material to report about celebrities, regardless of facts. Tom was being linked in various places with Ellie Goulding, half of The Saturdays, and more predictably with Jo-Jo from Echo. Of course, the latter was more likely than the others to happen, but it still wasn't true. Toby seemed to be linked with practically everyone in a skirt in the music business, but he wasn't bothered in the slightest.

'Cheryl Cole ... boom! If only it were true. Hey, Stan, can you get in touch with her and see if I'm entitled to a bit of action because the papers say so?' Toby laughed at another of the many gossip column stories about him. 'I wish I *was* dating Cheryl Cole ... that Ashley Cole must have a screw loose to let a hottie like her get away!'

Dale and Beth had made it very clear from the start that they were a couple. Beth had tweeted, 'We are together, end of story.' She'd said she wasn't allowing the gossip to even begin. Beth was becoming noticed by fans and the media for her upfront, no-nonsense attitude, and most people seemed to respect her for it. There was a recent rumour that Dale had been seen out with Leona Lewis. Her response on

Twitter was: 'Leona wishes it was true ... whoever made that up is an idiot.'

Luke thought about it from Melissa's point of view. She claimed to be OK with any gossip because she knew it was all rubbish, but it still wasn't nice to hear. The decision was made with Stan that they would make it obvious that Melissa was his girlfriend. They didn't need to act – they behaved the same way they always did, but they just did it in public a bit more. He didn't want to be fake – he promised himself that he wouldn't lower himself to that level. When he kissed her, it was because he wanted to. When he hugged her, it was because he wanted to. And when they laughed together, it was because they found something funny. They wouldn't put things on 'for show'. It wasn't easy for Melissa, but she realised that their worlds were changing and Luke would have to do as he was told for the benefit of his career. Within reason of course.

'It's fine. I want people to know I'm with you. You're mine, not bloody Jessie J's.' She looked fierce for a second as she said this.

******

Melissa and Beth were both miffed that they couldn't go to New York. But Ray, their new manager, was not changing his mind. He was a short, slightly chubby man. Life on the road hadn't been kind to him, but he wouldn't change it for the world. He was nearly fifty, but always wore a shirt and jeans more befitting someone in their twenties, and always looked like he needed a shave. He had a genuine 'music business' look about him.

Ray knew how to handle the guys and stood no nonsense from them. He understood they were young and new to fame and fortune, and tried to nag them only when it was needed. But he was well practised in exercising his brief from the record company, which was to look after them and make sure they were in a fit state to appear, perform and make money whenever it was required. Most importantly, the boys had felt comfortable with him almost straight away. He had spent some time with them at the beginning, both as a band and individually, to get to know them and understand them, and to gain their respect. This was important because it would make them much more cooperative later, when he needed them to be. Ray had quickly decided that his front man was easily distracted by one thing (person) in his life. He had always had a 'no girlfriend' policy when it came to touring, and he made it clear that it was definitely remaining – no exceptions. He made this point to try to set out where the boundaries would lie. The guys all joked that Melissa was the only person in the world who could demand Luke's attention without even asking for it, and that Ray would struggle to keep them apart. Ray told them that he hadn't met anyone yet he couldn't handle. But when Ray met her and saw them together, he understood what the others meant, and he realised he would have his work cut out.

Jay-Den was throwing everything their way – clothes, new phones and iPads, booze. He told them he would get them whatever they needed, within reason. But he wasn't a pushover, and in return he made it clear that he expected hard work and commitment. Just a few days before, the girls had been allowed to go and take a look around the studio where Jay-Den had lectured them about 'real life in the music business'. Melissa remembered it well.

'You do understand that those boys have to focus, and you'll need to take a back seat at times, OK?' He'd told them they had to occupy the 'back seat' several times and they'd nodded dutifully each time Jay-Den reiterated the point. But as the message started to sink in, Beth was starting to find it difficult to accept and Melissa wasn't sure if it was being told what to do that was annoying her, or being told she'd have to stay away from Dale. Both, she decided.

Beth worked hard to come across as someone who did what she wanted and answered to no-one. So the idea of obeying Jay-Den 'The Boss' Lake was alien to her. 'I'll see him when I damn well like, and Jay-Den can swivel on it,' she was thinking.

But Jay-Den was reading her expression like a book. 'I mean it – no tantrums. You can't be with them twenty-four hours a day, not if you want them to be successful. This is a once in a lifetime opportunity for them, and I'm sure neither of you want to be responsible for it going tits up.' Beth had pulled a face. 'Right there!' He snapped his fingers and pointed to her moody expression.

'OK! Jeez ... am I allowed to go for a fag or is that against the rules too?' Beth asked sarcastically, then got up and left without giving him a chance to answer. In a rare rational moment, she had realised that this would not be a good fight to get into, and knew she needed to leave the room to avoid saying something that would get them into trouble. She'd had to give him a small dig before she left though – having the last word was absolutely essential.

'Melissa, you do understand why I'm saying this?' Jay-Den asked softly once Beth had left the room. He could see that she would respond better to a friendly approach, and he was far more concerned about protecting Luke than the others, so Melissa was important. Indeed, she was also part of his plans. She noticed he was more casual than usual, wearing black cords and a blue shirt. She didn't know why that mattered, but it was her habit to observe people's fashion choices and use that to read something about their character. She still wasn't sure what to make of Jay-Den though, and she thought it was a lot to do with her preconceptions from him on TV and at Amplified playing the pantomime villain. He didn't seem that bad when you met him, but she hadn't decided which was the real Jay-Den.

'Yes, I know. I understand.'

'I haven't been this excited about a band in a long time; they are gold. We mustn't let them waste an ounce of their potential.' He shifted forward in his chair making Melissa feel slightly uncomfortable as he rested his hand on her leg. He was enjoying having a few minutes with Melissa – she was easier to talk to than Beth, who always seemed ready for a row. Melissa seemed to want to do what was best for Luke and in his business that made life so much easier. Plus, she was very easy on the eyes.

'How are you coping with the female attention he's getting?'

'I trust him.'

'That's good. Just be prepared – some fans can be a handful, so trust is important.'

'I know. I don't have any worries with that.'

Jay-Den raised an eyebrow. 'Really?' He was surprised by how comfortable she seemed to be about it.

'He's given me no reason to worry, so I won't until there's a need to,' she said, shrugging. She knew he loved her.

'Good girl. But you need to start growing a thicker skin. The fame world is a completely different game and you'll need to learn the rules. You have to be able to handle negative comments about him, about the band and about you. You'll get attention purely because of who you're dating, or you could be completely ignored for the same reason. And you need to have other interests apart from him and his music.' He reached over and patted her leg. He'd seen it all before, couples just like them, broken up because they didn't listen to him.

'OK ... but I'm fine with it all'

'That's good to hear. You're in for one hell of a ride if all goes well, so you'd better be prepared for everything to change. Never speak to the media or read anything about yourself, it'll make you paranoid. They don't know him or you, but that won't stop them telling the world what they think they know.' He laughed and reassured her that he was always there to help if they needed it. Then she went to find Beth.

Jay-Den watched her go, her long blonde hair swinging as she walked and the heels of her boots making that clicking sound. Her jeans hugged her tightly as did her brown waist-length jacket. He shook his head as she disappeared through the door. 'Lucky son of a bitch,' he whispered to himself. He was a little jealous of Luke Black right now, but he shook the thought away.

*****

Beth was pacing up and down outside, muttering about Jay-Den and how she hated being told what to do.

'Don't stress, babe, it's not that bad.' Melissa could see the frustration in Beth's eyes.

Beth hated having control taken away – she'd had total control of her life since she started to take care of herself at a young age.

'Sorry. I know, but he annoys me.' She realised it sounded ungrateful after all he'd done. But she had noticed how he looked at Melissa, even if nobody else had. It wasn't unusual – most men looked at her like that, but she thought he could have a little more respect for Luke, and make an effort not to leer.

'You know me, Liss, hate being told what to do.' Beth flicked her curls off her face and smiled. She wasn't worried. Melissa would never cheat – she didn't have it in her to do that to anyone, and she definitely wouldn't do it to Luke. Melissa laughed at Beth's observation but kept quiet about her chat with Jay-Den, not wanting Beth's mind to go into overdrive. Even if she were single, Jay-Den was too much in love with himself for her liking.

*****

'You've got a tear in your shoe!'

'What?' Melissa almost shrieked as she looked down and saw her black and silver heels were fine. Luke had been joking, and she threw him a horrified look.

'Oh, I have your attention now?' he said, sounding a little sarcastic.

'You horrible git. That was just mean.'

Luke frowned at her. He knew she had things on her mind but it wasn't the first time that day he'd had to take drastic measures to grab her attention. Melissa shifted her gaze back and forth nervously before resting her head on his shoulder.

'What's wrong?' he asked. 'Don't bottle things up.'

'Nothing.'

'Liss, I'm not an idiot.'

'It's just me being stupid. I worry that you'll meet someone else when you're away. Someone better than me.' She tried so hard not to feel that way. Most of the time she was fine, but sometimes it would creep into her mind.

'Shut up you muppet! Who's going to be better than you?' He laughed but realised that even to a beautiful girl like Melissa there would always be doubt. Melissa shrugged and pointed out that there were plenty of girls who could take her place. 'Well, I think I have a say in that. You've nothing to worry about Babe, OK?' He reminded her of the promise he'd made. He hadn't forgotten, and he had every intention of keeping it.

'They're lying in wait outside.' She remembered how different things were now, and stopped herself from kissing him, suddenly feeling like she was a circus act. Then she noticed some girls watching them while whispering to each other.

'Stop staring at us,' she hissed quietly through gritted teeth, 'god, is it too much to ask for one day with you?'

'Liss, don't stress out. It's fine. They're doing no harm.' Luke laughed and waved at them. It didn't seem to bother him at all, and he reminded her not to offend the fans. She sighed, knowing he was right, as usual.

'Just don't encourage them too much. Can we go soon?' Melissa whispered as the group giggled excitedly.

'Oh come on – I just made their day,' he laughed a little smugly.

Melissa counted to ten in her head, then turned to wave and smile at them too. Dutiful girlfriend bit done. She knew this came with the territory. The fans weren't really the problem – it was important that they had some. Most of them were pretty cool. But some girls would look at her like she was something they'd wiped off their shoe. The green-eyed monster was unable to hide on some of their faces. I should be smug about it, she thought. But it annoyed her more than anything.

'It's as if you'd be with them if it wasn't for me. I hate it when they look at me like that,' she would moan to Luke frequently.

Luke would nod – she was right. It would have to be someone

incredible to knock Melissa off her throne. The intrusion into their lives was only just beginning and already she was paranoid, and becoming very selfish about the small amount of time she got to spend with him.

Eventually, they left for their hotel. Melissa was blinded by a flash before she even stepped outside. The lens was right in her face. She was taken off guard, and she whipped her head up angrily.

'Shit. What the ...?' Then she remembered the paparazzi that were waiting for a final confirmation shot of Luke Black's 'official' girlfriend.

'It's OK, just keep walking,' Luke instructed quietly in her ear. He glared at one who had ventured too close. 'Back off mate,' he warned. He would play the game but he wouldn't stand for either of them being cornered like animals. They crowded around like predators – he hadn't expected it to be so intense. It was in that moment that Luke confirmed their relationship to the world without having to utter a word. He pulled her into his arms, shielding her. Melissa buried her face into his chest as he guided her to their waiting car. His kiss on her forehead as they settled into the back seat was captured clearly, giving everyone their answer.

The headline next morning was simple, 'Luke Black steps out with a beautiful blonde confirming his love status ... sorry girls but he is spoken for!'

*****

'Please come home soon,' Melissa begged down the phone.

'It's just a few more days, babe.' He was pleased to hear her voice because he hadn't had the chance to keep in touch as much as he'd hoped, due to their hectic schedule and the time difference.

Melissa decided not to nag him about his text-only contact, and let him get his career off the ground without having to worry about having a clingy girlfriend to please along with everything else. 'How many hotel rooms have you smashed up?' she joked instead. 'It'd better be impressive.'

'Oh, a few. We don't keep count.' He sounded so happy that she really didn't mind about the lack of calls. She smiled while she listened to him talk excitedly about New York and being ambushed by fans. The public were liking his music, but one thing concerned him. Melissa burst out laughing when he told her.

'What's wrong with a photo shoot?' Ray had arranged one with

*Highway* magazine. Luke wasn't keen and complained about having to wear make-up. That definitely wasn't going to happen. 'If I'd wanted to do bloody photo shoots I'd have become a model.' He didn't have an issue with having his picture taken, but this was a professional shoot and they'd been told they would have to wear make-up. Melissa was in fits of giggles.

'I am not putting that shit on my face. Not happening,' he ranted, getting himself more fired up over it. Melissa had a sneaking suspicion that Ray was having Luke on because he could be a bit of a joker sometimes.

Their phone conversation moved on to family commitments, as her parents wanted to see him and Melissa when he got back. Jean cooked a mean roast dinner so he was happy with that, knowing he would be well fed.

'I bet you're not eating well,' Melissa commented, knowing they'd be living off fast food and beer. It was the reason she'd started to cook more often. Her mother had taught her well. Cooking for Luke and the guys was something she enjoyed, when she could get them to sit down for more than five minutes. Cooking wasn't in their schedule because it just took up time when they could be drinking or playing. Their tour games didn't help matters – the game of Twenty-one was a regular in their activities. The rules were simple – just count to twenty-one. It sounded simple enough but included a host of complicated sub-rules, all of which led to drinking forfeits. It could and did descend into chaos very quickly. Then there was the card game 'Shithead' at which Tom was the champion, much to Beth's annoyance.

Another game invented out of sheer boredom when travelling was the retweet game. It had simple rules. Everyone tweeted something funny or random and then retweeted, seeing how many people they could get involved. No matter what the tweet was or who it was about, it still had to be retweeted. It caused all kinds of disagreements especially if it was insulting or embarrassing, and the game could go on for hours. Ray found it highly irritating and would cover his ears and ignore it. The girls loved it because with all the social networking they didn't feel completely cut off from the boys. They would get involved in the game at home, and it helped bridge the gap between them. Luke had won the last game and his tweet simply said, 'Dale is a prick'. It was retweeted twelve hundred times because the fans had joined in. They had to be reigned in sometimes, but it was all good fun and it helped their image as boys who liked to have a good time.

They loved chatting to fans, spending hours replying to tweets. Toby could get a little too friendly sometimes, and Ray would have to remind him that some girls might take what he said a little too seriously, so he had to be very careful.

'You know we don't eat well,' Luke said honestly. 'Nothing like *your* cooking anyway.'

'Hmmm,' Melissa replied. 'If you say so. More like you lot are too lazy.'

'We're way too busy,' he chuckled. 'I'm a rock star, not a chef.' The thought of Luke standing in a kitchen cooking a meal didn't seem right even to her.

'OK, roast lamb at my parents' house when you're back. And it'll stop them moaning about never seeing me any more,' Melissa laughed. Her parents adored Luke, and thought it was great how well things were going for him. Embarrassingly, they had started to listen to their music in an attempt to show their support. Her mother loved it – there was definitely a rock chick lurking inside her. She actually wanted to go to one of their shows. It made Melissa cringe but Luke thought it was cool. He assured Melissa that *his* parents felt the same about her. In fact Debbie Black couldn't have been happier with her son's choice.

'She's adorable, not to mention beautiful,' his mother had gushed after their first meeting.

They talked until Melissa was nearly at her car. She didn't want to stop talking to him but he was on his way to yet another interview.

'Don't forget that I love you to bits, OK?' She walked on, smiling at how happy he was. All she wanted him to do was what he loved.

*****

Melissa ended her day on a relatively good note. The cafe hadn't been too busy and her boss had been in a good mood – a rare thing because she was a miserable old witch. The fact that Melissa was dating Luke seemed to put her back up, and she always made a point of picking on Melissa so she would know she wouldn't be getting special treatment. But Melissa had never asked for or expected anything. It didn't help matters that at times people only came in to see Melissa or stare through the window. It didn't occur to anyone that she was in a difficult position, trying to keep her boss happy and her boyfriend's new following too. But her priority was the fans because it wouldn't be long before she could tell her boss to stick it. Despite missing him, she realised that their time apart hadn't been too bad. It proved that their relationship didn't fall apart the moment he went on the road, and this gave her confidence and hope for their future.

She'd parked her car, a blue Corsa, in a nearby car park. It was dark and deserted and only one street lamp was working, so there was only a dim glow lighting the street. She was halfway across the car park when she heard footsteps behind her. Thinking it must be the paparazzi again she turned, ready to yell at them. But she couldn't see anybody. I must be hearing things, she thought. But she definitely felt as though she was being watched. As she scanned the car park again she saw a figure by the entrance, standing still and appearing to watching. It made her jump, and she let out a low shriek. The person's hood was up, and the fur edges were pulled in so that the face was hidden, giving them a sinister look. The figure started walking in her direction, slowly at first and then picking up speed until he or she (she couldn't tell which) was running.

Melissa ran the last few steps to her car, pulling her keys from her pocket as she went. By some miracle she unlocked it first time and got in, then quickly locked the doors, her heart racing. The person jumped onto the bonnet of the car and stood there, staring down at her.

Fear had gripped her. Eventually, after what seemed like hours but was probably seconds, the person made a cut-throat sign and then jumped down. Melissa was sure she heard a laugh as he or she ran off. She thought it looked like a female, but she couldn't be sure.

Melissa was shaking like a leaf but she started the engine and once she'd caught her breath, and put her foot down to head for her best friend's house, and safety.

*****

'I think you're mental.' Beth was pacing around her flat, puffing on a cigarette and shaking her head at her best friend's decision. Melissa didn't want to make a fuss about what had just happened, and in particular she didn't want to tell Luke. She wanted to put it down to a jealous fan being a bit weird, and forget about it.

'It's nothing.' Melissa was trying hard to play it down, but in truth it had scared her to death.

'Oh yeah. It happens all the time,' Beth replied sarcastically. She wasn't amused in the slightest, and she definitely wasn't prepared to accept it as nothing. 'I still think you're insane.'

Beth's flat was a small one-bedroom place above a newsagent's, but it was hers and she was proud that she paid for it herself. It was her little piece of independence. It was decorated in a simple but homely way, and she was happy there.

Her hair was still damp from her shower making it go frizzy as it dried. Melissa giggled as she paced about in her yellow cotton pyjamas looking less like a rock star's girlfriend and more like a presenter on a kids' TV programme.

'Don't laugh,' Beth scolded. 'You caught me in the middle of my evening beauty ritual and it's gone to shit now.' Her voice cracked with the effort of trying not to laugh too as she caught her reflection in the window. 'Dear god, look at me,' then she cursed as she tripped over some of Dale's lesser used equipment. His acoustic guitar, which Beth had been instructed to take in for maintenance while he was away, was leaning up against the TV and Melissa reminded her she'd be in trouble if she didn't make sure she got it fixed. 'Me? In trouble?' Beth laughed. 'Have a word, babe. Anyway, I'm doing it tomorrow so it's all good.'

Dale had now officially moved in, and his stuff was already scattered everywhere. Melissa found it funny how things had worked out for them both – girlfriends of up and coming rock stars who had just fitted into their lives so easily. He had moved in without there being much of a conversation about it – it just sort of happened. It was as though it had always been that way.

Melissa was now used to tripping over guitars and amps on a regular basis.

Beth poured more wine as Melissa begged her not to tell anyone what had happened and she eventually agreed, on two conditions. If anything remotely suspicious happened again, it had to be reported straight away, and Melissa was to stay at Beth's flat until the boys were back, just to be safe. They considered it an emergency and used it as an excuse to call in sick for work next day.

*****

Their sick day was spent watching movies in their pyjamas and eating junk food.

'This'll be our little secret, he he' Melissa whispered as they snuggled together on the sofa, wrapped in a duvet with tea and biscuits.

'Yeah, just this once,' Beth promised. 'I mean it though. If anything else happens Liss, I'll call the police myself.'

Melissa nodded, accepting that what Beth was saying was fair enough.

The week ended with no more incidents, and Melissa began to relax a little. She started to believe that maybe it really had been a one-off incident.

Work kept her busy, and she'd started going to the gym again. There was also a weekly dance class at her gym that she had signed up to. She had always loved dancing, but it had been a long time since she'd done any. Luke would be away a lot more, so it was important that she had her own interests to keep her busy and keep her mind off the fact that he wasn't around, whatever gossip was being printed about her, and the threat of being accosted by weirdo stalkers.

*****

'Melissa and Luke are heading for a split after Luke flirts with mystery brunette in NYC bar! The newest star relationship is on the rocks, according to a source ...'

Luke screwed up the paper and chucked it over his shoulder, hitting Dale in the face.

'Who writes this shit?' he grumbled. 'Whoever it is, I'll shove it down their throat so they choke.' He called Melissa just to make she was OK, and he was pleased to hear her laugh about it.

'Oh man, it's the mystery woman again. Luke, you should really ask her name next time.' Melissa laughed, making him chuckle too.

She really is an amazing girlfriend, he thought. 'Sodding mystery to me too, seeing as though I didn't speak to any women that evening. I was too busy arguing with Toby about the football most of the evening as I recall.' He lit a cigarette. 'I guess that's not juicy enough.'

There had been several drunken nights back in the old days when they woke next morning surrounded by random items that had been 'borrowed' from various places – traffic cones, fire extinguishers, even a park bench once. But by far the most random had been a live goat. They still had no idea where it came from. They had to do some serious apologising when the RSPCA had arrived to take it away, and they only narrowly avoided being reported to the police. Their story of simply waking up to find her in the living room hadn't really washed with the officers...but she was returned unharmed to the farmer.

*****

The last few days of the trip to New York passed quickly, and eventually the guys returned home, much more famous than they'd been a week before. Four days after they left for New York, Melissa had realised how well known they were becoming when she returned home from work to find a group of six girls looking oddly nervous hanging around close to her house. They giggled nervously, whispering to each other as she parked her car. One of them walked towards Melissa as she opened her gate. It had been a very long, busy day with lots of demanding customers, and Melissa wasn't in the best of moods. She knew what was about to happen so she counted to ten, sucked in her breath and turned to them, smiling sweetly.

'Are you Black Eagles fans?' Melissa asked politely. It was easier that way for the girl concerned, to say something to break the ice slightly. Melissa understood how daunting it was to meet someone you're a fan of. There was always the fear that they might not be as nice as you had built them up in your mind to be, because this would smash your dreams to bits.

The girl stopped, a little unsure of what to say next as she looked down at the tiny girl who was dating her idol.

Melissa noticed that the girl was wearing black wedge-style Tom's shoes, exactly the same as the pair she was waiting for the postman to deliver.

'Wow, I like your shoes. I'm getting some of those.'

This made the girl's day.

The rest of the group gained confidence and came over. They asked a few innocent questions about Luke and the band, and Melissa chatted to them happily for a while, before realising that they had helped her forget about her bad day at work.

'You are so lucky,' one girl gushed, 'he's just amazing.'

Melissa smiled and thanked the girl, trying not to look smug about it. It was a bit odd to see a stranger almost having a meltdown about your boyfriend, flattering as it might be. They asked when he'd be home and Melissa gave a very vague answer, hoping to put them off. When Luke did get home, she wanted him all to herself.

Eventually, the group went on their way, smiling and laughing, happy that their journey hadn't been wasted. They knew Luke was away but meeting his girlfriend was the next best thing. Their pictures with her were soon all over the web but Melissa was slowly starting to get used to it.

# Hit the shelves

January 2014

'I'm so proud,' Melissa gushed as she held up a copy of *Highway* Magazine. It contained the boys' very first interview. She shook slightly as she stared at the picture on the front cover – the beautiful man staring out at her was her boyfriend, her Luke.

Beth snatched the magazine out of her hands, eager for another read, while Melissa straightened her hair ready for their night out. Echo were playing at The Roundhouse in London and had invited the two girls to join them as their guests.

'They come across really well,' Beth beamed as she pored over it again. Melissa saw the contented look in her friend's eyes. She stroked the page and her hand stopped and rested on Dale's face. For a split second the real Beth shone through, the loving girl who deep down was scared she would lose him. With a flick of her midnight curls, the front was back and she told Melissa to stop faffing around and finish her wine so they could go out. She didn't want to risk getting there late and missing the start of their friends' set. Beth packed the magazine into her overnight bag for safe keeping, and checked her hair again as Melissa stepped into her new killer heels and knocked back the last of the bottle of Pinot Grigio.

'Ready to rock and roll?' Beth asked excitedly. Melissa nodded and they headed out of the hotel.

*****

The evening didn't quite go to plan. Echo put on a great show but Melissa was subjected to several rude comments, including being called a slag, from people who'd decided that the rumours must be true about her sleeping with Toby behind Luke's back. Melissa tried her best to ignore it, but a particular group of girls were seemingly enjoying being bullies. It was a tough situation for Beth, whose natural instinct was to go on the attack. Nobody treated her best friend like that, but she was also trying to prove she could behave.

'I swear...if they carry on ...' Beth hissed, glaring at the group of girls who were huddled together as if they were back in the playground. They had made rude comments each time Melissa had walked past them, and one had barged past her, knocking her as she did so. One had commented loudly, 'she looks a little fat these days.'

This sort of thing was one of the negatives that came with her new life, and because of her new-found celebrity status it seemed that some people felt it was OK to bully her. She dabbed a tear away before it fell, not wanting to give them the satisfaction of knowing they'd got to her.

'Don't listen to those knobheads. You have what they want - that's all it comes down to,' Beth assured her. She gave her the smile she used when she was feeling all sentimental and protective. 'Keep your head high, and rise above it. These cretins don't care either way, they're just trying to feel better about themselves. Luke loves *you*, not them, so just remember that. It's jealousy, pure and simple.' Melissa nodded and smiled back at her friend, her expression saying, 'thanks'.

The Eagles' single 'Games' had reached number three in the charts and the album was days away from being finished, so she would just concentrate on the positives in her life. Screw those jerks, she thought as they knocked back more shots. Beth groaned as a flash went off – another thing they had to endure. It felt as though every move they made someone was being snapped by someone, but it was the things written about them that she hated most.

There were stories doing the rounds claiming she was in a relationship with Toby, and possibly other members of the band. She and Beth were lesbians apparently, and Cassie and Luke were cheating on Melissa as revenge for her Toby affair.

Cassie and Melissa laughed about it over a drink after the show. It made Melissa feel much better about things.

In a real-world development, Jo-Jo had asked the girls about Tom, and told them that she wasn't going to wait around forever.

'She totally wants him,' Cassie laughed. Their game of playing hard to get was becoming very irritating. They adored each other, yet seemed hell-bent on stringing the whole thing out. Cassie had told her that morning to 'shag him already ... you're driving me nuts', while Luke was saying pretty much the same thing to his bass player, three thousand miles away.

The girls chatted over drinks. Echo's single 'Run and Hide' was exploding up the charts, sitting just above the Eagles at number two.

Cassie had got a bit emotional while telling the girls about it. She'd written it years ago after her cousin had committed suicide aged sixteen, having suffered from nasty bullying. 'Run and Hide' was something he did day after day, until he finally couldn't take it any more.

Cassie took great pleasure in sending Luke smug messages each time they overtook them in the charts. The girls hadn't been offered anything by Sky Storm but Purple Velvet Records had signed them up, adding rival labels to the banter. They all had a nice friendship, and Melissa often thought about how it all came about, concluding that it was meant to be - written in the stars or something.

'Don't let them get to you,' Cassie said, referring to the 'bitch pack' as they called them. 'It's only because you're so fucking beautiful and Luke is your boyfriend.'

Melissa nodded, blushing. 'Thanks, Cass.'

'Let's pack up our shit,' Cassie called to the crew. 'Go somewhere without dumb bitches.'

They went on to a couple of bars and then a club, only leaving to head back to their hotel when things turned ugly. They were hounded as usual by the paparazzi, all spouting the usual rubbish. But Melissa had been worn down by the day's events, and alcohol had weakened her restraint, so she exploded at them, charging for one male photographer who had got too close to her, yelling at him to leave them alone. Beth and Cassie had to wrestle her into their minibus, and shortly afterwards Jo-Jo and Allie had arrived and helped calm things down.

'I'm not,' Melissa cried, referring to their accusations about her and Toby. It was driving her mad.

'Liss, we know that and most of all Luke knows that. Don't stress,' Beth said slurring a little before kissing Melissa on the cheek. 'They're just brainless morons – they don't even believe it. It's just to wind you up.'

Melissa slumped in her seat, angry and embarrassed at her little performance. A perfectly good night had been ruined right at the end, and her tears flowed at the hurtful lies that she couldn't stop them printing. Cassie noticed but didn't make a fuss. She just put her arm around her and told her it was all going to be OK. She texted Luke a heads up that Melissa might need a call from her loving boyfriend.

Naturally, Melissa had worried that Luke would be angry with her for showing him up, but he wasn't concerned about that – he knew very well how vicious they could be at times. She felt much better that he was sympathetic rather than annoyed.

'You're adorable when you're mad,' he joked, and she couldn't help but laugh.

'Thanks for making me feel better.'

'Anytime, beautiful.'

'Can I see you before I forget what you look like?'

'I'll be home soon, I promise. It's just I need—'

Melissa finished his sentence for him. 'I know ... I know you need to get the album finished.' It was just how he worked. He wouldn't rest till it was perfect. Every second he wasn't working on it, he felt like he was wasting time. This meant for the time being that she came second. It was hard, but she understood that it was his life's work. Even if he was with her, his mind would be on work, so it would be pointless anyway.

'You know I love you, don't you?'

'Yes, I know,' Melissa giggled. 'But will you hurry up and come back to me please?'

*****

'I hate this ...' Melissa growled as she threw the magazine to the floor. Their night out had hit the shelves and, as expected, Melissa was front page news.

'Eagle babe ... Drinking out of control, attacks male photographer ...'

'Now I look like a mental case!' Melissa complained, looking at Luke for reassurance. He picked up the magazine and threw it in the bin. Melissa looked deflated as she sat there in the kitchen, her legs pulled up and her chin resting on her knees. She looked like she was about to cry.

'You know me and Toby would never—' Luke cut her off by laughing loudly. 'It isn't funny,' she whimpered. 'People are believing this stuff. I was called a slut in the bar last night.' The hurt in her eyes made Luke stop laughing – he hadn't realised people were insulting her.

'Hey,' he said, sounding concerned now. 'I didn't know it was that bad, sorry.' He sat on the floor so they were at eye level and stroked her cheek gently. 'I know it's bullshit. I trust you both, and we don't care what anyone else thinks.'

'Sorry if I've shown you up by getting pissed.'

Luke shook his head before kissing her to show that he wasn't at all angry at her, or embarrassed by her behaviour. 'You're my very own mental case,' he sniggered.

The only time any of it would bother him was when the media

upset Melissa. He tried not to read any of it but it was impossible to ignore completely. When they were promoting, he would read enough to know the gossip doing the rounds. Then they would come up with funny or vague answers to the inevitable interview questions.

'I've got some good news,' Luke said, changing the subject. It was the reason he had rushed home after a meeting.

Melissa jumped up as she remembered his meeting. 'Oh my god, of course. Sorry, forget those idiots. How did it go?' She put her hands together like she was praying, looking excited but slightly cautious.

'They love it!' Luke said, before the biggest smile spread across his face. 'We've just signed off our first ever album.'

Melissa screamed, almost bursting Luke's eardrums. She jumped around the kitchen like she was on a pogo stick. Luke laughed hysterically. He knew the same thing would be happening with Dale and Beth. The record label were over the moon with the album and it had been passed for release without any quibbles or changes. Jay-den was the most impressed.

'I knew you boys were good, but Christ, I didn't think you were this good,' he had said just a few hours before. Their next step would be their first tour, around Europe first, then a short break before hitting the States. It meant almost three months away from home. There was still the matter of Ray's non-negotiable ban on girlfriends. Luke had tried to get him to at least let them join them for a couple of weekends.

'No' had been his final answer. He knew very well that he'd have a problem getting his front man out of his bed with that little beauty around. Despite his concerns, even Ray had to admit she was very easy to like. He even had a soft spot for Beth. They made his two main guys happy, giving him some comfort. The ban was staying in place regardless. He had a reputation to uphold after all.

'Miserable git,' Melissa complained, but deep down she knew it was important that Luke was fully focused. It had to go well. Melissa began to accept that it was nearly that time when she would be climbing into the 'back seat' Jay-Den always banged on about. 'Call me every day if you can,' she pouted a little.

'Your wish is my command.' Luke felt relieved that she had accepted Ray's decision so easily. He wasn't sure Dale would be having the same conversation and he laughed at the thought.

'You know Beth isn't going to take this well,' Melissa said, as if she had read his mind. Luke pulled something from his pocket, diverting the conversation immediately. Eyes wide, she screamed again. It was a copy of their album, plus an envelope containing tickets to Barcelona. A long weekend away to give them some time to themselves, before he went away. They would be back just in time for their very first album launch party.

Everyone agreed that the album listing was perfect.

The Black Eagles
*First Flight*

1. Fly High
2. Downfall
3. Broken Wings
4. Just Another Day Wishing
5. Games
6. Whiskey and Pills
7. Weekend High
8. Never Be Good Enough
9. Smashed
10. Bad Choices
11. Fuck Quiet, Let's Riot

*****

This is Melissa,' Luke said proudly as he introduced her to Sonny Lee, who had turned up at their launch party unexpectedly. Excitement was flowing through Luke as he attempted to maintain a 'cool' rock star image.

'It's a pleasure to meet you,' Sonny said, taking her hand gently.

It was Melissa's turn to act as though it was nothing at all, like she was used to mixing with rock stars every day.

Sonny kissed her hand like a true gentleman. His hair hung loosely from under yet another weird hat – it was just part of who he was – genuinely quirky. They exchanged the usual small talk, interrupted briefly by Sonny's wife, Saskia, who came over to say hello. She was working the room and mingling with several different groups, playing the dutiful wife like a true pro.

Ray called Luke over for another interview, this time with a local paper who had been lucky enough to get one of their reporters inside the event. They had five minutes to use as best they could. Melissa was left alone with one of the biggest stars ever to grace the music world.

'Thank you,' Melissa said feeling the need to break the ice again, 'for all the great things you said at Amplified.' The nerves took over and she began to ramble on before managing to shut her mouth, feeling rather stupid.

Sonny politely let her finish. 'No need to thank me. It was the truth.'

'Yes I do. You don't know how hard he'd worked.'

Sonny looked at her for a second, amused. 'Really, Melissa, don't I?' His tone was soft but with that raspy cracking sound to it.

Her cheeks flushed as it dawned on her just how stupid her comment was. Just because he had his status now, that had not always been the case. 'Of course you do, sorry.'

Sonny noticed Melissa's hands had started to shake and she clasped them together trying to hide it. She wanted Luke to come back. Messing this up wasn't what she had planned.

'You two remind me of our early days,' Sonny said referring to himself and his wife. They'd been together since their early twenties and Sonny could see that their paths were heading in the same direction. The look in Luke's eyes when he took to the stage – he had felt that too, and still did. It was a feeling that never went away. Melissa held the same stance his wife did back at the beginning. Trying so hard to be a good partner but deep down feeling like it would all end if they said the wrong thing or acted in the wrong way. And terrified they might lose their man to the temptations of another woman.

'Take care of each other, it can be a cruel world.' He kissed her hand again and winked before moving off to chat to some of the music industry VIPs, one being Jay-Den who had just arrived to reap the glory of such a find.

'I'm Jay-Den 'I love myself' Lake, pleased to meet you' Beth growled in Melissa's ear just seconds after Sonny had moved on. They both laughed. It was fitting because it was really quite sickening how he behaved around certain people. Luke had said a few times he thought his PA Megan did most of the work. Yet, she wasn't here. Luke had asked if she could attend – after all she had been working all hours getting things organised for them. She deserved it, he thought. And Toby had taken a shine to Miss May, as they liked to call her. But Jay-Den just said she was busy and wasn't available.

'Yeah, busy busting her arse for you. And you couldn't even let her come to one party. Asshole,' Beth said in Melissa's ear again. Beth had been eager to play Cupid with Megan and Toby. Melissa threw an arm around her shoulders and dragged her to the bar - she needed distracting. Beth's dislike of Jay-Den was increasing daily – she didn't trust him, but she didn't know why. It was just a sense she had. It irritated her that nobody else seemed to feel the same, but she didn't say anything around the boys, for now anyway.

The party continued into the night with over two hundred specially selected people. A few lucky fans had won a place at the event via an online prize draw and a radio competition. The album went down a storm, causing a flurry of excitement among label executives and investors. Melissa and Beth liked seeing the band spending time with their fans, but couldn't decide who was more excited – them or the fans. It shocked both girls when several came over acting just as starstruck towards *them*.

'Oh god, Melissa, I love you.'

'Beth, you're my idol. I wish I could be as brave and outspoken as you.'

'You're both so pretty. Wow, I cannot believe I've met you.'

That was surreal enough, but being asked to sign autographs was just mind-blowing.

'We're totally famous,' Beth giggled afterwards, as they headed home. The 'famous four' travelled in one car, while Tom and Toby had disappeared with several pretty hangers-on in tow, mumbling about finding another party. They were not done for the evening yet. However, Luke had noticed Toby had been obviously disappointed that a certain redhead hadn't been there.

'Dirt bags,' Beth sniggered as they drove past them, staggering down the road with a girl on each arm. 'It was a great night, I'm very proud of you,' she said turning her attention back to Dale. She kissed him passionately, not caring about their audience.

Melissa was sitting on Luke's knee. They were holding a long and unimportant conversation to divert attention away from the little show opposite them. But it was a bit uncomfortable all the same.

'Come here, you amazing, talented, adorable, sexy man,' Melissa purred as they headed to bed after what had seemed like a very long ride home.

'You like it?,' Luke whispered against her lips, wanting one last assurance that the album was good enough.

'I love it, but not as much as I love you,' she giggled, before kissing him.

*****

Tickets for their tour went on sale early the next morning, and there was no doubt in Melissa's mind that there wouldn't be a single one left by the end of the week, if not sooner.

The headline was a welcome wake-up for them all:

'The Black Eagles: 'Fledgling' tour has already sold out. The English band from Portsmouth have only been around for what seems like five minutes, but they are building a strong and devoted fan base. It took just twenty-nine minutes to sell out, leaving thousands of fans disappointed.'

'Thanks for everything, Miss May,' Luke whispered in Megan's ear as he passed her desk. They were at the record label offices, finalising a few things with some of the executives before heading off on the road. Jay-Den's PA smiled sweetly at him.

'Any time Luke, it's what I'm here for. Have a great time. And be good.' Megan blushed as he gave her one of his most charming smiles.

'Who, me?' he asked in mock outrage. 'Always.' He winked at her before disappearing out the door, while Dale and Tom both kissed her on the cheek as they left, making her blush even more. She was used to dealing with big names but despite being incredibly shy outside of her job, at work she was one of the best. It was one of the reasons Jay-Den kept her on, plus she did pretty much everything for him while he took all the glory. It was frustrating, but she enjoyed the job, even if her boss was an arrogant moron sometimes. Since this band had signed though, she looked forward to coming to work each day. Not so much today though. She carried on with her work despite her mood, and tried to bury herself in it to forget about things. She hadn't had a very nice evening the night before. It was something she hoped nobody ever found out about, and she was still very deeply hurt and embarrassed about it.

'Oh no, please don't stare at me,' she thought to herself. Toby Maxwell, their drummer, was always staring at her, but she wasn't going to fall for it. She'd promised herself never to succumb to the charms of a rock star ever again. So she stared at her screen, pretending he wasn't there and hoping he would leave quickly. 'Damn,' she thought as he sat down on the other side of her desk, messing with her pens in the pot by her phone. She couldn't ignore him. He was a client after all and she couldn't be rude, but he made her feel odd.

'Do you need some help? Did I miss something?' She asked, still keeping her professional voice on. Her green eyes looked at him briefly before looking back at her screen. 'Why does he make me feel so on edge?' She wondered again.

'No, I just thought I'd come and say hi,' he said as he checked her out a little more. 'What is it about you?' he was thinking at the same time. Her clothing was very 'geek chic' in an intelligent yet sexy way. She was the complete opposite of him, certainly not the type of girl he would normally go for, but for some reason he was fascinated by her. Infatuated, Luke called it. They had never really had a proper conversation, because Luke usually spoke to her when she called about band matters. He was the main man, so most things went via him first. It hadn't taken long before the guys had noticed the way Toby looked at her though. Tom had spotted it the second time they had visited the office. He could tell when Toby liked someone – it was in his eyes and his behaviour around that person. It was brought up in conversation later that day over a few beers.

'Just ask her out you muppet, it's bloody obvious you're into her,' Tom had blurted out.

Toby tried to deny it at first but after his fourth beer and a prolonged interrogation and plenty of jokes from his bandmates, he gave in.

'Fine. I like her, OK. Happy now? I suppose you're gonna take the piss for the rest of my life.' His defences went up, and he was ready to stick up for her as well as himself. It wasn't really Megan they were ribbing him about, it was just their way of getting him to admit it.

'No, you go for it mate. We think she'd be good for you. But don't scare her too much...' Luke smirked and patted him on the shoulder while Dale and Toby got the next round in.

As she looked up from her screen again, Megan could feel her hands shaking as she nodded and smiled.

'Hi,' she said, her voice quivering as she reached for her phone that had started ringing at a very convenient moment. Or at least it would have been, if she hadn't knocked her coffee over. 'Oh no,' she cursed, jumping up.

Toby spontaneously laughed out loud, making her flap even more. He then realised that she was panicking, and quickly helped her move her files and keyboard out of the way, before finding something to mop it up with.

'Thanks, but you don't have to do that.' Jay-Den would go nuts if he thought she was getting clients to clean the office.

'I don't mind,' he reassured her, still laughing at her meltdown. He knew it was a reaction to his presence, even if it wasn't quite what he wanted. But it was a great way to break the ice, although maybe not from her point of view, he thought.

'I don't want to hold you up. Are the others waiting for you?' She hoped he would just leave because she was mortified. But Toby just shrugged – they all knew why he was hanging back.

'There you go, good as new,' he said once the desk was clean and tidy again.

She smiled, warming to him. 'Thanks.'

'You're welcome. I guess I'd better let you get on with your work and go prepare for the tour then.'

'Yeah, you better,' she said, blushing again.

'Bye, Miss May,' he said as he turned and headed out of the door.

Megan watched him leave, and then without knowing why, she ran after him and called his name. Toby turned and looked back at her. The hood of his green sweater was up, shading his face slightly, and his ear piercings glinted from the reflections of the lights, mirrors and pictures that lined the wall. In that second, her heart seemed to skip a beat and she suddenly realised what a lovely, kind face he had if you just looked at him without the misconception that people already seemed to have of him. She didn't know what she was planning on saying, and could do nothing but stand there for what seemed like an hour, feeling her cheeks matching the colour of her hair yet again.

Toby waited for her to say something, but all that came out was a stuttered, 'Good lu-luck. With the tour. Not that you need it – that's not what I mean. Just have a good time,' she stammered on, knowing she was making herself look like a complete idiot for a second time in five minutes.

'Thanks – I guess I'll see you around.' He smiled and winked, then left her standing there, wanting the floor to open up and swallow her. 'It's a work in progress, but she's warming up a little bit. I'll marry that girl one day, you mark my words,' Toby said once he was back outside with the guys. They laughed at how smitten he was, but he didn't care.

'Sure mate,' Luke said, patting him on the back as they got into the car that was waiting to take them to a magazine interview. She might actually calm him down, if that was possible. Or he could ruin the girl forever, he thought, and laughed quietly to himself.

*****

As she left the gym after her dance class, Melissa cursed herself for parking so far away. It was dark and cold and she couldn't wait to get home and have a long hot shower, get into her comfy clothes and watch her favourite shows. Her satellite TV box was overflowing with recordings which had been building up for weeks. She'd been so busy, but hopefully she would be spending the next 24 hours with Luke before he went on tour. Tonight he was in London for a meeting with Jay-Den and yet another interview, then the boys were having a night out. Melissa was getting better with the idea of being famous, and she was learning to just get on with life – enjoy the good bits and ignore the unwanted attention. The dance group had helped, and they had welcomed her with no problem at all. Some were fans, but they knew her now so they treated her normally, so she felt comfortable with them.

*********

She sighed with relief when she finally saw her car, and quickened her pace to get there. As she pressed the ignition, she looked out the front window and gasped as she saw a hooded figure standing only a few feet away. It had been weeks since the first incident and she'd almost forgotten about it, but this was definitely the same person. What do you want? She thought. Was it money? Or was this a weird fan? She couldn't even see if it was male or female as the baggy clothes gave nothing away. She didn't hang around, but threw the car into reverse and backed away as the figure threw something at the windscreen. A knife bounced off the glass and fell into the road. Melissa choked on her scream, and screeched the tyres as she accelerated away.

*********

She raced home knowing she had to make a choice – either keep it to herself or tell Luke. He wouldn't leave her to go on tour if he knew, and she was sure that Beth wouldn't keep it quiet a second time.
The options raced through her mind. She couldn't tell them because it would make things difficult, and she didn't want to put the tour and the band's prospects in jeopardy.

But who was it and what did they want? Once home, she raced into the house, locked every door and window, closed the curtains and switched on every light. She searched every room to ensure there was no intruders lying in wait. She knew it was ridiculous but she even looked in the oven and the washing machine. She showered with the bathroom door locked, then threw on her grey sweat pants and one of Luke's jumpers.

She grabbed a knife from the kitchen drawer, and was curled up in bed, not really knowing what to do next. Her phone rang, making her jump. It was Luke. He sounded in a very good mood as he chatted. Melissa wanted so badly to tell him what had happened, but she had convinced herself that it would ruin things for him. So she kept quiet and let him tell her all about his day.

Luke was coming home in the morning, and he promised that she would have him all to herself for the whole day. So at least she had that to look forward to, if she could get through the night.

Luke kept his promise and was home by lunchtime. They spent the day watching films, which was perfect for Melissa because she had him all to herself for a change. She relaxed a little with him around again, and things felt a bit more normal. Again, she tried to forget what had happened, and hoped she had seen the last of the hooded stalker.

*****

'Melissa, it's not that long, don't get upset,' Jay-Den said as Melissa frantically tried to wipe away the tears that were threatening to spill down both cheeks.

It wasn't that she couldn't cope with being away from him – she wasn't that pathetic – but in the back of her mind she was still terrified about the stalker, and part of her was regretting keeping it to herself. But she couldn't tell Luke now, he was just minutes away from leaving to go on tour. No, she had left it way too late, this was something she was going to have to deal with herself.

'I know. I'm just being an idiot,' she said, trying to force a smile. She'd managed to put on a brave face until Luke had left, but then she lost her composure and just wanted to curl up and cry until he got back.

*****

The Eagles were flying to Germany first. They would be travelling by air for most of the trip, with a tour bus for certain parts. Sky Storm also had to get their crew and kit from one venue to the next, but that would be done using less glamorous means of transport. It was a huge logistical task, but they had a very professional team to take care of it.

Toby's old van, Alf, had now been officially retired, and they'd had a small party in his honour shortly after being signed. It was an emotional goodbye, and Luke had made a heartfelt speech to thank their old friend for so many happy and blurry memories. But Toby had assured everyone that there was no way he'd be getting rid of Alf – he'd be stored in the garage at home for now, and when they'd made enough money, he planned to have him restored 'to his former glory' as he put it. When Beth asked whether a 1989 Transit van had 'former glory', she was told in no uncertain terms by the whole band to button it.

*****

Jay-Den watched Melissa closely as she dabbed her eyes with a tissue. He had sensed that Melissa was struggling with the thought of the boys going away for an extended period, and decided he needed to get her to talk to him. Luke needed to be focused on the tour – it was crucial that it went well. Needy girlfriends were a nightmare, so she needed to be calmed down. At least the other one hadn't shown up due to her being ill, so he could talk to Melissa without her gobby best friend sticking her nose in. Beth was trouble with a capital T, he thought.

'Come on, let's get a coffee. There's a Starbucks just round the corner,' he said, buttoning up his jacket and giving her his most charming smile. Melissa agreed and followed him to the busy coffee shop. They found a table in the corner, and she hoped nobody would recognise them. But this was London and the sight of celebrities was not uncommon, especially so close to the record company's head office, so it wasn't a problem. Jay-Den got the drinks and a slice of lemon cheesecake for Melissa, her favourite.

'Thanks. I'll have to go to the gym for a couple of hours to work that off,' she joked, but it was sweet of him.

'There isn't anything to work off,' he laughed. She was looking stunning as usual and he understood why Ray had so much trouble getting Luke to put her down.

'Flattery will get you everywhere,' she joked, and then immediately wished she hadn't said that in case it sounded weird. They chatted for a while about the album and how good it was. Jay-Den was over the moon with what they'd produced. The album *was* incredible and Melissa knew now that it wasn't just her bias telling her that. She was as surprised as anyone by just how good it was. Some of her favourite tracks were included, changed and refreshed in places, but without losing the roots of the originals. What was really noticeable however was the huge improvement in quality that came from having the best in the business providing their expertise and top of the range equipment to optimise their sound, as Jay-Den put it. He spent some time explaining to Melissa how his team were able to use cutting edge technology to do this. She found it interesting, but didn't understand all of it.

'You must be very proud,' Jay-Den said, taking a sip of his coffee.

'So proud, of all of them. They're just incredible,' she replied as she cleared the last bit of cheesecake from her plate, and starting to feel more at ease with him.

'Are you going to tell me what's bothering you?' He asked, wanting to know why she was so upset and deciding he had broken the ice enough to cut to the chase now.

Melissa took a deep breath and looked at him. If she told him, at least she'd have someone to give her advice without being too close to home.

'Luke doesn't know, Jay-Den, and I don't want him to. Not yet anyway, not till he's home.'

Jay-Den promised her that whatever she told him would stay between the two of them. She told him everything.

'Wow, that's not good.' He was glad she had told him and not Luke. Luke worshipped this girl, so he would either spend the whole tour worrying about this, or he would have refused to go – either way it would be bad for business.

Melissa suddenly laughed loudly, and Jay-Den looked at her with a confused expression.

'It's funny when you think about it. If I walk out of a club, the shutter bugs are there like a pack of wolves. But when I get stalked and almost attacked and there's not a single one to be seen. Typical!' She threw her hands in the air.

Jay-Den laughed – she could be quite funny sometimes. Then he frowned. He knew she was worried about keeping it from Luke because it felt to her like she was lying to him, and this was the sort of secret that had a habit of coming out at the wrong time. But she knew the tour was so important to him, and she didn't want to ruin it, which was good.

'You're not lying to him – you just haven't told him. It's definitely different,' Jay-Den said as he reached over and placed his hand over hers, squeezing it tightly. A group of young lads at the next table looked over at them, and one smirked.

Melissa pulled her hand away, her heart almost skipping a beat. 'Jay-Den, don't!' She snapped. She was more than a little irritated with him. It was a stupid, inappropriate thing to do, especially in public.

'I'm just comforting a friend, don't worry,' he said calmly.

'That's not what they'll print, and you know it. I don't need this blowing up, not with everything else.' She got up and hurried outside. She knew that might make it look worse if people were watching, but she was angry with him.

'Melissa, wait!' Jay-Den tried to follow her, but she was already across the busy street and into the crowd. He cursed himself. She was right –that innocent little gesture could be made into something more than it was. He was normally much more professional.

# Idiot!

March 2014

'Woohoo, only two weeks to go!' Melissa shrieked down the phone, excited to finally hear his voice after what seemed like a lifetime. She did have to admit that the time had flown by because she had kept herself busy with work, the gym, dance classes and various nights out with Beth. They'd also had a girls' night with Cassie, Jo-Jo and Alli, which they manage to fit by finding a gap in Echo's busy schedule. She had still been missing him terribly though – and she noticed it most last thing at night and first things every morning when she went to sleep and woke up on her own.

He's called today because he had exciting news, which he was clearly bursting to tell her.

'You're coming home early?' Melissa joked.

'No ... but it's still fucking awesome.'

'What then?' Melissa laughed. 'This had better be good, if it isn't you coming home early.'

'Just listen ... if you could buy anything in the world right now, what would it be?' he asked cryptically.

There was silence for a few seconds while she thought.

'A pair of Jimmy Choos,' she said firmly. 'And Christian Louboutins, of course. But I guess that might be a while.' He laughed – he knew that was what she'd say. 'OK, tell me the news.'

'Jay-Den has sorted a deal for 'Games' to be used in the next David Cronenberg movie starring that Pattinson dude,' Luke said smugly, then waited for her reaction.

This was another element of his contract that was complicated because he was their sole songwriter. If his work was used in a movie or TV show then a fee would be agreed, plus any royalties. A very good deal had been negotiated by Jay-Den over the last few days. But Luke had decided not to mention it to her until it had been fully agreed and signed. The fee to use the song, before anything else, was £40,000, and that was after the label took its cut.

'No fucking way!' Melissa screamed, knowing enough to understand that this was a very good thing for them, and it would give their music worldwide exposure. Luke told her to buy the damned shoes. This was just the beginning.

'Are you sure?' She hesitated because it still all seemed a bit surreal.

'Yes of course,' he laughed. 'Get some things fixed round the house too. You don't have to make do now.' He was right; the house did need some repairs. 'Liss, get the bathroom done – you could do with a shower that doesn't involve running around in order to get wet!' It was true – her shower was rubbish.

It felt like their lives were finally changing for the better. She could go out next day and get what she needed without having to worry about how she was going to pay for it. They had their original advance from signing with Sky Storm, but that wouldn't last forever. She couldn't wait to fix up the house. Oh, and get the shoes. They talked excitedly for two hours before he finally hung up to prepare for the show that night.

Melissa called Beth and they arranged a shopping spree. The boring things could wait, they decided.

'I hate my stupid job. I can't wait to tell them to stick it,' Beth moaned. She worked as a hotel receptionist, but she wanted to do photography professionally. It was her passion and she was brilliant at it. She'd taken some amazing pictures over the years, and the snaps she'd taken of the guys in action were better than some of the professional magazine shots. Dale was arranging for a new camera and all the accessories for her, and he was going to help her start her own business. He had been waiting until he started earning a bit more money before he said anything. He'd been talking to Melissa a lot lately about Beth, worried that she wasn't happy. She'd been a bit down but wouldn't say why. Melissa knew the reason and had told him it was nothing to do with him. It was getting close to the date when her mum had left her. It was a date Beth struggled with, and she always got like this a couple of weeks before. Melissa was reassured to know that he cared about her enough to worry about things like this. She needed someone like him, someone who could love her flaws along with everything else. She could be misunderstood at times, but she was a friend you wanted in a crisis.

After speaking to Luke, Melissa spent a while trying to figure out what household items she needed, but it wasn't long before she was distracted by much more interesting things. Her mum would be better at helping her out with the boring household chores anyway.

'I'm picking you up at 10 so be ready. Jimmy Choos here we come!!!' was her last message to Beth before she went back to making her wish list.

*****

'What the hell?' Melissa whispered to herself as her online shopping was interrupted by someone knocking hard on the door. She froze. It was nearly midnight and she wasn't expecting anyone. The slow but heavy thudding sounded menacing. It speeded up, then slowed again. Melissa felt panic rising in her stomach because she knew who it was. There was no other explanation. She couldn't move – she was frozen to the spot. The bell started ringing and then more thudding, then silence. She quickly checked the peephole but could see nothing. Maybe it had just been a drunk knocking on the wrong door. She hoped so, as she headed back to the lounge. Then she jumped as the thudding started again only this time on the back door. Whoever it was, they were in her garden. There was a scraping, sound like something was being dragged down the glass doors.

Melissa took a deep breath and walked slowly towards the curtains. Her sensible side was screaming at her to stop being such a moron and call the police. But she had to know who was there, and confront them. She yanked the curtains open, then stumbled backwards, ending up on the floor, looking up at a picture of herself that had been taped to the glass. Her face had been scratched out of the picture. Then a movement caught her eye. Standing just a few feet back was the faceless, hooded intruder. They were motionless but the glow from the garden light highlighted him or her. Melissa was rooted to the spot with fear as she watched the blade spin in their hand – like whoever it was laughing at her.

'Please leave me alone!' she screamed, knowing it was a useless thing to do, but it was a human reaction. The stalker raised the knife and stabbed the picture, puncturing it where her heart would be, then let it drop. They then picked it up and scraped it up and down the door several times before running from the garden. Melissa was shaking but got to her feet and shut the curtains. This was getting serious, and it certainly wasn't going away. She knew she needed help. She grabbed her phone, hit redial and waited.

*****

'Melissa ... what's wrong?'

'Jay-Den, please help me,' she sobbed. Jay-Den gasped as she opened the door, shaking and sobbing, and ran into his arms. He guided her back inside quickly, before the whole street saw him arriving at her place at two in the morning.

'I'm so scared,' Melissa stuttered as she tried to tell him what had happened, but ended up sobbing on his shoulder, too upset to repeat it all.

'I want Luke.'

Jay-Den searched the garden but there was no sign of any intruder. The picture was still stuck to the door, and small scratches were indented on the glass, caused by the knife. Jay-Den removed the picture and shook his head. He went to the kitchen and poured Melissa a neat vodka to settle her nerves. He didn't like her suggestion to call the police.

'It'll be in the media quicker than you can drink that vodka,' Jay-Den advised her. 'I'd put my money on a fan just taking it a bit too far,' he reassured her, desperately wanting to deal with the issue as quickly and quietly as possible. Luke would have to be informed eventually - keeping it a secret from him couldn't go on much longer. Melissa would crack soon enough, but he desperately needed this tour to be successful.

'Could you stay with family?' Jay-Den suggested.

Melissa didn't want to drag her parents into this. Much as she needed her mum, she didn't want to involve them. She was scared of bringing that nutter, whoever it was, to their door.

'Could it be Amber?' Melissa explained about her to Jay-Den. He knew a bit about her but not the full-blown account of her history with Luke.

'It could be anyone,' Jay-Den said pouring another vodka, and this time one for himself.

Melissa lit a cigarette and threw one to her boyfriend's boss. Although he didn't usually smoke, he accepted it. He did have a cigar occasionally when he closed a big contract.

'I'm glad you called me.'

'I didn't know what else to do.' Melissa messed with her phone. She needed Luke and regretted her decision to keep it from him.

'Melissa, it's late,' Jay-Den said softly, knowing that calling Luke would be her next move. He reminded her that in Sweden it would be gone three in the morning, and she snorted with laughter.

'And?' Melissa could call him whenever she liked. What business was it of his?

'You'll just worry him. He can't do anything just now.'

'I want to speak to him, or I want him home,' Melissa demanded.

Jay-Den nearly choked on his vodka. 'Don't be ridiculous,' he snapped. 'Pulling out of the tour is out of the question.' Jay-Den knew she was young and inexperienced but the disbelief showed on his face. Calmly but firmly he explained the sheer amount of organisation and money that was involved in a tour like theirs. And how crucial it was to their careers. But he angered Melissa further by taking her phone from her as he continued to explain just how stupid her request was.

'You've no right to take my phone,' Melissa shrieked. 'I want it back and I *will* call my boyfriend.'

Jay-Den wasn't prepared to listen. 'Luke has commitments. Thousands of people have paid for tickets.' His tone was almost pleading. 'You love him. Right?'

'Yes,' Melissa snapped. 'That's not the point. I could be murdered in my bed!' There was panic in her voice and she grabbed Jay-Den's hand. 'Please let me go to him then, just for a few days?' Melissa begged. The tough record label guru gave slightly, drawn in under the pressure of her blue eyes, and realising that he needed to do something to calm her down. She could be dangerous in this state of mind. But she still had the most beautiful eyes he'd ever seen.

'OK, I'll call Ray in the morning and see what we can arrange.'

Melissa leapt up from the sofa, delighted, and hugged him.

'Now go and get some rest. I could stay on the sofa if you want the company.' Jay-Den assured her she had nothing to worry about. It was just silly kids playing a stupid prank. Later, as he lay wrapped in the thin blanket he thought long and hard about her situation, working out how to deal with it without too much fuss.

The next big problem would be Luke. Once he knew what had been going on, he wouldn't be happy to say the least. Things were made worse as Jay-Den listened to her crying upstairs. It took all his willpower to stay where he was and not run up to hold her and stop her tears. There was only one person Melissa wanted, and it wasn't him. Besides, he couldn't get too close to this girl, it wouldn't look good.

'So pretty,' he murmured to himself before drifting off to sleep.

*****

Melissa was woken by her phone vibrating on her bedside table. It was a 'good morning' text from Luke. She nearly called him right then, 'screw the tour' she thought, but then Jay-Den's words came back to her. She got up and stood in the shower for what seemed like hours, hoping somehow that when she got out, she would find it had all been a dream. But it hadn't.

'Thanks for coming over. I know you didn't have to,' Melissa said as she leaned against the kitchen wall.

Even after very little sleep and no effort, she still looked good, Jay-Den thought as he stared at her. Melissa made jeans and a baggy jumper look sexy. He knew he had to leave soon – being around her was driving him nuts.

'Any time. How are you feeling this morning?'

'Terrible. Like I was out clubbing all night,' she said sipping her coffee. She made them both some toast, but didn't eat much of hers. 'I have to talk to him now. I can't wait any longer. He needs to know,' she said.

Jay-Den sighed and Melissa knew he didn't have good news.

'Melissa, I called Ray before you got up and he isn't keen on you joining him. They've got gigs pretty much every night for the rest of the tour and they're enjoying themselves. Ray has asked you not to go spoiling things.' He put down his coffee and stood up, seeing that Melissa was clearly angry.

'You and Ray do not tell me what to do. You don't own me. Who the fuck does he think he is? I will fly to him, you can't stop me.' They weren't going to control her. He was her boyfriend and they couldn't tell her not to speak to him.

'Liss ...' he said, but Melissa stopped him.

'Don't call me Liss! Only Beth and Luke call me that, nobody else.' She knew it was childish, but she had seen red.

'Melissa, you have to calm down. You can't tour with him. You know that isn't possible,' he tried to reason with her.

'Why not?!' she yelled and threw her coffee cup so it smashed against the kitchen wall. She was so angry she couldn't stop herself behaving like a spoiled brat. But she was also terrified about what had happened, and she had decided that being with Luke was her best bet to stay safe.

'A tour is a major thing to plan and organise. Adding you in would just be more expense and planning. I'm sorry but it isn't possible,' he said firmly. Melissa took a deep breath and looked up at him. He was staring at her, looking torn, and she felt bad for her outburst.

'Sorry.'

She hoped he wouldn't be too mad with her. After all, he had done such a lot for them.

'It's OK.' She smiled, but the sadness was still there. Their eye contact was longer than it should have been and Jay-Den knew he shouldn't, but he couldn't stop himself. He leaned down and felt her soft lips on his. He put his hand on the back of her head, holding her to him. Her lips were warm but were frozen in place. It took a few seconds before it registered in Melissa's head what was happening. His fingers brushed through her hair and he grabbed her waist, pulling her towards him. As he forced her mouth open her senses clicked back into gear. Her hands flew to his chest to push him away, then she slapped him hard across the cheek.

'What the hell are you doing?' she yelled, completely shocked. 'Don't ever touch me again.'

'Shit. I'm so sorry.' There was panic in his voice. She shoved him away as he reached for her again. He knew he had just made one huge mistake and begged her not to tell Luke. But he knew that was exactly what she would do.

'Please don't tell him,' he begged. 'I'm really sorry, I wasn't thinking. You're just so beautiful, I couldn't stop myself.'

'Shut up. You've no right to talk to me that way,' she shouted, feeling even more uneasy.

Jay-Den backed away from her, frightened she might start screaming.

'I just misread the situation, that's all. I'm sorry. It won't ever happen again,' he promised.

'You're fucking right it won't. I was not part of any contract so just remember that, and get away from me,' she barked as she opened the door. She couldn't even look as he walked out. She slammed the door behind him, feeling even more scared and confused.

'What the fuck?' She murmured to herself as she slid to the floor with her back against the door. 'Luke is the only person I can trust,' she thought.

Jay-Den jumped quickly into his silver Maserati and sped away, angry with himself for screwing up big time. However, there was a little part of him that was disappointed, maybe even annoyed that she hadn't accepted his advances and kissed him back. There had been a split second when he had envisioned them tearing each other's clothes off and passionately having sex, right there in the kitchen. But unfortunately it seemed that she was committed to her boyfriend.

Melissa was terrified. She had to call Luke. She couldn't pretend this hadn't happened but knew he would be furious. She sat on the floor, sobbing, knowing that if she had just been honest with him from the start, she wouldn't be in this mess. What had she been thinking calling Jay-Den and allowing him to stay the night? How would she explain that to Luke? Even *she* knew it didn't look good. It felt like she had cheated in some way. She had lied to him, which wasn't a good way to build her case. It took her over an hour and several cigarettes to find the courage to call him and his good mood was smashed in seconds. Her fear of how he would react was confirmed, sending their perfect relationship into turmoil.

*****

'Luke, mate, please calm down before you hurt yourself or we get thrown out of this hotel!' Dale pleaded as he watched Luke storm around the hotel room, throwing and kicking anything in his way.

Luke was incensed by what had been going on behind his back. Melissa keeping it from him in the first place, then turning to Jay-Den. And that was before she dropped the kiss bombshell.

Tom and Toby were keeping well out of the way. They had company in their rooms and that was where they were staying until Hurricane Luke had calmed down.

'I'll calm down after I've smashed his fucking face in,' Luke raged as he kicked another chair over. This was a side of Luke that not many people got to see. Apart from his mum, Dale was the only person who could handle one of his tantrums. Even Melissa hadn't been prepared for his reaction.

'Has she been at it with him since the start?' Luke asked, almost pleading with his best friend to reassure him that his girlfriend hadn't been screwing his boss. The thought made him feel sick. Dale didn't think so, but he also agreed that it didn't look good. Beth had confirmed that she knew about the first incident. But she was just as angry about the other things that Melissa had seemingly been keeping from everyone. Turning to Jay-Den first had also angered Beth but because she loved her best friend, who was now a sobbing mess, she put all the blame on Jay-Den. It was much easier to be angry with him.

'She would never cheat on Luke – that I would swear on my life,' she had assured Dale.

*****

The truth about what had happened was confirmed for Beth later that day when she arrived at Melissa's house to comfort her. Melissa cried on her shoulder as she explained how angry Luke had been, accusing her of sleeping with Jay-Den the whole time and questioning her motives for all the things she had done for him. That cut her like a knife because all she had ever tried to do was make him happy. Luke's anger and hurtful accusations tore at her heart as she feared she had just lost the best thing to have ever walked into her life. She hated herself for allowing herself to get into this situation.

*****

'I really can't see her cheating – she adores you, mate,' Dale said, trying to calm his best friend, who was still pacing the room. He clenched his fists before punching the door. The room was wrecked and his phone was ringing again. No doubt it was Melissa. She had tried several times since Luke had hung up on her.

'Talk to her.'

Melissa was now calling Dale's phone and Luke knew it meant she was desperate. 'No. I'm too pissed off with her.' He held his head in his hands and as the rage and confusion clouded his judgement he headed outside onto the balcony to smoke and pace some more.

Dale answered his phone to a hysterical Melissa. 'Please, Dale, I need to talk to him. I haven't slept with Jay-Den. I promise!' she cried down the phone.

'I know. Just let him calm down.'

'I love him. I would never do that,' she cried.

'Melissa, you don't have to convince me. Jay-Den should have kept his hands to himself. I promise you I'll talk to him. Just stop calling and give him some space to think it through. You should have told him, babe, you really should have!' Dale said, fuming with Jay-Den and disappointed in Melissa. But his best friend was his main priority right now.

'Please tell him I love him,' he heard her sob as he hung up.

Luke was shaking his head – he wasn't in a talking mood. Shocked and angry, he felt sick at the thought of her with another man. She should be turning to him for help, not Jay-Den fucking Lake. It made him look like an idiot. He'd never imagined ever being angry with Melissa but he was absolutely livid with her at that moment and if she had been cheating, it was over.

*****

'Zoe, I think you need to get going, love,' Ray ordered a few hours later. He had already got rid of the blonde from Tom's room. She'd been refusing to leave and causing a scene, and quite frankly Ray was fed up with drama for one day. Enough was enough. His front man was having a meltdown and he didn't need crazed groupies adding to his stress. Anyone who wasn't part of the crew was now being banned from the hotel.

Zoe was what you might call a 'friend with benefits', and was one of several girls Toby would call when he felt like some company. She was in Milan for the show but had flown out a day early to spend time with him. She would sometimes go with him on the bus – she was well known to Ray and was allowed to do this as long as she kept quiet about it and followed his rules. But Ray was putting his foot down this time. She wasn't any trouble and she knew when she needed to leave. Toby wasn't an idiot and knew he wasn't the only one she gave her 'special time' to – they weren't a couple and never would be. She flitted between a few bands, but only picked out a specific member of each one to ensure there were no awkward situations. If Luke hadn't already been spoken for she wouldn't have given Toby the time of day, and she had decided she'd make an exception to the rule if Luke did become available. There was something about Luke that made you want to break all the rules, and Zoe didn't care what people thought of her. She was adored by some very famous men, and one or two women.

'OK I'm going Ray, don't have a heart attack,' she laughed and patted him on the bum as she picked up her coat. He blushed. Zoe was tall and skinny – a rock chick with a hint of Goth. She had long tar-coloured hair and was covered in jewellery. She bent down to kiss Toby goodbye then struck one of her very seductive poses while he took a picture on his phone.

'I would tell you to behave but that'd be stupid,' Toby laughed. He knew she would find some other mug to entertain her while she was in Milan. Zoe was never alone for long.

'Toby, I don't ever behave. See you, big man. Call me whenever you want me again.'

He watched her go; the pretty, confident girl who would do anything he asked her to. And vice versa. He wondered what was wrong with him - why wasn't he thinking about her. She was certainly his type, if you ignored the bed-hopping. Yet the whole time he had been with her, it was Megan May's beautiful green eyes he pictured looking at him and her flame-red hair spread out on his pillow.

*****

'Zoe, keep this shut,' Ray warned as they walked to the lift together. He was making sure she left, and he didn't want her shooting her mouth off about the day's events.

'My lips are sealed, Ray.' Zoe may have been a bit wild but she wasn't a gossip. She wouldn't talk about people's private lives – her 'arrangements' with these and other famous people depended on her reputation of trustworthiness being maintained. The four guys had always been friendly towards her, and they had looked after her with endless meals, drinks and cigarettes, so she wouldn't stab them in the back. Zoe had met Melissa once and had thought she was a sweet girl. It was annoying as it would have been easier not to like her. If they broke up and she moved in on Luke, she'd feel like she was kicking a puppy. She knew she'd do it anyway though.

*****

The yelling coming from Russell's office was not pleasant. Russell was Jay-Den's boss and Sky Storm Records' CEO. Megan had just come back from a meeting and wondered what was going on. Everyone had their heads down trying not to look like they were listening, but whatever it was, Jay-Den was not very popular.

'Fix it, Lake. Now!' Russell's voice boomed as the door opened, and a very red-faced Jay-Den headed back to his office.

'Megan, get in here,' he ordered as he sat at his desk, looking flustered. Megan hurried in, bracing herself to be given a long list of instructions.

Jay-Den told her she needed to organise flights to Milan for Melissa Webb and Beth Watkins for a few days. Megan would also be personally dealing with Luke Black as of now. Luke was their biggest name at the moment and Jay-Den would never hand over responsibility for someone like him just like that. This meant there was something big going down.

Once she had everything organised, Megan headed to the kitchen to make some coffee. It wasn't long before Jack, her friend and colleague from the legal department, followed her into the kitchen. He looked around to make sure the coast was clear, even checking under a coffee cup for comedy value. Jack was a funny guy. He loved a bit of gossip and by the way he was acting it seemed that was exactly what he had. 'You must have heard?' His expression was bursting with excitement.

'Heard what?'

Jack ran his hand through his hair. He couldn't believe his friend was unaware of the gossip that the whole office was talking about – Jay-Den's major fail.

'No way,' she shrieked a little too loudly after he had filled her in.

Jack was nodding affirmatively. This had made his day. He didn't like Jay-Den, mainly because of the way he treated Megan.

'She knocked him back, and slapped him by all accounts. Thank god the girl has sense. She called Luke and told him, and apparently he went apeshit.'

That would explain everything. Of course Luke wouldn't want to deal with Jay-Den after he'd hit on his girlfriend. Megan smiled that he'd screwed up. So the sun doesn't always shine out of his backside, she thought.

'You, lady, are one lucky bitch,' Jack said.

Megan looked smug. 'I know. Check me out, rolling with rock stars.'

'So ... you and Toby Maxwell ... spill,' Jack whispered. He'd caught her off guard, and she blushed. Jack noticed and took it to mean that something really was going on. She tried to change the subject but it didn't work.

'Megan, it's about time you had some fun. Go for it.' He sensed that her lack of confidence was getting in the way as usual, although everyone in the building had seen how he would watch her when the band came in.

'I'd better take this to His Majesty,' she said, before hurrying out. It was not a conversation she wanted to be having.

'Damn you, Toby Maxwell.' She didn't want to, but she couldn't stop thinking about him. As if to rub it in, she'd got back to her desk to find an email from him saying:

'Hi Miss May, Just so you know, I'm having fun on tour, wish you were here with us though. Toby X'.

It made her smile and lifted her spirits even more. She didn't want it to, but it made her heart flutter a little too. 'Megan May, no,' she told herself. But it had made her feel good, and she wondered if Toby Maxwell was different to the others.

She replied to the email in a professional way but after much deliberation, decided to add a kiss at the end. She decided that she could easily explain it away as just friendly, if she needed to. She hadn't realised she was staring at her screen reading his email again and again until Jay-Den, still in a bad mood, hollered at her from his office, and she came back to reality with a thud before going in to see what he wanted.

Annoyingly, he wanted her to rearrange studio time for Death Wishes because as he put it, 'They're being fucking idiots again, don't ask.'

Megan didn't ask because she really couldn't care less about that band or their problems. They were vile, jumped-up, talentless assholes, and that was a generous description as far as Megan was concerned. She did everything for The Black Eagles gladly - they deserved her respect. She looked after Death Wishes only because her job required it.

The day passed quickly as Megan joked with studio staff and producers who all knew her well. Luke was his usual lovely self when she called to confirm details of Melissa and Beth's visit, despite what had happened. He made her blush by asking if she was single, saying his drummer wanted to know, but she dodged the question like a pro. When she told him she needed to check something with Jay-Den, his response confirmed that there were issues.

'No need, Jay-Den won't argue.' He sounded agitated at even saying Jay-Den's name and she laughed to herself again at the hot water her boss had got himself into.

# Flapping their lips

*March 2014*

'Move out of the way,' yelled one of the security guys who had been hired just to get the girls from the airport to the hotel. There was a swarm of paparazzi following them as they were ushered through Milan airport into a waiting car. Both girls wore sunglasses and the four big security guys formed a circle around them as the swarm closed in.

'Melissa ... Melissa ... Luke's been seen out with a fan. Did you know that?'

'Are you and Luke fighting? Are you here to patch things up?'

'Beth. Beth. Give us a smile!'

'I hear Dale was out with a model last night!'

Melissa could feel her friend tense up next to her, so she shot her hand out and grabbed her.

'Don't react,' she instructed. They didn't need any more drama, not now.

*****

Luke had finally called her back, after ranting and stewing for hours. He still wasn't completely happy with her, but had accepted that nothing had been going on with Jay-Den. They would talk about it when she got to Milan. Luke had yelled at Jay-Den, asking him what had been going on. Jay-Den had backed Melissa up, and took full responsibility for it.

'Luke, I'm sorry. It was my fault,' he'd said. He explained how she'd been worried that telling him about the stalker would jeopardise the tour, and they all thought they were doing what was best for him and the band.

'Kissing my girl isn't best for me. You stay the fuck away from her.'

Jay-Den had assured him it was just a moment of madness and would never happen again. Luke told him he'd kill him if it did. He was too pissed off to carry on dealing with him, and wanted Megan to look after them.

It was clear now that Melissa hadn't cheated, but he couldn't help still being angry with her. She had kept a secret from him – something he had never expected from her. The Jay-Den situation was awkward. He wanted to cause him some damage but being stuck in a contract with the man was making things tricky. When he calmed down, he realised that he had others to think about, not just himself.

*****

'Losers,' Beth said when they were finally safe in the car. She was cursing one of the mob for scuffing her new black and white Vans shoes. 'I only got these yesterday. Fat idiot,' she cursed, then gave him the middle finger as the car pulled away. She didn't realise that the car had tinted windows, so he was none the wiser.

Melissa took off her leather jacket, realising how hot it was. She was both excited and nervous about seeing Luke.

'I never learn to wear sensible shoes,' she moaned as she kicked off the purple heels Beth had given her for her birthday. She tried to stop thinking about the conversation she'd be having shortly.

'They're cute though. I should have got myself a pair,' Beth said, picking one up and admiring it. 'Why do you have to have such small feet? If you were normal I could borrow them and we could save money and luggage space. Size threes aren't feet – they're more like stumps.'

'Better than walking around on those massive clown feet of yours,' Melissa shot back.

'Size six isn't that big, you cheeky bitch,' Beth retorted and flicked Melissa on the arm playfully.

The journey took twenty minutes, and before they knew it they were checked in and heading for their rooms. Luke's room was wrecked after he had, as Dale put it, 'Gone into full-on rock star mode.' The chairs were all in one corner where he had just dumped his clothes. Bottles littered the floor, and several had been smashed against the wall it seemed. She tried to tidy the room, putting his clothes in order as well as clearing up the bottles to make the place at least half decent.

The bed was unmade, and laying in the middle were Chloe and his notebook. Melissa poured herself a whisky and lay on the bed flicking through his book. There was enough material for two albums, she thought as she made the bed so she could sit on it more comfortably.

'Do you ever stop writing?' she whispered to herself as she read.

The band were doing another interview so she had a few hours to kill before he arrived back. Beth was in the next room catching up on some rest because she claimed she always got sleepy after a flight. Melissa thought that was probably because she had put away enough wine to send most people into a coma. But she was on holiday so why not? Melissa was hungry so she called room service. And thinking about wine made her fancy a glass. She took a shower while she waited then put on a summer dress and sat on the balcony, looking out over Milan. She needed the wine for a bit of courage as she was certain Luke was going to shout at her, and she was dreading it. To make her feel even worse she checked her Twitter account and found the rumour that her and Luke had split was already circulating. This was what bothered her – how had this got out? Someone somewhere had heard there was an issue and had started flapping their lips. She knew that people didn't care about the facts, just the gossip. Yes, they'd had a fight but they hadn't split up – at least she hoped not. Melissa thought she would send her own little message out, her tweet simply said, *'Finally in Milan and looking forward to watching my lovely boys in action tonight!'*

She had over ten thousand followers herself so, as expected, it only took seconds for it to be retweeted hundreds of times. People tweeted back, most leaving positive messages saying they hoped she had a good time. It made her smile that at least some people liked to see them happy, even if others didn't. She didn't spend too much time looking at Twitter if she could help it, and she knew she shouldn't draw too much attention to herself. But sometimes the ridiculous gossip needed to be shut down.

She dozed on the sun lounger, tired from her flight, but it felt like only seconds before she was woken by warm lips on hers. Opening her eyes, she saw Luke looking back at her. 'Hey,' he said, frowning at her.

He was still annoyed with her, but at least she'd got a kiss so maybe it wasn't all bad. She stood up and threw her arms round him. 'I'm so sorry. I will never keep anything from you again.'

He pulled her inside shutting the doors and closing the curtains blocking out the world. Melissa told him everything, even down to Jay-Den trying to hold her hand in Starbucks, making him explode all over again.

'Why keep it from me?' he shouted at her. 'Why was he in our home?' The anger still bubbled inside him and he couldn't help but let it pour out even though he could see Melissa almost jump and then quiver under his verbal assault. Beth and Dale were in the next room and Dale had to stop Beth from getting involved as she was getting upset at how bad it was. She could hear Luke shouting and Melissa crying, begging him to listen.

'Have you been shagging Jay-Den?' he bellowed at her. There was real anger in his tone.

*****

In the room next door even Beth flinched at the shouting and she looked at Dale with a worried expression.

'He won't hurt her, will he?'

'Of course he won't hurt her,' Dale assured her, feeling a little annoyed that she would even think that about their friend. 'He's just angry. But please, just for once, wind your neck in and leave them to sort it out,' he warned, knowing her urge to defend her friend would be in full force.

Beth eyed him for a few seconds as she thought about his request. She wanted to charge next door to stop Melissa crying.

'Please, Beth,' Dale begged. 'Let them deal with it.'

'OK,' she huffed and stepped onto their balcony to light a cigarette. The noise from next door wasn't so loud outside.

*****

The crew were under instructions to keep well away while all this was going on. Only Dale, Beth and Ray stayed close by, just in case they were needed. The scene inside the room wasn't a happy one. Melissa, head in hands, sat shaking on the bed, while Luke paced round the room. She'd hurt him so badly, and she feared he would tell her to go home and that he never wanted to see her again. That thought ripped at Melissa's heart. Losing him was her ultimate fear.

She jumped up from the bed and grabbed him frantically as her sobs broke through, causing him to stop mid rant.

'I was so confused – I didn't want to ruin your first tour.' She almost screamed the words in panic. 'I didn't know what to do. I thought if I told you it would complicate things.'

'I could have made sure you were safe before I left.' Luke seemed to calm down a little as he stroked her cheek. 'You could have been seriously hurt and I didn't have a clue it was happening. But *he* did, and it makes me feel like a fucking idiot.' Luke felt he should be the one to take care of her, nobody else.

'I'm the idiot, not you,' she admitted, happy to take full blame for all of it. She almost choked on another sob.

'Don't cry,' he begged. 'I hate seeing you cry.'

'So stop shouting at me,' she begged, hoping he was beginning to believe her.

'Promise me you haven't been sleeping with him ...'

'I promise you! God no!' Her tone was strong as she looked him fully in the eyes. Her gaze didn't falter as a liar's would. 'Listen to me – I would never cheat on you. I love you. I was scared and confused and he took advantage. I slapped him and threw him out.'

Luke knew she was telling the truth. It was just something in his heart that told him to trust her. He tugged at her dress, winding the white cotton in his fingers, pulling her to him and feeling relief. But then the realisation of her scary ordeal finally began to sink in and he started to realise that she should have his support and protection, not anger.

'I don't know what I'd do if anything happened to you, or anyone took you away from me. He could give you so much more than I can ...' He admitted his concerns about Jay-Den, who was a very wealthy and powerful man. He also wouldn't be forced to leave her alone for months on end, as Luke had been.

'Luke, shut up. Yes, he could give me everything material,' - she rested her hand over his heart – 'but he couldn't give me this.' She smiled at him, yet she was still tearful. 'It wouldn't matter if you don't make another penny from music. We could be living in a cardboard box and begging, I don't care. I just want you, nothing else.'

'I love you so much it hurts,' Luke whispered, as he pushed her against the wall. He didn't want to argue any more. He wanted to stop her tears and make her feel safe again.

'I know the feeling. I've missed you so much.' She was breathless as they kissed, desperately tugging at each other's clothes.

'If he ever touches you again – I swear I will break his legs.' He picked her up, carried her to the bed and threw her down much more roughly than he would normally. But the emotions racing through his body were a mix of love and jealousy. For the first time in his relationship with Melissa, he felt threatened. What had happened had floored him, and for a while made him see Melissa in a slightly different light. She was just as desirable to other men as he was to other women. She constantly worried that he would leave her for another woman, but now he knew that she could leave him for another man if she chose to. It was a scary thought, but mostly it made him want her so much more. He almost tore off her thin dress as she kissed him. The world outside didn't exist as they forgot about everything.

'Nobody will ever take me away from you,' she promised.

*****

The shouting had stopped, and Ray was relieved. He stood outside the door, ready to go in if he had to. The others were either in their rooms or in the bar, keeping well out of the way. As Ray heard their angry shouts die down and then turn into passionate moans, he realised that all was well again in Paradise, and he quickly scuttled off before he heard something that might give him nightmares.

Toby was just heading back from the bar and raised an eyebrow at his manager. 'Ah, the making-up stage. That took longer than I thought. Damn, I owe Tom a tenner now,' he laughed then banged on Luke's door.

'You owe me a tenner, Black, you slag,' then headed back to the bar, laughing loudly and knowing they had plenty of time to chill out. Those two weren't going anywhere for a while.

*****

'We have to get going in less than an hour,' Ray huffed, frustrated.

Luke still hadn't surfaced and wasn't answering his phone. The entire hotel must have heard their domestic, not to mention their passionate making up session. Ray messed with the spare key, which he kept for emergency reasons. His long experience as a band manager had taught him always to be prepared. He shuddered at the memory of his first ever job – a young up and coming band. They could have had everything, but Ray was young too, and didn't react quickly enough to the signs of addiction. He found his first ever front man dead in his hotel room after taking an overdose. Twenty-four years old, with the world at his feet, and his life cut short. That experience had never left him, but it had helped make him the manager he was today. The Black Eagles were his fourth major act. He'd managed a few smaller bands along the way, but he was in his element when he had a challenge on his hands.

*****

'You look hot, come on, babe!' Luke said, a slight irritation in his voice as he waited for her to finish putting her outfit together. Melissa had opted for one of her signature looks – purple skinny jeans, tight fitted vest top and killer heels. Completed by her birthday locket.

'Leave the make-up,' Luke told her. 'You don't have time – you look beautiful without it anyway.'

Melissa dropped her make-up bag and took his hand. He really did make her feel like the only girl in the world sometimes. Luke threw on his usual black hooded jumper and they were finally ready. The show was already going to be over half an hour late starting.

'Will everyone be angry with me?' Melissa worried as they walked to the lift. She kept hold of his hand.

Luke reassured her she had nothing to worry about. 'Nobody will say a goddamned word to you,' he promised.

Everyone was waiting for them at reception. Ray didn't look at all happy, but decided to keep his mouth shut for now, considering the day's events so far. Luke was ready and in a better mood, so overall it was good news. Rocking the boat at this stage wasn't sensible, he decided. Their friends seemed to find the whole thing very amusing, he noticed, and so maybe he shouldn't stress too much. Beth smirked, and smiled, giving Melissa an 'I'm glad you've fixed things' look.

'I was going to ask if you'd made up but we kind of gathered that you had, three times,' Dale sniggered, along with the rest of the crew who hadn't yet headed off to get their equipment set up.

Melissa went bright red and looked at the floor, mortified. Luke shrugged, not caring right now what people had heard.

'Slut,' Beth sniggered.

'Right, get on the fucking bus.' Ray was getting more and more wound up as the minutes passed. 'We might as well cancel tonight's gig if we stand around here any sodding longer. Come on, move it!'

They were all eager to get going now. Toby ruffled Melissa's hair, but her emergency brush was in her new Chloe bag. She almost felt guilty for spending such a ridiculous amount of money on a bag, and it was so pretty she almost didn't want to use it. It matched her equally expensive shoes.

'Glad you two made up. He's been a right twat the past twenty-four hours. Nice to have some good karma again.' Toby smiled, then offered to rip off Jay-Den's balls – Melissa only had to say the word. It was a tempting offer, but she declined.

'I think I've caused enough trouble for one day ...' Melissa trailed off as the boys' state-of-the-art tour bus came into view. 'Wow!' It was essentially a hotel on wheels with everything they could possibly need, and more. The Wi-Fi, games consoles and Blu Ray players were the most well-used, and they were complemented with high definition TVs.

Beth was already helping herself at the bar. Melissa sat down next to Luke on the black leather seats in front of one of the TVs. He put his head on her lap and closed his eyes as the bus got going. Toby sat next to her, laying out the familiar whites lines ready for each band member. Luke would have his at the last minute. She resisted nagging him – not in front of his boys, she told herself.

'The offer's there if you change your mind,' Toby said as he opened a beer. He was relieved that the situation had been resolved between the two of them, at least for now. They had all been a little concerned, because if things hadn't worked out it would have turned the tour on its head. Melissa definitely brought a calmness to Luke and this was the perfect example. Yesterday, he'd been smashing up hotel rooms, screaming blue murder. Of course they didn't blame him, Lake had crossed the line. But it had taken all three of them, plus Ray, to talk him out of catching the next flight home to have it out with Jay-Den, and that wouldn't have ended well for anyone.

'Sorry I made you all late,' Melissa apologised timidly. She thought they were all mad with her.

Toby laughed and ruffled her hair again. 'It's cool, don't stress about it. Ray just worries too much, like an old woman.'

'I'm paid to worry, and no it isn't OK,' Ray shouted from the other end of the bus.

Luke stopped him mid rant, telling everyone in no uncertain terms that Melissa had been put through enough, and he didn't want it mentioned again. 'The name Jay-Den Lake is fucking banned as of now. Right?'

There was silence. Although it was nice that he was defending her, Melissa felt awkward again. Worried that Luke was going to have another meltdown, Dale came over to check on him and handed him a joint. He accepted it, assuring his best friend that there was nothing to worry about.

Toby left them alone and went to sit next to Beth who was getting a card game ready.

'I'm so sorry,' Melissa whispered to Luke. 'I'm ruining everything.'

Luke shook his head. 'No you're not. At least I have you here for a while and you made being late *so* worth it.' He pulled her to him and kissed her. 'Now get me a beer, woman.' Melissa punched him playfully on the chest, telling him to get it himself. 'Ouch! Now that's assault. I'm going to be late for the gig and beaten black and blue as well,' he joked. Their giggles were a welcome sound to the rest of the bus.

Toby watched them, wishing he had someone loyal like Melissa who he could eventually settle down with. When he did, he didn't want a groupie or a fan. He wanted a nice girl he could trust. As he thought about it, those lovely green eyes filled his mind again. He wanted Megan May more as each day passed. He shook the thought away.

'While you're up, Webby, get us all another beer,' Toby called, much to everyone's approval. Melissa felt happy again that normality had officially been resumed.

'Deal me in gobby,' Luke called to Beth, deciding to join the game. He was feeling much better now.

'Up yours, Black,' Beth threw back at him.

It wasn't long before the good-natured bickering started over the rules of the game. Beth's excuse for being rubbish at cards was that Tom always won because he cheated.

*****

They arrived at the venue just before ten, with Ray red in the face and thoroughly stressed out. The road crew buzzed around them. Dean, who was one of the guitar technicians and responsible for all Luke's guitars, waved to the girls as he walked past. He had been in the business for fifteen years and Luke trusted him with his prized possessions. They all had someone who took care of their kit and did their sound checks. It was just as well tonight because they were straight on stage when they got there. Luckily for them, Silver Daggers, their support band, had covered for them as long as they could with several encores.

Dean gave Melissa and Beth beers, and they chatted for a few minutes. The crew were all becoming like family, and the girls had a free reign back stage. Dean was the only one who had the guts to make a joke. He'd grown very close to Luke so he could get away with it. 'You causing trouble, Miss Webb? Tut tut.' He'd just turned forty and had the scruffiest dark brown hair Melissa had ever seen.

'You know me, Dean, I just have to be centre of attention.' She flicked her hair dramatically.

'I think you're in Ray's bad books. He doesn't look happy,' he whispered to her, grinning.

'I know, I'm such a bad girl,' she laughed as he walked away.

'Better clear the air, lady.'

Melissa knew Dean was right, so she put on her most innocent and apologetic face.

'Sorry Ray, for causing so much trouble.' She felt bad that they were so late, but it wasn't all her fault.

'That's exactly my point. They can't do this.' He shook his head at her, frustrated. 'But I know it wasn't all your fault. Sounds like a big misunderstanding on everyone's part.' He'd given Jay-Den an ear full earlier, and he wasn't very pleased. But Melissa was hard to stay mad with – she just had to look at you and you melted.

'You have to admit he's in a better mood. Anyway, I read that it was getting cool for bands to be late on stage.'

Their manager didn't agree, but she was doing her best 'please don't shout at me' act, and Ray softened. This girl was impossible to dislike - no wonder his front man was hooked. Even if it was mostly her fault that they'd made several thousand fans wait for them to arrive. But he knew that if he upset her, Luke would kick off again.

*****

Luckily, the show was fantastic and their lateness was forgotten. If anything, it just added to the drama, after the stories that had been circulating about them, and Melissa's unexpected arrival in Milan.

They were just finishing 'Weekend High' when Luke, still playing his guitar, jumped from the stage and danced towards the now delirious crowd. He stopped in front of a young girl of about sixteen, who was already crying, and made her almost faint as he kissed her on the cheek. He then walked all the way along the front row giving high fives, before jumping back on the stage to do a guitar solo. The crowd went wild and Melissa could feel her naughty streak rushing to the surface. Beth looked at her, and knew she knew she was going to do something mad, not caring what anyone thought.

'Liss ... what are you going to do?'

Melissa winked at her friend and looked at Ray, who was completely unaware of what Melissa was planning. She waited a few more seconds then kicked off her shoes and ran onto the stage. Luke saw her coming and smiled just as she knew he would. He couldn't stop her as she grabbed his face and kissed him. He kissed her back without stopping his solo, proving again just how talented he was. She could hear the roar of the crowd and the vibration of his guitar, and the sound was deafening. Luke was clearly enjoying himself. She didn't care what people thought – she could stay there like that forever.

'You are a bad girl,' he said when he pulled away briefly. Melissa smiled and pulled him back. She wasn't finished yet.

'Wayhay. Go on, girl,' she heard Dale shout. He was killing himself laughing.

'Hold it, Luke ... don't fuck it up,' Tom heckled.

But he didn't and Melissa knew that was why she had done it. If she'd thought for a second her actions would embarrass him in any way she wouldn't have done it. But he thought it was awesome.

The crowd went wild, giving Melissa her first experience of being on a stage.

'You nutty bitch,' Luke joked, with the biggest grin.

'I couldn't help it,' she yelled as she ran off. 'You're so goddam sexy.'

Ray shook his head, thinking what a handful these girls were, but at the same time the crowd had loved it, so how could he be angry?

'That was wicked,' Beth screamed and high-fived her. 'Love you, girl.'

Melissa felt quite liberated; it was like sticking her finger up at all the gossips. Melissa and Luke were perfectly happy, so they could all shove it.

'See.' Melissa winked at Ray as they closed the show to the biggest standing ovation of the tour so far.

*****

After the show, they all headed to a club for a few drinks. They had the next day off to spend in Milan before flying to Norway. The girls would then have to head home. The whole Jay-Den disaster had been forgotten for now, but Luke was still very concerned about the stalker situation. Melissa assured him it was just a crazy fan who would soon get bored. If they had really wanted to hurt her, they would have done by now because they'd had three chances and hadn't done anything other than scare shit out of her.

'I know, but it's still worrying me,' Luke said as he leaned against a wall.

'You both take care of each other when you go home,' Dale said as he wound his arms around Melissa. She patted his hand and promised they'd be fine. Luke didn't react to Dale being so affectionate towards his girl – they were like brother and sister so it was no problem. He was the same with Beth, who was leaning against the wall next to Luke, tweeting as usual. He leaned over to see what she was doing. She put her arm round his neck and he kissed her cheek. They were a family, pure and simple. But it hadn't gone unnoticed. The paparazzi were circling. Melissa always felt better about things when the boys were around. They made it seem like nothing at all because they had accepted it and barely even noticed what was going on. They had taken over the club with all their entourage. As time went on, the crew started to run riot and it descended into one hell of a night.

Ray, Dale and Tom had to carry an unconscious Toby out, even though they themselves could barely stand. Beth got into a scuffle with one of the bar staff who'd flirted with Dale right in front of her, clearly doing it on purpose. After drinking more whisky than Melissa thought humanly possible, Luke's feisty side came out briefly, and he called Jay-Den, leaving a very abusive (but barely coherent) message on his voicemail. Melissa wrestled the phone from him, before he said something really stupid.

*****

Melissa was mortified when the pictures from the night out surfaced next day. 'Eagles run riot in Milan' was the headline, with over fifty pictures of the night, none making them look good. Of course it was Luke and Melissa who looked the worst. The photos looked much worse than the reality but it backed up the story of them trashing the bar. It wasn't true, but the truth was rarely ever written. And it was much too late to worry about it anyway.

*****

The following day, two very delicate girls flew home and the guys continued with their tour, amid new rumours that Melissa was heartbroken because Luke had dumped her after another row, this time over her stage invasion. The truth was that Luke wasn't at all angry. The crowd had loved it and so had he. The truth was also that she was just very hung over and sad to be leaving him.

There was a part of Melissa that just didn't care any more and she stuck her fingers up as the girls walked through the airport. 'You want the classic rock chick ... have that you bastards,' she shouted.

# Hospital (3)

October 2014

'You should have reported this sooner, Miss Webb.'

Melissa shrugged, too tired to argue with Fox. Besides, he was right. It had nearly cost her relationship with Luke, but she hadn't really understood back then how serious it was. She'd just thought, or hoped, the problem would go away.

Liz came back in. Her timing was perfect as Melissa was running out of energy. She was also getting sick of being told how stupid she'd been.

'I need to change your dressings my dear,' Liz said, looking round at the visitors and making it clear that they needed to leave.

Melissa wanted Beth and her mum to stay, but having Dale and the police there was too much. Beth looked over at Jean. They hadn't seen the wound yet and Beth wasn't sure she wanted to. She wasn't sure how bad it would be, and she didn't want to react in any way that would upset Melissa any more then she already was. Jean moved to stand closer to Beth and held her hand. Liz removed the dressings and Beth sucked in her breath as she saw the black and deep purple bruising that covered the entire left side of Melissa's face. But it was the wound that stood out. Her once beautiful face was now stitched together like a football. Beth had to get out of the room, but she couldn't run now. She had to wait for a good moment.

Liz chatted away as she worked. Beth didn't trust easily, but she liked how caring Liz was with Melissa, taking good care of her. When Liz had finished and Melissa was comfortable, Beth made an excuse to leave, saying that she had to make a phone call. Once in the corridor she moved as far away as she could, but only made it half way down the corridor before collapsing to her knees, sobbing. Dale was outside waiting and went immediately to her, wrapping his arms around her.

'What happened? What's wrong?'

'Her face, Dale, you should see her face.'

Beth couldn't stand there any longer. She ran to the toilets, into the first cubicle, and threw up. Eventually, she composed herself, washed her face and rinsed her mouth out. She sighed at her reflection in the mirror – it wasn't up to her usual standard but she really didn't care. The yellow and white checked shirt she was wearing was creased and her blue cords needed a wash, but again she didn't care. Her phone rang and she answered it. It was a client. Beth was doing the photography for someone's wedding. She couldn't back out now, so she assured the worried girl she would be there.

The door opened and Dale popped his head round, looking worried.

'You've been in here ages. Are you OK?'

'Not really, but I'll be fine. What about you?' Dale was taking care of everyone. But she had to remember that he was suffering too.

'It's really that bad?'

'Her beautiful face ...'

Dale saw the distress in his girlfriend's eyes, and felt a wave of guilt rush over him.

'I feel guilty, B. I should have gone with him instead of staying for another drink. I should have been there when that psycho attacked her. I should have done something.'

Beth wrapped her arms round his neck.

'Don't you dare blame yourself. No way is this your fault and I won't have you carrying that around with you,' she said firmly. Dale nodded, and crouching down he kissed her stomach. Beth knew it was a messed up situation, but blaming themselves wouldn't help. This was all Amber's doing. The police would find her and lock her away, and Melissa and Luke would be safe. Dale placed his hand on her stomach and very gently she rested her hands on his head.

'We will find your Uncle Luke, I promise you,' he said gently before standing back up, keeping a tight hold of Beth.

'I want our baby to have an uncle ... and Luke will be the closest thing to one.' Dale was going to be a dad and he couldn't even tell his best friend. Beth kissed him, grateful for a few minutes alone after the intense atmosphere in Melissa's room.

'The baby will have its uncle Luke, I just know it,' she reassured him, although deep down she was terrified for Luke. Deep down, she also feared that she would be a terrible mum. But now wasn't the time to think about that. Opposing emotions ran through her and she fought the urge to throw herself on the floor and cry. She told herself that she was stronger than that, and she knew she had to stay strong – there was no choice. The quiet moment alone was interrupted by Dale's phone going off.

'Here's a quote for you ... drop fucking dead!' Dale yelled before hanging up on another journalist wanting a story.

Beth switched his phone off and then hers. They had always coped better with the media attention. It didn't faze Beth much, and Dale took everything in his stride. But this was a different type of situation. The world was on the edge of its seat waiting for the next part of the drama. It was like a movie, only they were the real life unwilling stars of the show.

'You'll be an amazing mum,' Dale said, changing the subject. He promised her they'd be OK, they would be a family and would always be together. He would never leave her. He could read her like a book and he knew she had doubts, most likely stemming from her own bad experiences as a child.

'What about when you tour?' She joked, looking up at him. 'You have to leave me then...'

'You know what I mean.'

'What about when I'm all fat and pregnant with swollen ankles?'

Dale kissed her forehead and laughed. 'You'll be carrying our child, you're allowed a little bulk. I'll rub your ankles and feed you chocolate.' As he laughed, a few loose strands of his hair fell forward.

They had found out about the baby the day after Luke went missing, so they hadn't told anyone yet. They hadn't even seen a doctor. Beth was struggling with morning sickness but they wanted to have this little secret for a while. Nothing they did stayed secret for very long. Beth wanted to tell Melissa so much, but now wasn't a good time.

'I love you,' he whispered before they headed back to their friend's side.

*****

'So, did anything else happen after you visited Luke?' Fox was back and the questions had already started when Beth and Dale got back to Melissa's room.

'No, it was about a month later. Do I really have to talk about it?' Melissa asked. Her voice cracked and she welled up just thinking about it.

Beth sat on the edge of the bed and took her friend's hand. This was going to be one of the hardest parts to talk about. If Fox thought the incident with Jay-Den was bad, he hadn't heard anything yet.

Melissa didn't want to talk about it – the whole business was in the past now. It was a chapter of their recent lives they wanted to forget. They couldn't change it, but they had got through it, eventually. Luke had wanted to erase it, make it go away, but being in the limelight meant nothing you did ever went away. The whole world knew about it, so that was never going to happen. Everyone had read it, or a version of it anyway, but nobody knew the full and true story.

The two police officers were about to hear what really had happened. Lee Noels was silently excited. This was the best job he'd ever been involved with. He couldn't believe he was sitting in a room with Melissa Webb, the most famous rock girlfriend in the world. Not to mention Dale Baxter, one of his idols. But he had to stay professional, and he realised that it obviously wasn't at all exciting for those involved.

'Please … I do need you to tell me everything,' confirmed Fox.

'Fine, if I must.'

# Go for it, you said!

May 2014

'It's perfect.' Melissa skipped around the lounge area of the top-floor apartment. They'd been searching for their new home since Luke had returned from their tour just over a week ago. After a day resting, he'd called an estate agent to get things moving. Once he had something in his mind he wouldn't settle until it was done. They had agreed that London was better for Luke because when he wasn't touring he spent most of his time in various London-based venues. The record label and most of their studio work were based in the capital. Last Track Recording Studios were one of the best, and Luke was spending a lot of time there, recording and experimenting.

Although the décor in the apartment was a little too colourful for their tastes, it was nothing a bit of painting couldn't fix, and they both felt right at home the moment they walked through the door.

Melissa was already jotting notes for the makeover, which was made all the more exciting because she didn't have to worry about cost. The tour had been such a success that the payout, along with record sales, had set them up nicely. They weren't millionaires, far from it, but they had more money than they had ever dared dream about. Luke had been asked if he'd consider writing for other artists or bands, but at the moment that wasn't his focus. His priority for the time being was *his* band. He'd also been approached by several magazines who were after 'rock couple' features, and wanted to find out more about him and Melissa. But again he had shunned that idea after he sensed that Melissa wasn't too sure about it.

'I'm not ready for that yet,' Melissa had said when he'd mentioned it.

Luke wasn't overly keen on the idea anyway. As far as possible, their life together was their business, nobody else's. After the Jay-Den incident, he wanted her all to himself. His team had tried to convince him to rethink some of the offers, but he'd reminded them he was in a band – he made music. There was nothing else to it.

'You really want this place?' Luke checked, but the look on her face gave him his answer.

The agent had been waiting outside while they looked round on their own and Luke called him back in and confirmed they wanted to rent it, with an option to purchase later. The band would be heading off on their American tour the following month, and Luke wanted Melissa to have somewhere to feel safe while he was away. Melissa felt very happy as they made their way back to Luke's other new toy – a black Audi S3. Luke was also planning his next guitar-buying spree, and he was much more excited about the guitars than anything else.

'I love this car.' Melissa almost purred as she got in and took Luke by surprise as she jumped onto his lap.

'Wow, babe ... seriously? This is a little public,' he laughed as Melissa twisted her finger in the collar of his T-shirt and, pulling him towards her, kissed him passionately. Luke ran his hand through her hair as she teased him, rubbing her hand up and down his stomach. He stopped her from getting too carried away, sensing her wild streak was coming out to play again. This was way too public, even for him.

'Ease up, Liss,' he laughed, peeling her off him. 'Let's go home.'

Melissa giggled as they noticed an elderly lady shaking her head and looking disgusted at the public display of affection she'd just witnessed.

'Some people have no sense of humour these days,' Melissa joked, pulling his lips to hers again for another kiss before they drove off. She waved and blew a kiss to the lady as they went by.

'Thank you,' she whispered, knowing that his talent and hard work was giving her the life so many others could only dream of. Luke kissed her forehead and stroked her cheek.

'Thank you, for believing in me.'

Life was good for them right now, and they were enjoying every second of it. They both knew things could change in an instant.

*****

'What's his problem?,' Tom asked as Ray, who was looking pale, suddenly stopped everything and ordered everyone except Luke out of the studio.

They were working on material for their second single, and Ray never interrupted studio work, so they knew something was up. Luke shrugged as Dale looked at him as he left, along with the others. Even the engineers and producers had to leave. Ray pulled Luke out of the booth and switched everything off. He was now starting to get anxious as Ray looked really worried.

'Ray, what's wrong?'

Ray put his hand on Luke's shoulder and patted it, not sure where to start. This was going to be a big problem. Luke was his priority, and he was about to tell him something that would turn his life upside down. There was also a young girl who was about to have her world torn apart, and Ray couldn't stop it. He wanted to bury it and protect them both, but he couldn't. All he could do as the band's manager was be there to guide him, and try to limit the damage. But that was not going to be easy.

'Luke, I'm not paid to judge. What you do in your private time is your business. But who is the girl?' Luke looked blankly at his manager, waiting for the punch line. 'Come on, talk to me. If you're honest, I can help you.'

'Help me with what exactly?' He felt a pang of dread in his stomach because Ray had never acted like this before. There was something about him that told Luke this was definitely no joke.

'OK, I'll spell it out. The guys in PR have just taken a call from Amanda Green, the top editor at *Juice* magazine, and they've got photos of you and this Kelsey bird.' Ray went on to say that there had been a bidding war going on for the photos and *Juice*, according to his sources, had paid over £50,000 for them.

'What photos?' He asked, shoving Ray's hand off his shoulder as the realisation of what he was saying began to sink in. Ray explained that the photos showed him and a girl, who claimed to have been with him after their gig at the O2 on the last stop of their tour.

'Fucking stop them. You're my manager, stop them.'

But it was too late. They were already going to print.

'Liss,' he breathed her name. How would he tell her this? It would destroy her and would destroy them. 'No ... Liss.' Luke looked at his manager, his eyes begging for help. But Ray couldn't help. Luke's claim that the photos must be fake had already been denied. The photos were not fake. The girl had taken them and the evidence was on her camera. They had not been tampered with either.

'Luke, I really don't know what to say about whatever did or didn't happen. The point is, what they show will be the truth in the public's eyes. You need to accept the reality and deal with it.'

'Ray, I don't remember that night, I really don't.' He remembered waking up alone the next day, but the night was a blur. He remembered coming off stage, having a few drinks and a few lines with the crew because it had been a successful tour, but he didn't remember much else.

Ray pulled out his phone and showed Luke the photo of himself on what looked like the bed in his hotel room. He was propped up against the headboard, shirtless, with a short-haired girl on his lap. The only item of her clothing you could see was a red bra. He had his hand on her waist and she was leaning down, her lips on his. Luke flinched as he looked at this.

'No!' Luke hadn't realised he was still holding his guitar until he let go of it. It dropped to the floor and he kicked at the wall.

Dale came flying in on hearing the crash.

'What the fuck's going on?!'

Luke was staring at his manager, hoping for a miracle.

'Home ... Luke ... now. You can't wait any longer. Melissa needs to know before they hit the shelves.

'Luke, what have you done?' Dale asked as alarm spread through his body as he searched his best friend's horrified face, and found nothing but confusion.

'I didn't, Dale. I didn't do anything.'

*****

'Packing is so boring,' Melissa complained on the phone to Beth while she took a break from putting her things into boxes, ready for the move. The job was half done, and there were boxes piled up everywhere, and it was starting to feel like she was making progress. The new place was almost theirs – just a few more days to wait.

'It'll be worth it for several reasons...you'll have a beautiful home in the middle of London, and more importantly you'll have a bit of privacy back,' Beth reminded her.

Melissa wanted to be away from her current neighbours. She was sure it was one of them tipping off the press about her movements. She'd lived there for eighteen months and only since Luke became the public's newest fascination had any of them even attempted to say hello. But now they all seemed to want to be her best friends. She couldn't wait to get out of there. She had no problem with being nice to people when they were at a gig or an event, but she would never be comfortable with it in her home life. As long as she had Luke and they took care of each other, then she'd be fine and she didn't want or need randoms hanging around. Melissa asked Beth how their search for a place was going. Beth told her that they couldn't decide what sort of place they wanted, or where they wanted it to be, so were going to wait before making any decisions.

'I'm not staying here though. It just doesn't feel like home.' They were renting a place in Notting Hill, but Beth wasn't keen on it. It was fine for the time being though.

Toby still had his house. He didn't really care much, because most of the time he stayed in hotels. Tom still lived with his parents and put up with a lot of teasing about it. He was looking for somewhere for himself, but wasn't in any rush and had taken to gatecrashing Dale and Beth's on a regular basis if he wasn't hanging out at Toby's.

Melissa heard Beth shout hello to Dale, and then heard her tone change. She could hear Dale in the background asking if Melissa had spoken Luke.

'Liss, is Luke home yet?'

'No ... why?' Beth said she had to go. Dale was telling her to get off the phone because Luke needed to talk to her.

*****

It was over an hour later when Luke, looking awful, finally arrived home. Melissa had been getting worried about Dale's strange behaviour; he normally shouted hello down the phone or would take over from Beth and have a conversation with her. He would sometimes pretend to be Beth and mock their conversations, which always made Melissa giggle.

'What's wrong? Melissa asked.

Luke was just staring at her and he looked like he had seen a ghost.

'I don't even know where to start,' he said as he walked over to her. Taking both her hands in his, he kissed her forehead.

'Luke, you're shaking. What's happened?' she asked, her voice full of concern.

'I need you to sit down and listen to me.' He guided her to the sofa.

Melissa started to panic as she ran through her worries. Had something gone wrong with their new home? Had he fallen out with the guys? Or was it something to do with their contract? Luke said all those things were fine. The way he looked at her, she thought he might cry.

'Luke, tell me what's wrong. You're scaring me.' Her heart pounded because something told her this was bad. He looked shell-shocked.

'Liss, I love you – you know that, right?'

Melissa nodded and said she loved him too. He pulled her to him and kissed her, cherishing the moment for as long as possible thinking it could be their last. It was at that moment he realised just how much she meant to him, and his heart was breaking because he remembered how she had told him about her ex and how he had hurt her so much with his cheating. He had promised her he would never break her heart and now that was exactly what he was about to do.

'I'm sorry, I'm so sorry! I swear I don't remember.' Melissa pulled away, looking at him, waiting for him to explain. 'She's lying,' he whispered.

'Who is lying?' Melissa said backing away from him and removing his arms from around her waist. He told her about the girl and the pictures.

The world seemed to slow down, and her heart felt like it had been ripped open.

'No!' she yelled as he tried to take her hand. 'Please don't do this to me, Luke, please.' Luke begged her to believe, him but he wasn't thinking straight and was not making a good case for himself. Insisting that he couldn't remember only upset her more. 'Fucking try to remember! Please tell me this is a joke,' she begged. 'You promised me.' Luke wished it was a joke. The pain in her eyes was killing him. 'Everyone will see those pictures. Please tell me the truth – at least be man enough to do that.'

She tripped over a box as she backed away from him. Luke went to help her up, but she pushed him away, crying now.

'Don't touch me!' she screamed as tears stung her eyes, and everything blurred.

Luke could do nothing but just stand looking at her, breaking down on the floor. He had no idea what to do he felt helpless, numb and terrified. The girl's story hadn't even come out yet. He had no idea what she was going to say. She hadn't even looked that attractive. Even if he was going to cheat, which he never would, this girl would not be his choice.

'What did I do wrong?' he heard her whisper as he picked her up off the floor. She struggled at first but he held onto her until she calmed down and let him hold her as she sobbed.

'Nothing ... you did nothing wrong.'

'If I'm not good enough for you ... how many more?' She felt so humiliated.

Luke turned her around to face him and took her face in his hands. Her tears were flowing and he wiped them away.

'I've never cheated on you, and I never would. You're all I want.' He pressed his forehead against hers, holding her face close to his. 'Please believe me.' He could feel the prospect of losing her already tearing at his heart.

'Promise me she's lying,' Melissa whispered as her tears fell again at the thought of losing him.

'I promise,' he replied.

Melissa reached up and kissed him. She ran her hands through his hair, holding him tightly, too scared to let him go. This was what she had always feared, and she couldn't believe it was happening to them. She didn't want to see the pictures or read the story, but she knew she would have to.

*****

The next forty-eight hours were torture. Melissa couldn't eat or sleep. Luke watched her, worried, as she paced the house, waiting for her worst nightmare to come true. They didn't go out and had made all their friends and family aware. As was to be expected, their parents were upset and worried. Luke's parents naturally didn't believe a word of it. Jean and Mick were furious, but didn't know what to believe. Either way, their daughter was the one who would be left heartbroken and humiliated.

Luke was adamant that he was innocent, and rigidly stuck to his story. Dale backed him up. 'Melissa, I spent over a month practically in his pocket and he never showed any interest in anyone else. He spoke to fans, of course, I won't lie. There were girls around but I never saw him once be anything but sociable. There were nights when things got rowdy, but I know my best friend and he didn't cheat.' But even Dale couldn't explain the pictures. He believed that Luke believed what he was saying, but the trouble was that he couldn't one hundred per cent say he hadn't done something with this girl, and the pictures were about as incriminating as they could be.

It felt like a tidal wave of heartache when the story broke. Melissa had no idea how to prepare for her world to be torn apart, and even though she tried to brace herself, it still hit her like a sledge hammer.

'My wild night with Black Eagles frontman. We had sex three times in one night, and he still couldn't get enough,' by nineteen-year-old Kelsey Gibbs ...

Melissa stared at the pictures, hoping they would change or she would realise they were fakes if she looked long enough. But the images stayed the same. It was him, no question about it. The tattoos alone were a giveaway, but the pictures had captured him clearly. Kelsey Gibbs was kissing *her* boyfriend, and it was happening to her all over again. Feelings of betrayal and hurt swept over her as they had done when she was cheated on before, only this time they were much stronger. But the worst feeling of all was of worthlessness. The girl claimed that Luke had called his relationship with Melissa 'boring and stressful' and that *she* was more beautiful. This added insult to injury and it crushed her completely. She'd thought she gave him what he needed, but she was clearly wrong. The feeling of not being good enough was shattering because she had never loved anyone the way she loved him, and she thought he felt the same. It made her feel as though their whole relationship had been a lie, and she'd been totally taken in by it. She'd never felt such intense pain.

'You lying cheating bastard! How could you?! How could you say she's more beautiful than me?' Melissa screamed as she pushed Luke towards the door. 'You screwed her three times!' She lashed out, catching him and almost clawing at his face.

'She's lying!' he shouted back, the rage bubbling under the surface at the thought of losing his angel.

'Look at the pictures!' Melissa was hysterical as she threw the magazines at him and then the paper which had the full story on the front page. 'What the hell is that bitch doing on your lap in nothing but her bra and knickers? Explain it to me now!' she screamed as tears ran down her cheeks and her heart-wrenching sobs nearly choked her. 'I hate you, I hate you!' she yelled repeatedly as she pounded his chest with her fists until she wore herself out. The words cut him like a knife. Hearing her say she hated him was much worse than the punching. He caught her as she collapsed to the floor. 'Don't insult me even more by treating me like an idiot. I want you to leave.' She stood up and looked him right in the eyes. How could he do this to her after the accusations about Jay-Den and how bad she had been made to feel?

'I trusted you ...I believed in you,' she cried. 'I sat and cried over Leon and what he did to me, how he made me feel worthless. You promised me you would never do that ... you promised me.' Her words choked her again.

'I didn't do it,' he sobbed. 'I love you. Please, Liss, please listen.' He stopped as she covered her ears with her hands and screamed for him to stop talking.

They argued for what felt like hours as the anger grew and the insults began to fly, making this their worst fight ever. There would be no passionate making up this time. Luke, now annoyed that she was not accepting his denial, had brought up the Jay-Den incident and he knew it had fuelled the flames.

'Don't you dare throw that at me. I did nothing wrong ... I didn't have sex with him unlike you and this dirty whore!' She hit him again, which shocked her as much as him. Luke was on the defensive again, realising that he was the one with the explaining to do here. He had never begged a woman in his life, but the fear of losing her forced him to do just that. But Melissa had seen and heard enough, and pushed him out of the front door. He slipped in the rain on the steps, but she didn't hang around to see if he was OK. Shutting the door, she threw herself on the floor and sobbed as her world crumbled around her.

'Melissa! Don't do this, please.' He hammered on the door, realising that he himself was experiencing a real relationship heartbreak for the first time in his life. Eventually, he gave up and headed to his car. A couple of photographers stepped out of the shadows and began clicking away.

'Fuck off!' Luke yelled as he got into the car and locked himself in. He put his head on the steering wheel and counted to ten to stop himself from getting out and kicking the shit out of the guys laughing at him. His phone rang and he knew it would be his mother.

'Luke, where are you? This isn't true, is it? Please tell me you didn't just break that girl's heart?'

'Mum, I'm coming over. I'll talk to you then.' He'd prefer to get this over with sooner rather than later, but his mum would be so upset. She adored Melissa too.

*****

Melissa tortured herself by reading the article over and over. She wouldn't talk to anyone, not even Beth, and had locked herself in her home. She wouldn't even face her parents. They had called and banged on her door, but she didn't want to see anyone. It had been three days and the loneliness was getting to her. Ignoring the frantic calls from friends and family was now just cruel of her, and she realised that she shouldn't punish them. She was angry with the world, but she realised that it wasn't their fault. Luke called her several times a day. He was the last person she wanted to speak to and at the same time he was also the only person. He still maintained his innocence, but he couldn't explain any of it, so he was fighting a losing battle.

Melissa had given up her job. She'd also nearly lost her home, but luckily her landlord hadn't got anyone lined up to move in, so he let her stay. But how she was going to pay her rent was something she would have to think about, and soon. How was she supposed to find a job with the whole world laughing at her? She still couldn't believe he had done this to her.

The boxes still sat in the hall, waiting to be unpacked. She should have been in her new home now. But Melissa knew they were over. There was no way she could stay with him after this because she could never trust him again. She had to tell him face to face and end things properly. The next time her phone flashed with his name, she answered.

'We need to talk, here, tomorrow at two,' was all she said, giving him no chance to speak before she hung up. She boxed all his stuff up, ready for him to take away, then burst into tears again.

*****

'I don't believe what that girl is saying about our son,' Debbie Black raged.

Luke's dad read the paper again. Stuart Black looked like an older Luke, only with slightly less hair and a few grey patches.

'Why would this girl lie? Look at the photos, Debs.'

They were horrified by what was being printed about their son, but his mum wasn't having any of it. Stuart knew what young lads could be like and with the lifestyle Luke lived, he could understand if for once he'd given in to the attention from another woman. Not that he condoned it, but he wouldn't judge his son either.

Debbie had never liked any of Luke's previous girlfriends so this was just as heart-breaking for her.

'Money, that's why she'd lie!' She snapped. 'Luke says he doesn't remember and he hasn't done anything, and I believe him.' Debbie had brought her son up better than that. Melissa was a beautiful girl, and her son loved her and would not have cheated. A mother knows these things, she assured her husband. It wasn't true, it couldn't be. Debbie knew she sounded like a biased mother who didn't want to believe her son was anything but perfect. She wasn't stupid, she knew he was far from perfect, but the way he was behaving over this made her believe him. He had never been able to lie to her – he may have thought at times in the past that he'd pulled the wool over her eyes, but she had just let him believe that sometimes.

'He isn't lying, Stu.' Debbie hadn't seen her son cry since he was a child. He had cried like a baby the morning he arrived home after the story broke. She could tell that he was genuinely shocked and upset by the whole thing, and this was a different reaction to someone who was sorry they'd been caught.

He was still staying with them, even though his new place had been ready for two days. He had been trying to keep himself busy, but it wasn't working out too well and Debbie was glad that Dale was such a good friend. She wasn't too happy with Beth though, after she'd turned up shouting and screaming at Luke, and had even hit him. Debbie had soon put a stop to that. She understood that Beth was angry and was looking out for her friend, but she wouldn't have that sort of behaviour, not in her home and certainly not directed at her son.

The whole band were fully behind Luke, giving him the support he needed. Ray had been brilliant and had told Luke to keep working and keep busy which Debbie thought was a sensible idea.

The band's publicist, Stan, was already throwing things out there, trying to divert attention away from the scandal. Luke hated being branded a cheat, but it was the damage it was doing to Melissa that upset him most. Dale was his only connection to her and every time Dale saw her, he reported that she was crying.

Luke wanted Kelsey Gibbs found. He wanted to look the girl in the eye and ask her why she was doing this. Even if he had cheated in a moment of drunken madness he would never say those things about Melissa, never. That was what had hurt her most –that he had apparently been so cruel about her. Jay-Den had tried to track her down, but she had vanished. Melissa didn't have a team of people to help her as he did – she was on her own, and that thought was tearing Luke apart. Even if she wouldn't even speak to him, he still wanted to protect her from it all. But it had hit the news like a nuclear bomb and Luke felt blown away by it.

'You need to eat,' his dad said, not really knowing what else to say. He was worried about Luke's beer intake and chain smoking.

'Not hungry.'

'Well at least have this,' Stu said handing his son a coffee.

Luke took it and held it in both hands staring at the steam rising from it. 'I don't remember that night. If I could just remember something...' the frustration in his voice was clear.

'What, there's nothing at all? You must have seen this girl, even just to say hello to?' Debbie asked.

Luke shook his head. He'd woken next day feeling awful but put it down to exhaustion and a hangover. They had done a gig almost every day for nearly two months and it was hard work.

'Luke, I want the truth...' She hesitated. 'Were you doing drugs?' He knew that lying wasn't going to do him any favour so he nodded. She asked what.

'Does it matter?'

Debbie decided she didn't want to know, but it was something she worried a great deal about. 'Did you speak to Melissa?' she asked instead.

'No.' He sounded choked up, and looked away from his mum's gaze, trying to hold back the tears he could feel welling up again.

'I can't believe how much I miss her.' He hadn't expected the pain in his heart to be so bad. 'She'll never forgive me.'

'Give her time. That girl loves you, but right now she's hurting, and you can understand why. Let her come to you when she's ready,' she said softly. 'Don't push her.'

'Don't you think I'm feeling the same?' he snapped.

'Yes, but think of it from her side of things. She'll be fighting with her emotions; the Luke she knows and this Luke.' Debbie pointed at the paper hanging out of the bin. 'Everything she knew and loved has just been ripped up and stomped on. Every fear she had just came true. She won't know what to believe any more.'

'She should trust me ...why isn't she listening to me?' There was a hint of anger in his voice.

Debbie frowned at her son. 'Don't be angry with her. This isn't her fault.' Luke knew that, and he knew he was frustrated and angry at the situation, not with her.

'You should move into your new home. It's yours and you have to get it ready for her because I believe this will all be sorted out. Melissa will come back if you've done nothing wrong. You just need to work out how to prove it, and fight for her.'

'Maybe,' he said, sounding unconvinced. He got up and grabbed another beer from the fridge before opening the back door and leaning against it while he lit another cigarette. How do you fight something like this? He wondered. He didn't have the answers, so where did he even start?

'The image of a rock star might be drink and drugs, but you don't actually have to live that way all the time,' Debbie lectured him. 'Luke Black, don't roll your eyes at me.' She took the beer from him and poured it down the sink. Luke had to sort this mess out, and drinking wasn't the answer. She left him to his thoughts, and went into the garden.

'Get out of my garden,' she yelled as she spotted someone hiding by a bush by the back gate, obviously trying to get a picture. No doubt they'd managed to get a shot of Luke when he had opened the door.

*****

'Oh, Melissa, darling ... I'm so glad you finally let us in.' Jean hugged her distraught daughter, followed by her dad, who was not at all happy. He and Luke had already had words over the phone, and they hadn't been pleasant ones.

'I'll rip your head off for doing this to my baby,' Mick had said, among other threats. They'd argued as Luke pleaded his case, but as far as Mick was concerned the damage was done.

They both sat with Melissa while she sobbed and tried to find reasons for why it had happened – maybe she wasn't pretty enough, or she didn't give him what he needed perhaps. Both were ridiculous, they told her. It was not her fault. It was his, for not keeping it in his pants.

'You've done so much for him... he should be grateful.' This was not how Mick expected his daughter to be treated. She never hurt anyone, so why did people keep letting her down?

Beth arrived later, almost knocking Melissa over as she bounded in through the front door and locked her in the world's tightest hug.

'Don't shut me out babe... I've been going mental.' Beth was on the verge of tears as Melissa apologised but explained she just needed time to herself to think it through. She was still completely blindsided by everything that had happened.

'He called me that night, said he loved me and he would be home the next day. So was he with her while he was feeding me that shit?'

There wasn't anything they could say to her. No one had any answers. She told them that Luke was coming over the next day and that she'd made her decision – it was over. The trust was gone, and things could never be the same. Just the same as screwing up a piece of paper – the creases would always remain. Beth's face fell.

'What?' Melissa snapped at her, looking annoyed.

'Nothing. I just think maybe you should hear him out before making your decision.'

Melissa glared at her. 'Oh, I see. You're on his side?'

'No!' Beth explained that all she meant was that Melissa should talk to him first then make her decision. If she still felt the same then of course she would support her. She just didn't want to see her making rash decisions. Beth was angry with Luke too, but she also knew how much Melissa loved him and she wanted her to be sure before walking away and possibly regretting it later. 'You know I'm always on your side.'

Melissa wasn't listening to reason and she shocked everyone by yelling at Beth for forgetting where her loyalties should lie.

'This is good for you – you can have the full limelight now. The only fully fledged Eagle girl. Don't worry, you can still be with Dale if that's what's worrying you,' she ranted as she paced the room.

Melissa's phone rang and she picked it up and threw it across the room, and Jean watched her daughter fall apart right in front of her eyes. 'For fuck's sake, why won't they just leave me alone?' If it wasn't Luke, it was a journalist wanting a juicy quote.

'Liss, don't be a bitch. I know you're hurting, but don't blame me!' Beth had spotted the empty wine bottle and knew Melissa was drunk. Her parents clearly hadn't noticed but Beth knew this was the drink talking. She tried hard to stay calm as Melissa took all her fury out on her.

'You can continue being the awesome girlfriend that everyone thinks is cool, and Luke's fans can rejoice now he's single. I was never good enough for him anyway. And Kelsey fucking Gibbs isn't even that pretty!' Beth could see the complete devastation in Melissa's eyes and knew she was more than upset and heartbroken. She was utterly destroyed. 'He'll be fine because he's a rock star! But the world is laughing at me.' Beth just sat quietly staring at her as the nasty comments poured out and she puffed on yet another cigarette. 'Go for it, you said, because you wanted Dale so much – I knew even then he would break my heart. And you pushed me to do it.' Melissa couldn't stop. 'Some best friend you turned out to be.'

'Melissa, stop it now.' Jean couldn't bear to see them fall out and had to stop this.

Beth was shaking, tears rolling down her face as her only true friend tore strips off her for no good reason.

'Liss ... please don't,' Beth begged her.

'No. Beth can take my spot now until Luke finds someone else. That bitch can take the shit off me. Maybe it's a good thing. People will eventually forget about me and let me breathe again,' she cried as she stormed out of the door. The cameras started snapping immediately. 'This lot can find some other mug to hound. Leave me the fuck alone ... get away from my fucking house,' she screamed into the wind as her dad pulled her back inside. The anger and hurt chipped away at her heart and the feeling of betrayal was too much to bear. She was lashing out and trying to transfer some of the hurt she was feeling to someone else. 'Don't worry, when Dale fucks you over we can cry together.'

That was the last straw for Beth. She leapt from the sofa and slapped Melissa hard across the face, making her stumble backwards into Jean.

'Melissa Webb, you stop this now. It's Beth for god's sake,' Jean begged.

The two girls eyed each other across the room but there was silence. Mick looked lost as his family fell apart in front of his eyes.

'You take that shit back, Liss, or I swear to god I will walk out that door and never come back.' Beth had come to support her, but Melissa had broken her heart with just a few words. She was getting the blame for everything, or so it seemed.

'I'm so sorry,' Melissa wailed, holding her arms out to Beth who ran into them. 'I didn't mean it. I'm so sorry.' The slap had snapped her out of it. It had been totally deserved and she didn't mean any of it. Beth hugged her, crying too because everything was such a mess.

Melissa was shaking like a leaf as all her emotions escaped.

'I believed in him ... I helped him achieve his dream and this is how he treats me. I'm such an idiot.' She spent the next hour apologising until Beth started to find it annoying and told her to stop or she'd slap her again.

Her parents headed home around midnight, promising to be back next day once she'd seen Luke. They would help her out with her rent for a couple of months, so she needn't worry about anything for now.

'Your parents really are amazing,' Beth commented once they had left. Melissa was well aware of that, and very grateful to have them. Beth grabbed her bag and retrieved her iPad. She messed with it for a few seconds then handed it to Melissa. On the screen was a Facebook fan page which made her smile. It wasn't one for the boys but one for her and Beth. She hadn't known they had one of their own. Beth pointed out that was just one of twenty pages for the girls, but this was the most popular.

'Melissa Webb & Beth Watkins Fans ... 8345 likes
This page is dedicated to Melissa Webb and Beth Watkins (Girlfriends of Luke Black and Dale Baxter from The Black Eagles. We quite like them too). They are beautiful and stylish and we think they both rock.'

Their status update from one hour ago read:
'We are still devastated over the news that hit the press a few days ago. We don't know what is really going on, but we will always be fans of Melissa Webb. We pray that the stories are just lies, because they are perfect for each other. It has to be Luke and Lissa always, and wherever Lissa is we hope she is being looked after. Beth, we hope you are kicking ass right now ...'

'Wow,' Melissa said, feeling slightly overwhelmed. It was sweet, she thought, but also strange to think that so many people liked and cared about her when she'd never met any of them. But it was comforting in a strange sort of way.

*****

Once Melissa was asleep, Beth called Dale. He was with Luke, who wasn't coping well either. Debbie had come home from work to find Luke so drunk he hardly knew his name. She couldn't get hold of his dad so in a panic had called Dale and he'd driven straight from London to help sort him out. Debbie had found him lying on the kitchen floor after downing a whole bottle of neat whisky. He hadn't even hidden the fact he'd been doing drugs. Dale had carried him up to his room, dumped him on his bed and stayed with him to make sure he didn't choke on his own vomit.

'He's hurting too, B, so just back off a bit ... he could have killed himself today.'

'I know... she isn't good either and I don't have a clue how to fix her broken heart. I've never seen her like this. This is 100 times worse than when that other idiot stitched her up.'

Dale had never seen Luke upset over any woman in his entire life. He would always just shrug and carry on.

'I don't know how to fix them either.'

*****

'I need a fag,' Luke called to Ray as he headed outside. Just as he did, he received a message from Melissa. It wasn't what he'd expected and his mood immediately dropped.

'Sorry but I can't see you today. I'm not ready. I need more time to think ... I can't look at you ... it will just make me cry.'

The cameras clicked away. 'Hey Luke, how's Melissa?'

'Oh yeah, that's right ... you wouldn't know since she kicked you out.' The cameras carried on clicking.

Luke gritted his teeth and tried to ignore them. But that was never going to happen, not in the mood he was in, and feeling like he was at death's door after the previous day's bender. He'd taken it very close to the edge yesterday, and scared the life out of his mother, not to mention Dale who'd done nothing but nag him all morning about being an idiot.

The two reporters were hell bent on getting him to react, and he decided not to let them down. He chucked his cigarette aside, throwing insults as he charged for one who was wearing a black beanie. He seemed to spend his life following him or Melissa, and he had been pissing Luke off for ages.

'You want a reaction, mush ... here have this one,' he screamed in his face before head butting him and leaving his face covered in blood.

'Get him inside, now!' Ray yelled as Dale and Toby struggled to get control of him. He wriggled and kicked out as they dragged him back into the studio building. 'Beanie Guy', as they had come to know him, picked himself up and smiled smugly at his fellow vulture, who'd snapped every second of it.

'Let go of me. I'll kill the bastard. The tosser deserves it,' yelled Luke as he disappeared inside.

The work on their second single had been delayed, but Ray feared that it was completely buggered now. He cursed to himself knowing he would have to drop everything and sort this mess out now. He dialled Stan and Jay-Den – it was a PR nightmare and they would need to nip it in the bud. Stan was the master at putting a spin on things and Jay-Den was well skilled at turning a bad situation into a good one.

'He isn't worth the court case,' Toby said dragging Luke backwards.

Dale was yelling for the guy to back off as he continued to wind Luke up.

'Ahh, missing your little lady are you? Should have kept it in your pants then, son.' The clicking of cameras was continuous.

'Smashing his head in will make me feel better.' Luke was bursting with anger and the red mist had descended. 'I should fucking kill him and feed him to the dogs.'

Tom was hanging back because the other two had Luke covered. He smirked as he walked over to where Beanie Guy was about to pick up his camera which he'd dropped in the scuffle. As his hand was almost touching it, Tom stepped in and flicked it up in the air with his foot, then volleyed it into the busy traffic, where it was smashed to pieces. Beanie Guy wasn't laughing now. He had a week's worth of snaps on the memory stick in the camera, and they were now lost. That represented a week's income.

'You'll regret this, you idiot. I'll have you all for this,' he yelled at Tom as his mate captured the whole thing.

'Oh I'm quaking in my boots. Fuck off,' Tom said shoving him into the wall before turning to walk away and flicking his half-smoked cigarette over his shoulder. It landed at the furious guy's feet and Tom gave him the middle finger as he walked on.

Tom had a quiet personality, and he did not say much, but he let his actions do the talking. This was his way of showing he had his friends back, and he was always ready to look out for them.

'Luke, I know things are rough for you right now, but you have to calm down,' Ray said while Dale held him against the wall. 'You do realise he could have you for assault? And *you're* making it worse,' he snapped at Tom. It fell on deaf ears as Tom just shrugged.

'The guy's an idiot ... I'll buy him a new fucking camera if he's still crying about it tomorrow,' was Tom's response. 'Let's make some music and forget about all this shit.'

Luke was taking deep breaths, trying to swallow the urge to run back out and finish the guy off. Dale asked everyone to give them some space for a while, so he could talk to him.

'Liss cancelled on me.' Luke almost choked on the words.

Dale now understood the sudden outburst from his best friend, who had been looking forward to seeing her and hopeful they would be able to sit down and talk about things, even if they didn't sort everything out straight away. Mostly, he just wanted to see her.

'Sorry, mate, I'm sure she'll come round soon. She obviously needs a bit more time.' Dale hoped so anyway. He hated this situation, mostly because it just didn't make sense. Luke was too cut up to be lying and had shown no signs of straying. He loved Melissa and wouldn't risk everything for a drunken shag. That girl wasn't worth losing Melissa over. There were always a few lasses hanging around after shows and he showed no interest in any of them, other than just a bit of friendly banter.

'Love, you're blocking my view. I can't see the footie. Go and dangle those things somewhere else,' he had said once, before a gig in Germany when one girl had draped herself over him, clearly thinking she was in with a chance if she thrust her massive boobs in his face. It was just embarrassing for all concerned. Dale had been her next target.

'I don't think so, love,' he'd answered. Like Luke he wasn't available, yet she seemed hell bent on trying to break them both down. Eventually, she'd been removed when she became abusive to Ray, who had just been doing his job - he could see she was trouble. Luke said he was sick of random tarts hanging around and anyway. Portsmouth had lost again that day, so he had the hump.

'Come on, let's finish up here, then we can go for a beer and talk it through,' Dale suggested. Luckily the press had moved on and they headed back into the studio where Luke took out his frustrations on his vocal chords and guitar strings.

*****

A couple of hours later, they had finally finished. They were all over the moon – it was some of their best work yet. It also helped that the single fitted the situation. 'Broken Wings' was about love and loss. There was so much emotion coming through in Luke's voice, complemented by his guitar work - even his Black Fender sounded like it was crying. Dale supported it on rhythm guitar, and Tom brought in the deep, rhythmic undercurrent of bass that sounded almost like a heartbeat. The three were an impressive combination, but with the addition of Toby's brilliant drumming skills, their sound was complete. They had produced a piece of music they were all proud of.

However, their good mood was short-lived because on their way out of the studio, they were met by two police officers, who arrested Luke on suspicion of assault. Ray had to intervene to ensure that he wasn't going to have to bail out the entire band, as they tried to defend their front man and argue his case.

'The guy's lucky he still has his teeth. He's a scumbag. If I see him again I'll deck the little prick,' Dale shouted at the arresting officer

'I would advise against that, Sir,' the officer responded, trying not to smirk. It was a good day for him – arresting a famous rock star was a change from dealing with petty crimes that were more paperwork than anything else.

'Bollocks,' Dale snapped before Ray jumped in and gained control.

*****

'You are one lucky son of a bitch,' said Ray two hours later, after finally getting Luke off on a caution. It was his first offence – at least the first he'd ever been caught for.

Beanie Guy had caused a fuss for a few hours, but then dropped his complaint after a visit from Jay-Den – obviously money had talked. Luke didn't want to know, so he didn't ask. Instead, he headed straight out for a few beers with his friends.

'See you later, mate, you take care. I mean it, *I'll* call her if I have to and make her listen,' Toby said, patting Luke on the shoulder as he and Tom left them in the pub and went off to a club to meet some of Tom's friends. 'Stay out of trouble, for fuck's sake,' he lectured. Toby would call Melissa if he was asked, because the situation worried them all. They all loved Melissa. She was one of their girls and it didn't seem right that she was not around. In truth, Toby missed her because she was also his friend. But most of all he hated seeing Luke like this.

'I'll behave for the rest of the day, scout's honour,' Luke forced a cheeky smile.

Outside, Toby looked at his phone, trying to decide whether it would be a good idea to call Melissa. He thought maybe he could at least get her to talk to him. Tom was shaking his head, fearing it was a stupid idea. He thought Toby should keep out of it. But Toby ignored him. That was no surprise to Tom, but he had at least tried.

'Melissa Webb, don't you hang up on me,' was his opening line when she answered.

'Hi, big man, how's things?' There was no denying the sadness in her voice. 'You're not going to force me to forgive him.'

'I'm not ringing to force you to do anything, relax. I'm just asking you to talk to him before he does something completely stupid.' He filled her in on the day's events, and heard her sigh.

'Cheating on me, head butting people, getting arrested. He really is so rock and roll these days.'

'Babe, look, I don't know what happened with this Kelsey bird ... I don't remember her. But then again, I was wasted so who knows ...' he trailed off as he said this, realising from Tom's look of horror that he wasn't helping the situation.

'Luke clearly didn't remember *me* that night ...' she stopped herself before she really went on a rant and said something she would regret.

'Please ... he needs you, and so do we. We miss you.' There was silence from Melissa, and Toby waited as she thought it through.

'Fine ... I'll call him. But I'm promising nothing.'

*****

Luke was relieved to have a bit of space. It wasn't that he didn't want to be around Toby and Tom, but sometimes he liked to spend some time with Dale, who was like a brother to him. He was his sounding board when he needed to talk about things. Dale told him the truth, and Luke respected his opinion. Dale had always been the more placid, laid-back of the two, and he rarely got stressed over things. He was a calming influence on Luke. If left to his own devices, Luke could analyse things way too much, and wind himself up.

Dale grabbed more beers from the bar. They were in a pub near the studio which was becoming their local. The landlord knew who they were, but treated them like any other customer. The locals left them to it, either because they didn't know who they were, or didn't care.

Luke took a large gulp of beer and checked his phone, making the mistake of looking on the internet. It was definitely a bad move. He learned that in some people's eyes, he was Satan's spawn, and of course now he could add assault to his list of misdemeanours. He considered deleting every account he had, so he didn't have to read all the crap. But that would change nothing, he realised.

'As if I'm going to answer these idiots!' He said to Dale. He was referring to the questions people were leaving on the social networks. People thought he would actually reply to them. He would interact with fans to say hello or discuss music, but this was not up for discussion.

He took to Twitter: 'My personal life is my business. Oh and by the way, Broken Wings is ready for release if anyone is interested.'

The genuine fans who cared about their music and didn't give a damn about the soap opera of their private lives were quickly out in force, pleased to hear the news about the single.

'Do you know if she's doing any better?' Luke asked Dale, hoping to hear some positive news about Melissa. He didn't want to discuss the day's other events. As far as he was concerned, it was done with.

'No, mate, she isn't I'm afraid.' Dale couldn't lie and say she was OK.

Beth had spent every day either with her or on the phone checking on her, and the previous night had been one of the worst since they'd split. Melissa had sobbed her heart out, and she'd been drinking again. In the end Beth had gone to her and was now staying there for a few days.

'Does Beth still hate me?'

Dale shrugged. It was hard for him because he loved Beth, but he didn't like her bad mouthing of Luke, which she'd been doing since this whole thing broke. He understood why she was angry but she had to understand that he wouldn't abandon Luke. Regardless of what he had or hadn't done, he didn't like hearing some of the things she said about him, particularly when nobody knew what really happened.

Dale had been so angry with her after her little show at his mum's. She had shouted all kinds of things at Luke and when she slapped him and then went to punch him, Debbie had stepped in. Dale had to drag her out of the house and calm her down. They'd fallen out, and hadn't spoken for the rest of the day. So it wasn't just causing problems for Melissa and Luke, it was affecting everyone.

Dale knew Luke better than anyone, and the things people had been saying about him were untrue. It was all so wrong.

'Sorry this has caused you issues.' Luke didn't want to see anything come between Dale and Beth, and had already forgiven Beth for the slap. She was standing up for Melissa and he expected nothing less.

'Don't worry about us. We're fine,' Dale assured him.

Luke told him not to be too hard on Beth as she was only doing what any other best friend would do in that situation.

'She's a good girl. Don't worry, she might hate me but I don't hate her.' Dale was relieved – another reason Luke was his best friend was because he had a good heart.

The news about Melissa worried Luke, so he called her again. To his surprise she answered this time.

'Hi, Luke.' She sounded miserable and his instinct was to drop everything and go to her. Hearing her made him realise how much he had missed her lovely voice – the one he would hear after every show, meeting or interview, and every night and morning. Melissa was the person he called when he wanted to share the good things in his life, and she calmed him when he was worried about something. Dale was a great help as a best mate, but it just wasn't the same. The thought of never hearing her voice again made him shudder.

'Liss, I know you wanted space but I need to see you, just a few minutes, please,' he begged. 'Five minutes is all I'm asking for.'

'Have you lost your mind, Luke?'

'Yes, I have,' he answered. 'This is wrecking my head.'

'Yeah, it sucks ...'

After a few awkward minutes she agreed to see him the next day. His spirits lifted a little, but Dale secretly knew where this was really heading and he just didn't have the heart to point it out to him.

*****

Luke sat outside the house he used to share with Melissa, both scared and excited about seeing her. The street seemed oddly quiet – maybe for once he was being left alone. But he doubted it.

The door opened as he approached, and he ducked in quickly. His heart skipped a beat as he saw her. He thought she looked as pretty as ever, but tired, sad and thinner. Her navy cords, which normally hugged her figure, hung off her. He knew she wouldn't be eating properly. Melissa wasn't a comfort eater, in fact the opposite. If she was sad or worried she couldn't eat, but instead chain smoked to get her through.

When she saw him, Melissa thought about running to him and forgetting everything. They could lock the doors behind them and hide until the world forgot about them. But the doubt and the hurt would be locked in with them. Luke looked so hopeful that she almost felt cruel.

'Hi, beautiful.'

'Don't say that,' she snapped. She didn't want him to be nice to her because it would make what she was about to do so much harder. Seeing the hurt on his face made it easier, she thought. They went through to the lounge and she offered him a beer. He took it then she sat on the floor in front of him.

'I miss you,' he said reaching down and stroking her cheek. But she pushed it away.

His touch made her realise how much she missed him too, but she couldn't let him get to her. She'd made her decision, and she had to stick to it. She asked him again to be honest with her but he said the same thing he had said all along. He couldn't remember.

They talked it through for over an hour but ended up going round in circles and she still didn't get the answers she wanted, so she decided enough was enough. Luke had hurt her and she was hurting him now by giving him false hope. This was the end.

He'd be leaving in two weeks to start their American tour so she had to let him go. If he wanted that life then he could have it, and he needed to be free from all this – they both needed to start rebuilding their lives.

'Luke, I still love you, but you've broken my heart.' She looked at the floor because looking in his eyes would make it worse.

'Liss, please don't.'

'I'm sorry. I've tried, but I can't get the image of you and *her* out of my head. It makes me sick. I can't bear it, that slut's hands all over you. You promised me that I was the only one you wanted.'

He told her again that she was, and it was all a pack of lies, but it was no good. Melissa told him to go to America and enjoy the tour, without her holding him back. He could live that life and maybe one day when they'd grown up and he'd got it out of his system they could at least be friends. But right now she wanted him to leave her alone, and move on. It was killing her to be so close to him, and she felt confused by all her emotions. The part of her that loved him and wanted him was fighting with the part of her that hated what he had done, and wanted him gone. These emotions raged against each other and his begging didn't help. He looked so lost, and she wished she didn't love him so much.

She stood up, grabbed her purse and pulled out her credit cards. She gave them back to him, then grabbed Chloe from the spare room and handed her back to him too. She walked to the patio doors and stared out. 'Please, if you have any feelings for me, prove it by doing as I ask and leaving now.'

Luke placed the cards on the coffee table. He told her they were hers and she could use them if she ever needed them. She shook her head, but he left them anyway.

'I meant it when I told you I loved you, and that never changed. But I guess you never knew me at all,' he said before he left.

'No, I guess I didn't,' she whispered.

Melissa waited until he'd forlornly packed his stuff into his car and driven away, then she let it all burst out as she collapsed to the floor. Her life had just walked away. She cried till her throat was raw and there were no tears left.

Luke put his foot down, and tried not to cry. It wasn't permanent. He would win her back, he thought to himself as he drove to the only person he could trust right now.

*****

'Bee, I know you don't like me very much right now, but I need to see Dale,' Luke said as Beth opened the door to him. He looked so awful that she took pity on him.

'Fine, come in,' she said as she shouted for Dale to come and deal with it.

Dale ran down the stairs, but his smile faded as he saw the look on Luke's face as he stood numbly in the doorway. Dale ushered him inside, and he immediately broke down.

'I've lost her. She won't listen to me.' Melissa had reduced him to tears. The only other girl who had ever done that was Chloe, but that was different.

'Why can't I remember anything?' He smashed his fist into the wall. 'This has hurt her so much, and I don't know how to fix it.'

'I'm sure in time it can be fixed,' Dale assured his friend.

Beth didn't answer, but she was confused. Luke was devastated about losing Melissa and she could see the sheer shock in his face. Beth knew that if Luke couldn't prove he hadn't cheated, he would never get her back. Melissa had made a promise to herself that she would never take a cheat back, no matter how much she loved them. Beth knew she wouldn't make exceptions, not even for Luke. If she didn't have absolute trust in someone, it was over.

Beth watched as Dale talked to him. The famous front man, the up and coming king of rock, crying over a girl, and Beth didn't know what to believe any more. The fact that Luke loved her with all his heart was clear. You could see it in his eyes when he looked at her. So why would he be so stupid, when he knew very well that in this day and age, celebrities couldn't put a foot wrong without being snapped?

# Kicked

May 2014

'Please ... stop!' Kelsey begged as the boot of her attacker made contact with her arm. Rather than stopping, she laughed and did it again.

'No way, skank,' the girl hissed at her. The attacker was a big girl with ash blonde hair, pushed under a pink baseball cap. She glared down at her shaking victim.

'Give her some more...she deserves it,' her friend laughed, egging her on, yet not actually taking part in the violence. The friend was shorter, with bobbed auburn hair. Both were wearing distinctive black hoodies, with Black Eagles gig dates listed down the back, and a band logo on the front.

Kelsey knew she was in trouble as soon as the girls followed her into the toilets. She hadn't been out in weeks, and now wished she'd stayed hidden. But Darren wouldn't have it. She had run out of excuses, and she had to 'be nice to his friends', as he put it.

Kelsey still owed him £3,000, but that was just a way to keep her chained to him. Darren said he was her boyfriend, and that he loved her, but in reality he was her pimp who had trapped her when she was sixteen. She'd had nothing, she was lonely and scared when he found her on the street, cold and hungry. She wasn't a bad person, she had just made bad choices. Darren was nice to her at first. He took her in and showered her with presents, giving her all the things a girl wanted in life. Then he started taking her to clubs, and got her into drugs. Kelsey felt as though the life she suddenly had was like a dream come true, and he was her knight in shining armour.

But what she didn't realise at the time was that nothing comes for free.

They'd been 'dating' for four months, when Darren suddenly turned. He told her that she had to repay him for all the things he'd given her.

'I'm not made of money,' he'd said.

Kelsey had no money, and he knew that. He said she could pay him back in other ways by helping out some of his friends. She begged him not to make her do those things, but he had a hold over her, and she knew she had no choice. He reminded her that she needed to help him, and she had to repay her debt. He gave her more drugs to help her get through it, and she was becoming addicted.

'Kelsey, baby, do it for me. You know I love you but he'll give us three hundred just for a couple of hours with you. All you have to do is be nice, do whatever he asks then I'll come and get you later,' he would say.

Kelsey was so young and naïve then, and she believed what he told her. She thought Darren actually loved her. But in reality, he was an evil predator who abused vulnerable girls. No matter what she did, she would never clear her debt, and nor would the other four girls under his spell.

Luke Black was supposed to free her from all this, but no, she had failed there too.

It was all such a mess. She didn't realise how bad she would feel after going through with it. It wasn't as though she knew Melissa Webb, so what did it matter, she'd thought. But it did matter, because what Kelsey did destroyed an innocent girl's life. Seeing her boyfriend like that must have been heartbreaking, and Kelsey wished she could take it all back; rewind to that night and walk away from the hotel and Luke Black.

'Girls like you are disgusting. Melissa's worth a million of you,' the girl taunted before kicking her again.

'Have you seen yourself? I mean, look at her, and look at you!' The bigger girl pulled Kelsey in front of the mirror and held up a magazine with a picture of Melissa and Luke leaving a bar, hand in hand, smiling. 'Look at them, look what you did!' the girl said shoving another magazine in her face. These were recent pictures of Melissa on one of the rare occasions she'd left her house, looking a shadow of former self.

Melissa looked miserable, heartbroken. Even the pictures of Luke made her feel bad. He looked shell-shocked, his handsome face lost.

Despite what she'd been through, Kelsey had never regretted something more than this. She had caused it, and she couldn't change it. But her need to survive was important, and she had needed the money.

She needed to try to escape from Darren's clutches. And she still needed more.

'I know what I did was wrong, but it wasn't just me. I'm not the only one to blame in this. You don't know anything about it...I never meant to hurt anyone!' Kelsey yelled, kicking out in defence.

The girl's friend joined in the attack, laughing while they punched and kicked her until they finally got bored and fled, leaving her battered and bruised, crying on the floor.

She finally managed to sit up, every part of her body aching. She held some tissue to her split lip, and reached for her phone which had been kicked across the floor. Calling a number she hadn't used in a while, her anger flared up again.

'I want money, or I will cause so much more damage. Don't think I won't open my mouth. I could drop you so far in the shit there'll be no coming back from it. You know I don't bluff. So pay up in two days, or I'll start talking.'

# Hospital – Dale (4)

October 2014

'Do I have to talk about this? I can't go over it again.'

Melissa begged for a break. Her knuckles were going white as she gripped the sheets, and the distress was clear on her face. Beth suggested that Dale took over for a while. Only Dale could explain the next part anyway. The Eagles had been on tour after the split, and Melissa had cut off all contact with Luke, so she couldn't tell that part of the story anyway, not fully.

Fox thought some insight into Luke's side of things would be useful. He needed to get a picture of him that wasn't from the devoted or scorned girlfriend perspective. He needed to know if there was anything else that might help their enquiries, and it was quite often the seemingly small things that held the biggest clues. He certainly hoped so this time.

'Mr Baxter, I'm aware of your loyalty to your friend but can I ask you to be completely honest about Luke's behaviour while on tour. How did he take the split?'

Dale looked at the floor then at Melissa. She nodded, giving him full permission to say what needed to be said.

'I know everything important – not much can shock me anymore,' she whispered.

Luke had held nothing back from her since they had reconciled their differences. She shivered, knowing that she was about to hear more upsetting things. Dale sat forward in his chair, his hood hiding most of his face. Melissa wanted to reach out and hug him – he looked so sad, but mostly he looked tired.

Beth must have been thinking the same because she took his hand before whispering in his ear, 'Luke isn't a bad person, he isn't.'

Dale's tone was already defensive. He knew that what he said next would not paint Luke in a positive light. He explained how Luke had pulled himself together in time for the tour, and initially seemed surprisingly focused. Nobody suspected there were any problems, apart from the obvious one that he seemed to be starting to deal with. They all knew Luke was hurting over losing Melissa but, as the saying goes, the show must go on.

The tour itself was a success because on stage Luke was always on fire. But they could all see as the tour progressed that he wasn't himself. Dale explained that about half way through the trip, while they were in Chicago, he began to worry about Luke's behaviour. After forcing him to open up, which caused a great row, he finally got him to crack. The truth had spilled out, and the full extent of Luke's breakdown had been confirmed – to those on the inside anyway.

'How bad was it?' Fox asked

'Luke's no angel – I won't sit here and lie. His drinking increased, but his drug use was the real problem. Cocaine mainly, but whatever he could get his hands on really.' Dale shifted uncomfortably in his chair like a naughty schoolboy in front of the head teacher. None of them were angels.

Luke had wanted to forget his hurt, forget how much he missed Melissa, so he made himself feel nothing instead. He was either drunk or on drugs, but mostly both.

'People assume we shag anything that moves, but it's bollocks. He isn't like people think he is. There's this image that we all have, just because we're in a band, but it is a false one.'

Dale explained that as much as they loved what they did, it was hard work. 'Every night you have to give the same amount of energy, give each new crowd the same good show. It's a lot of pressure. People forget we're human beings and after a while it takes its toll.' He explained how Luke's moods changed from one day to the next, and he didn't trust anyone.

'Then, in Chicago, he had slept with a fan. He picked her out of the crowd and took her back to his room without even asking her name. Next morning she left and he didn't even mention her. It was as if it hadn't happened. He'd slept with several more over the next few weeks.'

Melissa sucked in her breath. It wasn't a secret, but she didn't like to hear about it again.

'I thought that was the life of a rock star,' Lee Noels chipped in, without thinking. He hoped the others got the joke, but they didn't. His boss glared at him, giving him a clear message that it was not appropriate. Noels face flushed red, and he apologised.

Fox was beginning to see into their world, with no PR spin or unfounded rumours tainting it for the world's entertainment.

Dale shook his head, irritated. He hated the assumption that if it had a pulse and tits, they would shag it. 'I've known him most of my life, and I know the real Luke.' He explained that Luke had always been picky when it came to women, and he had no interest in sleeping with just anyone. 'It takes someone very special for Luke to show any interest. Amber was a rarity, and a mistake, and we all wish he'd never met her. But you live and learn. Luke is always thinking and writing. He finds it so hard to switch off that he needs someone who understands him and accepts his passion for music. Someone who will be there for him when he needs them, but give him the space to do what he loves one hundred per cent, without stress ...'

Dale trailed off, looking guilty. 'He was in a bad place ... just a bad place, that's all. He really isn't a bad person.' Dale hated talking about Luke like this. It felt like a betrayal. But finally he continued, knowing he had to explain about how their tour rows got worse.

'Arguing sometimes is normal when you tour, and it isn't an issue. Living in each other's pockets, sometimes you just piss each other off and need space for a bit.'

Dale explained how Luke became a time bomb. They never knew what mood they would find him in each day. He became paranoid to the point that he convinced himself the rumours about Toby and Melissa must be true and it had been Toby that had screwed him over, in order to have her all to himself. This was right before their show in Portland, and it caused the biggest row in the band's history. It was a miracle the gig went ahead.

Ray and some of the bigger members of the road crew had to restrain Toby, who was obviously incensed by the accusation, but mainly hurt by it.

'It was a mess, but we have a good manager who sorted us out, and made us bury it for the show. He reminded us that we couldn't let our fans down.'

It had been hard for them all. It was the first show where they had to fake everything. Each smile and bit of banter was forced. Luckily, Toby could just hide at the back and let the three front guys run the show. He did what he needed to do, and when their last song ended, he got up and left the stage. He was still raging and even though his drum kit had taken a severe beating, the feeling of hurt was still raw.

Ray made them sit and talk it through afterwards. Luke knew full well he had been out of line and after much apologising, Toby accepted it. The official reason given for the late start to the show was that Toby had been ill, but after seeing a doctor had been given the all-clear to carry on, not wanting to let the fans down.

'I should have seen it coming. Looking back it was obvious.' Dale's shoulders slumped and he looked at the floor as the memories of that horrible time came rushing back.

'I seriously need some air and a fag.' Melissa went to the bathroom and threw on some jeans and one of Luke's jumpers. Wearing his clothes wasn't something she did very often outside the house, but right now it was the closest she could be to him. It still smelled of his aftershave and she breathed it in as she pulled up the hood and tucked her hair underneath. She pulled the cords to try to cover her face as much as possible. Her Ray-Bans covered her eyes, like a shield from the world. Luke had said to her once, 'Your eyes are the doors to your soul. If people can't see them, they can't get to you.'

Her hand caught something as she pulled it from her holdall. It was the *Highway* magazine that had featured their first interview. Luke stared at her from the front cover. Her legs shook and she steadied herself against the wall. Dale leapt from the chair hearing the quiet sobs, and pulling her towards him, he held her tight.

'I feel so empty. I just want him home safely.' Melissa sobbed against Dale's chest.

Jean swallowed her emotions and joined in the embrace, as did Beth.

'We all miss him,' Jean whispered and kissed her daughter on the top of the head.

Beth wiped a tear away. Jean had noticed a change in Beth. There was something different, but she couldn't put her finger on it. She could tell that Beth was holding back on something. There was a pleading for help in her eyes. She looked scared as she comforted her best friend. Melissa would be her first point of contact in a crisis, but she couldn't rely on her now because she was in the mist of a crisis of her own. So whatever it was, it couldn't be discussed now. Jean decided she would talk to Beth later when she thought the time was appropriate. She wasn't happy about Melissa leaving the room, but she had to keep busy. She would also prefer it if Melissa didn't smoke, but she was an adult and could make her own choices. And she was worried about the attention Melissa would get from outside. The fans were not the problem, it was the photographers.

'There are fans outside?' Melissa asked, spinning round to face her mum, who nodded. 'How long have they been there?' Jean told her they had been there since she was brought in, and had refused to leave. 'They must be freezing!' She wanted to see them. They might listen to her and go home. The band had some loyal and devoted fans, and although some were a bit weird, most were really cool people and Melissa felt a duty to make sure they went home safely. But Mick reminded her that it wasn't her job to look after every stray fan she came across.

'Dad, I know that. But if they'll listen to me and it gets them home and off the streets then I should do it. The boys have some young fans and I couldn't forgive myself if they got ill or something happened to any of them.'

Mick wasn't happy about it, but he agreed to go with her. Deep down he knew that Luke's fans were also her fans, and she felt a responsibility to make sure they were safe. They would listen to Melissa.

'I'm coming too!' Beth called, grabbing her jacket from the chair Dale had been sitting on. He grabbed her arm gently and pulled her to him, whispering something before kissing her softly on the lips. Melissa noticed that his eyes were searching hers for something, hope maybe. Beth stroked his cheek giving him her confident smile before whispering something that Melissa couldn't hear.

'Just be careful,' Dale said as they left the room. He wanted to go with them, but Fox needed more answers from him. Besides, he wasn't in the right frame of mind for it and he knew that nobody would want to have to bail him out for assaulting one of the pap's, which under the circumstances was a possibility.

Melissa took a deep breath as they approached the doors to the outside world, which at the moment seemed almost alien, scary even. It would be the first time she would be facing all of this without Luke to help and comfort her, and protect her if they got too close. Her dad was there by her side, but she wanted her boyfriend to come home.

*****

'Melissa!' The shouts began instantly. A group of fans were standing just a few feet from the entrance. Melissa held her hand up as an indication to just give her a few minutes. But she had acknowledged them, so they quietened a little. She lit a cigarette as she saw the press pack heading her way. She stood her ground and smoked her cigarette, trying to ignore them as Mick held them back as much as possible. His daughter would never be left alone, but she was learning to deal with it much better these days. After what she had been through, it didn't seem quite so bad.

'Melissa, what's happened?' Click click.

'Where's Luke?' Click click click.

'Who attacked you?' Click click click.

'Did Luke do this to you?' Click click click.

She froze for a second at the last question but closed her eyes, counted to ten and swallowed the urge to scream at the idiot who had said it. Eventually, she made her way to the fans, recognising Tess straight away. Tess threw her arms around her, the relief echoed in her embrace. She asked Melissa about Luke, tears spilling from her eyes. Tess was their first official fan and ran one of their biggest fan websites.

'Tess, I'm fine – you must go home, darling.'

'No.'

'Please, Tess, for me.'

Tess begged to know about Luke, her tone a little demanding, and Beth glared at her. Melissa was fragile and didn't need any more stress. Beth's look made that very clear.

'Luke is...missing,' Melissa said, her voice low and weak. The colour drained from her face and her vision blurred then everything went black. Mick caught his daughter before her head hit the floor, cradling her as he carried her back inside, yelling for help. Beth followed, shouting at Tess to tell the fans to go home. To the waiting pack of reporters, her message was loud, clear, and full of venom.

'Drop dead you heartless bastards!'

*****

'Luke Missing! Melissa hospitalised, collapsed ...' was the headline next morning.

Mick watched his daughter sleep. Her breathing was steady and calm, and he wished she could stay that way until all this was over. Her doctor had said there were to be no more questions until the next day on medical grounds, and definitely no more excursions out of her room. She was suffering from exhaustion and needed nothing but rest. Mick rested his head against the wall, feeling sleep start to take over, but it only lasted a second.

'Mick,' Jean's voice cracked under the strain as she returned from calling Luke's parents to see if there was anything to report. The news wasn't good. Jean was pale and her eyes looked empty. Mick stood up and led her out of the room and into the corridor, where Jean burst into tears.

'Oh, Mick,' she sobbed as she struggled to get the words out. Mick's hands flew to his face in shock.

'Please, god, no.'

*****

'Luke, no!' The scream from Melissa sent chills down her parents' spines. They saw what bit of strength she had left drain from their daughter as the words registered. The devastating news tore her heart out and crushed it.

A body had been found floating in the Thames.

It couldn't be Luke, she told herself over and over.

Luke's parents had been asked to go and identify the body . Her confused face searched her father's for answers. Everyone knew Luke, so it couldn't be him if they needed his parents to identify him. She cried, lashing out at her dad, the messenger, who had just torn away what tiny bit of hope she had been clinging on to.

Mick gripped his daughter's shoulders to steady her, as the words stuck in his throat.

'Princess, I'm so sorry.' Mick had to explain to her that although the young man fitted Luke's description – age, hair, build and even tattoos, he had been very badly beaten. The injuries to his face were so severe it was difficult to tell. Melissa went deathly white and the sound that came from within her made her parents jump; it was like an animal being tortured. She was hysterical, and had to be restrained as she threw herself on the floor screaming for Luke. Her parents struggled with her, begging her to calm down but she had snapped. Everything she had been subjected to rushed to the surface and boiled over. She was unable to control herself any more. Her medical team rushed in and quickly assessed the situation. Due to her state of mind, they decided that sedation was the only way to calm her down and prevent her from causing herself harm.

'Do it, doctor – now!' Jean yelled as she struggled to hold her broken daughter.

# Sirens

October 2014

'Any news?' Megan asked as she arrived, out of breath, at Luke and Melissa's.

'No nothing yet ... I just can't believe this is happening!' Jo-Jo whispered. Her cherry brown hair fell loosely around her shoulders and her eyes looked sad and scared.

Tom came in from the balcony, where he'd been having a smoke with Toby, still trying to take in the news. Megan noticed he didn't have a hat on, and his hair hung messily around his face in untidy curls. He nodded in Megan's direction as Jo-Jo went straight to him, took his hand, and guided him to the sofa to sit and wait.

'Toby's outside, babe,' Tom said quietly as he put his head on Jo-Jo's lap and closed his eyes. She ran her hand through his hair, and sighed.

Megan gasped at how beautifully the living area had been decorated, assuming that it must have had Melissa's work. The colour theme was of course black and white. The walls were white, with a black leather sofa and chairs, state of the art TV and surround sound. The room needed nothing else. The main feature was a picture that covered half of one wall. It was Luke's acoustic guitar, with a blonde girl. She had her back against it and was holding the neck of the guitar. Her nails were beautifully painted with black and silver swirls, and her face was turned ever so slightly showing just enough of her face to know it was Melissa. The only item of clothing was a black silk lingerie set. Her blonde hair rained down and pooled around the bottom of the guitar. It was so beautifully done, it could have been an album cover. But this was definitely a personal thing. The two things Luke cherished most captured in one frame – sheer perfection.

Megan headed for the balcony, seeing and smelling the smoke that rose above Toby's head as he leaned over the balcony railing, in his own little bubble, watching the world go by.

'I'm sorry,' Megan said as she rested her hand on his arm. She felt his muscles tense just for a second then relax when he heard her voice.

He turned and pulled her into one of his warm bear hugs, but this time it was more for his benefit than Megan's. He brushed his lips against her neck.

'Thanks for getting here so quickly. Jay-Den didn't give you any trouble, did he?' Toby had called Megan as soon as he heard the news, wanting her to be there with him while they waited for Luke's parents to call with news, dreading it but at the same time desperate to know.

'Even Jay-Den has a heart. He's just as shocked as everyone else,' Megan assured him. 'Everyone's in shock, and they send their love and support.'

Toby smiled and leaned down to kiss her softly. 'Good, because I need you.'

With a little help from Melissa, Toby had eventually won Megan over, and things were going well. They were taking it very slowly - Toby was fully aware that Megan was shy and rather insecure. He asked about her day, just to pass the time. Her eyes were sad as she explained that it had been a hard day, cancelling all their scheduled work. She missed Luke too, and she was feeling their pain.

Toby noticed her expression change. 'You're hurting too.'

'Of course. Luke has always been good to me. You all have, and I don't always work with such nice people.' Toby noticed a slight change in her tone as she looked away and her cheeks flushed. He asked her what she meant.

'It's nothing,' Megan answered, dismissing it. He had enough to be dealing with without her whining about non important stuff. But Toby knew that something was wrong. 'Honestly Toby, it doesn't matter. Don't worry about it,' she insisted, but he wouldn't leave it. He was already very protective of her, and she wasn't used to it.

'If someone has upset you, then you need to tell me, or I'll have to punch everyone I see in case it was them.' He wasn't joking.

'You're a freaking nightmare. If I tell you, promise me you won't start a band war,' she begged.

'Nope, can't promise that. Look, as long as it isn't Aiden Bailey from that bunch of dickheads Death Wishes, then it won't be all-out war,' he laughed.

Megan's face fell and her hands went to her face as she tried to stop the tears. But it was too late. There had been several rumours about Bailey and his band and how they would lure girls to their hotels by pretending they liked them, only to be cruel to them when they arrived, and Toby suddenly had a bad feeling about what he was about to hear.

Toby never believed everything he heard as he knew full well what the media were like. But was this story about Death Wishes true? Was his girlfriend one of these girls?

'What the fuck did he do?' She could hear the anger already building in his voice as he assured her that they already hated that band, so she wouldn't be causing a war because Aiden and his merry band of idiots had already started one.

'How?' This was something she didn't know about.

Toby told her about Amplified and how he'd been rough with Melissa. She felt a bit better knowing that she would already have their backing. She turned and rushed back inside, wiping away her tears. She still didn't want to tell him because it had been a horrible experience, and she still felt so stupid.

'Hey, what's the problem?' Jo-Jo asked looking up from the sofa where she was sitting with Tom. Toby followed her inside, looking very angry.

'It really doesn't matter. I don't want to cause any trouble. Toby, please don't push it. You're stressed out and this won't help you.'

But he was not going to let it go. 'Tell me. Now!' he yelled, making her jump and immediately hating himself for doing it. It was not going to make her feel better.

'Toby, don't shout at her. What the hell is going on?' Jo-Jo asked as she hugged the shaking girl and asked again what was going on.

'It really doesn't matter, Jo. It really isn't all that important.'

'It clearly is. Come on, it can't be that bad,' Jo-Jo said softly.

Megan knew it was best to get it over with. Maybe if she finally spoke about it she could move on. Toby crossed the room, picked her up and sat her on the sofa. 'I'm sorry I yelled at you. Come on, just talk to me,' he said.

Megan took a deep breath. 'Aiden Bailey is the reason I took so long to say yes to you,' she whispered. She noticed him tense a little just at the mention of Bailey's name.

Tom turned round and sat up. 'Toby, deep breaths.' Tom knew this wouldn't make the two bands any closer to sorting out their issues.

'He told me to meet him outside his hotel...ohhh, I feel so stupid, I can't tell you,' she sighed and looked at her boyfriend.

'You have to tell me,' he pushed. He really wanted a reason to smash Bailey's arrogant face in. Megan went on to explain that after Death Wishes had also signed to Sky Storm, Aidan would come in every week to see Jay-Den. He would stop and talk to her, and he seemed nice. One afternoon he asked if Megan wanted to go for a drink. He told her he liked her and wanted to take her out. She agreed because she was flattered and it had been a long time since a man had shown an interest in her. He told her which hotel he was staying in and to meet him there that night. She'd arrived at the hotel and went to reception as instructed and was met by one of his hangers-on and taken to his room. Aiden was there but so were the rest of the band. They were all drunk and Aiden had a brunette on his lap. The door was locked as she entered. There must have been about twenty people in the room.

'Look, guys, she came just as I told her to. She thinks I like her,' Aiden had said. The girls laughed loudly and pointed at her then he whispered something in the brunette's ear. 'Ah, Megan, you silly cow, nobody wants you. Have you seen yourself?' Aiden laughed and pointed his finger at her moving it up and down.

Megan had asked why he had done this to her and his response had been 'Because I can, and because you're stupid enough to fall for it'.

They made her stand there for fifteen minutes while they made horrible jokes and generally humiliated her, before finally letting her out.

'So there you have it. That night destroyed any confidence I had, and there wasn't much to start with. I didn't really like him, but is it so wrong to be wanted?' she whispered.

Toby scooped her up. 'Evil son of a bitch. I will kill him' he said, angrily.

'No, you won't. I don't want you getting into trouble. Promise me, Toby?' She begged him. He didn't answer her, because that was another promise he couldn't keep.

'I know I'm not pret—'

Toby cut her off before she could finish her sentence. 'Shh, don't you dare say that. You are beautiful.' He was frustrated with her for always putting herself down. OK, she wasn't stunning like Melissa, who barely had to try, or like Beth who was attractive in a scary kind of way. Or like Jo-Jo, who was the ultimate rock chick. But she was pretty in a shy, quiet way. There was a personality in there desperate to jump out, but her fear of rejection held it back. 'I want you,' he whispered in her ear and promised her that nobody would ever treat her like that again.

Jo-Jo hugged her and told her that Aiden Bailey would shit himself when he found out who she was dating.

'Really?' Megan asked, starting to feel better.

Jo-Jo explained that Death Wishes were scared of the Eagles. Luke had practically ripped Aiden's head off at Amplified. And Toby was, well, Toby. One look was all it took to make people back off. Even Beth had her own weapon of mass destruction – her mouth.

'You don't mess with our women, or our friends,' Tom said suddenly. He walked over and put his hands on Jo-Jo's shoulders. They made a great couple, even if they did have a somewhat competitive element to their relationship. Jo-Jo was the bass player for Echo and they liked to outdo each other. But they were good together and kept each other grounded. Jo-Jo took Tom's hand and they went onto the balcony to smoke, shutting the door behind them.

Toby kissed Megan and from the way he did so, she was left in no doubt that he wanted her. For a few minutes, they forgot about the sad situation. She made him feel like the world wasn't such a bad place after all.

'He will be found. I just know it,' she whispered, taking her turn to comfort him.

*****

'Mr and Mrs Black, are you ready?' The young policeman asked the distressed couple.

'No ... not really,' Debbie replied. Her heart raced and her whole body was shaking. She gripped her husband's hand as they were led down the grey corridor towards the viewing room.

They stopped outside a door and the policeman turned to them and explained that they didn't need to rush. They could take as long as they liked.

'When you're ready, they will lift the sheet. I must warn you the young man in there is in a bad way. I know this is terribly difficult, but you must be sure before you answer.'

Debbie asked for a minute, and he left them alone as requested. They were just seconds away from knowing for sure that their son was dead. Debbie wanted to run and hide, but she couldn't. She had to be brave. If it was Luke, then she had to claim him and say goodbye.

'What if it is our baby?' She cried. She was shaking so much she thought she might have to be carried in.

'Shh, don't say that. It's not him.'

'I can't carry on if it's our Luke...I feel sick, Stu.'

'Come on, Luke needs us to do this,' Stuart said, trying to give his wife hope, but inside he was also fearing the worst. 'Debs, come on. Let's not be here any longer than we have to.'

As the door was opened for them, Debbie felt her heart beating so fast and loud she thought everyone in the room could hear it. The room had grey walls and no windows. A single bed stood in the middle of the room, with a white sheet covering the body. A man waited for them, and greeted them solemnly.

Debbie took a few deep breaths, before walking over to stand right next to the poor boy on the bed, with her husband at her side. A selfish thought ran through her mind that although she wouldn't wish losing a child on any parent, right now she hoped this boy was another mother's son, and not hers.

'I'm not ready to say goodbye,' she whispered and felt the grip from her husband's hand tighten as he sensed her urge to run. He could feel it too.

'He has so much more to give, he can't be gone,' Stuart whispered back. It was then he realised how proud he was to have a son like Luke. He hadn't thought much about it before, but now all he could think about was how many people would be devastated if this was him. His son was a hero and a role model to a lot of people, and he had earned that status with hard work and sheer determination. Stuart wished he had been to see him play more. They had been to a few shows but not as many as they should have, at the time not wanting to cramp Luke's style. He realised he would give anything right now to watch his son on stage doing what he was born to do, and he felt empty at the thought it might be too late.

They both nodded to indicate they were ready, and the man stepped forward and lifted the sheet. They both stared for a few seconds, taking in the sight of the poor boy who lay lifeless in front of them. They were unable to make out the boy's face.

Debbie looked the body up and down, before her legs gave way. She steadied herself against a wall, and then doubled over as she threw up.

*****

'Dale, please talk to me, don't bottle things up,' Beth said. She was supposed to be resting but she couldn't. Dale was taking care of everyone, but nobody was taking care of him because he wouldn't let them.

'I'm fine.' He picked up his acoustic guitar and started to play.

Beth sighed. This was what he did when he didn't want to talk about things. But she wasn't having it.

'Dale, stop playing, please just stop.' She wrapped her hands around the neck and held the strings down. 'You are not fine.'

'Let go, B.' He really didn't want to talk.

'Please, Dale, he's your best friend. I know how important that is.' She could see the sadness in his eyes. Luke and Dale were so close, having spent half their lives together. She didn't know what he was thinking, and she was hurting for him.

Dale touched her face and shook his head.

'I can't.' He told her that if he started talking about it, then he had to accept it was really happening. And at the moment, they didn't know if it was true. It was helping him having Beth to think about. He could just focus on her and keeping her and the baby safe.

'I miss him too,' Beth said, and burst into tears. In truth it was she who wanted to talk about it. But she couldn't speak honestly to Melissa because they had to focus on keeping her positive. But everyone was slowly losing hope.

Dale removed her hands from his guitar and placed it on the floor. She rested her head on his shoulder and sobbed. It took only a few seconds before he gave in and his tears fell too. He mourned the loss of his friend and his career - he didn't want to work with another band. Luke could never be replaced as their front man. But more importantly, his best friend could never be replaced.

'I love you, Beth. You and the baby are keeping me sane.' He lifted her up and held her. She might be loud and feisty, but he was one of the few people who truly knew the real Bethany Watkins – the girl who just wanted someone to love her. Dale loved her, and he couldn't wait for their child to be born. But it should be a happy time and instead it was nightmare.

'I wanted to give you everything, but it's all over,' he said.

Beth looked up and kissed him. His hair tickled her face but she didn't giggle as she normally would. 'Don't worry about any of that. I just want us to be a family. I love you so much. Just promise me you'll never leave us,' she said, patting her stomach.

He kissed her and whispered, 'Never.'

They talked and cried together and Dale finally opened up about how he was terrified Luke was dead and about something happening to Beth or the baby. Beth assured him that if anyone tried to hurt any of her family, she would knock them the fuck out.

Dale laughed – he loved her kick - ass attitude.

*****

'I don't know what to say, or do, sweetheart,' Jo-Jo said. She stroked Tom's face as he blew smoke rings into the air.

He shrugged. 'There's nothing you can do.' He took her hand and kissed it. 'People think I don't care, but I do.' He had always been the same when it came to his emotions – he found it hard to express how he was feeling.

'I know you care – it's just the way you are,' Jo-Jo said. It had taken a long time to get with Tom but that was down to his quiet nature. He was a nice guy, but he just didn't like being the centre of attention. People called him the moody Eagle who never smiled, and he'd been accused of being ungrateful of their success. But that wasn't true. He just didn't show it all the time. He wasn't shy - he could be quite the wild one at times. But he was more comfortable with people he knew and trusted.

Tom was just as worried about Luke as everyone else, but he didn't really know what to do. Screaming and shouting wouldn't help, and crying about it wouldn't change things either.

Jo-Jo opened his jacket and wrapped her arms around him. He covered her with the rest so they warmed each other. They were still on the balcony, giving Toby and Megan a bit of time alone after Megan's revelation. Jo-Jo was supposed to be in the studio next day, but she really wasn't in the mood, and Cassie and Allie were also worried sick. But their manager reminded them that time was money, and they should be keeping busy to take their minds off things.

'I'll come with you,' Tom said. He didn't want her out of his sight until this was sorted. He had a weird feeling that it wasn't over. Amber had gone too quiet, and he just knew she was lurking somewhere.

'I'll be fine,' Jo-Jo assured him.

'I don't care. I'm not leaving you alone until that freak is off the streets and locked up,' he said firmly.

Tom had known Amber was trouble as soon as she walked in that night. It was the creepy way she watched Luke. There was a dark aura surrounding her, and Tom didn't think she was normal.

It was heartbreaking for all involved and the void was already being felt. The future looked bleak for them, but Tom knew it was Melissa who would suffer most. She had already lost him once, and now this could be permanent. He worried how she would cope.

'She's already been through so much,' Tom said.

'You care about her, don't you?' Jo-Jo had never heard him talk so gently about his friends.

'I care about all of you. But yes, I do care about her, she's like a sister.'

Jo-Jo nodded. The girls looked up to Melissa, even if they didn't say it, because she just handled everything that life threw at her. She didn't walk around like a diva who could have it all, demanding whatever she wanted. She just wanted Luke to live his dream and anything else that came with it was a bonus. Or maybe not, as it seemed right now.

Sleeping with random women got boring very quickly, and Tom was happy he had his own girlfriend now. He knew JO-Jo liked him because he was Tom, not because of what he did. They were in the same business, so she understood what life was like for him.

'OK, you can come along to the studio watch me in action – you might learn something,' she giggled, trying to lighten the mood.

'I look forward to it.'

Tom thought Jo-Jo and a bass guitar were the sexiest thing on the planet. He was very proud of her and loved to watch her play. But he'd almost lost his chance with her by playing hard to get, until Luke had told him to stop being a twat and just call her.

'I'm still better than you,' he joked.

'In your dreams, loser,' she shot back and pinched him. He *was* the better player, but she wouldn't give him the satisfaction of agreeing with him.

He was still worried about her being out of his sight.

She leaned in and kissed him softly. 'So ... don't leave me then.'

*****

'What do we do if it is him?' Jean whispered to her husband. He tried to reassure her, but in truth he didn't know the answer to that question.

How could one mad girl cause so much trouble? Mick thought to himself. Luke had become a massive part of so many lives, and if he didn't return, the effect would be felt not only in their lives but worldwide.

But Mick was more concerned about the damage this would do to Melissa. She had been through so much and he wondered how much more she could take. He was very proud of her for the strength she always seemed to find when it was needed most, but he feared this would be a bridge too far for her.

Jean lay down on the bed and closed her eyes to try and rest, but too much was going on in her head and she found it hard to switch off. She had only just dozed off when she heard the door open and assuming it would be a nurse to check on Melissa she ignored it at first.

'Jean,' a voice broke through her sleepiness and she was immediately alert. She sat bolt upright as Debbie and Stuart Black walked into the room, looking shell-shocked and dazed. Jean felt a stab of panic. It wasn't good news, she just knew it. They had come to break it to them in person.

Debbie sat down on the bed next to Jean. Mick could feel the sweat on the back of his neck as he waited for them to speak. Debbie broke down, sobbing as Stuart stood next to her, looking equally lost.

'Oh no, I am so sorry,' Jean said, sensing from their expression that it must be bad news. It couldn't be anything else.

Debbie waved her hands in front of her as she caught her breath and realised that Jean had jumped to conclusions.

'Sorry ... god no, it wasn't him.'

'Oh thank god!' Jean said, and embraced them both.

Debbie explained how awful it had been, and that the dead boy belonged to some other poor mother. But it wasn't Luke. It was a relief, but she still didn't know where her son was, so her torture was still going on. It didn't make her feel much better.

In a way, it made it worse because they might have to go through that all over again. Debbie explained about the boy, and how although the face was badly injured, she knew it wasn't Luke because the tattoos were all wrong. Also there was a small birthmark on the boy's left hand and Luke didn't have any birthmarks. A mother knows her child.

Debbie stopped talking and leaned over Melissa and kissed her forehead.

'Hi, Lissa.'

Jean explained that she had been sedated. 'She just screamed for him and they feared she'd hurt herself. This is such a mess. Dale's trying his best to stay calm but I can tell he's struggling too,' Jean said.

Debbie threw her hands in the air. 'Oh shit,' she cried out. They had come straight to the hospital and she hadn't even called the boys. She scrabbled frantically around in her bag looking for her phone and dropping everything all over the floor.

'Debbie, I'll do it. You just have some tea and relax,' Jean was already calling Dale's number because he was the first person who should be told.

*****

'Thank fuck for that. So where is the little bastard?' There was huge relief in Toby's voice, but now they were back to knowing nothing. Dale and Beth had raced round to tell everyone in person, and deep down Beth wanted to have everyone together. Jean had given them the keys to set up base at Melissa's. It was more private and would stop her from worrying about her home. Dale spent some time in Luke's studio checking over his guitars and equipment. It wasn't really needed but it made him feel like he was doing something for his best friend.

*****

'I'll make some coffee for you all,' Megan said, feeling the need to do something and get out of everyone's way. She was so relieved at the news and had been crying again.

But she struggled with her thoughts, wanting to talk to Toby about something else that had been playing on her mind. She wanted to be sure about her suspicions before doing anything, but she was worried about how to find out if she was right. As the kettle began to boil, a movement behind her made her jump. It was Beth.

'You don't have to fuss over us. You're not at work now,' she said as she leaned against the fridge, looking both pretty and fierce at the same time as was her trademark.

Megan wished she looked as good as Beth did in those blood-red skinny jeans.

They talked while Megan lined up the mugs, and messed with coffee and sugar feeling relief and more stress at the same time.

'Megan May, when will you start to relax around us? You need to start enjoying your new relationship. Toby adores you. And so do we.'

'I know, thanks. I am enjoying it, or at least trying to,' she said, blushing.

Beth reminded her that there were millions of women around the world who would kill to be in her position, so she should stop hiding and be proud of it.

'I've never had any proper friends before and Toby is my first proper boyfriend. I suppose I just don't want to get too comfortable, in case it all goes wrong. I've no experience at all and I worry about not being good enough.' Megan blushed again and went quiet. Great, she thought, another secret to be exposed tonight. She hadn't even told Toby as she was worried he would think she was a loser.

'Good enough?' Beth asked.

This was Megan all over, always feeling like they were better than her, and thinking that she was just being accepted because she was with Toby. Beth wished she had more confidence. That prick Aiden hadn't helped. Beth had been alerted to the Aiden situation because Jo-Jo was fuming about it and had texted her. Revenge was already being planned. The saying that the female of the species is deadlier than the male was true – the Eagle girls were definitely not to be messed with.

Beth sensed that there was more to this than just Megan's nervousness around them as a group, and she asked what else was bothering her. There were several things, but Megan had already revealed way too much for one day. However, she knew she had no chance of keeping Beth at bay.

'I've never ...' Megan whispered, then quickly turned away.

Beth moved to stand closer to her new friend so she could whisper to her without the whole place hearing them.

'Oh, you mean you've never...?'

Megan shook her head. She was worried that he would be expecting her to be something she wasn't. Only she had no idea what that was, because she had never done it. It was no secret that Toby had played around a lot, and it didn't bother her. She just wanted to live up to his expectations, and she worried she would be a disappointment.

'Does he know?' Beth asked.

Megan shook her head.

'Talk to him. It'll be fine, but you need to be honest. Toby won't expect anything, he just wants you to be you.' Beth told her that she was there for her if she needed any advice.

Megan smiled, thinking maybe she had finally found a little happiness.

'Thanks, Beth. Oh, damn.' Megan had opened the fridge to find no milk, just plenty of beers and two bottles of Moet. She laughed – this was Melissa and Luke all over.

'What do we do?' Dale was asking as Megan went back into the living room.

Tom and Jo-Jo were holding hands. 'We stick together,' Tom said. 'I don't want that head case going for anyone else.' Jo-Jo told him to stop worrying. She knew *she* was safe. Amber had done what she wanted, so why would she go for anyone else.

Megan grabbed her coat and said she was going for supplies. It seemed like everyone was setting up for the night. Melissa had her parents and a police guard at the hospital, so she was safe. They all planned to visit her again the next day.

'I'll come with you,' Toby said, but she shook her head and promised him she would only be ten minutes, no longer. Megan was the last person Amber would go for. It was doubtful Amber would even know who Megan was, so surely that made her the safest person of them all.

'No, I'm paying. I'll use the company credit card. Don't worry, I'll be back before you know It,' she said as Toby tried to give her money.

*****

Megan pulled her coat tightly around her as the icy air bit her face. The car park was nearly empty. Luke's Audi had been standing idle for some time, and next to it was Toby's toy – his black Suzuki with talons painted across the front. That was something she would have to deal with – his love of bikes. Trust her to pick a speed freak, she thought.

Toby wolf whistled from the balcony, and she giggled as she blew him a kiss.

Next to Toby's bike was Dale's black Golf GTI. That was more to her taste, and it made her laugh how they had all gone for black. Next to that was Tom's BMW – black of course. She arrived at her car, a white Mini, and fumbled around for her keys, dropping them because her hands were so cold.

As she stood up, a reflection in the window made her gasp for breath. The hooded figure grabbed her from behind and held her tightly.

'Just stay away, and keep your mouth shut,' whispered the voice.

Megan struggled but the assailant held her tightly while whispering threats in her ear.

'Toby!' she screamed as a knife was lifted up, then brought down heavily, sinking into her stomach. It felt like a punch at first, and it took her breath away. The knife was pulled out and she felt the wetness of her blood soak around her stomach and run down her trousers. Her hands clutched at the wound as the pain seared through her body. Her vision blurred as she was shoved forward, hitting her head on the car door before collapsing, gasping, to the floor.

'T-To-Toby ...' she tried to shout, but it was more of a gasp. It felt like she'd been there forever before his voice grew closer, then footsteps and then his arms picking her up.

'Megs, no!' she heard him shout as he cradled her, kissing her.

'Al ... Lu ...' Megan tried to tell him something, but she couldn't do it.

'Don't try to speak. Stay with me, do you hear me?' he begged, as her blood pooled around his knees.

'Shit!' she heard Tom shout as he held something against her wound. 'Why?' she heard him yell into the night air.

Beth screamed her name, but it was further away. Beth was closely followed by Jo-Jo and Dale, both girls hysterical as they watched the two guys, covered in Megan's blood, trying desperately to keep her alive.

People from the other apartments had heard the shouts and ran out to help. Luckily, a doctor who lived two floors below Luke and Melissa took over and did what he could, while Toby held her head on his lap.

'Inside, now!' Dale yelled. They couldn't risk anyone else getting hurt. He scanned the building and car park, his hand resting on Beth's stomach as the fear rose in his stomach.

The doctor's wife helped Dale get the hysterical girls inside, and some people who were visiting another resident formed a circle around Megan to shield her from the photographers who had been waiting in the shadows for a glimpse of the rock stars. The attacker seemed to have appeared from nowhere and vanished just as quickly.

'The girl's been stabbed. Have you no fucking respect?' One of the guys who formed the circled yelled. Toby hadn't noticed what was happening around them. His focus was on Megan's face, which was now colourless and her eyes showing nothing but fear.

'Jo-Jo, back inside, now!' Tom yelled at his girlfriend, relieved to see her not arguing as Dale took her back into the flat. She looked terrified and he wanted to comfort her, but he couldn't leave Toby or Megan until the ambulance arrived.

Toby had witnessed the attack from the balcony, unable to stop it. 'I'm sorry,' he sobbed, feeling guilty that he hadn't gone with her. It was a stupid move and he would never forgive himself if she didn't make it. Then it hit him, as the blood slowly ran into the gutter that she could die. His Megan was dying in his arms, and her gasping for breath was only making it more real.

She reached up and touched his face, smearing blood on his cheek as she tried again to speak.

'Sssaa ... Luu ... Ro ...' she made a frustrated sound and tried again. 'Check ssss...' Tears rolled down her face. 'Toby I ...' was her last attempt before her eyes rolled back, and she lost consciousness.

'Megs, please stay with me, stay with me ... please,' he cried as they finally heard the sirens approach.

*****

'Mum,' Melissa gasped as she opened her eyes. She felt awful, like she was in a bubble.

Jean smiled down at her daughter, relieved that she was awake and she could finally tell her the news. Melissa wept with joy when she heard that the body wasn't Luke's, even though they still had no idea where he was. But at least she still had hope now.

Jean knew that with good news often came bad, and she told her about the attack on Megan, sending Melissa back into a depression, and blaming herself again. Melissa was going mad in the hospital room, and wanted out. They were only keeping her there because of the circumstances now - it wasn't as if she was at death's door.

Melissa called her doctor and asked if she could go home. He wasn't concerned about her injuries now - they would heal just fine. He agreed that she could go later that day.

'I wish you would come home with us,' Jean said. She wasn't happy with Melissa going home, when she could just as easily stay with them so they could keep an eye on her more.

'I know, but I want to be in our home. I want to sleep in our bed and have our things around me.' She wanted to go straight away, and she felt frustrated at having to wait.

Jean realised that she wouldn't change her mind, and she understood that Melissa wanted Luke's things around her.

'Megan will be OK, won't she?' she asked her mum.

Jean assured her she was being taken care of, and it looked like she would be fine thanks to the boys and the doctor. Their quick reactions had saved her life. Jean fussed and told her over and over again that she was to go straight to bed once she got home, and definitely no housework.

'Housework's the last thing on my mind. I want a hot shower and a good sleep in my own bed.'

'Jay-Den's been around today,' Jean said. He'd been to see Megan and had also stopped by to check on Melissa. She didn't say anything. They both felt awkward now, and it was easier to avoid each other.

'I'm glad he at least showed some support for Megan,' was all she said after a few minutes silence.

Jean nodded. She knew about their little incident.

Melissa went to see Megan as soon as her mum had stopped nagging her. Toby had been a bit off with her, and she hoped it was just stress and not that he blamed her. But she could see how angry he was.

*****

Later that day, Fox and his team arrived at the flat. They wanted to see everyone who'd been there at the time Megan was stabbed. He was now looking at another attempted murder case, and had more questions for Melissa. He was getting concerned over the wasted time and added complications, but it made him think there was much more to this situation than he first thought.

'Let's continue, Miss Webb.'

# Until we die

July 2014

Melissa had been going out more on her own and trying to put her break up with Luke behind her. She'd been to a club the previous week with her cousin. Libby was an air hostess, so getting together was always a bit of a mission to organise but she'd made time to take Melissa out after her mother had called her, worried. Libby was the daughter of Jean's sister and was worried sick about Melissa's recent reclusive behaviour. She didn't think it was healthy. Melissa hadn't been keen to go out, but Libby wouldn't take no for an answer. Besides, she reminded her, it had been nearly two years since they'd caught up properly, and there had been quite a lot going on since they last saw each other.

The night wasn't as horrific as she'd worried it would be, and she'd been chatted up by a guy called Curtis who seemed nice. At the end of the night he had walked them to their taxi. Libby had got in and told Melissa to go for it - it was time to move on, she suggested.

'Thanks for the drinks,' Melissa said as she stood awkwardly in front of Curtis.

He stared at her and nervously messed with his hair. 'You're welcome...err, sorry about asking personal questions about...well you know,' he said awkwardly.

Melissa shrugged. 'It doesn't matter.' She could see the paparazzi clicking away waiting to capture something to confirm that she was moving on from Luke Black. She wanted to feel OK, but she didn't want to kiss this guy in view of the watching pack, so she asked him back to her house for a coffee.

It surprised her and disappointed her at the same time. Melissa had never done that before with a guy she had just met, but she was lonely and just wanted to feel something again. Curtis made her feel nothing though. His kisses didn't make her heart race, nor did his touch spark any kind of emotion. So before she made a huge mistake, she stopped things before they got too far.

'You prick tease,' he accused as he left.

'I've been called worse,' she responded. His insult barely registered.

But Curtis made himself feel better with his story a few days later. Melissa had been waiting for it – nothing surprised her any more.

'Melissa led me on for drinks to get over split from Luke Black ...'

Melissa didn't read it all. She wasn't interested in what it said. It was nothing compared to those pictures of Luke, and nothing could hurt her more than they had. Luke saw it too and it pissed him off. It wasn't completely made up, as she was snapped with this guy in a bar, so he knew she had definitely had contact with him.

Luke tried to call her but again she ignored him. The result was that he drank too much before appearing on a TV show, and had threatened to punch someone in the crowd who heckled him. The producers shut the show down as the guy accepted Luke's challenge, and they'd scuffled with each other briefly, until security pulled them apart. Dale gave the guy a dig in the ribs in the melee, for good measure. Luke was labelled a thug, but he pointed out that things the man was shouting about his personal life were out of order.

Luke had gone into meltdown again, and Dale called Melissa, once again begging her to speak to him. But again she refused. She couldn't pick up the pieces for him when she was still trying to mend her own broken heart.

Beth was still stuck in the middle. She'd been a rock for both Dale and Melissa, but it was hard for her. She had to stay civil with Luke because it had threatened to come between her and Dale. She didn't want to have anything to do with Luke but that wasn't practical. She had to see him sometimes, and she couldn't stop Dale from seeing his best friend. Melissa didn't want anyone feeling they had to take sides, and she'd told Beth not to worry about her – she was going to be fine. But deep down she hated being on the outside now, and missed them all so much. Melissa was angry with Luke and hurt, but at the same time she couldn't help missing him. And as each day passed it got harder to stop herself from picking up the phone and calling him. It didn't help seeing his face everywhere. It was torture every time she switched on the radio and heard his voice.

*****

‘I wouldn't take him back, if I were you,’ the woman standing behind Melissa in the queue at the newsagents commented. ‘Yeah, the guy’s a cheating scumbag. I’d have cut it off if I were you,’ said the woman's friend. Very helpful, Melissa thought.

She paid for her cigarettes, and without even responding quickly left the shop, ignoring the magazine racks which were still dominated by stories about them both. This week’s big rumour was that Melissa was starving herself and was devastated that Luke had moved on with Ivy Lovette, an American model. It was complete rubbish - he was still single, and Melissa knew that for a fact. She had her best friend on the inside so she knew as usual it was a fabrication.

The sun was shining for a change, so she went home and changed into her running gear. She grabbed her iPod and turned the music up loud so she could drown out the world. It didn't start off well. It had been a while since she had even picked up her iPod and her heart sank as a familiar voice sang into her ears. She flicked to the next album and Cassie’s voice sang to her. She left the house and ran down the street and along the seafront, feeling the stress slowly drain from her body. She had missed running and was determined to go back to her dance class next week. It was time she accepted her decision and began to live again. Ignoring the stares and pointing, she ran for over an hour, enjoying every minute of it, even though she was a bit out of shape.

*****

As Melissa arrived back home, her phone rang. It was Beth, calling to demand that she ‘get her arse up to London asap’ for a few drinks and late lunch. She showered and dressed the way the old Melissa would have done. She hadn't done anything wrong, so she didn’t want to hide any more.

An hour later, she looked and felt ready to rock. She put on her favourite heels, tight denim jeans and grabbed the Chloe bag which Luke had bought her – she deserved that at least. She had put on a very small amount of make-up, wanting the slightly natural look. Luke had always told her she looked better that way. ‘You can do this ... don’t be a loser,’ she told herself as she left the house, doing her best to hold her head high. She headed for London - the old Melissa was back.

*****

'You had a good night I see,' Dale commented as he walked into Luke's room and saw the rolled up notes and empty cans on the table.

'It's too early, come back later,' Luke said as he stumbled around the room, shaking the girl who was asleep in his bed. He looked like a man who had not had much sleep and the room looked as if there had been at least twenty people partying in it, not two. 'Hey, darling, you have to go. I think your boyfriend will be sending out a search party soon. Your phone hasn't stopped,' Luke said to her as she stirred.

The girl sat bolt upright as she looked at her watch. 'Oh shit, he'll kill me. Listen, thanks for an awesome night, Luke, but it never happened, right?' She jumped up and dressed quickly.

Luke called Ray and asked him to get the girl home for him. Ray did as he was told –he wasn't going to be telling anyone about Luke's night with her.

'Your secret's safe with me,' Luke said.

'Remember what I said – if you want something, fight for it. I hope you get what you want,' the girl whispered in his ear. He nodded as she left.

Dale thought she looked very much like Melissa, only she had much shorter hair and was at least a dress size bigger.

'Shagging fans is not going to win Melissa back mate.' Dale was growing concerned about his friend's behaviour.

'She isn't going to take me back, so I might as well accept it and have some fun. People seem to think I'm a player, so I might as well act like one. At least I remember this one.' He smiled at his friend, but it was a fake smile. He wasn't OK with any of it, but he didn't know what else to do. Melissa had made her decision and made it clear she wouldn't listen to him. She wouldn't answer his calls and had cut all contact. He missed her more than he would admit and that guy's story about her had made him feel even more hopeless. He knew he was spiralling out of control but he just didn't know how to stop it.

'You're happy with that, are you?' Dale asked him.

'Who wouldn't be...girls on tap and living the dream?' Luke replied unconvincingly as he threw his stuff in his suitcase ready for their final stop on their tour – LA.

'If you say so, but you don't fool me. I've known you too long.' Dale could see right through his act. Luke was hurting and was doing everything he shouldn't be, in an attempt to mask it.

Luke looked at him and shrugged, knowing his best friend was right.

But then he worried him even more by rolling up a note and starting his day the same way he had ended the one before. The girls meant nothing to him but sometimes he just wanted some company.

Ray popped his head round the door and told them they had two hours before they were due to leave. The girl who had just left Luke's room had been put in a cab and sent on her way safely.

Ray also worried about the change in Luke's behaviour. His cocaine intake had tripled on this tour and he had more or less swapped cigarettes for joints. Once they finished this tour, Ray knew he would have to sort him out before he really did self-destruct. Luke was too much of a talent to end up like so many others before him. He was a nice guy but he had been shown the darker side of fame and was learning hard lessons in the life of a celebrity.

'I'm going to the gym while we have some time,' Luke said as he headed out the door. It was mainly to take out his frustrations there – fitness was the last thing on his mind.

*****

'Are you sure about this?' Beth asked, for the fourth time that afternoon.

Melissa smiled and sipped at her glass of wine. 'Yes...go and have fun. I'm fine.'

Beth was flying out to LA to meet Dale and be there for their final show in two days' time. It irritated Melissa that Ray was softening a little on the whole girlfriend thing, now it made no difference to her.

'I hate leaving you. I hope Luke's calmed down now.' Beth had been worried after the last few phone calls from Dale, getting the impression that things weren't great.

'Yeah,' was all Melissa said in reply.

They were having lunch in Covent Garden before she left. Beth hated this part –leaving Melissa behind when she should be at her side. Even though Melissa always pretended she was fine, Beth could see the pain in her eyes when Luke or the band were mentioned. Beth and Luke had spoken so many times about Melissa that she knew, regardless of the situation, that he missed her just as much as she missed him. Beth had even begun to wonder about the scandal and whether it was all it seemed at the time, but if she tried to bring it up with Melissa it would look like she was taking Luke's side so she knew she couldn't do it. She was too afraid of losing her friend.

'Say hi to everyone for me,' Melissa said, as she finished her wine.

'Everyone?' Beth wondered if Luke was included as normally it was just say hi to Toby and Tom for me.

Melissa shrugged, but didn't say no, so Beth took that as a yes but didn't push it. They had another drink and chatted about anything but Luke or the band. It was a lovely afternoon and Melissa felt better than she had done in a while. It helped that so far they had been left alone.

But that was ruined when a group of men sitting at a table nearby started to look over at them. The men whispered and laughed then one stood up and took off his jacket. He had spiked dark brown hair with blonde highlights, and he turned to walk towards them. Melissa thought he was attractive, in an arrogant way maybe, and she immediately thought of Jay-Den. Beth could see where this was heading, and prepared herself for it. She straightened her back and put on her 'don't mess with us' expression.

'It's Melissa and Beth, right?' He had clearly already had a few drinks.

Melissa smiled politely and nodded, then continued her conversation with Beth, hoping he would take the hint and go away. But he didn't. He sat in the empty chair between the two girls.

'What would you like to drink?' he asked, but they both declined politely.

'Oh, come on. I've had a bad day. Won't you girls help cheer me up? He went on to say that he'd been robbed earlier that day and had two hundred pounds taken while he was at Waterloo Station. He continued to intrude on their lunch, becoming more and more annoying as the minutes went by, and Beth quickly started to find it hard to stay polite.

'Seriously mate, leave us alone,' she finally said, but he ignored her and carried on staring and talking at Melissa.

'So, do you want me to make you feel better? Your ex is a stupid fucking idiot. I would never cheat on you. Damn you are hot. How about you come home with me? I tell you what, come home with me and my friends and we can have a little party,' he slurred. The man's hand was on Melissa's leg and she hit it away.

'I don't think so,' she snapped. He laughed then asked her again, saying she should stay away from rock stars and hang with the big boys who actually made decent money.

'Oi, cretin, she said no,' Beth snapped, and glared at him. The day was completely ruined. What Melissa did not need right now was some moron treating her like a cheap whore. He then became rude, saying they thought they were better than him but in fact they were nothing but a couple of druggie cast-offs.

'You can do better than some cheating druggie scumbag.'

'He isn't a scumbag...you don't know him.' The words jumped out of Melissa's mouth instinctively, surprising her.

Beth leapt from her chair, calling the guy every name under the sun.

'You don't know them or us, so keep your evil comments to yourself...if you believe everything you read in the papers then you really are fucking stupid.' She jabbed her finger in his face, forcing him to take a step back. The guy was having his very own 'Beth Watkins experience' and it wasn't fun. The bar had come to a standstill, and all eyes were on him as he was put in his place by a girl.

'Look, it was just a joke,' he tried to say.

'It wasn't very funny. Now leave us alone. Anyone else want to comment on our lives?' She turned and shouted across the busy bar, but predictably there was silence while everyone suddenly felt the need to look at their feet.

'Good. None of you know shit about us. So keep your opinions to yourselves. My friend doesn't have to answer to any of you.' She turned and grabbed her coat and bag, and they stormed out, leaving the audience open-mouthed and the guy wanting the ground to swallow him up.

'For fuck's sake,' Beth cursed as they were chased down the street by cameras. Clearly the tweeters had been at it, telling the world exactly which bar they were in, and that there had been an incident unfolding. She pulled Melissa across the road, losing themselves in the crowd of tourists, before ducking into a quiet street where they finally lost their tail.

'Don't cry babe. Remember, keep smiling. That's what those bastards want, so not in the street, Liss, not in the street.' She could cry all she wanted behind closed doors, but not in public for the world to laugh at. Melissa took a few deep breaths and swallowed her tears.

'I'm trying so hard to be strong' she said, but it was almost a whisper. Beth told her she was doing great and everyone was proud of her. 'But it's not working, Beth. I know I should just move on but I can't.' She sat down on the pavement and lit another cigarette. She was still chain smoking, and drinking too much. A bottle of wine in the evening helped her sleep, she said, but for most people this would be just a glass.

Beth looked around them then crouched down beside her. They

seemed safe from prying eyes for now.

'You're going to be fine...you know I'm always here for you. Best friends forever, OK?'

'Until we die,' Melissa replied.

'Even after that – we'll haunt people together.' Beth did a rather lame impression of a ghost, making Melissa laugh and feel slightly better.

'I miss him, Beth. I think about him every day and I cry because it hurts so much. I thought it was going to start to get easier, but the longer it goes on, the more I miss him. I don't know what to do.'

Beth wrapped her coat around Melissa, sensing that they needed to have an honest talk before she headed to LA. She'd suspected for some time that Melissa wasn't coping as well as she tried to make out. She had lost her spark.

Once they were back at Beth's, Melissa admitted that there was a part of her that wanted to believe Luke. Their connection hadn't broken, but was just strained. She couldn't break free from it, no matter how much distance was between them.

'I'm falling in love with him more every day.' The love she had for him was still strong, and in her heart she wanted him back. But until he finally came clean and told her the truth, her head knew that there was no chance for them. She didn't believe that he'd said those horrible things about her, but clearly something had happened that night. She just wished she could know for sure if he had slept with her.

'I just want the truth from him ...'

*****

Once Beth had left for the airport, Melissa headed home. She felt better for being honest and talking it through. Beth had told her to talk to Luke if that was what she wanted. But she wasn't ready, and she knew it would be better to wait until he was home.

Jay-Den had tried calling her again. He had called a few times over the last month, but she had always ignored him and deleted his messages. He was the last person she wanted to speak to. His last message had been ridiculous. 'Melissa, please talk to me. I know you're hurting and I know it's him you love. I realise me and you will never happen. But I'm here if you need anything ... I just want to help.'

She poured herself a glass of wine and smoked another cigarette while she ordered a takeaway. She hadn't cooked in weeks and she knew she wasn't eating properly, but she couldn't be bothered. Cooking for one just seemed pointless, she thought, and it made her realise how lonely she was.

Cassie called later that evening to check on her. She'd been so supportive. She made it very clear that she cared about them both, and she wouldn't take sides over what had happened between them – she just wanted to be there for each of them as their friend.

'I'm doing OK, Cass ... I think,' Melissa said.

She didn't tell Cassie how she really felt because she had a feeling it might in some way get fed back to Luke, even if she didn't intend it to. And although Cassie was being a good friend to Melissa she had been honest and told her that she did not believe that Luke did or said what Kelsey claimed. But she understood that it was up to Melissa to make her own decision.

'He's a mess, Liss. Won't you please just call him, even if it's to call him a twat?'

Luke would phone Cassie a lot when he felt down, because she was a good listener, and for some reason he felt that with her he could open up about how he was feeling. He told her that he felt like a loser for being so cut up over a girl, and worried that he was losing the respect of the rest of the band. He also felt guilty because of his recent behaviour.

'I don't know, Cass ...'

'At least think about it, yeah?'

'OK. Maybe.' It was all she could give right now. In truth she knew if she heard his voice, even for a second, it would make things so much harder. If there were issues with the band, that wasn't her responsibility. It was Ray's job, she kept telling herself. But deep down she knew she could change everything with just three words.

'I forgive you,' wasn't something she was ready to say yet, even if it seemed lately that she was losing everything and everyone around her. She wasn't really part of the group any more, and she felt like a burden to Beth and her family. The thought of losing the friends she loved so much made her feel even more depressed. She would miss Luke most because deep down she loved him no matter what had happened. He had been such a huge part of her life. She would see Dale because of Beth, so she would always have him in her life. But she loved Toby and Tom like they were her big brothers too. Her heart sank all over again as the realisation dawned on her that even Cassie would eventually move on from her as her career and life on the road took over.

She knew she couldn't go on like this.

# Brass neck

July 2014

The taxi ride made Kelsey feel even more nervous and she thought she might be sick. She'd been walking around for hours, trying to find enough courage to go through with her plan. This was the last place she thought she would ever visit.

'Just drop me here,' she said to the driver, and threw a handful of notes at him before getting out without waiting for her change.

The walk up the street gave her a little time to compose herself, although she nearly turned back a few times. But she had come this far, and knew she had to go through with it. It was the right thing to do.

The lights were on and through the window Kelsey could see Melissa was on the phone in deep conversation with someone, only she didn't look happy. Kelsey was scared but she had come a long way and she couldn't back out now.

'Oh damn ... sorry, Cassie, I have to go,' Melissa ended their conversation as she heard the doorbell ring, promising to call back in a few days. She promised again that she would think about talking to Luke.

'Mum, if this is you checking...' her sentence was cut short and she fell silent for a moment as her brain processed what she saw in front of her. This was the last person she expected to see.

'What the fuck do you want?' Kelsey stood in her doorway, and immediately held her hands up, explaining that she wasn't there to cause trouble, she just wanted to talk to her.

'Talk to me about what?' The glare from Melissa was almost murderous.

'About what happened with me and Luke.'

The mention of his name made Melissa look and feel as though she had just been punched, but Kelsey felt even worse as she looked back at her, because she could now see first-hand the damage her actions had caused.

'What is there to talk about? What more do I need to know apart from you screwed my boyfriend, took photos, told the entire world in exchange for cash, humiliated me and ruined my life?' Melissa's tired mind had caught up with the situation, and she bellowed at Kelsey before moving to slam the door in her face. But Kelsey stopped her by putting her foot in the way, and yanking it back open.

'Melissa, please five minutes, just give me five minutes to explain it all, there's more to it than you think,' Kelsey begged her. She had to tell her the full truth.

'I'm not interested in the gory details of your amazing night with *my* boyfriend!' She hadn't thought for a moment the girl would have the brass neck to show up on her doorstep. It was unbelievable.

'You're nothing but a whore...now get away from my house or I'll call the police,' she snapped as she tried again to slam the door shut.

'I lied!' Kelsey yelled. 'I'm so sorry, Melissa, but I lied.' She backed up a few steps and fell silent, to let this sink in.

Melissa was momentarily dumbstruck.

'Get inside,' she ordered as she grabbed her and dragged her into the house. This was not a conversation to be having in the street.

'Lied about what exactly?' Melissa snapped, as she pushed the girl through to the living room. Kelsey stood there, looking pathetically at the floor, like a child in trouble with her parents, too ashamed to look at Melissa.

'Well?' Melissa yelled.

Kelsey jumped, and tried to compose herself as Melissa stood waiting. She was shaking like a leaf. She finally looked up.

'I'm sorry, but I never slept with Luke,' she whispered.

Melissa heard her words as clear as a bell, and she listened as Kelsey explained how she had set him up. Luke had never cheated, and he was telling the truth about not remembering. She'd drugged him with enough GHB to knock out a horse.

'You did what?' Melissa shrieked as she charged across the room and punched Kelsey so hard, she fell back onto the sofa behind her.

Melissa shook with rage. She had been wrong all along, and felt sick that she hadn't believed and trusted Luke. After all that had happened, it was actually she who had destroyed their trust, not him.

'I really am so sorry,' Kelsey pleaded as she rubbed her face where a bruise was already beginning to show. For a small girl, Melissa certainly packed a punch, Kelsey thought.

'Sorry? You're fucking sorry?' she screamed. 'Well that's just all fine and dandy then isn't it? Why the hell would you do an evil thing like that?'

Kelsey sat up, tears streaming down her face, and explained that she'd been begging outside Waterloo station when she was approached by someone who said that if she did them a small favour they would pay her four grand. All she had to do was take some photos and hand them over then disappear for a while.

'I didn't know who it was at first. I just thought four grand to take some pictures -brilliant.'

She went on to tell Melissa that the photos were taken and handed over, but she never saw a penny of the promised money. She admitted that going to the newspaper wasn't part of the plan, and she had done that off her own bat. They paid her £1,000 for the story.

'You drugged him, then what? Staged those photos while he was passed out?' she asked.

Kelsey nodded and looked at the floor. Melissa leapt at her, holding her down, screaming at her while she shook her violently.

'You sick twisted, evil bitch! You don't know what you've done! You could have killed him,' Melissa screamed. 'Have you seen the mess he's in?'

Kelsey knew from the reports in the media that he was in a bad way. It was one of the reasons she couldn't continue with her lies.

'I know. I hate myself more than you could ever imagine,' she murmured, breathless. 'I don't really know what you did to this Amber but—'

'Amber!' Melissa shuddered at the mention of the name.

Then it all fell into place as Kelsey explained how it was Amber who had approached her. She'd told Kelsey her deluded story of Luke being her sweetheart, and being stolen from her.

'That girl is scary. She talks to herself loads, and she's got hundreds of picture of him,' she said, laughing out of nervousness and fear.

Melissa wasn't laughing, and Kelsey stopped quickly.

'I don't understand how you even got to his room.' Melissa wanted the full story from Kelsey before she decided what to do with her.

Kelsey told her that she'd been instructed to meet Amber in a car park a few streets from the hotel. Amber had handed over a spare room key and the bottle of GHB. The plan was to wait in the hotel bar until they left for the O2, then get to his room without being seen, and find a way to hide until he returned. Amber knew Melissa and Beth wouldn't be there because it was Melissa's mum's 50th birthday and they were celebrating with her, so they were well out of the way. Kelsey had to wait until around two in the morning before she heard Luke and Dale heading back to their rooms.

They were laughing and joking and seemed to have been having a good time. Luke was a bit drunk, and staggered into the room alone. He'd opened a beer then phoned Melissa, but she'd been asleep so he'd left her a message simply saying that he hoped her mum had enjoyed her birthday, he missed her and he would be home tomorrow. And that he loved her.

'He left his beer inside and went out onto the balcony,' Kelsey continued. And that was when she crept out and put the GHB in his beer. She didn't know how much to put in, so she had tipped half the bottle in, then hid back in the wardrobe.

'He eventually came back in, picked up his guitar and sat on the floor, playing for a bit.' Kelsey stopped for a second and looked at Melissa who was just speechless.

'He's really good. I watched through the gaps as he scribbled in his book and tried different chords. You have a very talented and lovely boyfriend.'

'I did have. But you ripped us apart,' Melissa hissed.

Kelsey said he seemed drunk, but had no problem playing. Melissa laughed for a brief moment as she thought about him - he could drink gallons of beer like it was water, and still be able to play perfectly.

Melissa missed hearing him play, she missed the stopping and starting, the note taking and muttering, even if back then she'd found it irritating.

'Just play the goddam song, babe,' she would say.

'Hush, woman, I'm working on a masterpiece,' would be his usual response.

She realised she was smiling, but it only lasted a second.

'Get out of my house!' Melissa yelled, her blood coming back to the boil. She had given this girl enough of her time already. She had to get to Luke and fix things.

'Melissa, have you ever been scared?'

'What has that got to do with anything?'

'Everything. It has everything to do with it. I wouldn't have done this if I wasn't desperate and scared. I watched him and saw how different he was to what I'd read about him. And then that message he left you proved how close you were. He called you before he went to sleep – he wasn't partying with groupies like we were led to believe. I argued with myself but when you've no other option, you'll do anything to survive. If you'd been in the situation I'm in, you'd understand.'

Kelsey sobbed again and explained that Luke drank his beer as he played, but then his behaviour quickly changed as the drug took effect. It was awful to watch. He didn't seem to be able to focus, and he couldn't walk properly. It took about ten minutes before he was knocked out completely and collapsed on the bed.

Then she'd set up a camera and taken the photos, making sure they looked bad enough, to be credible, but good enough that he could be clearly recognised. All the while, he was out cold, and had no idea what was happening.

'What else did you do to him?' Melissa yelled, feeling sick at the thought of him being treated like this. It was sexual assault. If it had been a woman subjected to such an attack, they'd throw away the key, she thought. Kelsey assured her that she didn't do anything else, and she would now do anything to put it right.

'You can't fix this, the damage is done. You stay away from him, from us.'

Melissa stopped yelling and sat back down. She felt terrible that she had pushed him away when he needed her most. She had let him down.

'I don't know what else to say, but sorry,' Kelsey whispered. Melissa was about to grab her and throw her out, but the sobs poured from her and she collapsed to the floor, crying like a toddler. It was a horrible, desperate sound and Melissa stopped.

'Please don't make me go back to him. I am so sorry. Please forgive me. I've nothing and no one at all, and I'm so frightened. I'll do anything. I'll shout it from the rooftops if I have to,' she wailed.

'Don't make you go back to who?' Melissa asked, kneeling down next to the sobbing girl as her awful story poured out. She told Melissa about the way Darren called himself her boyfriend but in reality was her pimp, how she couldn't get away from him and that she didn't want to do those things any more. But saying no was not an option. If she upset Darren or his friends, he would beat her.

'That doesn't excuse what you did. We didn't deserve it. Couldn't you ask your family to help you?' Melissa was trying not to weaken at the sob story, but it was hard not to feel some sympathy for her. She seemed to be telling the truth now.

Kelsey explained that she didn't know who her parents were. Foster home after foster home had been her life from an early age.

'You can work things out with Luke, now you know the truth,' Kelsey said.

'Let's hope so,' Melissa replied.

The two girls sat on the floor and Kelsey told her the rest of the details of the story, warning Melissa to be careful because she really thought Amber was nuts. Amber had gone off at Kelsey a few times.

'She isn't going to be pleased with me for telling you. She said she'd kill me if I did.' Threats were part of daily life for Kelsey, so one more didn't phase her at all.

Melissa didn't want to feel sorry for her, but the more she listened the more she was beginning to. She told herself to snap out of it though, because she knew she had her own life to put back together. 'Don't forget what this bitch did to you and Luke,' she told herself sternly.

'I want you to leave, now!' Melissa pulled the girl up from the floor and dragged her to the door. Kelsey begged her to help her, but there was no way. Not after all her lies, not to mention the crime she'd committed. Kelsey grabbed Melissa by the shoulders. 'Please, I want to apologise to him, in person,' she begged again.

Melissa's anger got the better of her and she slapped Kelsey one last time before throwing her through the door and into the street, yelling as she did.

'You stay away from him!' She slammed the door behind her.

Kelsey hadn't expected anything else, but she felt better for telling the truth. She meant what she'd said about going public if that was what they wanted. The only thing left to do now was head back to Darren before he got suspicious about where she'd gone.

She had nothing else, and running away wasn't worth it because he would find her. The whole mess had been nothing but a huge mistake. She'd come out worst from it all as she never even got the four grand, and Darren had taken the thousand from the newspaper story towards her debt. Her life sucked, she thought as she pushed the note with her phone number through the door. She'd written it in case Melissa wouldn't see her.

It read, 'Luke and Melissa, I'm so sorry for what I've done to you both. I didn't sleep with Luke, it was all a big lie. I drugged him and took the photos while he was out cold. I'm disgusted with myself and I know you will never forgive me but I don't expect you to. I'm not proud of what I did, but I had my reasons. If you want to report me then go ahead. I'll accept whatever you throw at me. It can't be any worse than the situation I'm in now. My number is on the back of this letter. If you want to talk in person I will be happy to meet with you. I truly am sorry for the hurt and pain my lies have caused you. Kelsey.'

Melissa was pacing around the kitchen, her hands shaking while a confusing rush of emotions pulsated through her. Her mind raced. She was relieved, happy even, that Luke was not guilty, and there was excitement at the thought that maybe they could be together again. But she also felt terrified that everything had gone too far. She feared that Luke would be just as hurt and angry with her for not believing him as she'd been with him when she thought he had cheated.

She now knew that he was the victim in this, and she needed to see him, to kiss him and tell him how sorry she was for doubting him. That was all she could do, and she would have to hope that he was able to forgive her.

She decided that she had to go to LA and see him, even though she knew Ray wouldn't be pleased about her turning up and causing a scene. But she didn't care. She called her mum to explain what had happened. Jean was relieved, but also worried about what it meant for them now. Melissa packed a small case and got the first available flight, disguising herself as much as possible to avoid any fuss at the airports. She had enough going on in her head.

# Double Trouble

July 2014

'OK boys, this is the last one, so let's bring the house down,' Dale said in his team talk as they prepared to hit the stage at a packed LA venue.

'We always do,' Luke replied. Dale playfully punched his friend on the arm, who returned one equally hard. They laughed together, avoiding the elephant in the room as long as possible, but Dale knew he had to say something.

'Luke, I don't mean to sound like your mum, but you need to ease up on the white stuff and the booze.' Dale was concerned that Luke was heading for trouble. He knew it was hypocritical after doing a line himself, but Luke was obsessive and could become dependent on things. None of the others did it as much as he did.

'It's all good, I'm living the dream!' Luke said, smiling his cockiest smile. The crowd roared as Silver Daggers finished their set, making way for the headline act. They waited a few extra minutes to whip up the excitement in the crowd a bit more. Luke was 'totally buzzing' as he put it as he and Zac, the front man for Silver Daggers, chatted for a few minutes. Zac's girlfriend, Lyla, waited patiently with a group of girls who had tagged along for the evening, pretending to like her. Amongst them was a blonde, trying to look like Melissa, who seemed to be following Luke around. It was embarrassing, he'd told Zac. But he knew she was wasting her time because he was done with all that. He would be heading home soon and he wanted one girl and one girl only. He needed her back before he completely lost the plot. He was only truly happy when he was with her. When he was on stage, he could forget his issues for a few hours because he was in control. They were like gods on that stage and nothing could hurt them. But as soon as the shows ended, he was lonely again.

'Get on with it lads, that lot are going to riot soon,' Ray yelled, looking irritated. But then, he always seemed to look that way.

Beth was chatting to Dean about Luke. Everyone was worried about him, and talking to Dean was better than mixing with the hangers-on that had been invited backstage who didn't have a clue. Besides, most of them were awkward because they were intimidated by her, or they were jealous bitches. 'Pathetic,' she complained to Dean, and he laughed.

'We miss her too,' Dean said, knowing that Beth was missing her sidekick. Everyone missed Melissa - she had won over the whole crew.

'It sucks, Dean, but you can't blame her. He is such an idiot.'

Dean didn't answer, and walked off to check on a few things with the equipment as Ray yelled at them again.

'Get your asses out there!'

'Take the roof off, babe,' Beth said and kissed Dale.

'We always do,' he replied with a wink, then followed the others out to a huge ovation.

This was Beth's favourite bit – the roar from the crowd sent a shiver down her spine every time. But this time, it felt a little empty because she didn't have her best friend with her. Things were just not the same any more. But maybe one day, she hoped, as she sent her a message, 'I miss you, girl.'

*****

'I landed fine, Mum, don't worry. I'm in a cab and I'll be there in a few minutes.' Melissa had smiled at the text from Beth then had called her mum who was worrying as usual.

'What will you do – or say?' Jean asked, panic in her voice. She really wished Melissa had made more arrangements before jumping on a plane at the drop of a hat. Luke had no idea she was even on her way to LA. What if he didn't want to see her? Jean knew he had been just as upset when they split, and she feared that Melissa could be walking into more heartache.

'I don't know what I'll say yet. The plane was delayed so I'll be late getting there and they'll have started already. Don't worry, I'll be fine,' she promised. She'd decided not to tell her she didn't actually know how she would get in. It had dawned on her mid-flight that nobody would be expecting her and she didn't have a ticket because she never usually needed one. The plan was just to get to him – she hadn't worked out the details. It wasn't a conversation they should have over the phone, but on reflection, she was also a bit concerned that surprising him might not be a good idea.

'You that Eagle girl?' The cab driver said suddenly, and Melissa nodded, hoping that would be enough. But he was very excited about her being in LA, and in his cab. He knew the full story.

'Are you back with Luke?' he asked. Melissa said nothing and let him jump to his own conclusions. She couldn't be bothered to get into it.

The cab ride seemed to take hours, and it was gone ten by the time she paid the driver and stood outside the venue with no idea what to do next. They were in full swing, and she could hear his voice.

She had to get in there.

'Sorry, but I can't let you in. You don't have a ticket, and your name isn't registered,' the security guy said. He had a job to do, and he refused to budge on his decision.

She almost used those dreaded words, 'You know who I am, right?' but stopped herself in time. That would have been a major fail.

'Beth!' She realised that Beth was her only hope. After they'd finished screaming down the phone to make themselves heard, Beth got the message and hung up, telling her to stay where she was. True to her word, within ten minutes the security guard called her over. The man was massive, with dreadlocks that hung past his shoulders.

'Looks like this is your lucky day, baby girl. Come with me.' He took her round to the back entrance where Beth and Ray greeted her.

'Liss!' Beth screeched, and Ray smiled at her, seeming genuinely pleased to see her. They took her inside and Ray got her a drink.

'What the hell are you doing here?' He asked.

Melissa explained about Kelsey's visit and what she'd done. They both sat and listened, open mouthed in utter disbelief.

'It's disgusting,' Beth said, but was glad Melissa had given the girl her marching orders. Melissa was a sucker for sob stories.

Ray looked deep in thought. 'I think you need to speak to Luke, and let him decide what he wants to do. Liss, I really am glad to see you. He needs a kick up the ass.' He knew that Luke wouldn't take this well. But who would?

Melissa asked Ray how someone could get his key, but it was a mystery. He felt uneasy about it because only the boys and Ray himself had access to their rooms – and it certainly wasn't down to him. Melissa looked towards the side of the stage then back at Ray.

'Come on,' Ray said and took them both to watch the rest of the gig.

Melissa's heart pounded as she saw Luke. He was doing his thing, and she felt at home again. Beth hugged her and handed her a beer as there was a shout from behind them.

'Hey, trouble ... you're back!' Dean rushed over and picked her up. 'Great to see you.'

'Good to see you too, Deano.'

He asked her what had changed. 'Long story, Dean. You'll find out soon enough, but I need to talk to Luke first.'

Dean put her down, smiling, and headed off. He seemed just as relieved as Ray and Beth.

There were several shouts from the crew.

'Huh oh, double trouble are back.'

'Alright, Liss ... you here to give him a kick up the arse?'

'He's been a right miserable bastard.'

It made her feel like she was back where she belonged, and this time she knew she had to make sure she stayed for good.

'Who are *they*?' She asked as she waved and smiled at Lyla and her boyfriend's band. She didn't know them, but it was polite to acknowledge them. Naturally, everyone backstage was confused by her sudden appearance, and there was plenty of whispering and pointing going on.

Beth cursed silently as she noticed that one of the groupie girls looked upset that Melissa had shown up.

'She's looking at you like that because you just stamped all over her chances with Luke. You walked in, and she knew it was game over,' Beth said as she threw the girl a smug look.

'But the game never started. Luke hasn't even blinked in her direction.'

'Is she trying to look like me?' Melissa laughed.

'Pathetic, isn't it?'

'She's got the hair all wrong, and I would never wear shoes like that. And Luke hates that much make-up.' She knew she was being a bitch, but she had every reason to be defensive. The girl was clearly after Luke's attention so she was fair game and Melissa wasn't having it.

'Let me pap you,' Beth said, and took a photo with her phone. It was so quick it caught them both looking at each other and laughing.

It was the perfect picture – best friends, together again. Then they posed, putting on their famous pouts.

'You know, I feel like setting the tongues wagging!' Beth said as she uploaded the photos to all her social networks.

'Bliss in LA rocking it backstage. The Eagle Queen is back where she belongs!'

'See what people think about that!' Beth chuckled.

Bliss was the name some of the tabloids had given the two girls, combining their names like celebrity couples. It was pretty cool, they thought. The photos went viral in seconds.

'I'm so glad you're here, Liss, he needs you,' Beth said.

Melissa was worried about how Luke would react to seeing her like this, and how he would take the news. Beth assured her she needn't worry. They did have a lot to talk about, but she had a feeling things would be just fine.

'He looks thinner, and tired,' Melissa pointed out, worried. He didn't look right and she didn't like it.

'It's exhausting doing this most nights ... it's a better workout than the gym,' Beth replied.

The crowd sang the lyrics loudly to 'Weekend High' making Melissa smile and forget her concerns for a moment.

But she felt uneasy. Luke definitely didn't look right. His voice didn't seem as strong and he didn't look focused. He would normally interact with the crowd during this song because it was a fans favourite, but he wasn't doing it tonight.

*****

The sweat was pouring from Luke, much more than usual, and his guitar suddenly felt very heavy. His vision was blurred, and the faces in the crowd moved in and out of focus. The noise was like an echo in his ears and he knew he couldn't continue the song. He knew the words, but he couldn't sing them. It was as though the connection between his brain and his body wasn't working properly. His legs felt like jelly, and he felt sick. He was getting hotter, and he started to panic as he felt his chest tighten and a pain shoot through his left arm. He needed air, but he couldn't move.

He could hear Dale shouting, 'Luke! What are you doing? What's wrong?' But he couldn't answer him. The guitar strap was digging into him, and he had to get it off. Using what little energy he could summon, he pulled it over his head and threw it aside before dropping to the floor, gasping for breath.

The sound of his guitar hitting the stage made a terrible sound that vibrated through the amplifiers and around the stadium. Dale's and

Tom's guitars followed made similar noises as they were thrown aside. They ran to his side, and Toby yelled for help.

Backstage, the road crew burst into action, running on to disconnect the equipment. They thought he'd been electrocuted by the way his back arched before he hit the floor. The medical team took no time making their way to the stage and the security guards and stewards focused on the crowd. An eery silence fell across the venue, apart from the voices of those on the stage. Melissa's screams echoed as she ran to his side.

'Luke! 'Luke!' she sobbed.

Beth wanted to go with her, but Dale told her to let the paramedics do their job. She shook as she watched her friend sprawled on the stage. Melissa was led back to them by one of the crew, and Dale held her tightly as she called Luke's name over and over. He didn't have a chance to wonder why on earth she was there, because Luke was motionless. Ray took control and cleared them all from the stage.

The crowd watched in silence as the drama unfolded before them.

'What's wrong with him? I have to talk to him! Luke!' Melissa sobbed.

'He's going to be fine. He's just being a drama queen,' Dale whispered, trying to make a joke, but more for his own benefit than hers.

'You don't know how glad I am to see you, girl.'

'I need to apologise for punching him,' Beth said suddenly. He looked so ill and she'd been so mean to him.

'I don't think that matters at the moment babe,' Toby told her.

Silver Daggers stood, equally shocked, at the edge of the stage and Zac comforted Beth while Lyla helped Ray remove the other girls, who were all hysterical, while the medical team concentrated on Luke.

It looked serious, and after what seemed like a lifetime he was wheeled to a waiting ambulance with an oxygen mask attached to his face, then rushed to hospital.

The band released a statement just hours after the incident.

'We are all very shocked by what has happened tonight in LA. We are sorry to our fans for cutting the gig short, and we thank you for your amazing behaviour and understanding. We are concentrating on our friend, who is receiving the medical treatment he needs. Luke is now our main priority, and we will update you on his condition in due course. Dale, Toby & Tom.'

*****

'You've been putting yourself through a lot of stress lately, both physically and mentally,' the doctor said.

Luke had suffered an angina attack, caused by stress and his lifestyle. After treatment, he was ordered to have at least a month of complete rest, to relax and recuperate. Definitely no work, and most importantly, he had to lead a healthier lifestyle to avoid this happening again.

'Thanks, doc.' Luke sat up, feeling terrible. But at least he was alive.

The doctor left, and a few minutes later he was surrounded by his friends and manager.

'You're a lazy bastard. Why do you have to be such a drama queen?' Dale asked, deciding that he was out of the woods, so the mocking could start. Toby and Tom jokingly accused him of forgetting the lyrics and faking the whole thing to avoid looking like an idiot. Luke laughed and reminded them that he didn't have to worry about being the idiot when he was on stage next to them. This was how they showed each other affection.

'I just needed a lie down,' Luke chuckled, but he knew he'd scared everyone, including himself.

Ray looked like he was himself on the verge of a heart attack. He told Luke that his parents had been kept fully informed. They were naturally worried, but were alright. The boys were due to be heading home in a few days so they had been told not to fly out because he'd be home soon. Luke called them straight away, to prove he was OK, and to stop them worrying. His mum cried throughout the phone call, telling him off, and telling him that she loved him, all at the same time. Luke wondered if Melissa knew or even cared, wherever she was.

Beth was standing next to Dale, holding his hand. She looked extremely shaken and upset, Luke thought. Then, she unexpectedly moved forward and threw her arms around him.

'I'm so glad you're OK, you scared us to death you idiot,' she said, sounding totally genuine. Luke found it surprising, considering how angry she had been with him over Melissa. But it was heart-warming to know that deep down she still cared, and he hugged her.

'I'm sorry I scared you,' he said. Beth whispered that she was sorry she'd punched him, and he told her he'd forgotten about it. They chatted and joked with him, all relieved that he was going to be OK. But they all warned him that they'd be watching him with eagle eyes from now on, and would kick his ass if he didn't sort himself out.

'I promise I will,' Luke agreed. He then came out with the important question that was on his mind – had Melissa been told?

Beth nodded and told him she'd spoken to her, and Melissa had sent him a message saying she hoped he was OK and she was thinking about him. His heart sank because part of him was hoping that she'd flown to LA to be at his side. She obviously still hated him.

'I can't keep this up, it's cruel,' Beth whispered to Dale. He looked at her and nodded. Everyone had seen Luke's expression, and could see what he was thinking.

'Oh, you do have one other visitor. But they didn't want to come in because they wanted to give us time with you first,' Dale said walking to the door. Everyone followed him, leaving Luke wondering who else would want to see him. Maybe it was Jay-Den. When the door opened, Luke thought he was dreaming as Melissa peeped round it, and then gingerly came into the room.

She was still in her clothes from the previous night, her jeans were creased and Dale had given her his jumper which was way too big for her. Her eyes were puffy because she'd been crying almost non-stop, and hadn't slept a wink. Add in the jetlag, and she definitely wasn't looking her best. She was still a sight for sore eyes though.

'Liss!'

'Luke,' she bursting into tears as she ran into his arms and buried her head in his chest. The emptiness he'd felt for so long was suddenly gone as he held the love of his life in his arms again.

'Thank you for coming. I know you didn't have to because...'

Melissa looked up and kissed him, cutting him off mid-sentence.

'She lied, that bitch was lying – she set you up. I am so sorry.'

She told him about Kelsey's visit. 'You need to feel better before I tell you the rest. It isn't nice.' He wasn't ready for the full truth, not today anyway.

'I told you!'

'I know you did, and I'm so sorry. Can you forgive me? I have missed you so much.' She asked him if she could come home, if he still wanted her. He looked at her, his face expressionless, and she feared that there was too much water under the bridge and he wouldn't want her back. Then he pulled her closer to him and kissed her forehead, knowing there was nothing he wanted more than for them to be back together.

But they had so much to talk about before they rushed into things. Luke knew he had to tell her everything, including the girls, if they were to move on with a clean slate. They had split up, so in theory he was free to do whatever he wanted, but he was worried she wouldn’t see it that way.

‘We need to talk first, babe. I have things I need to tell you, and if after that you still feel the same, then of course you can come home with me.’

Melissa had an idea what he would say, and she had already decided that she didn't care what had happened while they were apart. She had pushed him away, so she had to accept whatever had happened since then.

‘I don't care, I want you back. I don’t want to spend another day without you,’ she whispered, holding him so tightly he had to remind her that he had a heart condition.

‘I have missed you too, so much.’ Luke said, as he held her against him.

# I get it now

July 2014

'Luke, I'm so sorry ... I should have listened.'

Luke was in horrified by what he was hearing. He had no words to describe how he felt. 'If I had done that to her...I'd be banged up.' His hands clenched into fists.

'Bitches,' he cursed.

Melissa watched him as he took another puff of his cigarette, trying to calm down. He was leaning forward as if searching the floor for something that wasn't there. The lightning streak in his hair seemed to point at the floor. His frame was thinner, and she could see his ribs sticking out slightly. He looked so weary and his jeans and jumper looked much baggier on him than before. But it was the only clean set of clothes he had left.

They were staying in LA for a few extra days after Luke had been released from hospital, to give him more time to recover. Besides, the weather was much better than back home. They knew they needed to go home soon and see their families, but they had a lot to talk about first.

The conversation was intense as the truth was revealed to Luke about what Kelsey had done at Amber's request. Luke had also admitted what had been going on since their split.

'Liss, I'm so sorry about the girls ... they meant nothing.' He'd told her.

'I don't care about them. I just want us back together. We can start again ...'

It hurt that he had turned to other women, but she wasn't angry. It wasn't cheating because they weren't together at the time, and that had been her choice. She knew he had been in a bad place.

'I told you it was over, so you could do what you wanted. That was my mistake. No, actually, my monumental fuck up.'

Melissa's main concern now was the drug problem, and she wanted to confiscate everything. He knew she would search everywhere, so he might as well be honest and hand over his stash.

'Is this all of it?' She asked as he handed her a small plastic bag. Tears stung her eyes as he produced bags from several other hiding places, including one inside one of his guitars. Luke told her he hid it so that when Ray would check what he was doing or snoop in his room, he could pretend it was only a small amount.

'Yes, that's it now.'

'Promise?'

Luke nodded. Melissa looked at the stash in front of her. There must have been about £500 worth, and that was just what was left of his last purchase.

'Oh, Luke.' She was close to tears, and felt angry with herself. This had been coming for a while before they split. She had sensed it in Milan but did nothing, and now she realised that his heart had been broken just as much as hers, maybe even more.

Luke laughed when she suggested rehab. No way was he doing that.

'Waste of time. I just want to go home tomorrow with you.' He took her hand and kissed it. 'I just need you, and I'll be fine.'

Melissa closed her eyes as she felt the warmth of his lips on her hand.

'One day at a time,' she said. 'But I'm back now. I promise you I'll help you get back on your feet.'

'Who's Curtis?'

The question threw her because she'd completely forgotten about him. 'Curtis is no one, a guy in a bar who bought me a few drinks.' She paused briefly. 'I did take him home but I don't know what the hell I was thinking, and I quickly realised it was stupid. It went no further than a kiss, I promise.'

Luke felt relieved, but even if she had gone further, he was in no position to judge. 'He wasn't you,' Melissa explained. 'He kissed me and all I could think was ... it's not Luke...it doesn't feel right.'

'I was thinking about you when I was with those girls,' he admitted, knowing it sounded pathetic. 'They were nowhere near as good, and in truth they made me feel worse. I felt like a scumbag afterwards, because some wanted more from me and I couldn't give it to them.'

'I guess we're both pathetic losers,' Melissa laughed.

'I can live with that, if we can be losers together' he said as they cuddled up on the bed.

'Let's start again....' he whispered, before he fell asleep properly for the first time in months. Melissa waited till she was confident he was properly asleep then took the cocaine to Dale and Beth's room, where they flushed the lot away.

Dale asked Ray, Tom and Toby to his room so they could talk properly, now that Luke was finally resting.

An hour later, everyone felt much better that they'd got things off their chests and had been told about everything that had happened. They all agreed to support Luke in whatever way they could.

The first change was keeping drugs of any kind away from him. Drugs had never been a problem for the rest of the band, just an occasional pastime, so nobody had any objections to knocking it on the head for good.

'It'll have to be tequila shots instead then,' Toby laughed. 'I'm down with that.'

'What does Luke want to do about this Kelsey chick?' Ray asked Melissa. 'We should get the police involved, especially since Amber was behind it.'

Melissa shrugged, and told Ray she would prefer to worry about that once Luke was on the mend properly.

She realised she was still shaking, and it all hit her over again. She broke down

'I'm so sorry for ignoring you all when you asked me to talk to him, to help him. I'm such an idiot.'

Toby was there like a shot with one of his comforting hugs.

'I've ruined this for you, just like Milan,' she cried, feeling as though all she did was cause trouble for everyone. 'You must hate me.'

'Don't be stupid,' Toby said as she let it all out. 'We couldn't be happier to see you and Luke back together. You were tricked, and it's terrible what's happened to you both. But none of it is your fault' Toby felt her skinny frame in his embrace. She'd lost weight too, and it was sad to see.

'That girl can't be allowed to get away with it, Melissa,' he whispered.

'Don't bother with the police. I'll rip the little bitch apart.' Beth was on the warpath and wanted nothing more than to confront Kelsey. 'I'll teach her a lesson, along with nut-job Amber.'

Melissa smiled at her best friend, wishing she could do just that. Ray, along with everyone else, was pleased that Melissa was back and there seemed to be a sense of calm now.

'I promise he'll be back, better than ever, he just needs some time,'

Melissa said before heading back to check on Luke.

She was relieved to find him still asleep. He was smiling as he slept, and he looked so peaceful, almost angelic. Melissa quietly tidied up the mess in his room, packing his stuff ready to fly home next day, and feeling like it was just a tiny start towards moving on together. She suddenly realised that she was one of those girls she'd read about in magazines, who years later told their stories of how they coped with the crazy, surreal life of a rock star boyfriend. She'd never understood why they would put up with it.

'I get it now,' she thought.

*****

'Are you ready?' Melissa asked Luke. They were about to get out of the car as it pulled up outside the airport, and the local paparazzi were already there waiting, relentless in their quest for an exclusive.

Luke nodded. He still wasn't fully recovered, but he wanted to go home.

'Let's just get the fuck on that plane,' he said. His hood was up, sunglasses on and he looked down at the ground.

Melissa was feeling a renewed strength and confidence, and took control, standing up for them both. Luke still felt slightly embarrassed that a girl like Kelsey had been able to do that to him, and he was still thinking about what to do about it. Melissa had given him the note, which he read then screwed up and threw in the bin. She couldn't blame him but she had quietly retrieved it later, in case Luke decided to talk to her. Melissa knew he would, once he had calmed down. She also realised that the police would want it as evidence.

Dale leaned forward, ready to get out first with Beth, looking fierce as ever, beside him. Toby and Tom would get out last, to help surround them. Ray would cover one side of Luke, and Melissa the other. Stan, the band's publicist had gone in all guns blazing in order to clear up the lies about Luke. His fans were outraged and Kelsey Gibbs was now in hiding. Darren was furious that it was bringing unwanted attention his way. Kelsey had been very profitable for him since the story broke – all of his 'friends' wanted to spend time with the girl who slept with Luke Black. But all of that had changed now that she had been exposed as a liar.

'Keep your head down. Don't listen, just stay calm,' Melissa whispered as he stepped out, his face completely hidden.

'It's OK, son, we're here.' Ray patted him on the back and his bandmates encircled him as he was guided through the swarm.

'Go fuck yourselves,' Luke heard his drummer shout into the crowd, as the clicking of cameras and the sound of frantic footsteps echoed in his ears. He was front page news for all the wrong reasons, again. But at least some of his reputation had been restored.

The fact that the small, delicate hand he gripped was Melissa's was the only thing keeping him calm. He ducked into the terminal through the security door, where airport staff and security waited to guide them to the specially-chartered plane that was ready to take off as soon as they were on board.

Melissa had one last thing to do. She knew it was childish and would only create more drama, but she did it anyway. She turned to the swarm and looking right into the sea of lenses with a smug but triumphant smile filling her face, she shouted.

'Amber, I know everything – I win.'

It caused a flurry of questions because Amber had never been mentioned before. Who was she and what connection did she have to Luke?

Ray grabbed her arm and dragged her inside. 'Melissa, shut up.'

*****

It had been tough getting back on track with Melissa after the initial euphoria of being reunited. But she'd now settled into their new home and they had both kept themselves busy, making it their own. They were moving on, and they couldn't have been happier. Kelsey had admitted everything during her court case and had been given twelve months for assault. No sexual offence could be proven. But going to prison was actually a blessing for her, because it gave her a chance to be free from her old life. Darren's little empire, including several girls all under sixteen, had been discovered and brought down. He was going to prison for a very long time. By the time Kelsey was released, the world would have forgotten about her.

*****

'There wasn't any need for that, Jay.' Toby snapped after a very awkward moment during their meeting to discuss the next steps in their career. Luke was feeling much better – happier, stable, drug-free and ready to get back to work.

'No more fucking around then, we can finally get back to business!' Jay-Den had said, rubbing his hands together. He didn't seem to realise how disrespectful he was being to his best employee, making light of everything that had happened.

Jay-Den sat arrogantly back in his chair, talking about getting back in the studio and getting to work on their next single. He rattled on about needing to divert attention away from all the attention on their private lives of late, and prepare for a second album in due course. They listened dutifully, nodding in the right places – or at least Luke did. He hadn't forgiven Jay-Den over the incident with Melissa, and at times it was hard to be civil with him. But he had other, more positive things to concentrate on now, so he decided to leave it in the past along with everything else.

However, Jay-Den's little performance with Megan during the meeting hadn't helped Luke's opinion of him. There were times he wished he wasn't locked into a contract with the man. He'd seen a side to him that he didn't like, but he just had to grit his teeth and bear it.

Toby watched as Megan rushed from the room, and had to resist the impulse to run after her when he saw her distressed expression.

'Toby, my PA is none of your concern.'

Toby glared at him but decided to drop it. Megan had accidentally spilt a glass of water all over Toby's jeans as she passed it to him. She'd frantically and nervously tried to clean up the mess.

'S-s-sorry,' she'd stuttered, feeling her boss' glare aimed at her, not to mention feeling doubly embarrassed for spilling something for the second time in front of Toby.

'He really must think I'm a complete moron', she thought to herself.

'No harm done. Don't worry,' Toby said kindly, before Jay-Den began his humiliation of her.

Jay-Den was in his macho, showing off mood, and he gave her a thorough and public dressing-down for neglecting her work, and for arguing with him (when she'd dared to remind him that the work he was talking about was the same work he'd told her to leave in order to concentrate on The Black Eagles).

Toby saw how upset she was, and it enraged him. Luke had noticed his drummer's expression and prayed that Toby would keep cool, even though he felt like smashing Jay-Den's head on the desk.

They continued with the meeting until all the details of their plan were ironed out and agreed upon, then, free from the clutches of their boss, they went on their way.

*****

Toby had gone looking for Megan, but after almost giving up and heading home, he smiled when he saw her getting out of her car.

'I'm so sorry about that,' Megan mumbled, hoping to clear the air.

Toby shrugged and laughed. 'It was just water – I'll live.' He took her hand and led her to a bench just to the side of the building, where they sat down. He noticed her blush again, and she was trembling slightly.

'I only have a few minutes.' Megan felt on edge, scared even. It reminded her of a recent event which had turned into a bad experience, and she told herself to run from him to avoid more heartache. If recent events had proved anything to her, it was that men like him weren't interested in girls like her, not for the right reasons anyway. She shouldn't kid herself otherwise.

He reached over and pulled the clip from her hair. It fell like flames around her shoulders and he smiled. Megan froze momentarily before her hands flew up in panic to put it back in place.

'Leave it down, it looks pretty like that,' Toby said softly, slightly amused at her panic. He found her cute, and the shyness seemed to make her more appealing.

'I hate my hair.'

Toby didn't hate it at all, quite the opposite, but he handed the silver clip back and let her put it up again. She thanked and apologised again. Toby noticed that she wouldn't look directly at him and it bothered him. He could see her hands shaking, although she tried to cover it by fiddling with a bag of grapes. She was the one person he didn't want to feel afraid around him. Without taking his eyes off her, he watched as she put her hair back in place. He searched his mind for the right words to say. She wasn't like other girls, and getting her to go out with him wouldn't be easy. It was a challenge, but then he loved a challenge.

'Do you have a boyfriend?'

The question was so unexpected that Megan almost choked on the grape she was eating. She shook her head.

'Good. You can join me for Luke's birthday party this weekend then.'

Luke would be twenty-three, and Melissa was pulling out all the stops for a big celebration, with help from Beth and Ray. There would be a lavish party the night before in a top London club, with everyone important to him invited. Her plan for his birthday itself was to have

Luke all to herself. Nobody blamed her for wanting that, after all they'd been through. Despite their outward smiles, they were still recovering and rebuilding their relationship, and they needed the space and quality time together to do that.

'I'm sorry, I can't.' Megan hurried back inside, leaving Toby sat on the bench alone. He didn't follow, and instead headed back to his bike, feeling dejected. He could usually walk into any room and take his pick of women, but the one he actually wanted would hardly even look at him.

Luke had been waiting in his car, watching them. He wanted to help in some way, but he thought it was more Melissa's sort of thing. He opened his window and shouted to Toby to follow him back to his place. It was Monday and as they had nothing else planned for the day, they were going to have some beers and a jamming session.

*****

'As if...you've seen yourself, right?' Megan whispered to her reflection in the reception window as she watched Toby leave. Her boring, plain image stared back at her as the words and memory of that horrible night hit her again like an arrow through the heart. Putting on her best fake smile, she sighed and went back to work. Back in work mode, she called Francis Colt, the boys' producer.

*****

'Liss, stop worrying,' Beth told her as she tucked into her chips. Melissa was fretting again about Luke; his health, his birthday and everything in general. 'Luke's fine. He's back with you where he belongs and that's all he needs.'

'I know, but he isn't completely right. I mean he is better, but he's quieter. He seems on edge all the time.' She messed with her pasta, pushing it round the plate.

'It'll take time. What that girl did was awful. He might be a man, but it must feel horrible having someone take control of you like that.'

Melissa hadn't really thought of it in that way and for a man it must be embarrassing too. She shivered at the thought.

Luke was still smoking, but had cut down on his drinking. He had also stopped the drugs altogether, and although it had been a shock to his system at first, quitting had not been a major problem.

But he seemed constantly worried, and Melissa would catch him watching her. He laughed it off and said it was because he liked looking at her, but she felt it was something else, as though he was checking she was still there.

'He'll be fine. Dale will make sure of that. I take it there's still no news of Amber?' Beth pushed her empty plate away. Melissa was bound to worry, and after LA, she couldn't blame her. She would be the same if Dale had been through an ordeal like that.

'Nope, no news,' Melissa replied. She leaned back in her chair and pushed her Ray-Bans down over her eyes. It wasn't helping matters that Amber was on the loose and nobody knew when, where or indeed if she would spring up again. They hoped she had been taught a serious lesson by the way her plan had eventually backfired, and had given up on her vendetta against them.

A group of girls a few tables away were whispering and tapping away on their phones, and two approached and asked for a photo with them. They both agreed, smiling. Melissa wasn't really in the mood but if she refused, she'd be branded a moody cow, so she played along and engaged in small talk with them for a few minutes. They asked how Luke was, when were they going to be touring again and when the next single would be out. Melissa and Beth answered in their usual way. 'Soon, hopefully.' Melissa didn't answer the Luke question. It was none of their business. The girls hovered around for a while then, left them alone.

'I need to think of a present to give him for his birthday, and it needs to be good,' Melissa said, looking thoughtful. It was difficult, she thought, because he had everything he could possibly need. Beth suggested a few things, but Melissa turned her nose up at each idea. They hit the shops, hoping for inspiration, but after buying two pairs of shoes and a leather jacket for herself, she still hadn't come up with anything exciting. She had some new clothes for him and some trainers, but they were boring. She also had the new guitar he'd asked her to pick up for him, but he'd ordered that himself, so it wasn't a present.

They had a quick drink before heading for home, and as they walked through the busy London streets, Melissa spotted a sticker in a car window that made her stop in her tracks. It was from a bird of prey sanctuary in the New Forest, called Wings of the Sky UK. She quickly tapped it into her phone and checked out the website. They offered sessions with a trainer where you could met, fly and feed a bird of your choice for a few hours, and they were also looking for people to sponsor or adopt the birds to fund their upkeep.

'This is just what I'm looking for. He'll love this! They have eight eagles...look at that beauty,' she said to Beth as she looked at the photos. The largest was a female called Black Rose – the perfect name, she thought.

'Liss, it's perfect, you have to get him a trip there,' Beth said.

Melissa called them straight away and asked how much it would cost to have a full day with the bird and also how the adoption worked. The guy on the phone talked through the prices, having no idea who he was speaking to. He explained that Black Rose cost several thousand pounds a year to feed and look after, and they just asked for small contributions from anyone kind enough to offer their support.

Melissa also asked if they would be happy for Black Rose to appear in a music video, possibly in a few months' time.

'Really? Sure, as long as the health & safety side of things was covered properly. As her trainer I'd have to be present of course. Can I ask who for?' The excitement in his voice was obvious.

'For The Black Eagles. I think Black Rose would be perfect for them.'

Melissa was excited too, because she was hoping to be in their next video as well. Luke had been sitting in her new dance room while she practiced one day, and said she would look amazing in one of their videos, if she wanted to be involved. She'd said that she would love to, but only if it was a 'proper' video which told a story. She wasn't up for just dancing around like a twat for no apparent reason for three and a half minutes. But maybe Black Rose could be the ideal co-star for her.

'Wow, my son and niece are huge Eagles fans. Wait till I tell them...' he laughed. Melissa smiled and asked the man to book in a day for a member of the band to meet Black Rose. He said he would need to check with the boss because they normally only did hour-long sessions, not full days.

'Can I take your name and number and I'll call you back? Do you work for the band?' he asked.

Melissa laughed. 'My name's Melissa,' she said then gave him her number. There was silence at his end for a few seconds, and she thought he'd hung up.

'Are you Melissa, as in Melissa Webb?'

'Yes, I am.' Then he asked her if the session was for Luke.

'Um, maybe,' she answered, although it was fairly obvious by now that it was for Luke. His love of eagles was common knowledge after all.

'OK Miss Webb, thanks for calling. I'll find out everything you need to know and ring you back,' he promised.

‘It’s just perfect!’ Melissa cheered as the girls did a little jig on the spot, followed by a high five.

‘He’s going to love you even more than he already does,’ Beth laughed. Melissa was delighted to have come up with something original, and special.

*****

The sound of hysterical laughter greeted the girls as they left the lift. The boys were back, and were cackling about something.

Dale was playing on his guitar, purposely being awful, and was managing to produce a truly horrendous noise. They were in Luke's studio, and judging by the empty bottles littered around the room, they had been drinking for quite some time. The girls dropped their shopping bags on the sofa, and they went in to see what the fuss was all about. Melissa told herself not to nag him in front of the guys about the mess or being wasted in the middle of the afternoon - it wasn't cool.

‘What’s so funny? Come on, share the joke,’ she said as she walked in to see Luke rolling on the floor laughing hysterically, and the others not far off joining him. Beth told Dale to stop the god awful racket, which only set them off all over again.

‘I can't even remember why we’re laughing,’ Luke roared, the tears running down his face. But it really didn't matter. It felt like a long time since Melissa had heard him laugh like that, and it was lovely to hear it again.

‘I have her,’ she said holding up the guitar case.

Luke stopped laughing instantly and rolled himself to his feet, smiling like a kid at Christmas. He took the case and opened it, flicking his hair out of his eye. He was thrilled with it. The boys spent the next hour discussing where it could be used in their sets, and what they could do with it in new material. Luke spent the rest of the day ‘breaking her in’ – it was definitely female.

‘I don't know why you need six guitars. You can only play one at a time,’ Melissa had said. The room went silent as all four boys turned to look at her like she was completely mad. Even Beth was shaking her head with disapproval.

‘Liss, darling, you can only wear one pair of shoes, but that doesn't stop you having nearly a hundred pairs,’ Luke replied, leaving her with no comeback whatsoever. All she could think of was to tell him to shut up, which just made everyone laugh hysterically again.

'You walked right into that one,' Beth chuckled.

Melissa stuck her tongue out at Luke, and he blew her a kiss and winked. Things were really starting to get back to normal, and she was finally feeling good.

To add to the good vibes, Carl from the bird sanctuary had called to confirm that Luke's birthday present was arranged.

'It's a birthday surprise, Carl. Can you please keep it to yourself until after the weekend? You know how things can be,' Melissa asked, hoping that someone would be capable of keeping their mouth shut, just for once.

'Of course, you have my word. You're helping us take care of Rose, so the least we can do is respect your privacy.' His work and the birds were his priority, not gossiping.

'What are you whispering about?' Luke asked, and she jumped. She hadn't heard him come into the bedroom and she spun round like a naughty child being caught out.

'I can't tell you. It's a secret,' she giggled. He shut the door, drowning out the noise from their visitors. He crossed the room to her, and wrapped his arms around her waist. Holding her tightly to him, he kissed her forehead, then her nose, and then her lips.

'I don't like secrets,' but she assured him he would definitely like this one.

'OK, I'll trust you on that.'

Changing the subject, he asked for her help with getting Megan and Toby together.

Melissa wrinkled her nose while she thought it through.

'Hmm, I'll see what I can do.' Luke suggested trying to get her to his birthday bash. Toby had been talking to them about it before the girls had come back, and they all agreed that a group setting was a good idea for a first date, to keep it as casual as possible.

'He really likes her?'

'Yeah he does big time, but the girl's so shy and we all know Toby can be a bit overwhelming if you don't know him.'

'I *will* get Cinderella to the ball,' she promised.

'Good girl. Thanks for arranging my party, but are you really sure you're OK with it all?' It would be the first real outing since they got back together. Stan had said that it was a big deal, and it would prove that their reconciliation was official. 'Just for one night let the people have their favourite couple,' he'd told them.

Melissa couldn't really be bothered with the whole 'putting on a front' thing. But as Luke put it, 'You want people to know we're happy, and stop the bullshit going around, right? We are together, and happy, and I'm proud of that.' So she'd agreed to let the photographers have a few pictures, perhaps even one of the two of them hugging.

The Echo girls were going to be at the party, and Tom and Jo-Jo were finally getting together after months of flirting. That was another big source of excitement in the media at the moment – Eagle boy and Echo girl hooking up.

Jay-Den and many other record label associates would be there too. Melissa didn't really want him there, but there wasn't really much choice. Beth reminded her that she didn't have to talk to him. Tom's older sister and husband were joining them, as were some of Luke and Dale's old school friends. Toby's brother Adam, who had just finished a tour of Afghanistan, was coming, and a few other artists and bands that the boys had befriended over the past few months would also be there. It was going to be a paparazzi's paradise.

'Let them snap away,' Melissa said, shrugging. What were another few photos in the sea of thousands that were flooding around the world anyway? And Luke was right – they were happy, so what was wrong with showing that off and having some positive stories about them for a change?

*****

'Is that really me?' Megan gasped as she looked at her reflection in the mirror. Melissa had shown up at her office unannounced earlier in the week, and taken her for lunch. She'd convinced her to come to Luke's birthday and get to know everyone properly outside of work. It wasn't a date, she assured her, so there was no need to worry. She had eventually said yes after Melissa had promised her it would be fun, and that she and Beth would look after her.

Melissa had agreed to help Megan get ready at her flat, and had pulled out all the stops to make her look like a film star for the night.

'Yes, that is you,' Melissa laughed.

'But I look—' Megan began to say.

'Hot,' Melissa finished her sentence for her. She had curled Megan's copper hair and done her make-up beautifully, but kept it natural. Melissa thought too much make-up looked tacky, and it was one of her pet hates. She had rooted through Megan's wardrobe and found dresses with tags still on them, hidden away at the back. Amongst them was a beautiful black pencil dress with silver sequins along the shoulders, which was perfect for a special occasion like this.

Megan explained that she often went shopping and bought nice clothes, but she never had anywhere to go where she could wear them. Melissa also found boxes and boxes of shoes too, and she quickly picked out some beautiful black kitten heels.

'Thank you, Melissa. It's been so long since I've been out or felt this good.' It was so nice for her to feel pretty for once, even though she knew she was nowhere near as stunning as the girl standing behind her, who was effortlessly wearing a black silk skater dress and black lace Jimmy Choo heels. Melissa's hair, not one strand out of place, hung loosely to her waist, and her outfit was completed by the pretty locket that Megan had noticed she always seemed to wear.

'You always look so perfect, Melissa. How do you do it?'

The comment took Melissa by surprise. 'I don't. You should see me first thing in the morning.'

Megan laughed. Melissa really was nuts if she thought she could ever look a mess, and she told her so.

'If you'd seen me a few months back, you wouldn't say that. I was a mess behind those doors.'

'I'm sorry. I suppose things aren't always as they seem.' Megan saw a flash of sadness in Melissa's eyes and felt sorry for her. She also felt awkward for putting her foot in it.

'Stay away from the gossip, Megan. They talk utter crap. I sometimes wonder who they're writing about, because it certainly isn't me or Luke.' Melissa could feel her temperature rise, just thinking about it all.

Megan wondered if she would suffer the same treatment if she even considered anything with Toby, and she asked Melissa what she thought.

'I won't lie. They will gossip, darling, they always do. Don't worry, they aim their guns at me and Luke most of the time so you're almost safe. You're not famous, so if you're lucky, they'll leave you alone. But if you ever need anything, you just call me.' They were both looking at the mirror as Melissa was putting the finishing touches to Megan's hair, making sure it was just right.

Megan often wondered how Melissa stayed sane with everything that went on around her. She could have anything she wanted, but she was just a normal girl with no diva tendencies whatsoever. She was so grounded. Melissa and Luke were just like any other couple trying to make it work. In the middle of a storm, they always managed to keep themselves calm. Megan asked her how she did it, how she handled being part of a circus the whole time.

'We just have to trust each other and protect each other as much as possible. I made a huge mistake over Kelsey...I'll never do that again. I love him, Megan. That's what it comes down to. It's who he is, so I have to take the rough with the smooth. Although there are many things that annoy the hell out of us in our lives, we don't lose sight of the fact that we are extremely lucky, and our 'problems' with people taking pictures of us or writing stories we don't like are really not that bad in the grand scheme of things, and there are a lot of people who have real problems. Like Kelsey and those other girls had, for example.'

Megan marvelled at her wisdom, for such a young woman.

'Listen, if you like Toby, don't be afraid to try getting to know him better. He really is a lovely bloke. I always say that you should regret the things you do in life, not the things you don't.'

Melissa stood back and admired her work – the makeover was complete.

They drank a glass of champagne together, cementing their new friendship, then left to join the party. Melissa told her again before they left that if she liked Toby, she should go for it. Megan admitted her fear that she would be just another notch on his bedpost, and she wasn't that type of girl.

'You're not just another girl. He *really* likes you. And that's not how I roll. If he was just going to mess you around I wouldn't be saying this. I know Toby, and I know you've got nothing to be scared of.'

Megan shook her head and told Melissa it wasn't him she was afraid of, it was men in general. But that was something she would have to get over, and she felt a bit more comfortable because Melissa seemed genuine about what she was saying, so maybe it wasn't as bad as she thought.

'You really think I look nice?'

'If you mean will Toby like it? ... then yes he will, he'll be blown away.'

'I hope so,' Megan said as she stepped into the car, smiling at her reflection in the window.

*****

'Damn!' Toby yelled across the table as he stared at the two girls walking in. One was his friend Melissa, looking lovely as ever, and the other was the girl he was definitely going to marry.

'Is that her? The one you're always talking about? The geeky one?' Adam, his brother, asked. He was the same size as Toby, and they would be identical if Adam had the piercings that Toby had. Being in the Army he didn't, but he did have a tattoo on his back similar to Toby's. He wolf whistled, and commented that she didn't look very geeky tonight.

'No, she doesn't,' Toby agreed, smiling as he watched her walk towards the table. She looked nervous as she waited patiently for Melissa, who chatted to guests as she crossed the room. Luke greeted Megan and hugged her as she wished him a happy birthday. He made her go and sit with them while Melissa finished her conversation with Sonny Lee. He had shown up uninvited, but Luke was thrilled. Then Echo arrived, closely followed by Silver Daggers with their girlfriends in tow, and at that point, the party really got started.

Melissa had hired the top floor of a Soho club, who had put on extra security to head off gatecrashers. She had invited all their parents, and they were all sitting together, enjoying themselves but feeling rather out of place. They were all very proud of their kids and got on like a house on fire, so they were quite happy to spend the night chatting about their kids' success.

Toby had told his mum about Megan, and his brother pointed her out. Jayne Maxwell thought she looked like a nice girl and gave her son the thumbs up.

'I don't want you marrying a trollop,' she had said on many occasions. Jayne was plump, but considering that she wasn't a tall woman and Mr Maxwell wasn't a huge man either, it was a mystery where Toby and Adam got their size from.

Tom had finally called Jo-Jo the previous week, and they had finally gone on a date. Now, it was like the dam had burst, and they were draped all over each other in their own little bubble, confirming a new couple in the group. Beth and Dale were already on the dance floor and everyone else soon followed.

Cassie hugged her friends and told them all how much she loved them as she did a little dance around them, and falling over. Luke attempted to helped her up, but she was laughing so much they both ended up in a heap on the floor, giggling like schoolgirls.

'I love you guys!' she said again, hugging Luke and kissing him on the cheek. He picked himself up and then helped Cassie to her feet. She grabbed Melissa, pulling them both in for a hug.

'I'm so glad you two sorted things out. And I'm sorry that I wasn't around much.' No need to apologise, Melissa told her. Her phone calls and support were enough, and they knew she cared – the feeling was mutual.

They had left Toby alone with Megan, and it looked like things were going well. They had been deep in conversation for the last hour and she'd laughed a number of times. She seemed to be relaxing, and to everyone's surprise she allowed Toby to take her onto the dance floor. Her nerves were slowly slipping away, and she seemed to be really having fun. Hopefully she'd be going home with a smile tonight, and not tears. Toby winked at Melissa and mouthed, 'Thank you.' She smiled and blew a kiss back to him.

'My work is done. The rest is down to him,' Melissa whispered to Luke.

'I think it's in the bag,' he replied. His arms were round her waist and he rested his chin on her shoulder as they swayed to the music.

'I'm so proud of you,' Melissa said.

Luke had done so well since LA and hadn't touched drugs of any kind. And although he was still drinking and smoking he had cut down and he felt much better for it. Melissa had been his rock. She had been very vocal on the two occasions he had come close to slipping after LA, but she reminded him why he had stopped, and how he felt when he had the problem. He didn't like to think about where he might be now without her.

'It's getting easier because of you.'

'Whenever you feel that urge again, just look at me or think about me. You made me a promise to stay off it, so when you need a distraction, I will be that distraction for you.'

'You're my angel – you know that, right? You look so pretty tonight ... can we go home soon?' He had really enjoyed himself and it was nice to have fun again. But he really wanted to pick his girlfriend up and take her home.

Eventually, the night began to wind down. Jay-Den came over to say goodbye, along with Ray and his wife, and Sonny Lee. Luke's old school friends staggered over to say farewell shortly after.

'It's been an awesome party, Luke ... happy birthday, man, love you' Tim slurred as he hugged him, before heading off to see Dale and Beth before he left. Tom and Jo-Jo had already gone, soon followed by Allie. She could barely remember her name thanks to the amount of tequila she'd put away. Cassie had taken her home.

'Melissa, it was really nice to meet you finally. Take care of him.'

This came from a girl she didn't know. Tim's wife, Lisa, had known Luke and Dale since their school days. Melissa promised her that she would, and Lisa gave Melissa her number and suggested they keep in touch.

'I'll take you home,' Toby told Megan. It wasn't a question, and she didn't argue. It wasn't for any other reason than to make sure she was safe, and Megan had come to realise during the evening that he was a gentleman. Toby wouldn't rush things with her. She was too important to him, and he wanted to get to know her first, sensing that she wasn't very experienced.

They made their way over to say goodbye, and Megan hugged Melissa and whispered in her ear, 'Thank you for convincing me to come.'

'You had a good time then?'

'The best.'

Luke and Melissa watched them leave, smiling as Toby put his arm protectively around Megan. She giggled, looking happy and relaxed for once.

'Do you want your presents when we get home?' Melissa asked once they were in their car and Luke laughed.

'That is not what I meant. Don't you men ever think of anything else, but sex?' She playfully slapped his arm.

'No, not usually.'

'OK ... I want to know what you've been whispering about,' he said when the car had dropped them off. Melissa couldn't wait to finally show him.

'Sit down, and I'll go and get them,' Melissa ordered. Luke sat patiently on the sofa and a few minutes later Melissa reappeared. She had changed out of her dress and into shorts and a vest top, and was holding five parcels, all beautifully wrapped in black and a huge envelope that was almost as tall as she was. She passed him the four packages that contained clothes, and the card. The card was black, with just a simple heart on the front. The message read: 'To My Brilliant Boyfriend, Happy Birthday.' Inside she had written him a message.

'Luke, Happy Birthday. I hope you enjoy every second. Things have been tough, and we still have a long way to go, but we can do it. I am so proud of you. I still feel so guilty every day for not believing in you when it mattered most. I will always be here for you. I love you more every day, although those three words don't seem enough. If I could write as well as you I would write you a song, but for now just know that I have so much love for you, I sometimes don't have enough room in my heart to hold it all. You are my soul mate. The One. I promise I will never doubt you again, EVER! Liss XXXXX'

'You don't have to feel guilty, or keep apologising,' he said, as he wiped away a tear that was threatening to slide down her cheek. She couldn't help it. The whole nasty episode still haunted her. Luke clearly loved the card, and he put it on the coffee table. Then she handed him the last package. She was very excited as he ripped off the paper to reveal a black and white gift box. Inside the box was all the paperwork that Carl had couriered over to her. Luke read through it while Melissa watched for his expression to change as it sunk in that she had effectively given him his own eagle. His smile grew into a huge grin as he read it again.

'I love her,' he said then placing the paperwork carefully back in the box he picked Melissa up and spun her around. 'You got me my own eagle! That's the best present I've ever had! When can I meet her?' he asked, looking just like a kid. She told him that a date hadn't been set yet, but all he needed to do was call Carl to arrange it.

'She is amazing, and so are you.'

'Happy Birthday babe...you deserve it.'

He carried her to their room, kissing her and placing her on the bed, where they stayed for the rest of his birthday.

# Stay Calm

October 10th 2014

'Melissa!' 'Luke!'

The flashes and the yelling came at them from all angles, and Melissa clung to Luke while trying to keep the smile on her face and avoid tripping over in front of hundreds of people. Fans lined the carpet, and the sound was deafening. They had been invited to attend the premiere of Diana Sweeney's new horror film, *Ward 7.* Luke and the boys were wearing black suits and they looked good, even if they hated being dressed like penguins, as Toby put it. Melissa wore a beautiful silver Armani gown with her hair in a low plaited chignon, with silver bands entwined in it. Luke kept hold of her as they moved away from the flashes, and Beth and Dale took their place.

'Melissa ... Luke, please!' The fans screamed. Luke walked over to a group of girls while she hung back a little, trying not to get in the way. But after a few minutes Luke waved her over. She crossed the red carpet and grabbed his outstretched hand. The girls were almost crying at seeing her, and Melissa noticed that they were the girls who ran her fan website – the page that had cheered her up during the scandal. Melissa was thrilled to meet them and thanked them, telling them how their words of support had really helped her.

After posing for photos with Luke, and calling Beth over to meet them, Melissa moved along the red carpet. Once the guys were free from the sea of adoring fans, Ray steered them through the line of reporters. They charmed their way through the throng, apart from one very awkward moment when Luke was asked how things were with Melissa since the scandal.

Luke wasn't in the mood for personal questions. 'Are you blind?'

'Are you back with Melissa for good?'

'No, I just bring along my ex-partners for a laugh,' he snapped.

'How are things with you both?'

'None of your fu—'

Ray grabbed Luke's arm, and dragged him away before he got himself into trouble, trying to keep him calm while calling Melissa over for extra back-up. Luke was clearly irritated.

'They like to push their luck sometimes - there's always one moron,' Ray reminded him, patting him on the back and keeping him moving forward towards the sanctuary of the cinema.

Beth and Jo-Jo were causing their own stir, further along the red carpet. Beth was wearing a red cocktail dress and Jo-Jo a yellow and black dress. Both were in heels to match their dresses and were posing for anyone and everyone with a camera.

Those who were there were sorry that the rest of Echo hadn't been invited, and that Megan had fallen ill that morning with a bug. It would have been nice to have the whole gang there.

They were nearly at the theatre entrance, when Melissa made one last stop to sign a poster. A flash of chocolate brown caught her eye and she looked up, nearly choking as, through the crowd, those unmistakable steel-coloured eyes bore into her. She froze as Amber raised her hand, doing a throat cutting motion with her finger, then pointed at her. She had an expression of pure hatred on her face. Melissa desperately called out for Luke, and she stumbled backwards as her heel caught on her dress. A member of security was there quickly to help her up, and Luke was back by her side in seconds. He thought she had just fallen, until he saw her terrified face.

'What's wrong?'

Melissa pointed to the crowd, but she was gone.

'Amber!' Melissa gasped.

Ray jumped into action, and more security guards quickly arrived and they searched the crowds for Amber. But as usual, she had vanished without a trace. Luke was shocked, and furious. Yet again Amber had managed to ruin something good.

Melissa was taken inside, shaken but angry with herself for reacting as she did. Why hadn't she jumped the barrier and taken her down? The truth was that Amber really scared her. And this had just proved how much.

'She's gone. Damn, that girl is fast,' Ray said on his return. There were beads of sweat on his forehead and he looked worried.

Beth was hovering next to Melissa, like a viper ready to strike, and

Luke had his arm protectively around her trying to calm her down. Tom and Jo-Jo were talking to security, to find out if anyone saw Amber. Dale watched his best friend closely. He could see the anger bubbling, and he knew that if anyone made the wrong move or said the wrong thing, Luke would flip. They were both on edge again. Toby stood like a wall on the other side of Melissa, eyeing anyone who came anywhere near her, trusting nobody.

The police were informed, but as she hadn't actually done anything, there wasn't much they could do without witnesses. Conveniently for Amber, with all the excitement and noise, nobody had noticed her little performance.

'Ray, I want that bitch found. Enough of this shit,' Luke raged. Amber didn't give out warnings. She just struck and clawed at their lives whenever she pleased, and they were helpless to do anything about it.

Melissa was messing with the bottom of her dress and cried as she saw the rip where her heels had caught the hem. There were flecks of blood along the bottom and she noticed a scrape on her ankle caused by her heel catching her as she fell. To add to it all, there would be hundreds of pictures doing the rounds of her sprawled on the red carpet.

*****

'Lock the doors, I won't be late,' Luke said as he put Melissa in the car. Ray was taking her home. Amber had ruined her evening, and she had a stress headache. 'Walk her to the door and don't leave until you hear the door lock behind you,' Luke instructed his manager. He had to mingle for a few more hours before he could go home. 'I'll call when I'm outside.' He kissed her quickly before shutting the door and heading back inside to the after party.

'Beer?' Dale shouted over the buzz of the crowded venue, and handed one to him without waiting for an answer.

*****

Melissa kicked off her shoes once she had securely locked herself in. She heard Ray's footsteps going down the hall, and the sound of the lift doors opening. She changed into her comfy nightwear, took some painkillers for her headache, and had a cigarette while calling Luke to say she was home safely.

Irritated that Amber had ruined her evening, she went to bed. She cursed as she tripped over Chloe, left on the floor of their room by Luke, and put her back in the studio. She cursed again as she tripped over his loop pedal.

'Luke, how many times have I told you to move it,' she muttered to herself before crawling into bed where she was asleep before her head hit the pillow.

*****

'Boring bastard!' Dale mocked Luke as he said his goodbyes just before 1.30, keen to get home to Melissa after Amber's little performance earlier. Melissa had been so excited about the premiere. She'd looked so beautiful and happy as they'd left home and Luke was annoyed that yet again that girl had ruined it. After one last drink, he left to find the car that had returned to the venue after taking Melissa home.

*****

Melissa woke hours later, feeling very thirsty. The apartment was quiet and she checked the time, and frowned when she saw it had just gone five. She got up and checked to see if Luke had fallen asleep on the sofa, but it became clear that he wasn't home. She assumed that he'd crashed at Dale and Beth's but was annoyed he hadn't even bothered to tell her. He wasn't answering his phone either, which irritated her even more. By around 6.30, she started to worry. Knowing that she was probably going to have her head bitten off, she called Beth to ask where he was, just to put her mind at rest.

'I'm sorry to wake you so early,' she said as soon as she heard Beth's sleepy voice.

Beth said there had better be a good reason as she'd only been in bed two hours and wasn't available for early morning wake-up calls. Melissa could hear Dale complaining in the background. Beth told her that Luke wasn't with them and that he'd left around one-thirty saying he was going home.

'He isn't here. Are you sure he said he was coming home?' she checked. Beth confirmed that was definitely what he said, and he was in a relatively good mood despite Amber. Melissa started to panic.

'Stay calm. Maybe he got talking to someone after leaving us and went on somewhere else,' Beth said, trying to reassure her. But Melissa had a horrible feeling in her stomach. She knew he wouldn't just wander off in the middle of the night. He wouldn't do that to her after everything they'd been through. Not without at least letting her know.

Dale took the phone from Beth and told Melissa they were due at the studio at ten. Luke never missed studio time, and when he saw him he would make sure he called her.

*****

But Luke didn't show, and the studio time was cancelled. All calls were going to his voice mail, and at around midday, his phone was switched off.

'He's been hurt, I know it,' Melissa cried. She had called the police but they couldn't file him as a missing person until he'd been AWOL for twenty-four hours.

Beth watched as Melissa paced up and down, lighting yet another cigarette. 'Liss, you have to eat. You'll collapse soon...'

Melissa shook her head. She couldn't eat now. She looked at Beth while she tried calling him again.

'Luke, where are you? Please call me. If something's happened then talk to me. We can work through anything. Don't worry if it's the drugs. I promised I would stand by you. Just call me, please, baby, I'm worried.'

She hoped there would be a simple explanation. Maybe he'd relapsed with the cocaine and was hiding, because he felt bad. She knew it wasn't another woman, and he hadn't left her.

'I hope he's not gone on a bender. He was doing so well,' Dale said, but he knew it wasn't that. Even if it was, he wouldn't just go off radar like this, because he knew Melissa would support him. Luke had left the party and just vanished. Dale picked up a sobbing Melissa from the sofa and hugged her.

'He will turn up, don't worry.' But deep down he wasn't convinced.

The hours dragged by slowly, with no news. Melissa called his phone every hour but it was useless, and hearing his voice mail was just upsetting her even more. Ray called every few hours to check on her, and her parents and Luke's were calling frequently.

Jay-Den called her, and this time she answered.

'Melissa, have you heard from him?' He sounded worried. Things were still a bit awkward but he had stuck to his word and kept it strictly professional recently.

'No, something's wrong, Jay-Den, I just know it.' Her words rushed out, the panic evident. 'People keep telling me to be calm and wait. But what if he needs me now?' It had been twelve hours since she'd seen him, and nine since his last sighting. She had to wait a further fifteen hours until the police could do anything.

'This is torture. Amber was at the premiere – what if she has something to do with it?' Jay-Den emphasised that anything was possible.

'Melissa, you have to accept that it could be another woman,' he said, knowing it would add to her stress.

'No!' she yelled. 'No! He wouldn't do that to me, he wouldn't.' She hung up and flung her phone across the room. Jay-Den called again but she ignored him, but listened to the message he left.

'Melissa, I am so sorry, I never meant to upset you. I don't actually think that either. Of course he wouldn't. I'm just an insensitive moron. If you need anything just call.'
She deleted it immediately.

She finally got some restless sleep, and woke around six. She checked her phone, and also checked around the house that he hadn't arrived home. That was ridiculous as he obviously hadn't, but she had a tiny hope that she would find him working away as if nothing had happened, or asleep on the couch.

Luke was gone; he wasn't coming home and she knew it.

*****

The police came to take some details. They needed to know what he was wearing, and his last known movements. As Dale had been one of the last people to see him, he filled them in on everything he knew. He told them that Luke had stayed until around half one, then said goodbye to their group before heading home. He wasn't staggering drunk, although he'd had a fair bit, but there was nothing unusual about him. They already knew about the incident with Amber, and said they would look into it. But as she hadn't approached them or caused them any actual harm there wasn't an awful lot that could be done. The driver booked to take Luke home confirmed that he had waited for nearly two hours, but he never arrived. The CCTV was checked, but it didn't show a clear angle of the entrance. It hadn't even caught Luke leaving the venue.

It was a complete mystery.

'Miss Webb, I know this is hard, but you must stay calm. He is now officially listed as missing, and we will do everything we can to find him. I'll be in touch,' the police officer promised as he left.

Melissa sank to the floor. 'This can't be happening.'

'Liss, I am so sorry,' Beth whispered. Hadn't they been through enough? She thought. Were they not allowed to be happy? Melissa wasn't the only person who would be affected though – she had Dale to think about too. Luke was her boyfriend's best friend as well as her best friend's boyfriend, which was confusing in itself. She wasn't sure who to comfort first.

'I need to lie down. My head's hurting again,' Melissa muttered as she wandered numbly to her room. She buried herself in their sheets, which the scent of his aftershave still clung to, and cried as she held them to her face.

Dale was putting on a brave face, but was obviously worried sick, and the cries from Melissa were heartbreaking. To keep himself busy, he called anyone who hadn't already been told what was going on.

Cassie burst into tears when she heard the news.

'What the hell? Dale, he wouldn't just walk off like that,' She made him promise to keep her informed. She would call Melissa later, once she felt able to talk. Next, Dale called Luke's mum, to check on her.

'Dale, was he back on the drugs?' She asked frantically. He assured her that he wasn't – at least he hadn't seen any evidence of it. There was only so many crying women one man could take, he thought, and he was frustrated that he didn't have the words to make any of them feel any better. He shared their concern, but he needed to be strong for Beth and Melissa. Beth couldn't be too stressed out in her condition. They had only found out they were going to be parents a few hours ago, and they were still getting over the shock of that news.

Dale and Beth stayed until the evening when Melissa insisted they'd done enough for her, and they should go home.

*****

'Mum, honestly I'm fine. Don't drive tonight, it's late,' Melissa's parents had been away for a long weekend in Italy, only landing in Gatwick that night. It would be the early hours before they arrived, so they agreed to stay put. They promised to be there the next morning.

The quietness of the house got to Melissa very quickly, so she put the TV on for some company. The half bottle of wine she found in the fridge disappeared quickly, so she opened another bottle and wandered into Luke's studio, closing the door behind her as if to shut out the world. The studio was all she had, and even the mess was comforting. His new guitar stood proudly in the corner, still plugged in, and his notebook sat open on the table. His scribbles made her cry, and she wondered if she would ever see him write in it again.

The words jumped off the page. They were new, but she wondered if they would ever be finished.

'See me, the man before, I stand here still, yours all yours

Let them lie and scheme, for a score.

You are my wings, for me to soar ...'

Melissa sat on the floor and cried, unable to read the whole thing. He was her world and she knew she couldn't be without him. When they were together everything made sense. He knew her better than anyone, including Beth, because when you give yourself to someone absolutely, and you trust them without exception, you tell them all your hopes and dreams and fears. He knew things about her she had never told anyone and he made her feel safe. Nobody had ever made her feel the way he did, and when he kissed her, touched her, she wanted nobody else. She had always believed in soul mates, and he was hers, she was certain of that.

*****

Drunk and emotionally exhausted, Melissa had fallen asleep on the sofa. She didn't hear the sound of the key in the lock.

'Mmmmmmhhh,' was the only sound that came out of her mouth, as she woke to feel pressure on her chest, and something covering her mouth. It took a few seconds for her to realise what was happening.

'Surprise,' Amber said smugly, her face almost touching Melissa's. She couldn't move under the weight on top of her. Amber smiled wickedly, then lifted her hand away.

'Amber, how the fuck did you get in?' Her heart raced and beads of sweat formed on her forehead, and a headache from the wine began to take hold. Fear raced through her as Amber waved a hunting knife above her face, and Melissa noticed that she had dyed her hair blonde.

'Just thought I'd stop by. Luke sends his love, by the way,' she sniggered. Hearing her say his name made Melissa struggle to free herself.

'Where is he?'

Amber shook her head and dug her knee into Melissa's stomach, making her retch.

'Amber, please ... stop.' She winced as she felt another dig. Amber was clearly enjoying this, so begging wouldn't stop it.

'I didn't mean it, I didn't mean for him to get hurt!' She said suddenly, panic and desperation in her voice like a child scared of being punished. She yanked Melissa up by her hair, still begging her to believe that she had never meant to hurt him.

'Amber, what have you done?'

'I just wanted to talk to him, that's all. I wanted to say sorry for Kelsey and that I did it all because I love him. I never meant it.' The emotion in her voice was genuine and for a moment, she sounded truly sorry. But just as quickly, her expression changed again, and she whipped her arm around, catching Melissa on the side of the face. There was so much force behind it that Melissa fell against the wall.

'Get up, now!' Amber screamed, grabbing Melissa's hair and pulling her to her feet. She clamped a hand over her mouth and held her against the wall, the knife brushing against her neck. The changes in Amber's character from one moment to the next weren't normal. Melissa could see it now, how she seemed to flick back and forth between the childlike, scared Amber, and then the aggressive, dominant alter ego who would suddenly take over.

'Do as I say, Melissa. You need to be a good girl if you want to help him.' Melissa didn't know if this was just Amber lying, or she really did know where he was.

Amber laughed. 'Of course we know where he is. We put him there.' She pulled her phone from her pocket and showed Melissa a picture. Melissa gasped, and begged Amber to tell her where he was. The picture showed Luke bound at the wrists and ankles, laying on a stone floor. His eyes were closed and there was blood down one side of his face. Melissa couldn't tell if he was even alive.

'Just shut up. We're going to leave without a fuss.' Melissa noticed that Amber had Luke's keys in her hand, explaining how she had got in. She held the knife to her side and they walked to the lift, then out into the car park, to Luke's car.

'Good, you listened to me. It's a first, but it's a start,' the calmer Amber was back. She rooted around until she found Luke's iPhone connector and plugged her phone in.

'Don't you just love their album?' She said, nodding her head as 'Games' boomed out through the sound system. Melissa tried to think of a way to escape, but she had no ideas. She only had the clothes she was wearing – purple sweat pants and white jumper. She didn't even have any shoes on. Her phone was charging at home and she felt helpless without it.

'This is my favourite ... what's yours?' Amber asked as though they were best friends. Melissa's mind was racing, and songs were the last thing on her mind. Luke needed help. 'You don't care about him. You don't even know what your favourite song is. I know every word to every song. Do you?!' Crazy Amber was back. She whipped her left arm out, the knife stopping next to Melissa's throat.

'Sing,' she demanded.

'What?' Melissa gasped. Singing was even lower down her list of things to do. This was the most insane situation yet. All she could focus on was the knife at her throat, and the fact that the car swerved and skidded as Amber tried to control it with one hand.

'If you know the words, you can sing. If you don't, I will cut your throat.'

The hand holding the knife was shaking, and she hit a small bump in the road, but she kept the car under control somehow. But it meant using both hands, and Melissa breathed a sigh of relief as the blade was pushed back into her jacket.

'If you've hurt him I will kill you.'

'Shut up.' Amber shook her head frantically as if trying to dispel a memory.

'Amber, what do you want from us?' Melissa yelled. Then something on Amber's arm caught her attention. Luke's leather cuff was too big for Amber's skinny wrist.

'He wants me. I'm the only person who truly knows him.' Amber sobbed. 'He wants me...he wants me...'

Melissa was getting more and more irritated at this girl and her delusions.

'It was just one night. No strings attached, you told him.'

Amber wouldn't listen. As far as she was concerned, Melissa had stolen him, and was keeping them apart. Melissa decided that it was no good trying to reason with her. 'He never came back for more? Melissa taunted smugly, glaring at Amber.

Amber's lips twitched. 'What?'

'You know what I mean; he never came back for more. If he wanted you like you've convinced yourself he did, then once wouldn't be enough.'

Amber twitched again, and her eyes seemed to glaze over. They had been driving for over an hour and Melissa had no idea where they were going. Suddenly, they turned sharp left into a dark dirt track. Melissa started shaking. If Amber dumped her here, she would freeze to death.

'You stopped him coming back to me,' she snarled.

'I didn't and you know it!'

'Shut up now!' Amber screamed.

'It's true. He always wants me. He tells me he loves me every day. I share his life, his bed, his money and he can't keep his hands off me. The sex we have is electric. I will never give him up. He is mine. He will never leave me, for you or anyone,' Melissa bragged smugly because it was true, and she could say it without any doubt.

Amber slammed on the brakes, jolting them both forward. Melissa may as well have ripped her heart out of her chest and stamped on it. But the worst thing for Amber was that she knew it was true. The memory of that night came flooding back, but again she shook the thought away and replaced it again with her perfect image.

'Shut up, shut up!'

There were no lights around, and it seemed as though they were in the middle of nowhere. Amber gave another ear-splitting scream as she punched Melissa, knocking her head into the window and dazing her for a few seconds. But Amber was coming at her again, the blade glinting in the moonlight before she slashed downwards. Melissa shrieked as it ripped at her cheek. Amber grabbed her hair, lifting her upwards and then slammed her head down against the window again.

Melissa had to get out, so using all her strength she managed to push Amber backwards, giving her a few seconds to find the door handle. But it was locked. Amber grabbed her hair again and pulled her back. Blood dripped down Melissa's face and onto her clothes. She felt sick with pain and the fear of what damage had been done to her face, let alone her boyfriend.

'I want you dead,' Amber whispered in her ear but at that moment, Melissa flicked her head backwards, smashing it into Amber's face and making her lose her grip. She scrambled into the back seat, yelping. Amber jumped forward again, flipping Melissa over. Raising her hand again, she brought the blade down and ripped at Melissa's cheek a second time.

One of Luke's guitars was on the back seat. She noticed that it was the same one that had started off the whole feud with Amber. The one she had almost smashed at Ruby's when she first met Luke. The strings dug into her and it felt like her back was being ripped open as Amber pushed her down onto it.

Melissa grabbed at Amber's arms, and finding the wrist with Luke's cuff, she gripped it. The cuff tore from her wrist and Melissa held on to it as if her life depended on it. 'Amber, stop this,' Melissa sobbed. 'Please …' she was sure this was it, and she was going to die.

'Not so pretty any more lady, and it's your fault he's gone, too,' Amber hissed, just inches from her face.

He was dead because of Melissa. It wasn't *her* fault.

'You ki-killed him?' Melissa stuttered, tears stinging her eyes.

'I have him now, back in our special place where I first met him.' She rolled Melissa over, grabbing her hair, lifting her head up, and smashing it down on the guitar. Then she smashed it down again, but this time holding her face down so the metal strings and bridge cut into her cheek again. Amber sat on Melissa's back, her weight pinning her down. Grabbing her round the throat, she ripped the locket from her neck and threw it over her shoulder. Then she grabbed her neck, squeezing so hard, Melissa couldn't move or scream. Amber's grip was like a vice. Blood ran down the neck of the guitar pooling round the letters that spelt out 'Eagles'. This was going to be her last memory, Melissa thought as her body went limp.

'Say hello to that other little bitch who got in my way … I win!' Amber breathed in her ear as it all went black.

# Hospital (5)

October 15th 2014

'That's it. The next thing I remember was waking up here,' Melissa said, relieved to be finally done with the story, and realising she didn't know how she had got to the hospital.

Inspector Fox explained that a farmer had found her. Melissa didn't even know what time it was that Amber had dragged her from their flat, but they had looked at CCTV and seen them leave around 3.30. Melissa had been dumped like a piece of rubbish in his field.

'The farmer had found her around 7.00. He was an elderly man and was so shocked that he nearly had a heart attack. He thought you were dead. Then he turned you over and knew immediately who you were. His grandson has pictures of you on his wall.'

Melissa asked if he was OK, and said she wanted to send him a message thanking him for finding her. The inspector assured her he was fine.

'What happens now?'

Fox explained that they would take all the information back to the station and continue from there. Searches had already started, and they would be in touch when they had any updates. Before he left, Melissa asked if her locket had been found. She felt naked without it. He shook his head, but promised that if it turned up he would make sure she got it back.

Inspector Fox was a very busy man as Megan May's stabbing was now also part of the investigation. It was obviously connected somehow, but there didn't seem to be a logical explanation. Megan held no threat to Amber, so it was a mystery. But Fox felt sure it meant that there was something that hadn't been uncovered yet, or that someone wasn't telling the whole truth.

Dale got up and silently left the room. Beth followed him and tried to comfort him. But he gently pushed her away.

'Don't. I'm barely holding it together.' He punched the wall, nearly breaking his hand.

'He's coming back, I know he is.' Beth said, taking his hand and kissing it. She was trying to keep some hope alive, but it was hard when all the facts and details pointed to the worst case scenario.

Melissa finally got the all clear from her doctor to go home. He lectured her about resting and Liz had told her that she didn't need the dressing on her face any more. The stitches were enough, but the truth was that Melissa felt better covering them up for now.

'Thank you for looking after me,' Melissa said and hugged her tightly. She was sad to say goodbye to Liz and it seemed that Liz was sad to see Melissa go too.

'It was a pleasure. I really hope you find him safe and well. When you do, I want to be on the front row at his next gig.' Melissa promised her she would be their special guest and treated like a VIP.

She made one last stop before leaving. She couldn't leave without checking on Megan, who was still in a bad way and yet to wake up. Toby was still there, guarding her like a hound from hell, but was pleased Melissa was getting out. Melissa blamed herself for all of it.

'I bet you wish he'd never met me.' she said and gave Megan's hand a little squeeze.

Toby gave her one of his bear hugs and assured her it would have happened whoever Luke had met. 'Melissa, we all love you. Don't blame yourself,' he said and kissed her cheek.

'Love you too. I'm so sorry about Megan, but she will be fine.' Toby nodded and sat back down at his girlfriend's side. Melissa could see the anger and worry back on his face. She was full of anger herself. This sweet, innocent girl, who lay there pale and motionless, didn't deserve this. Amber had stabbed her, and they all knew it. The question was, why? It made no sense, Melissa thought as she left the room, and headed home.

The entrance doors opened and Melissa stepped out into a sea of lenses and shouts.

'Where's Luke?'

'Is he dead, Melissa?'

'Did you kill him in a jealous rage?'

She kept walking, head down, her parents and friends at her side. But they couldn't get to the car. They should have called Ray who could have arranged some security, but she had just wanted to go, and hadn't thought about it.

Jean screamed at them to leave her alone. Melissa's mind went blank, and she didn't know whether to just get to her dad's car, or run back inside. Her legs were frozen to the spot. She was surrounded by a flock of vultures, tearing the last bit of her away. Her sobs turned to screams as she sank to her knees in the middle of the chaos, her hands over her face, giving up...

'Get up,' Beth ordered in her ear. Melissa shook her head. 'I said get up,' she said again, grabbing her arm and trying to yank her back to her feet. Beth wasn't going to let them win or let Melissa give up when she had so much to fight for. The pushing was getting out of control, and Beth almost lost her footing but Dale steadied her, cursing the crowd. He wrestled a camera from someone's hand in the chaos. If Beth fell, it could hurt the baby, and only he knew about it. He had to protect her, but he had to help Melissa too. He couldn't do both.

Toby must have heard the cries, because suddenly he was storming through the doors, pushing aside anyone in his path.

'Leave her the fuck alone, you pieces of scum,' he roared as he scooped up his friend and cradled her in his arms, carrying her through the crowd and finally placing her in her dad's car.

'Thanks, Tobes,' she said through sobs.

'No problem. Now go home. Me and Megs will see you very soon.' He patted Dale on the shoulder and kissed Beth as he shut the door. Then he turned to the swarm of photographers and walked straight through them, pushing and shoving them out of the way. They were lucky that was all they got. But he had someone much more important to take care of, and getting arrested for assault was not going to help.

Dale stuck his finger up as the car drove away. But the press now had their story. It had been almost a week since one of the most famous musicians in the world had last been seen. Melissa's public breakdown just added to the drama.

'Jesus, I think the kid might be dead. Shit, this is one hell of a story,' Jimmy said, straightening his black beanie and turning to his colleagues. His new camera, paid for by Tom, hung around his neck.

They were excited yet shocked. The rumours now had some substance and they all needed to get the exclusive on it. The chase was on.

*****

Toby returned to Megan's side and sat watching her motionless face, taking in every part of it. He was heartbroken, and angry with himself that he hadn't gone with her to get supplies for the group. Had he done so, this would never have happened. He could have stopped the attacker or taken the blow himself. It would be a tragedy if, having found the girl of his dreams, he lost her like this.

'Son, I'm here now.' Jayne Maxwell, Toby's mum, had arrived. She hadn't even met Megan properly but whenever she spoke to her son lately he seemed happy, which told her everything she needed to know. He looked tired, Jayne thought, and she told him to relax and close his eyes for a while. She promised him she wouldn't let anyone near Megan, and he knew she wouldn't because Mrs Maxwell was not a woman you messed with. He nodded and went for a cigarette before returning and finally dropping off to sleep, for a while at least. He was leaning back in his chair, still holding Megan's hand.

The minutes ticked by as Toby slept and Jayne read her book, occasionally sending a text message to update the rest of the family on the situation. Toby's family was large and if they all turned to see him, there would be a queue outside his door to the end of the corridor. Jayne was the head of the family, and she was in control of the situation. She took no nonsense from anyone. The vultures outside had just been introduced to Mrs Maxwell and their ears were still ringing from her foghorn-like voice. One reporter's arm still hurt after she had swung her bag at it because he was in her way.

The flames of red hair lay wildly around the girl's pale face. Such a sweet and kind looking face, Jayne thought, and smiled at her son's choice. But she then frowned at the awful after-effects the attack had caused. Toby had always wanted kids, but he wouldn't be having them with this girl. Jayne leaned forward, staring at her. She could have sworn she moved a little and edged closer and stroked her face.

'Megan,'

A few seconds passed before Megan slowly turned her head towards Jayne. 'Toby,' she murmured. Her eyes opened but she couldn't focus at first and looked around, feeling a sense of panic because she couldn't think straight and she didn't know where she was. The last thing she remembered was arriving at Luke's house.

Toby woke up as his mum shook him.

Megan became calmer as she saw his face. 'What happened?' she asked, then she realised she was in pain, and this began to jog her memory. 'Is everyone OK?' She was worried that she wasn't the only one who had been attacked, but Toby assured her that everyone was fine.

'You're not hurt?' she asked him and he shook his head

'Don't worry about me ... I'm sorry, I should have gone with you,' he said as he leaned down and kissed her dry lips.

'It's not your fault.' She winced at the pain as she tried to move.

Jayne leaned over and introduced herself and Megan smiled up at her. It wasn't the best way to meet your boyfriend's mother, but then being stabbed wasn't a welcome experience either.

Toby called Doctor Howard, who was also in charge of Megan's care, and Liz. They wanted to keep the level of interaction to a minimum and they already had gained the trust of these famous people. It was not a case of giving them special treatment, but more about ensuring they prevented intrusions from the press and leaks of information – there was a criminal investigation going on, after all. They checked Megan over and were pleased at her recovery so far. Then Toby told her the bad news that after her attack they'd discovered that her womb had been so badly damaged it had to be removed, meaning she would never be able to have children. It was the worst thing he had ever had to do. Megan took it better than he thought she would. She didn't say much, just nodded her head and then asked if Luke had been found yet. She cried when he told her he was still missing.

Toby called Tom to tell him that Megan was awake and was doing well. It was some good news at least.

*****

'She's physically and emotionally drained, but she's stronger than you think. She'll get through this,' Beth said about Melissa, who had now been discharged from hospital and had arrived home. Tom and Jo-Jo had been at the flat just seconds before Melissa arrived home. Beth had called Tom on her way back because she wanted to see them both. She was worried about everyone and didn't really want her friends too far away. They had both been concerned by how Melissa looked. She was so thin, her tiny body was covered in bruises and she'd hardly said a word.

Melissa had showered and almost been force-fed by her mum who wasn't having her daughter starving to death along with everything else. Melissa didn't have the energy to argue as Jean then put her to bed. Luke's aftershave smell was there again and after tossing and turning for a while, she eventually drifted off.

Beth was struggling to keep her secret to herself. She felt dreadful and she'd had to run to the bathroom to be sick three times since getting back from the hospital. Jean had already worked it out. Beth was just coming out of the bathroom for the third time when Jean appeared and gently ushered her back inside.

'Bethany Watkins, how far gone are you?' Beth tried to deny it but Jean wasn't having it. 'Darling, I am not stupid. Throwing up, tired, no cigarettes or alcohol?' Jean smiled and told Beth she was delighted for her and just wanted to help.

Tears flowed down Beth's face and she frantically wiped them away. 'Stupid hormones. I'm so scared.' Her knees buckled under her and Jean caught her and sat her carefully on the floor. Beth thought she was five weeks but she hadn't seen a doctor yet. She told Jean that they'd found out the day after Luke went missing and she hadn't really had time to think about it. Then she'd been booked to attend a wedding the next day as the photographer, and she felt that she couldn't let the couple down. Jean agreed she would go with her for moral support. Dale wanted to go, but it was decided that he should stay away because it would just cause a stir if he was spotted. Mick would stay with Melissa so she didn't have to worry about anything.

Beth admitted it wasn't planned, and they were scared. She knew it wasn't an ideal situation but she wouldn't have an abortion, no way. 'My baby will have everything I never had. I'll cherish it and protect it and be everything my parents weren't.'

Jean had no doubt she meant it. 'You'll be a great Mum and Dale will be a fantastic dad.' She reminded Beth that she would always have her and Mick for support and she didn't have to make up for the shortcomings of her parents. 'You may not be biologically my daughter, but I love you just the same,' she said, wiping Beth's eyes again. She was effectively going to be a grandparent and despite everything else, she was very excited about it.

'I'm so worried about Luke. Please don't let him be dead.' Beth buried her head in her hands, the hormones taking over again. She had never really thought about her feelings for Luke until now. He was just Luke, who was always there. But now he was gone she realised how much she cared for him. She loved him like a brother, and just like Dale, she wanted their child's uncle to come home. Beth had cried more in the last week than she had in years, and she hated it. Jean held her and comforted her, telling her that it was healthier to cry and let her feelings out, rather than trying to be brave and bottling things up.

'Thank you, Mum, for everything,' Beth said, before getting up and going to the bedroom. She curled up next to her sleeping friend, and immediately she was asleep too.

'Look at them, Mick.' Jean and Mick stood in the doorway looking at the sleeping girls. 'They're just kids. The world thinks they know them but they don't. No amount of money or fame can erase loss and pain,' Jean continued, a tear escaping down her cheek. They looked just like they had done when they were little, sharing a bed when one was scared or upset.

'Everything's going to be OK. I'll give that boy a piece of my mind when he finally rolls home.' Mick tried to make a joke of it. Jean smiled and patted his arm before going to check on the others. She found Dale in Luke's studio. He was sitting and staring at Chloe, with sadness in his eyes. He was missing his best friend. He turned as she entered the room, but there was no hint of the smile he would usually greet her with. Jean explained that Beth was fine but sleeping, and that she knew about the baby.

'Dale, I know you want to be strong, and you feel that you need to be the leader while Luke isn't here, but you don't have to pretend with me. You know you can talk to me in confidence, if you need to.'

Dale looked up at her and just for a moment, he looked like a little boy. 'I'm terrified,' he admitted. He was twenty three, and hadn't even thought about having children for a long time yet. That was something grownups did, not him. He still felt exactly the same as he did when he was 17, and although legally he was an adult, he often didn't feel like one.

'To be honest, I'm freaking out.' Jean patted his shoulder and took a seat opposite him, taking his hand. 'I'm not sure I'm ready for this. There's too much going on in my head. I need my best mate to talk to. Where the hell is he?' He began to panic.

'Everything you're feeling is normal. It's a huge commitment, and nothing can prepare you for it. You have to be completely honest. Do you want this baby – can you get past your initial shock and rise to the challenge? I'm asking because that girl is like another daughter to me, and I don't want her left alone in this..' Dale's expression answered the question.

'I wouldn't do that to her. She's my Beth, and as scared as I am at the moment, that's my child. Of course I want it. I'm just scared and confused, and I need to get my head around it all which is not easy with everything else going on. I thought you knew me better than that?' He snapped, and immediately felt bad. This was Jean after all. There was a smile on Jean's face as he apologised.

'No need to apologise that was the answer I was hoping to hear.' It had reassured her that his response had been so fierce. He loved her and the baby, no question about that. Jean still held his hand. 'I'm here, whenever you need me, and I think you should consider telling people about it. It will make it easier to be able to talk openly about the things that worry you.' Jean also suggested his own parents might appreciate the good news at this awful time. Talking to Jean had taken a weight off his shoulders and helped him put it all into perspective.

'Thanks Mrs Webb, I'll speak to Beth when she's awake. She worries that telling people early will jinx it, but perhaps you're right. It will only be leaked to the papers somehow soon anyway.' He paused, and looked up at her before saying 'And, I just wanted to say that Melissa means a lot to all of us, and no matter what happens, the boys and I will always be there for her.' Jean smiled again, this time with a tear in her eye, and patted his hand.

'Thank you, let's just hope Luke comes home soon. I'm really not sure what Melissa will do if he doesn't.'

Dale didn't even want to think about the possibility of Luke not coming back. He couldn't imagine life without his oldest friend, especially since he was now going to be a father.

*****

'Jay-Den and Stan are taking care of everything. They're working with the PR team to get a statement out, so you don't need to worry. But for god's sake keep your mouth shut, Beth. Don't go anywhere near Twitter!' Ray was pacing around his lead singer's living room. To his surprise, she didn't argue. Tom and Jo-Jo sat on one sofa, Beth and Dale on the other and Melissa's parents hovered behind them. Melissa was still sleeping, and they were happy to leave her that way.

'I think they're going to keep it simple. Melissa fell and hurt herself, and Luke is away for a few days, taking a break.' Ray said he knew nobody would believe it, particularly because of the police presence at the hospital, but they couldn't say too much until they themselves knew more about what was going on.

'No!' A voice boomed, making everyone jump. Melissa had woken up and come to find out what was going on. 'Luke isn't away taking a break; he's been kidnapped and he might be dead!' Her voice was firm and the room went silent at her unexpected appearance. Melissa never usually spoke to anyone like that, but she had to make herself heard this time. This was *her* life and Luke's life. She didn't care about PR or publicity – they weren't important right now.

Ray tried to explain that telling the full truth would open up a 'shit storm' but Melissa yelled this time. 'I'm already in a shit storm!'

She turned to leave the room, but as she did, the next thing Ray said almost sent her over the edge. He started talking about the boys spending some time in the studio to keep things ticking over, maybe doing some mixing. They could work on the things that didn't need Luke immediately and if there was material here then he could take it and make a start on it. Dale looked up and saw the fury on Melissa's face. 'Are you kidding me?' Melissa seethed as she stormed across the room and glaring at Ray, who backed away.

Dale stood up and moved between them. Ray would never offend her intentionally. 'Melissa, he meant nothing by it, calm down.' Dale held his hands out towards her.

Melissa jabbed a finger in Ray's direction. 'You and that fucking label don't give a shit about him, only the money he makes you. Nobody touches his stuff, right? It goes nowhere until he comes home. Get out!' she screamed, shaking with anger and emotion as Dale held her. For the first time, she regretted ever seeing that flyer. It had changed everything and right now it hadn't been for the better.

'Melissa, I do care about him, of course I do. I'm sorry.' Ray said he hadn't meant to upset her, and he cursed himself for not thinking before he spoke. He immediately realised how insensitive it sounded. Melissa said nothing as she removed herself from Dale's embrace and left the room, shutting herself in Luke's studio. She sat behind the door so that no one could come in, and ignored every attempt to coax her out. She was seething and although she knew she was overreacting to what Ray said, at that moment she felt she had every right. This was her home, so people could just back off.

But Beth wouldn't give up and eventually Melissa let her in. Beth sat down next to her, against the door. 'Are we holding a protest? We'll need food if we're in for the long haul. Peaceful or rowdy?' Beth asked, smiling.

To Beth's surprise Melissa laughed loudly. 'Rowdy, if anyone sets foot in here. I don't care about the album or the damn record label's time or money. They can bloody well wait.' Without Luke, they had no album anyway so they could shove it. She was ranting, which was good because she was able to let off steam. Her head banged against the door as she gesticulated.

'You just threw a proper diva fit. I'm very proud,' Beth said and laughed. Then she noticed Melissa was now rubbing her bandaged face, deep in thought. 'Do you want to look at it?' She asked. Melissa knew she had to face it one day, but she shook her head, saying she wasn't ready. Beth reminded her that there would never be a good time, and the sooner she could accept what had happened, the sooner she could start to heal. She pulled her up, and into her bathroom where they stood in front of the large oval mirror.

'I can't,' Melissa said, terrified.

'Yes, you can,' Beth assured her.

They stood for a few minutes as Melissa tried to pluck up courage, before finally indicating that she was ready. Beth gently pulled off the dressing, and Melissa closed her eyes as Beth turned her to face the mirror. Feeling sick with dread, Melissa counted to ten and took a deep breath as she opened her eyes. The face that looked back at her was not her face, and her heart thudded in her chest as she tried desperately to stop herself from screaming. The left side had two deep slashes, both only centimetres from her eye, and ending just above her lips. Through the middle of the two cuts were six lines made by Luke's guitar strings. There was a dip just under her eye where the bridge of the guitar had pushed into it, and stitches were all that held her cheek together. Her skin was purple and black and her eye was swollen and bloodshot.

'Look at me,' Melissa cried. She was mutilated and she knew she looked hideous.

'I think it's healing fine. It looks better than it did two days ago, and in another two days it will look even better. Give it a month, and you'll be good as new.' Beth tried to make her feel better, but it didn't work and Melissa begged for it to be covered up. Beth reminded her that the doctors were confident it would heal fully and leave very little scarring, if any.

Unfortunately, Melissa saw a different image looking back at her. She touched her cheek, her hand shaking as she traced the lines held together by stitches. 'What will he think of me now,' she whispered. Beth hugged her and told her not to worry. Luke would still love her whatever she looked like. Melissa leaned forward and placed her hand on Beth's stomach, taking her by surprise. 'I can't wait to meet my niece or nephew,' she said.

Beth looked at her wide-eyed. 'How did you know?' Melissa laughed and said the first time she had refused a cigarette it could mean only one thing. 'Dammit, am I that obvious? Your Mum said the same thing!' Beth said, laughing. She realised that it was going to be impossible to keep this a secret for long.

'It's so exciting. A baby, wow!' Melissa's emotions were a mixture of happiness and sadness. Kids might not be part of her plans right now but they would be one day, and she could only imagine having babies with one person. She was pleased for Beth and Dale, and she knew they would make great parents.

Beth knew it wasn't going to stay a secret much longer, so she decided that all of their close friends and family should be told. At least she would have more support during this nightmare situation. When they were told, everyone in the house was thrilled, and the guys christened the baby their 'little fledgling'.

They felt bad about telling Toby after what had happened to Megan. But Toby couldn't have been happier for them. 'Congrats mate.

We're all already trained in sleepless nights, so you'll be a pro. But nappy changing? You're on you own son,' he'd said to Dale when they'd phoned him at the hospital.

Melissa told Dale and Tom to go and be with Toby. He needed support as well. Toby had been pleased to see his bandmates, and Megan asked them if they were OK. Tom was still quite shaken up over the stabbing and couldn't get the image out of his mind. But as usual he said very little, preferring to keep his feelings to himself. Megan had thanked Tom as he hugged her - she remembered him with Toby as they desperately tried to keep her alive. It was an image she would never forget.

*****

The Black Eagles' official statement to their fans read as follows.

'To all our fans, from Dale, Tom and Toby. We are very sorry to say that at this present time our dear friend and front man Luke has now been missing for five days. His girlfriend Melissa has been released from hospital after being subjected to a serious attack, but thankfully she is making a good recovery. Unfortunately, our friend, and Toby Maxwell's girlfriend, Megan May is still in hospital also having been seriously injured in a separate attack. There is no further information we can give you until we know more but they are both being taken care of and have all of our love and support. The police are now investigating, and are using all available resources to find Luke. These have been dark times for our Eagle family over the past few days and we ask for some peace and privacy while we come to terms with what has happened. We would like to thank you all for your support and kind words, which have been overwhelming. Please stay calm, and pray that we find our friend safe and well. As a band, we have stopped all work and cancelled all engagements until this situation is over.'

Stan had listened to Melissa after she had called and begged him to do as she asked, and to her surprise he wasn't hard to convince. Even *he* knew the world was catching on quickly to what was really happening. The fact that two of their girlfriends had almost been murdered was something that could never be contained. Luke was never out of the public eye for five days, so it was obvious that something was wrong. The internet went crazy after the statement was released, and within two hours, the entrance of their building was covered with bunches of flowers and letters of support. Tess and her fan group sent a beautiful bunch of flowers for Megan too.

Melissa activated her accounts again to say, 'The Black Eagles have the best fans, thank you all. At times like this, you don't know how much your support brightens these dark days. #FindLuke'

Later that evening, Melissa finally persuaded them all to let her have some time alone. She was so grateful for all the support but she needed space to think. She stood in front of the mirror again, staring at her reflection, and turning her head to different angles. But it was no use, she thought, her face was destroyed. There was nothing she could do but hope it would calm down and heal as time went on, as the doctors seemed to think it would. As the tears fell, she pulled the mirror off the wall and threw it to the floor, sending shards scattering everywhere. Melissa stood barefoot in the middle of the sea of glass looking down at her now fragmented reflection. Her emotions getting the better of her, she did the same with every mirror in the house.

She finished off the bottle of wine in the fridge along with Luke's half bottle of whisky and a whole pack of cigarettes. Then she found Luke's stash of weed and smoked that too, as she called his number over and over, just to hear his voice. Listening to their album only added to the torture, and at four in the morning Melissa was violently sick. By late morning, feeling like death warmed up, she had given in and called Beth. The hangover was the worst she had ever experienced. Beth came over and helped Melissa shower, sobbing as she whimpered about ending it all. She'd had enough, and she felt as though she couldn't fight any more.

'Don't you dare say that again,' Beth yelled, shaking her by the shoulders. 'You get dressed. Don't you dare give up, not now. Luke needs you, my child needs its aunty and I need my best friend.' Beth's voice was full of hurt. 'Don't you dare leave me too,' she begged.

Melissa sucked in her breath, realising suddenly how selfish she was being and how much hurt just that one sentence would have caused her best friend. She got dressed properly for the first time in what seemed like weeks and Beth brushed her hair until it was perfect.

Beth had borrowed Dale's car for the day so they went for a drive. It felt good to get out even if they had been ambushed as soon as they left the building. But they kept their heads downs and their mouths shut. Melissa's hangover headache was still raging. They called in to see Megan, who was putting on a brave face and insisting she was fine and didn't want any fuss. Melissa was furious – enough was enough - this had to end, and soon. Amber wasn't this clever, surely, Melissa thought.

She was starting to think that maybe she was receiving help in some way.

Toby's mum was there, in full mothering mode, fussing around Toby and Megan and then the rest of them, treating them all like her own kids. They were important to her son, so they were important to her too.

# Like Lightening

October 16th 2014

'They've found nothing! This is ridiculous, what are they playing at?' Debbie ranted as she stomped around her son's kitchen. She needed to feel like she was doing something, so caring for Melissa was helping her, but nothing could keep her thoughts from her missing son. Luke's dad wasn't coping very well and wouldn't leave the house in case Luke called or turned up. He'd been pulled away from the photographers quite a few times and had almost been arrested for assault. He was frantic with worry, and the lies about his son had finally got too much for him to cope with. He knew his son better than anyone, and the most recent rumour, that Luke had attacked Melissa and caused her injury was the straw that broke the camel's back. People were calling Luke a woman beater solely on the basis of one ridiculous article suggesting the possibility. But that was enough to start the story spreading like wildfire, and being repeated as though it were fact. Stuart was so proud of his son, and these people were tainting his name when he wasn't around to defend himself. Luke despised men who hurt women, and he would never raise his hand to Melissa, no matter how bad things got. Showing his emotions with words and music was the way he coped when things got tough. That was why he was so good – people could relate to his music because it was so honest and personal. He turned bad things into good, and he shared it with the world. So many fans had said his words had saved them when they were low, and that was something money couldn't buy.

It had been six days now, and there had been no news. The investigation was still ongoing but it was as though Luke had been erased from the world, and Amber too. The trace on both phones had drawn a blank. They'd been dumped in a bin in Camden Town, completely wiped of all data, definitely making it start to look like Amber was receiving some help. From what they knew about her state of mind, they didn't think she would think of little details like that. And Luke's car was still missing despite a national alert, including all ports and airports.

Melissa heard the smash as Debbie dropped a mug. She was on her knees in the kitchen clearing it up, apologising and promising to buy another one. Her hands were shaking. 'Don't be daft. Leave it, Debs.' Melissa led her up to her feet.

'No, I made the mess, I'll clean it up,' she insisted, so Melissa let her carry on. It wasn't worth arguing.

'I just want my baby back', Debbie suddenly began sobbing. 'Sorry.'

'Don't apologise for being upset, we all are. You're his mum, so you're closer to him than any of us.'

Debbie hugged Melissa tightly, scared she might lose her too. 'I'm glad he has you.' She knew Melissa loved Luke the man, not Luke the rock star. They sat on the sofa and she picked up a carrier bag she'd brought with her. She pulled out an old grey photo album.

'What's this?' Melissa asked.

'It's our family album. I started it when Luke was born and kept it going up until ...' Debbie trailed off. She explained that she couldn't have any more children after Luke. She could conceive, but she always miscarried before twelve weeks, and eventually she and Stuart had agreed to stop trying. 'He was meant to be,' Debbie said quietly. It explained how she was with him. Nagging, Luke called it, but he loved her all the same.

Melissa opened the album. It started the day he was born and the last photo was just a few weeks ago. There were articles and interviews, just like any other proud mother would have as memories. They laughed at the pictures, and for a while forgot he was gone. Melissa loved seeing this part of him and Debbie told her she had never shown the album to anyone outside family. Melissa asked her why not.

'Because they're my private memories and only people I trust completely get to share them,' Debbie replied. Melissa smiled, knowing for certain she had been accepted.

'That's a nice picture.' Melissa pointed at one of Luke holding Chloe. Debbie explained that it was his twelfth birthday and his first guitar. His smile hadn't changed and he looked so pleased with it. Melissa asked if they had ever thought Luke would become a rock star. Debbie smiled and said she always knew he had a gift. He'd written his first song at thirteen and she knew then he was talented. He never had a guitar lesson in his life, he just watched his idols and mimicked them. When he turned sixteen he suddenly found his own style, saying he didn't want to be a copycat. He wanted to be himself.

Debbie was also very proud of Dale. He was a bit older before he started playing the guitar, and he wasn't as naturally talented as Luke.

But with a few lessons and a lot of practice, he was soon jamming away with Luke and dreaming about one day being a rock star as well.

'What's amazing is that they actually did it. And you are his angel, my love' Debbie said. She wasn't sure if she was happier about Luke having achieved his childhood dream, or finding the perfect girl in Melissa. She did know that it was important for Luke to have someone other than his mum and his best friend believe in him. He'd needed a very special girl to understand him and accept his commitment to his music, which was at times all-consuming.

'I don't understand,' Melissa wasn't sure exactly what Debbie meant when she said that she was his angel.

She took Melissa's hand. 'Tina, his ex, was a bitch. She didn't even try to understand him. She always wanted his attention and complained when he just wanted to write or play. She would put him down, just to cause an argument and get his attention. She only ever watched him play twice, and never said anything positive - she just made jokes.' It was obvious that Debbie really didn't like her. 'Then you came into his life and changed everything. I knew you were good for him before I met you, just seeing the change in him.' Melissa blushed and asked why that was. 'He smiles much more now. He couldn't stop talking about you the weekend you met, and he must have told me the story about Amber, the guitar and the slap at least twenty times!' She laughed, and Melissa noticed Luke had his mum's blue eyes. Her jet-black hair hung to just below her shoulders with no hint of grey. She didn't look fifty-one, although lately the stress lines were more evident. Debbie Black was a very attractive woman. Luke got his intense look from her, and his cheeky smile from his dad. You could never doubt they were his parents. When you looked at each one it was like Luke staring back at you. They were a beautiful family.

'I love watching him write and perform. It's the most amazing thing. Tina must be an idiot,' Melissa said. She hadn't known that about her. Luke just said that it hadn't worked so he ended it. He didn't really talk about his exes much and would just say, 'They're not my problem any more.'

Debbie wiped away a tear. 'Where is he?' She cried again, and they shared another hug, before Debbie went to make yet more coffee.

Melissa was flicking through the photos when one in particular caught her eye. 'Is this Chloe?' she asked.

Debbie put down her coffee and looked at it. She nodded. 'Such a shame. Luke was heartbroken when she was killed in the fire.' Debbie looked at the photo for a few seconds then looked away. It had been such a horrible tragedy. Chloe was always at their house having dinner and watching TV. 'She was such a sweet girl.' Debbie shook her head. The photo showed Luke and a small girl who had light-brown hair in two pigtails, tied with pink ribbons. Both children were six years old and Luke's eyes were just as blue and mesmerising back then. They were both sitting on a blanket in what looked like a playground. Chloe was smiling with her arm round Luke's shoulder, and he was laughing and holding his hand up in a peace sign. There were children playing in the background.

'That's a nice memory to have,' Melissa said, feeling sad for the girl in the photo. As she was about to close the album something caught her eye. Melissa went cold and stared at the photo, thinking that she must be seeing things. She rubbed her eyes in disbelief and looked again, closely. There was no mistake.

'Melissa, what's wrong?' Debbie asked her.

Melissa checked the photo again. It was still the same, she wasn't going mad. 'Debbie, where was this taken?'

'Rosewood Primary School.' Debbie had been a dinner lady for a few months, and had taken the picture.

Melissa pointed at the photo, not at Luke or Chloe, but at the child in the background, looking at Chloe with a familiar and unmistakable cold stare. The same stare that she'd seen all too often over the last few months, and most recently when the guitar strings were cutting her flesh just a few days ago.

It was Amber! Amber had been a pupil at his school, and this photo proved that she was just as obsessed with him back then. Then a thought struck her like a bolt of lightning. 'Oh no, Chloe...' Her blood ran cold. The photo album fell from her hands as she remembered the words Amber had said during the attack:

'Say hello to that other little bitch that got in my way...'

*****

'Don't bottle it up, you can talk to me,' Toby said, taking hold of Megan's hand.

She smiled and said again that she was fine. 'Talking about it won't change things. I'm more concerned about you.' That was typical of Megan, always putting others first. Toby assured her that she didn't have to worry about him, but the person who had done this to her had plenty to worry about. 'Stay out of trouble,' she warned him, but he told her that he couldn't promise that. One of the things she liked about him was that he never made promises he couldn't keep. But on this occasion, she would have preferred a different answer.

'Do you remember that you were trying to tell me something after the attack? What was it?' Toby asked. Megan pretended to think about it, but played dumb, saying it must have been the shock. In reality, there was something, but she still wasn't sure she was right. She needed to be in the office to look into it. But that wasn't going to happen any time soon.

Toby told her that he had tried to find her parents but hadn't had any luck. They'd been travelling for eight months and had hardly been in touch. 'They'll be in some remote place. But thanks for trying.' She leaned over and kissed his cheek. 'Could you get my phone? I just want to text Melissa. And I could really do with a hot drink please.'

Toby found her phone then went to get her a drink. 'I'll just be a few minutes, but I don't want anyone in there unless I'm with her,' he told the policeman outside her room. The officer nodded, although those were his orders anyway.

Megan switched on her phone and called the one person she thought might be able to help her. Jack, her colleague and friend, answered immediately. He was relieved to hear from her. He'd been so worried, and nobody would tell him anything.

'Jack, I'm fine. I could do without the hole in my stomach, but that's not my main concern right now.' She didn't have time for small talk, so she quickly explained what she needed him to do.

'You want me to do what?!' Jack yelled down the phone. 'Are you insane? I could lose my job, and so could you. Are you even sure?'

Jack was the only proper friend she'd had until she had met Toby and the rest of his group. He had always been nice to her, unlike a lot of men she'd encountered in the past. Megan explained that she wasn't sure about anything, but there was definitely something odd going on. She needed proof before she even attempted to tell Toby. He was already on the edge and if she was right, this would send him right over. Jack was torn between his friend who desperately needed his help, and the job that he loved. She assured him that nobody would know it was him. She would give him all her log in details so all traces would come back to her. If she was wrong, she would take the fall, but if she was right then the risk was worth it.

'You really like him, don't you?'

'Yes, I do ... please, Jack.' She was risking everything for Toby.

'Fine ... I'll see what I can do.'

'Thank you.' She hung up just as Toby came back in with tea and some biscuits for her. She held her arms out to him, asking for one of his giant hugs that were so comforting. He held her gently, and she kissed his cheek, still thinking about Jack's mission, and hoping she was wrong. Because if she was right, it meant that the man she was falling in love with was being lied to.

# Vital Signs

October 18th 2014

'Thank you, but you don't have to keep checking on me,' Melissa said as she stomped around the living room, her cigarette smoke filling the air.

'Yes I do. When Luke gets home he'll want to know you were properly looked after. We'll all be in the shit if we don't.' Ray laughed and tried to lighten the mood. Melissa felt sick at the change in tactics that had been agreed upon after she'd spotted Amber in the photograph. It had made everyone realise just how determined and dangerous Amber was. They didn't know for certain that her comment had anything to do with the death of Chloe James all those years ago, but they couldn't rule it out either.

Stan, Jay-Den and Ray had agreed with the police to hold a press conference, hoping to draw Amber out of hiding. It might not work, but nothing else was happening and they were at a loss as to what else to try. The police had scoured London and the surrounding areas endlessly, and had even carried out searches in Luke's home town of Portsmouth, all to no avail.

Melissa and his parents had agreed to take part in the press conference, along with Inspector Fox. Dale and Tom would be there for support, but not part of the conference itself. Everyone had agreed that it wouldn't be helpful if they lost their tempers and said the wrong thing.

'You need to eat before we go.' Ray hadn't seen her eat anything in days and was concerned about her weight loss. She was looking very pale, and her clothes hung off her. The constant nagging about food irritated Melissa. She'd never been a big eater and she wasn't hungry now. 'Please, love,' he begged. 'What would Luke say, if he was here?' Those last few words worked because they reminded her that Luke wouldn't let her do this to herself. 'He'd want you to stay strong, and you know it. He needs you. Starving yourself won't help him,' he lectured.

'Ray, I'm lost ... I can't eat. I've barely slept in a week and when I do I have nightmares that he isn't coming back, or Amber coming at me with a knife. Or both.' She hadn't told anyone that until now.

Ray put down his phone, crossed the room and hugged her. 'I know. Everything will be fine, I promise.' He made her sit and relax while he cooked her a huge fry-up. She played about with it at first but then she realised that she really was hungry. She finished the lot.

'Better?' Ray asked, and she nodded and smiled.

'Thank you for everything, Ray. You're a fantastic manager.' He shrugged – it was what he was paid to do. 'I'm sorry for all the trouble I've caused you.'

'You've certainly kept me busy.'

'Sorry.'

'Melissa, you're a rock star's girlfriend. You're meant to run a little wild now and again,' he said and winked.

Feeling better after getting some food inside her, she got dressed, settling on black cords, a white lace fitted blouse and black heels. She didn't put any make-up on and let her hair hang loosely so it covered her left cheek, which made her feel more comfortable.

'How do I look?' she asked Ray who was waiting for her in the living room.

He was impressed by how she had pulled herself together and right now it was perfect timing. 'You look great.' He really wanted to say that she looked beautiful, but he didn't want her to take it the wrong way. She did look beautiful, even with the damage to her face. Melissa just had a way of lighting up a room – she had a natural inner beauty that a scarred face couldn't change, and Ray wished she could see it herself. He could see why Luke was in love with this girl. Ray didn't fancy her - he'd been happily married for twenty years - but he had become close to these kids, and was fond of them all.

'Ready? It's time to go.' He held his hand out to her and promised he wouldn't leave her side if she didn't want him to.

She took some deep breaths and clutched his hand. 'For Luke,' she said as he guided her through the door, into the chaos outside, and onwards to the waiting car.

*****

'Amber ... I'm begging you, if you have Luke then please let him go. This has gone on too long. He needs to come home. You say that you love him, but you don't do this to the people you love. I am not asking you do it for me, but for Luke. Let him come home. We love him more than you could ever love him. Please ... I want him back! Plea ...' her voice broke and tears took over.

Ray waved his hand, calling time on Melissa. She had done enough. This was just too much. The world had what they wanted, the full story. The pleas from Luke's family and girlfriend filled news stations across the world. Stuart Black cuddled his distraught wife and Ray held Melissa in the same way he would hold his daughter when she was upset or scared.

Jean and Mick were watching at home. Melissa had asked them not to come because it would be upsetting enough for her without having them there too.

Fox ended the session by asking the public to come forward if they had any information, no matter how insignificant it may seem. He also warned against approaching Amber because she was considered dangerous. He also asked for anyone who knew her or any family members to come forward, to help find her. But apart from Jenny, the girl from Ruby's, there was no response. And she insisted that she hadn't seen Amber for months.

Jenny told the police that they'd fallen out just before Amplified because she refused to go with Amber. She had grown tired of her odd ways and had been relieved when she didn't hear from her again. Jenny didn't know much about Amber's family life. She had met her in a club a few years before. Amber never spoke about her family, just said they weren't important. Jenny had been concerned about her obsession with Luke, but never imagined she would go so far. She promised she would get in touch straight away if she heard from her.

'You did so well, but it's over now,' Ray said as he guided Melissa and Luke's parents into a private room. Dale and Tom were waiting for them and they hugged Melissa, telling her that Luke would be proud of her. Jay-Den was also there.

Stuart hugged Melissa too. 'You did good, kid. I'm so proud of you.' He kissed the top of her head.

'Do you think it'll help? Will it bring him home?' Melissa asked. Stuart assured her that his son was coming home soon, and she had done him proud.

Fox looked round the room, watching them all as they supported each other. Something suddenly caught his eye.

Fox had been in the force for thirty years and in that time had developed a sixth sense, which enabled him to pick up on things that others might not. There was somebody in that room who knew more than they were letting on. It was all in the eyes. He knew for certain it wasn't the girlfriend – she was too upset to be involved, and nobody was that good an actor.

'I messed it up, I said the wrong things,' Melissa was saying. Debbie patted her arm and told her not to be so silly. She had done just fine.

Jay-Den asked Melissa if she would like him to take her home. Ray could do with a break, to go and see his own family. She wasn't sure but he insisted. 'Please, I just want to help ... that's all.' Ray had done so much and had barely seen his wife since all this started so she agreed, telling him to go home and have the rest of the day off.

'Jay-Den, take her home and keep your hands off her,' Dale warned him. She was vulnerable and he would break his legs if he made a move on her again. Jay-Den assured him that was not his intention. He just wanted to help, nothing more. He needed them to believe him so he didn't have to walk on eggshells around her all the time. What had happened was in the past, and he wanted it left there. Dale accepted that he meant it – he seemed genuinely sorry. Dale was anxious to get back to Beth, who was really suffering with her morning sickness, and hadn't been able to be at the news conference.

*****

Melissa and Jay-Den didn't speak much on the way home, apart from a little small talk, and it all felt slightly awkward. Another press ambush was waiting outside the building, and Melissa knew she wouldn't get to the door on her own. Swallowing her pride she asked, 'Jay-Den, will you help me get inside, please.' He nodded and ushered her past the reporters, telling them that they'd been given all the information they were getting, and Miss Webb would not be making any further comments.

'Thanks,' she said once they got to the door. Jay-Den shrugged saying it was all in a day's work then turned to leave. Melissa stared at his back, feeling guilty that things were still so tense between them, after he had shown how sorry he was for what he'd done. Maybe he isn't so bad, she thought. 'Jay-Den,' she called out to him and he turned, expecting her to ask him for another favour, or tell him to keep away from her. But to his surprise she opened the door and asked if he wanted to have coffee and stay until her parents arrived later in the afternoon.

'Are you sure?' he asked, looking doubtful. Melissa laughed and said it was about time they put things behind them and moved on. His smile cheered her up and he seemed genuinely pleased by her offer.

'Just friends,' he promised as he followed her inside, where she made coffee and they chatted. He kept his distance as promised, keeping the conversation purely friendly and Melissa began to relax as he talked about how all the girls in PR were doing a great job. Also, Russ was doing all he could to ensure the guys had what they needed and he had a temp to cover for Megan. 'She isn't as good, but she'll do for now.'

'Yeah, Megan is pretty special,' Melissa commented.

Jay-Den looked sad about his PA's injury and Melissa thought maybe he did have a heart after all. 'I'm sorry that you've both been put through this. It wasn't meant to happen like this,' he said.

'It isn't your fault. Nobody saw this coming,' she assured him and patted his shoulder. 'Who would have thought we'd end up in this mess?'

'You're amazing,' Jay-Den said. 'Most people older and wiser than you wouldn't have handled it so well.' It was as if he had watched this young girl grow and become such an inspiration in so short a time.

'I have to ... but I do feel older these days.' She felt like she'd aged twenty years in just one week.

'I never meant to cause trouble, I really didn't. But you make things so difficult.'

Melissa still had her hand on his shoulder and his comment made her feel uneasy. 'What do you mean?' He grabbed her hand and held it tightly. Melissa saw his expression change as he looked at her, and he kept hold of her hand.

'Jay-Den, don't.' She tried to pull her hand away, but he held on to it, bringing it to his lips and kissing it. She jerked her hand backwards, but couldn't free it from his hold.

'Let me help you,' he whispered. 'I love you, Melissa. Please.' He didn't care any more, he just needed her to know how he felt, even though he knew in his heart that she would reject him. 'I know you're hurting ... that you love him.'

Melissa shuddered. This was not the first time he had said that to her. He had left her a message during their split saying it. She knew that inviting him in had been another mistake. She couldn't believe she had been so stupid again. 'Just friends, you said. You know it's never going to happen. And Luke is missing!' she yelled, yanking her hand away again.

This time he let go, shaking his head.

'But we would be good together.' Melissa almost leapt off the sofa and backed away from him, putting as much distance between them as she could. She felt her blood boil. 'I could give you everything, and I wouldn't be away from you for months on end like him!'

'Jay-Den, it's you who sends him away for months – he's in a band! That's what they do.' Jay-Den's face flushed red. Embarrassed, Melissa thought, and so he should be. 'I've got enough to deal with. I can't deal with your pathetic crush on me.'

Jay-Den looked up, and to Melissa's horror she realised that the redness in his face wasn't embarrassment, it was anger. 'Pathetic crush!' he yelled, as he stormed towards her and knocked her phone from her hand. 'Melissa, I can't stop thinking about you. You're driving me crazy. I've never wanted anyone as much I want you and I hate seeing you like this ...'

'No, Jay-Den, we are not doing this.'

'I'm not leaving till you hear me out,' he snapped, and they began to struggle. But he was backing her towards the wall.

'Get out!,' Melissa screamed. It was just like the last time. 'Now!' She couldn't let this happen.

'You ungrateful little bitch,' he yelled, grabbing her roughly and pushing her against the wall. She cried out, but her cry was cut off as his lips pressed against hers and he groped at her body. She tried to push him away, but he was much stronger than her. His lips moved down to her neck and he held her firmly by the hair so she couldn't move.

'Jay-Den, stop! Get off me!' she screamed and started to cry as she struggled in his iron grasp. He ignored her cries but started tugging at her clothes, whispering how he could give her so much, and that Luke didn't deserve her.

'Jay-Den, no! Please stop,' she begged.

'No,' he snapped, and threw her to the floor in rage. He flipped her over then held her down as he tore at her clothes. She tried desperately to push him off but after accepting she wasn't strong enough she kicked out wildly, hoping her heels would catch him. He cried out in pain as one caught his shin, and he let go, giving her chance to break free.

'You bastard!' she yelled, her whole body shaking. She had never been treated like that before, and in some way it felt much worse than what Amber had done to her. This was much more personal – it was a violation.

'I gave you everything. If it wasn't for me he would be nowhere and nobody, so a little gratitude wouldn't be too much to ask,' he said. There was no more Mr Nice Guy. His glare was menacing, and it terrified her.

'I don't do that kind of gratitude.'

Jay-Den grabbed her by the throat, yelling close to her face that he could ruin them. With one phone call he could damage them so much it would rip the band apart.

'Please don't, Jay-Den, please don't do this,' she begged as he told her he wouldn't cause them any more trouble if she pleased him. He would make sure Luke never found out.

Melissa felt like a piece of meat being offered up for a meal. 'No ... I would never degrade myself like that, and I would never do that to him.' Luke didn't need her to sleep with people to get anywhere. There were record labels desperate to have The Black Eagles sign for them, and Jay-Den knew it.

He demanded she got anything Luke was working on and gave it to him, including his book. 'Screw you! You're getting nothing,' she hissed back at him. Jay-Den reminded her that Luke had signed a contract and they owned him and his band, and all of their material.

'I don't give a shit what he signed. You do not come into our home and try to rape me! That is not in the fucking contract!' She screamed and lashed out at him.

He tilted his head slightly. 'Oh, Melissa, this could have been so much easier,' he said. She flinched as he ran his hand down over her chest again.

'Don't touch me,' she begged. 'Please let me go.' But it was no use. He wasn't listening. She could see her phone vibrating where it was lying on the floor, just out of her reach. She could see that it was Toby calling, and she cried that she couldn't answer and ask her friend to come and save her.

Jay-Den grabbed the phone and waved it in front of her face, laughing. 'Oh look who's calling you. Bet he would love to help you right now,' he sneered as he chucked it across the room. 'I think you should reconsider my offer. If you change your mind, Luke could be home by tomorrow.' He laughed, and it took a few seconds for the penny to drop.

'Oh my god ..! You!' Melissa cried as it all fell into place. Everything was making sense now. 'Where is he?!' She cried, suddenly feeling her energy and fight return, like a fire being ignited deep within her. Jay-Den had threatened the things that she would protect without question or hesitation – Luke and the boys. She loved them all and would do anything she could to protect them. But this was insane. All they wanted to do was make music – how did all of this happen? She wondered whether she had led him on, worrying that it might be her fault. Luke would be so angry with her for inviting him into their home again, after what happened last time. It *was* her fault, she thought, making her panic even more for being so stupid.

'Why are you doing this?' she asked, her whole body shaking.

'Because I can, and because it is giving us such great press coverage. It's the biggest story in the world at the moment, and you can't buy that kind of publicity. Look, it was never meant to go this far. I guess I never really understood just how crazy Amber was about him. It was only the scandal I planned, not the kidnapping, I swear.' He explained how Amber had done exactly what he wanted initially, but she had now taken things way too far.

'What?! You set him up?' Melissa bubbled with rage.

Jay-Den backed Melissa through the living room and the hall towards the studio and their bedroom. He told her how it was just to create attention. It was obvious Luke wouldn't cheat or be wild enough to be in the headlines, so he thought he would cause a little stir. It had worked better than he thought it would, and Luke collapsing on stage because of a drug problem was an added bonus. 'There's no such thing as bad press. He was a true rock star,' Jay-Den laughed.

He ran his hand through his hair as he bragged to her about how he could do anything, and control anyone. However, Amber had become unpredictable. He'd found her sobbing outside the office one day after Luke had ignored her after he left one of their meetings, just before departing for New York. Jay-Den told her he could help her get Luke back. He laughed about how she kept saying that if she took him back to their childhood, he would remember his feelings for her, and they could be together.

'You messed with her mind. She was already ill.' Melissa could not believe what she was hearing. She had suspected Amber had been helped, but she never imagined it was him. He boasted further that all he'd needed to do was tell her he could help her get Luke back, and she was under his control. He knew she needed help but he also knew he could get away with it, and because Amber was so unstable she didn't question anything he said.

'Who took Luke's key?' Melissa asked. She wasn't sure why she'd suddenly thought about that, but it had been the one thing unanswered about Kelsey getting into Luke's room before she drugged him. Amber had given her Luke's key, but who gave it to Amber?

'It's surprising what people will do when they have something to lose' he replied. Melissa demanded he told her and he smiled and said it was one of their road crew.

'Who?!'

Jay-Den threw his head back, laughing. 'Good old Deano.'

Melissa felt like she had been punched. He was Luke's friend and he trusted him but he had betrayed them both. Melissa would deal with him later, the backstabbing son of a bitch, she thought. It was true, they really couldn't trust anyone.

'Enough chit-chat. Let's get on with it.' Jay-Den grabbed her by the hair and dragged her to the studio. As he threw her to the floor she hit her head on Luke's loop pedal and the pain shot through the back of her head. Behind her, some of Luke's guitars stood proudly on their stands.

'What a cosy little set-up he has. I wonder what little gems he has hiding in here.' Jay-Den loomed over her, a sadistic grin spread across his face.

'Don't touch his stuff.' she warned.

Jay-Den leaned down, smirking. 'Do you know, dead musicians often make more money than living ones...'

Melissa seethed with hatred, and spat at him. She knew where Luke was now, but she had to get away. Jay-Den stood over her as she backed away. But for once, luck was on her side. She'd fallen by the monitors, and pretending to stumble and using her body to block what she was doing, she hit the switches she needed. The microphone went live, and she hit "Record". 'I'll tell the world what you did. That was attempted rape, and you know it.'

Jay-Den shrugged. 'You gave me mixed signals. You came on to me. That's what I'll say. I mean you have slept with the entire band, haven't you?.' Now it was obvious. He had been the source of every story that had been spread about them. He had set it all up, even the incident at her house. He knew she would call him.

'You are vile. You disgust me.' The contempt in her voice cut him like a knife and the words rang in his ears, and he slapped her across her uninjured cheek. Her whole face now burned with pain, but she didn't scream or cry, but instead grimaced and tried to suppress the pain. He would not reduce her to tears again, she thought.

'Don't say that, ever again.' He begged, closing his eyes as he said it. She saw that her comments had hurt him, and she was glad.

'She wasn't meant to do this,' he said, running his fingers over her covered face. He hated what Amber had done, and had been furious with her for attacking Melissa's face. Even though he had done all of this mainly for money and more exposure, he was in love with Melissa Webb, and the fact that he could never have her enraged him. In many ways he was just as unstable as Amber.

Amber hated Melissa, and Jay-Den hated Luke Black. In both cases, an unhealthy obsession was the reason.

'Did you get Megan stabbed too?' she asked him.
He closed his eyes and shook his head as if to rid his mind of the image. He admitted that he had. He hadn't wanted to hurt her, but she wouldn't stay out of his business.

'What did she have on you? Did she know what you were up to and she was getting too close?'

'If that idiot drummer had stayed away from her, she wouldn't have been snooping. I caught her looking through my emails the day before her little mishap.'

'Little mishap ... you nearly murdered her.'

'No, Amber did.'

'Toby will kill you,' she snapped.

Fear flashed in his eyes as he knew she was right. He knew he didn't stand a chance against him. He was realising that the only way out of this for him was if Luke didn't come home, and Melissa never told her story. If this got out, he would be finished. No band would trust him now and god knows what would happen to Sky Storm Records. Not to mention the time he'd have to spend behind bars. He knew he wouldn't survive in prison. 'I'm sorry, Melissa, I really am. You could have avoided all this.' He grabbed her again and threw her down. His weight kept her pinned to the floor while his hands were clamped round her throat. Melissa clawed at his hands as she struggled, choking. She managed to move slightly, all the time keeping her glare locked on him as she used all her strength to bring her knee up and catch him right between the legs. His eyes almost popped out as he screamed, loosening his grip and allowing Melissa to gasp for air. She reached over quickly and grabbed the loop pedal, then smashed it against the side of his head twice.

'Get your dirty hands off me!' Jay-Den's eyes rolled to the back of his head and he fell sideways. She untangled herself from his limp body and looked down at him. 'I will destroy you, Lake, and your fucking record label,' then ran from the apartment, grabbing her keys and her phone on the way out. She knew there was no time to lose.

'Shit,' the police officer said as he saw the girl he was supposed to be watching run across the car park towards him. He sat up and threw his coffee out of the window as she looked up at him and pointed towards her apartment. The bruise and the hand marks around her neck meant she had been attacked again. The only person he had seen that day was the band manager, who had left, and the record label guy. What had he missed? But she was already in her car and driving out of the car park. He called in, then raced up to her apartment. He found the door wide open and Jay-Den Lake unconscious on the floor of the studio.

*****

'What the hell is going on here?' Jimmy, the paparazzi photographer snapped away and muttered to himself as he watched his target speeding out of the car park. He pulled his black beanie on, started the car and set off after her. But he wasn't the only one. He had to be quick if he was going to be the one with the money shots.

Melissa knew they would follow, but she didn't have time to think about how to leave unnoticed, and right now she couldn't give a damn. 'Please let me be right,' she whispered to herself. 'Please be alive.'

*****

'Please stop this,' Luke mumbled. He was groggy and his head pounded. He still had no idea how long he had been there because he kept drifting in and out of consciousness. His wrists and ankles were bound so tightly, it was agony.

Amber gave him more water, which right now was the only thing keeping him alive because he refused to let her feed him. He wasn't a baby, but knew he needed the water. His surroundings were oddly familiar, but the room was dark and the only faint light came from two candles in the corner. The place was old and dirty, with old chairs and tables, toys and books scattered around the floor. Amber sat a few feet from him, cross-legged in denim crops and one of the Eagles' tour jumpers. Her hair was now blonde and she had attempted to style it like Melissa's.

'No, Luke. We have to stay here and play,' she whined in a childlike voice, whipping her head backwards and forwards oddly.

Luke shifted into a different position, wincing as he did so. The ties cut into his wrists, tearing his flesh even more. He begged her to untie him, but she refused, scared that he would run. They had been there for days and Amber kept knocking him out with an unidentified liquid, forcing it down him until he passed out.

She kept showing him the newspaper cuttings, so he knew something about what was going on. He had seen Melissa in one picture and she'd looked so tiny and frightened. He'd seen the press conference too. Amber had shown him the video on the new phone Jay-Den had given her. Luke was so proud of his girlfriend but he desperately wanted to hold her, to tell her everything was going to be OK, and most importantly that he was alive.

'Amber, they think I'm dead, for god's sake.' He begged her to stop and give herself up. He would never love her, and she needed help.

Amber screamed at him to shut up, and cried again. It was looking hopeless. She was in her own world, and she wouldn't listen to him. Luke had tried to reason with her, he had even been nice to her, but nothing helped him. She would switch from anger and fury to weak and sobbing in an instant, and at times he couldn't decide which was worse. 'I hate you, Amber,' he said finally.

'Melissa's lucky it's just her face. She should be dead. I thought she was, but no. She wasn't so easy to get rid of, not like Chloe,' she yelled. Luke went even paler, if that was possible, and his mouth dropped open. Amber, now in defence mode, paced the room back and forth, shaking as she tried to rationalise what she had done all those years ago. He should have noticed her, and Chloe shouldn't have got in her way. The boxes had caused the big fire, she hadn't meant it. And luckily for her, a few weeks later her parents had taken her away travelling, and the police never solved the case.

Amber was sixteen when they returned to Portsmouth. She had forgotten about Luke and erased what she'd done to Chloe from her mind. It was only years later when she met Jenny, who kept going on about some band she had seen and really liked, that she found him again.

'You walked on that stage and I fell in love with you all over again. I knew then that we were meant to be together,' she said. The look on her face was vacant, as if she was remembering something, or maybe creating another false memory. Luke didn't want to know. He was still trying to take it in the revelation that Amber had killed Chloe, his childhood friend. Adorable, funny, beautiful Chloe, who he had never forgotten, and never would. Melissa was his girl now, but if Chloe was still alive they would certainly still have been the best of friends.

'Drop dead, Amber. You're a murderer.'

Amber's heart collapsed on itself, as she realised that he would never love her now. Loneliness, rage, and many other emotions rushed through her body and exploded outwards. 'I love you. I did it all because I love you. Why won't you love me too?' she sobbed.

Luke wouldn't even look at her. He was so tired and had no energy left to argue with her. 'I hate you, you're insane.'

Amber shook and screamed, kicking out violently. She caught him on the side of his head, and it hit the wall, knocking him out. 'No! I'm sorry, Luke, wake up,' Amber shrieked in panic as he lay there, lifeless.

*****

'I knew Jay-Den was up to something.' Jack had called and confirmed that Jay-Den had been hiding something. From what he'd seen, he agreed with Megan that she was on the right track. But to prove it would take a long and detailed investigation.

Megan sat, frozen, as she listened to Jack, and the tears fell. He hated telling her. He couldn't believe what he had found. Jay-Den was so arrogant, or stupid, that he hadn't even hidden the emails between him and Amber. Jack had found a folder, created the day after the O2 gig, full of pictures from the Luke scandal. There were also emails between himself and Amanda Green, discussing payment terms for the exclusive. It seemed that *Juice* magazine had already sealed the deal before the bidding war even started. Jay-Den had personally pocketed £400,000 to break the hottest couple in the rock world, and he had nearly succeeded.

He had something on Dean, the guitar technician, from some years before and had blackmailed him to take Luke's key. Dean had to betray Luke or his secret would be published, and he would lose everything.

Megan switched off, unable to take it all in. Jack had also found photoshopped pictures of Megan, showing her face on another girl's body, appearing to do a line of cocaine. Jack and anyone who knew Megan would never believe it. She had never touched anything other than a painkiller in her life. But of course the rest of the world didn't know that, and the fact that she was dating Toby would make it more believable. The story he'd concocted would be about how Toby had turned her into a bad girl and got her into drugs. Toby knew how she felt about drugs and he was glad she didn't touch them. Jack had been so upset over the photos and wanted to protect her from them that he had deleted every trace of them so they could never be leaked.

'They're gone, Megan.' He heard her sigh with relief.

It hurt so much that she'd been right, but she had got much more than she bargained for and she sobbed hysterically. ‘He took my future away, and he hurt my friends.’ The pain flooded out. Her boss had betrayed them all, and she felt responsible, having been so loyal to him.

She would never be a mother now, and if Toby stayed with her, he would never be a father. Luke had nearly lost Melissa, now they had all lost Luke, and Jay-Den had planned on ruining her name and blaming it on Toby. God knows what else he has planned, she thought. He was selling all the stories and getting rich while their lives were being ripped apart. It was pure evil, and he needed to be stopped.

Toby heard her cries as he came along the corridor, and running into the room he took the phone from her and chucked it to one side. She told him everything through her sobs and he listened, numb with rage.

‘That was what I was trying to tell you,’ she admitted. ‘I just wanted to be sure before I opened my mouth.’ Toby held her tight as she sobbed her heart out. Jay-Den Lake was a dead man walking.

*****

Melissa focused on the road ahead. Her pulse raced because she had nearly reached her destination. The floodlights were on as she passed Fratton Park, home of Portsmouth Football Club. She could hear the ‘Pompey Chimes’ and the roar of the crowd. It sent a shiver down her spine as the familiar sound confirmed she was home.

A few minutes later, she pulled into a deserted car park. Her hands shook as she reached for her phone. She regretted not answering the frantic calls from her loved ones, but there was no time for that. Getting to Luke and ensuring his safety consumed her thoughts. She instinctively called Beth. She told Beth her location, and to get her some help, pronto. She had no time for a conversation, or to listen to a lecture on how stupid she had been for going out there alone.

Beth relayed the message to Fox, who contacted the local police and instructed them to despatch a team immediately, but it would take them a while to get there because of the manpower being used to police the football match, a feisty local derby against Southampton.

Luke's parents had been informed and told to wait at home with a family liaison officer, but they were naturally frantic with worry, as were Jean and Mick who had arrived to support them. They were all angry with Melissa for going alone. She should have called Fox and left it to the police. 'Stupid, crazy, idiot girl,' Mick raged, as his call was ignored again by his beloved only child, who he knew was in grave danger.

*****

The former buildings of Rosewood Primary School stood back from the road, hidden by an overgrown wasteland which used to be the playground.

It was the photo, and Amber's ramblings about 'going back to where they first met' that had given her the clue. Melissa now knew that Luke and Amber had first met here, so it had to be where she had taken him. The school had been abandoned for years, making it a perfect hiding place. From the road, the main building was almost invisible, obscured by the weeds, security fencing and all manner of rubbish which had been dumped there.

The school had closed down nine years ago because of poor Ofsted reviews and Government spending cuts, and since then it had been left to rot.

Melissa turned off the engine and took several deep breaths before getting out. At the front of the building, she noticed a green plastic sheet covering something large. It blended in and had been hard to make out, but as she got closer she could tell it was hiding a car. She lifted the plastic slowly and seeing the matt paintwork made her body shiver.

It was Luke's car.

*****

'Jay-Den, please help me,' Amber begged into the phone, frustrated to hear his voicemail. She needed him now. She checked Luke over again and again, terrified that she had gone too far. He was so cold and he hadn't moved for over ten minutes. She moved him away from the wall and lay him down on his back. She stroked his face, and whispered to him 'I'm so sorry.'

This was all such a mess. She never wanted to hurt him, but she just couldn't control her rages. Amber knew she couldn't keep this up and eventually they would find them. She hadn't looked after him very well – she knew that – and now he needed medical help. He looked so thin and his skin was white, but still she wouldn't give up her obsession to have him. It was a much stronger feeling than any other emotion she had ever felt.

'Please wake up!' she begged, shaking him. But there was nothing. She sighed with relief when she heard a noise behind her. Jay-Den had come to help her. She knew he would, he always did.

'Get your fucking hands off him,' Melissa hissed as she stepped into the light.

Amber spun round to face her, panic and confusion filling her face. 'What are you doing here? Get out!' She screamed.

'No chance.'

Melissa focused her eyes on Luke who was motionless and bound on the cold floor. Amber blocked her way and whipped the knife from her pocket, waving it around in front of her and making it difficult for Melissa to get anywhere near him.

'Amber, it's over! Let me take him and get some help,' Melissa said, staying as calm as possible. She was relieved she had found him, but fearful at the state he was in. She couldn't tell if he was alive and the blood that soaked his hair and shoulders looked like a mix of new and old.

'You can't have him back,' Amber yelled, jabbing the knife at her and feeling the fury ripping through her body and taking over again. 'I'll cut your throat this time. Don't even try to take him from me again.' She backed away, shielding Luke.

'Amber, he's dying. Open your eyes for once. Just stop and think about what you're doing,' Melissa shouted now, with panic in her voice. 'This isn't about you or me. He needs help or he'll die.' She was running out of time.

Amber shrieked loudly, and grabbing Melissa by the hair, dragged her across the room while screaming threats to kill her and anyone else who tried to stop her this time. She threw Melissa against the wall, then flipped her round and held the blade to her neck. 'I hate you so much.'

'The feeling's mutual love. You were nothing but a drunken shag - get over it,' Melissa snapped, throwing more insults at Amber. With each word, Amber seemed to weaken. Over Amber's shoulder, Melissa could see Luke, still motionless on the floor. He was her strength to get through this, and she wouldn't let him down again. But the air was turning colder and now his skin seemed to be turning blue.

Still holding the knife, Amber kept her pinned against the wall. 'Jay-Den did all this. It wasn't just me. He's obsessed with you,' – 'but it was more about the money with him.'

'What money?' Melissa asked, confused.

Amber was waving the knife at her again, smirking the way she always did when she switched between personalities. She tilted her head and then sighed as if she was bored with the subject already. 'Ask little Miss May. Jay-Den was furious when she got with Toby. Said it complicated things.'

'Amber, I know all about Jay-Den helping you, and right now he's being handcuffed. And locked up for a very long time, if I have anything to do with it.'

'Oh, it was much more than that,' Amber snorted, knowing now she was on her own she could do what she wanted. Nobody controlled her any more.

'Jay-Den has been getting very rich off your precious boys. That's all I'm saying. Don't ask me how, but he brags all the time about how he's making a fortune out of them, and how they're too stupid to realise.' It was like she was telling Melissa a joke, but they were the punch line. 'He's been ripping them off with unpaid royalties. That was what worried him about Megan ... she knew something wasn't right. She'd been snooping through his files and emails and found out he'd been doing deals behind their backs. I was meant to kill her. But I didn't have time.'

Melissa couldn't believe what she was hearing. But now she had to do something, and quickly, before it was too late for Luke.

'Amber, look, he's moving,' Melissa said, to distract her. Amber's eyes came to life and she turned her head to look at him, giving Melissa a perfect opportunity. She punched Amber in the side of the head, making her stumble sideways as Melissa kicked at the hand holding the knife. It took Amber completely by surprise and she dropped it. This time it was Amber who was dragged, kicking and screaming across the cold dirty floor, clawing at the hand around her neck. Every emotion coursed through Melissa as she picked up the knife and gripped it tightly. She screamed at Amber, letting all her feelings drain out of her for all the pain and betrayal she and her friends had been subjected to. Amber kicked out at Melissa as she threw her to the floor, catching her on the chest. She was covered in bruises; one more wouldn't matter in the slightest.

'Payback time, Amber. An eye for an eye, or cheek for a cheek in my case,' she sneered as she held Amber down. Then, grabbing her hair, she pulled her head up before smashing it down on the stone floor. Amber screamed out, and her arms waved around trying to claw at Melissa but failed.

'What are you going to do now, huh? You crazy bitch!' Melissa was in control now and Amber knew it. Something caught her eye in the struggle, seeming to gleam at her. Luke's guitar was standing in the corner, the same one that seemed to have been witness to everything dramatic that had happened recently. It still held the memories of Amber's attack on her, and Melissa's blood still stained the body and neck. Melissa pulled the struggling Amber up, and dragged her to the instrument. She knocked the guitar to the floor so its strings were facing up. Amber had pushed Melissa too far and in the heat of the moment she didn't care what people would say or think. She wanted revenge, pure and simple. The red mist had fallen and she had temporarily lost control.

'No!' Amber screamed as the roles were reversed. The strings and the bridge dug in to her face, and she yelped with pain. It only lasted a few seconds before she was pulled up again and flipped over again. Melissa sat on her chest, legs either side, holding her in an iron grip borne out of pure anger. Amber couldn't move as Melissa raised the knife and pointed it at her throat. She wasn't going for her cheek ... she wanted to put an end to Amber's evil. For Luke, for Megan, and for little Chloe.

'Game over,' Melissa roared as she held the knife above her head and closed her eyes, knowing there was no going back. Time seemed to slow down and she felt as though she was floating.

Suddenly, she felt strong arms hold her tightly, and a voice in her ear. 'Miss Webb, help is here. Let me take the knife.' She kicked out at first, her rage still at its peak. But then she saw the blue tint of the lights flashing outside, and was suddenly aware of the swarm of police officers storming into the room. Relief poured through her body as she was swiftly pulled away, and passed on to another officer. She knew that deep down she didn't want to kill another person, and she was glad she hadn't been given the chance to find out if she was capable of it. She would later come to realise that Amber was ill and needed help, and she would not have been able to live with herself if she'd committed the same terrible crime in revenge.

Members of the cavalry restrained Amber in an instant. A crew of paramedics were already by Luke's side, assessing him. Melissa ran to him, pushing everyone else out of her way. The bounds were being removed from his wrists, but they had left blood-red wounds where they had cut into him. 'Luke!' she sobbed, kneeling down and taking his face in her hands. 'Wake up, baby, please wake up.' He was motionless.

'Is he alive?' she sobbed. The paramedic checking him nodded his head. He had a nasty head wound, he was cold and weak, and he had been subjected to a high dose of GHB, so he was in a bad way. But he was alive, and his vital signs were still strong, considering what he had been through.

Amber was handcuffed and read her rights before being dragged away, kicking and screaming. 'No, don't take him away from me. I will kill you all. Luke!' she screamed, struggling like a wild beast.

'Amber!' Melissa yelled. The two police officers halted as Amber turned, her face bloodied, and twisted into pure rage.

'I win,' was all Melissa said before following Luke as he was taken to the waiting ambulance. By now, there was a swarm of reporters clicking away and shouting questions, but as she held her beloved Luke's hand once again, she hardly even noticed them.

*****

'Luke, don't you dare get out of that bed,' his mother warned as she put her hands on his shoulders. She could feel him shaking with rage, his eyes conveying anger, pain and disbelief. Debbie had decided that as his parents they should tell him what had been going on while he was missing. They had endured seven hellish days, thinking he might be dead. So yes, they now wanted just half an hour alone with their boy. Even Amber didn't know the true extent of the destruction left by her actions. Not to mention Jay-Den. Debbie hated telling Luke about Jay-Den's attack on Melissa. They were the last things she told him and she watched the colour drain from his face as he stared at his mum in disbelief.

'He did what?!' Debbie thought he was going to have another panic attack. He'd suffered a couple after the Kelsey episode, and Debbie could see another coming on if he wasn't careful. He tried to get out of bed but Debbie stopped him – there was nothing he could do because it was in the hands of the police now. 'He didn't ...' He couldn't even say the words.

'No, he didn't!' Stuart had to wrestle with him to keep him from charging out of the room. 'Luke, you have to calm down. I know how you feel,' he said.

Luke glared at him. 'No you don't, how could you? Is she OK? Where is she?' he asked, desperate to see her and hold her.

Stuart gripped his son's shoulders and looked him right in the eyes. Debbie cried as she watched yet more pain engulf her son. 'We're all angry ... we love her too. I know how I'd feel if someone tried to do that to your mother.'

'I should have been there to stop him.' He sank back into bed. His head throbbed and his wrists and ankles felt like they had been attacked with razor blades.

'She fought him off. You should be proud of her,' Debbie said as she once again pushed her son back down onto the pillows as he gripped his head. Luke had a linear fracture of the skull from Amber's blow. He had been hit twice but he could not remember any of it. His last clear memory was saying goodbye to everyone at the party, and then waking up at the old school. Amber would never say how she got him there, but now he knew Jay-Den was the man behind it all, Luke guessed that he must have helped her.

'Where is she?' Debbie assured him that she was just down the hall and was equally desperate to see him. But they had wanted some time with him first, to explain things. Melissa had understood that, but the wait was killing them both.

'I want to see her ... I need to see her. She should never have been put through this, my beautiful girl.' His mum nodded and said she would get her but before she did there was one more thing she needed to say.

'Luke, she's terrified you won't want her because of her face. She thinks you'll be mad at her for letting Jay-Den into the house and trusting him again. You've both been through some very traumatic events ... you'll need to fix each other. She's been through so much and she's lost so much weight.' Debbie had to be honest with him. Although things were finally settling down, the psychological and emotional impact of all of this would hit them hard and they needed to help each other through it.

'I bet she hasn't been eating while I've been gone.' He knew the answer before his mum confirmed it.

'You know she doesn't when she's stressed or worried. We all thought you were ... gone.' His mum cried again and she held him tightly, her miracle son. Luke was struggling with all this information, and hated to see her cry. The anger in him bubbled up again as he thought about how awful it must have been for them to go and identify a body, fearing it might have been their son. Luke needed to let out his anger, but the people who deserved to be on the receiving end were not there. He was surrounded by the people he loved and they had been through enough.

He was lucky to be alive, and lucky to be loved, so he should be thankful, he realised. The anger subsided for now, and instead tears rolled down his cheeks.

'She killed Chloe,' he cried as the exhaustion took over and the magnitude of what had happened began to hit him. He cried for Chloe, for Megan and for everyone else who had been caught up in the mess. But mostly he cried for Melissa, his soul mate, who he had failed to protect. He didn't give a second thought to the money Jay-Den had defrauded them of, he would worry about that much later.

'I want to see Melissa now.'

*****

'What is taking so long?' Melissa complained, pacing the room. She understood that Luke's parents wanted to see him first, but she was getting impatient. She turned to face the others in the room. They were sitting quietly, all looking shell-shocked. Dale got up from his seat, and took her in his arms.

'Stop pacing, you're making me dizzy,' he said, before asking again if she needed anything. A doctor to check her over, maybe. The new bruises around her neck made his blood boil once again. Melissa shook her head and insisted she was fine.

'I just want to see Luke. I don't want to talk about what that piece of shit did to me...' It made her feel dirty, and sick to her stomach. She had already told the police what had happened at their home, handed her clothes over and been checked over by medical staff.

'OK, of course you don't have to.' Dale reassured her, 'I still can't believe it. Son of a bitch!' he said, angrily.

'I told you he was a low life, but did anyone listen?' Beth piped up from her chair in the corner, where she too was seething. 'Those two pyschos are meant for each other. Sex for a record deal, Jesus fucking Christ! What planet is that man on?' Her eyes welled up as she looked at her best friend. 'I don't know what I would have done Liss, if anything had happened to you.' She let her tears flow. 'And, you're a stupid moron for going to find Luke alone.'

'I know, I'm sorry for putting you all through that.'

The door suddenly flew open, interrupting them. Toby and Tom burst into the room.

'He's OK?' Tom asked. The bandmates hugged and punched the air as Dale confirmed that Luke was going to be fine.

Then they remembered why all this had happened. How did they even begin to process it? They felt numb, and for once even Toby wasn't sure what to say. All they knew for sure, and what they needed to focus on, was the fact that Luke was home and he was safe. The fact that it had been Melissa who had solved the mystery and found him – before the police did - completely blew them away.

'You're a nutter, but you're an absolute legend' Tom told her. In a rare display of emotion he hugged her, and planted a kiss on her forehead. 'Jay-Den won't get away with this,' he promised her. 'I can't believe what he tried to do to you.' There was utter disgust in his tone.

'Oh, Tom, believe me, I won't rest until that man pays for the things he has done to us.' Melissa said, reaching out for Toby's hand. Their eyes met and she could see the sorrow in his eyes. 'And he won't get away with what he did to Megan either - for what he took away from you both.' Toby picked her up, holding her tightly.

'Bring that scumbag down. He took our chance of a family away, and nearly killed three of the people I love the most.'

'I am not resting until Jay-Den has everything ripped away from him. Sky Storm Records had better be prepared for a war. ' Dale roared.

'I'm totally in, nobody does this to us' Beth chimed, getting up from her seat. Her hand automatically rested on her stomach, patting it.

'You stay calm, you have to look after that precious little bump,' Toby said. 'It is the one bit of sunshine we have at the moment, so let's keep it that way.'

Beth felt a lump in her throat as she thought about what had happened to her friends. They were both such loving people, and she wished she could change it for them. Dale patted his friend on the shoulder, 'I'll tell you one thing, there won't be many kids around with such awesome aunties and uncles.'

There was a moment of peace as they watched Dale take Beth in his arms, kiss her and pat the bump gently. Scared as they were about the massive responsibility a child brings, it now felt 'right', and they were up for the challenge. Melissa threw her arms around them, and then the others joined the group hug.

They all congratulated Melissa again for her heroic (but stupid) rescue mission.

'Don't thank me, I just did what any of you would have done if you found out what I did.' She said. 'I just followed my instinct. I would do anything for Luke - or any of you. You're my family, and I love you all.'

There wasn't a dry eye in the room.

*****

Finally, Debbie popped her head round the door. Melissa looked at her, the worry showing on her face.

'Melissa, darling. You can go see him now. I'm sorry I made you wait— Melissa assured her she understood. 'Don't worry, he knows everything. Go, he is desperate to see you.' Melissa rushed from the room. The relief and the excitement bubbled up inside her as she reached out her hand to open the door to his room. His face lit up as he saw her, and he held his arms out to her. No words were necessary as they embraced ...

'Are you OK?' she asked, as he pushed her hair back so he could see her face fully.

'I am now. Hi, beautiful.'

Luke could feel her skinny frame and felt her shaking as she cried.

'I'm sorry ... I'm sorry ... I said no, but he wouldn't stop,' she cried. She didn't know how she'd fought Jay-Den off and it didn't matter that he hadn't got what he wanted, she still felt violated. She could still feel his hands on her skin, and she could see him glaring at her when she closed her eyes.

'Don't be silly, it's not your fault. I'm so sorry too, for not being there.'

'I've been so scared. I thought I had lost you forever' Melissa sobbed, as his hands stroked her face, wiping her tears away.

'Same here, but I'm home, and we're both safe now.'

Melissa begged him to rest and recover before even thinking about dealing with anything else. Luke promised her he would, and that none of them would be doing anything for that label ever again. They had a lot to answer for, and if they had any sense they'd be prepared for the backlash. He let her cry until she was exhausted.

Suddenly, she remembered the only good thing through all of this. 'Luke, there is some good news.' A hint of a smile lit up her face. He raised an eyebrow, wondering what good could possibly have come out of the nightmare of the last few weeks.

'You're going to be an uncle.' She waited for it to sink in, which took a good few seconds because his mind was still very foggy from the drugs in his system.

He looked confused, then the penny dropped.

'No way, Beth is pregnant?'

'Yep'

'Shit!'

Luke was thrilled for his best friends, although he had almost forgotten how to smile. He asked where everyone was. He wanted to thank them all for taking such good care of Melissa. He also missed his best mates. She assured him they were just down the hall and she would get them soon. He took her face in his hands again, and stroked her cheek. 'Let me see your face properly.'

'No, I'm hideous.'

'I doubt that.' Luke kept stroking her covered cheek, smiling, and his words calmed her. Melissa closed her eyes so she couldn't see his expression, then with shaking hands and holding her breath, she peeled off the dressings. The few seconds of silence felt like hours.

'You are still the most beautiful girl in the world, and I love you with all my heart. You saved my life, and I'm so proud of you. They will pay for what they have done, all of them, but the most important thing right now is that we're both safe, and we're together. '

Melissa smiled for the first time in what seemed like weeks as he trailed soft and gentle kisses over her cheek until she felt his soft, warm lips against hers once again.